Also by Jennie Marts

Cowboys of Creedence
Caught Up in a Cowboy
You Had Me at Cowboy
It Started with a Cowboy

WISH
upon a
COWBOY

JENNIE MARTS

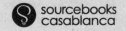
sourcebooks
casablanca

Published by Sourcebooks Casablanca, an imprint of Sourcebooks
P.O. Box 4410, Naperville, Illinois 60567-4410
(630) 961-3900
sourcebooks.com

Printed and bound in the United States of America.
OPM 10 9 8 7 6 5 4 3 2 1

This book is dedicated to my mom,
Lee Cumba.

Thanks for always believing in me
And for always being there.

I love you, Mom.

CHAPTER 1

THE CRISP MOUNTAIN AIR BIT HER CHEEKS AS HARPER Evans stepped off the Greyhound bus and gazed around the town where her son had been living for the past two months. She inhaled a deep breath of air that was better than the stale, canned stuff she'd been sucking for the last nineteen hours. It felt good to stretch her legs, and she rubbed at her hip, trying to get the feeling back into it. She swore her butt had fallen asleep two hours ago. Too bad the rest of her hadn't.

She'd spent the time staring out the window, alternately replaying the mistakes she'd made in the past and brainstorming ways she could fix them now and avoid making more in the future. Unfortunately, her brainstorming yielded few results. She couldn't accept that she was destined to make the same mistakes again and again—trusting the wrong people, trying to count on anyone other than herself—but the same piles of poo kept appearing in her life, and she kept stepping right into the middle of them.

It wasn't true that she couldn't count on *anyone*. She could count on Floyd—but he was only eight years old, so he wasn't that great in the support department. Although her son did have a way of dispensing fairly sage wisdom sometimes. She *had* been able to count on Michael and her grandmother. But now they were both gone. And so was Floyd.

But not for long. Because she was finally here. The small town of Creedence was barely a blip on one of the highways that crossed the Rocky Mountains of Colorado. They'd passed through Denver about an hour ago and had been steadily climbing ever since. Harper pulled the edges of her jean jacket together and sucked in another breath. The air felt different here—thinner and drier. She was definitely not in Kansas anymore.

Hitching her faded backpack further up her shoulder, Harper let out a sigh as she regarded the truck-stop diner the bus had dropped them in front of. A tall red-and-white-striped sign heralding the *Creedence Country Café: Home of the best chicken-fried steak in the county* nestled among a grouping of regal pine trees that rose against the backdrop of a snowcapped mountain range. The grand beauty would normally have struck her harder—she had always loved getting away to the mountains—but this wasn't a getaway, at least not yet. Not until she had her son.

Then they'd *get away* as fast as they could.

The air brakes squealed and hissed as the bus pulled away. Harper coughed through the cloud of exhaust and followed the other passengers across the asphalt toward the lure of the diner. A light dusting of snow swirled around the soles of her scuffed and worn black military boots. Well, to be fair they weren't really *her* boots. They'd been Michael's, but they were hers now. They were a little big, but along with being tall, she had clodhopper feet, so with a couple pairs of socks and a little cotton stuffed in the end, the shoes worked fine.

And Michael didn't need them—not anymore. She'd gotten rid of most of his clothes, saving some of her favorites, but she'd held on to the boots and just felt a little stronger when she wore them. As if he was still with her.

She swallowed, stuffing down the grief that burned her throat every time she let herself think about Michael and what they might have had, and fell in behind a mother and son, the towheaded boy clinging to his mother's hand. Harper knew the feeling of a small child's hand wrapped in hers—the tiny, sometimes sticky fingers twined through hers—so trusting, believing that their mom wouldn't let them go.

Except sometimes moms have to let them go. *Do* let them go.

Stuff. Stuff. She couldn't think about that either. No sense reliving the past. This was the time to focus on the future. She was here now. That's what mattered.

She pushed through the door of the diner. The sparse Christmas decorations and limp tinsel clinging to the side of the register with a piece of curled tape conveyed about the same amount of enthusiasm and cheeriness she had for the upcoming holiday.

The air smelled of stale coffee, hot grease, and despair. Not the kind of despair that came from being locked in a small cell that stank of urine and body odor, but despair just the same. She'd known that feeling. Had spent the last two months floundering between misery and rage, switching between the dull, constant ache of missing her son and bright-hot fury at her mother—and herself—for putting her in that cell.

Like mother, like daughter. No matter how hard she'd tried to fight it, she'd ended up just like her mom—flat broke, busted, and staring glassy-eyed at the world through the cold steel bars of the county jail.

Except that her mom wasn't in county lockup. She was

in the federal penitentiary, which was where they sent the real criminals. Harper shook her head, trying to dispel the images of the last time she'd seen Brandy. She couldn't blame *everything* on her mom. She'd been the idiot who'd let herself get roped in by another one of her mom's schemes. By the time she figured it out, it was too late. And she and Brandy had both gone down.

Thankfully, Harper had only been charged with a misdemeanor, but the county attorney she'd been assigned couldn't get her out of jail time. She'd missed Thanksgiving with her son, but Christmas was a few weeks away, and regardless of how festive she failed to feel, she was determined to have them both home for the holidays.

Because unlike Brandy, she was a good mother and was doing everything she could to get her kid back. *And* she was out now. Free.

And starving.

She dropped her backpack on the floor and slid into a seat at the counter as she mentally calculated the last of her money. She'd found a college student to rent the basement of her house for the winter break and had barely a hundred dollars remaining after she'd used that money to pay the December mortgage and the utility bill. Of that hundred, she had about eight dollars left after she'd purchased an apple, a jar of peanut butter, a cheap loaf of bread, and the bus ticket to Creedence. To her son.

Harper hadn't seen Floyd in two months—two months and fourteen days, to be exact—not since the night she'd been arrested, and her chest ached with the pain of missing him. She missed putting him to bed and smelling the sweet scent of his freshly washed hair. Missed smoothing down his cowlick, his goofy grin, and the sparkle in his hazel-brown eyes. His dad's eyes. He looked so much like Michael, a mini-me of the only man she'd ever loved.

Her unruly, curly dark hair and colossal stubborn streak seemed to be the only traits Floyd had inherited from her. That boy could dig in his heels like nobody else. Well, nobody except her.

She knew Floyd's similarities to Michael contributed to the reason Michael's mother, Judith, had taken him. And the reason Harper was here. To get him back.

Harper pulled the last of her money from the front pocket of her jeans, noting how the pants, which had been snug when she was arrested, were a little looser around her still ample hips. She'd lost several pounds while she was in lockup, but it wasn't a weight-loss program she'd recommend.

A sigh escaped her lips as she inventoried the cash—a five-dollar bill, two singles, and some assorted change. She'd been close. She smoothed the bills onto the counter. The sign above the register listed the day's specials: pot roast and potatoes for eight dollars, the cheeseburger and fries plate for three ninety-nine, and a cup of Creedence Corn Chowder for ninety-nine cents.

Fingering the corner of the bills, she knew she should save her money and order the soup, but her stomach howled in protest. She hadn't had a real cheeseburger in months.

"That hamburger sure smells good," Harper heard the towheaded boy say as he climbed onto the seat next to her. He was younger than Floyd, probably five or six, and his mother held her hand protectively behind his chair as she sagged into the stool on his other side.

"I know, baby, but the soup will be good too," she said as she pulled three crumpled dollar bills from a small coin purse. Its leather was faded and soft from wear, and Harper could see the few remaining coins left in the bottom.

A waitress appeared at the counter, her blond hair pulled into a messy ponytail and a friendly smile on her face. She held an order pad, the skin of her hand dry and chapped but her nails neatly painted a cheery pastel pink that matched the color of her uniform dress. Her name tag read Bryn. "Hi there. Welcome to the Creedence Country Café. What can I get you?"

"We'll have the soup," the mother said, "and..."

"A cheeseburger for the boy," Harper interjected, pulling the five-dollar bill from the stack and laying it on the counter in front of the child.

The mother jerked her head up, her expression guarded as she lifted her chin.

Harper knew that feeling—that gut ache of wanting to feed your child and still hold on to your pride and not accept charity. She gave a slight nod and looked directly into the woman's eyes. Their gazes locked as she tried to convey a message of understanding instead of condemnation. "I have a son too. I've been there." *I am there.*

The other woman glanced down at the boy, then back at Harper.

Harper offered her a sly grin and held up a fist. "Girl power. We girls got to stick together."

A smile tugged at the corner of the woman's lips. Then she nodded to the waitress and repeated the order. "Cheeseburger for my son, and a cup of soup for me."

"I'll have the soup too," Harper said. "And waters all around."

"You got it." The waitress scribbled on the pad, then ripped it free as she turned and snapped it into the order carousel for the cook.

"I'm Harper."

"Rachel," the woman said, automatically holding out her hand. Her sleeve pulled up, revealing a series of ugly purple finger-shaped bruises circling her wrist. She jerked her hand back before Harper had a chance to shake it.

"I'm Josh," the boy piped up. "We're on an adventure. That's why we took a bus and only have two suitcases." He grinned up at Harper, his missing left canine leaving an adorable gap in his smile.

"Adventures are good."

"Are you on an adventure too?"

Not a very good one. "I guess you'd say I'm on more of a quest. I'm here to find my son. He's a little older than you."

The boy's eyes widened. "Why do you have to find him? Did you lose him? Or did he let go of your hand and wander away? My mom always tells me to hold tight to her hand."

"That's good advice," Harper told him around the lump in her throat. Floyd hadn't let go of her hand or wandered away. She'd been the one to let go. It had only been for a moment. But it had cost her everything.

The bell on the counter dinged, and the waitress hustled by, then plunked three cheeseburger plates on the counter in front of them.

The scent of the crispy pile of fries had Harper's mouth watering, and she was tempted to snatch a fry and cram it between her lips before the waitress caught her mistake. She clasped her hands tightly in her lap. "I think there's been a mistake. I ordered the soup."

"So did I," said the boy's mom.

"I know. But we're running a special today—three burgers for the price of one." The waitress grinned and offered them a conspiratorial wink as she held up her fist. "We girls gotta stick together."

The three women smiled at each other, strangers bonding over life's struggles.

The boy, oblivious to the situation, picked up the burger and took a giant bite. A glob of ketchup squeezed from the side of the bun and hit his plate. He closed his eyes in bliss. "Best burger ever."

Harper took a bite of her cheeseburger, the sharp tang of the cheddar blending perfectly with the grilled meat. "I couldn't agree more."

Logan Rivers winced at the string of swear words he heard coming from the kitchen as he stepped into the house. He barely contained a sigh as he looked around the messy living room at the eight or nine housekeeping chores that had been started the day before but still weren't anywhere near finished. The front curtains had been taken down and were spread across the floor, assorted laundry had been separated into piles on the sofa, and the vacuum was still in the same place it had been left the night before.

He'd thought hiring housekeeping help would alleviate some of his stress, but once again, he'd made a dumb decision and now had an even bigger problem to solve—how to fire her. His house was a wreck, and where he should have had holiday decorations and a brightly trimmed Christmas tree, he had cleaning supplies and dirty laundry. Not that it mattered. He'd barely had time to think the last few weeks, let alone worry about putting up a tree or untangling tinsel.

He hung up his hat and scrubbed a hand across his whiskered chin. His jaw already carried a five-o'clock shadow, and it was barely noon. Forcing a smile, he walked into the kitchen. "Hey, Kimberly, something sure smells good in here," he told the woman standing at the stove stirring a pan of gravy.

It didn't actually smell good at all, and the kitchen was a disaster. But he knew the woman had a temper hotter than anything she was cooking, so he tread lightly. But holy cowbells, she must have used every pot and dish he owned. The sink was piled high with them, and crumbs and some kind of brown goop littered the countertop. A blackened glob that he could only guess was a meat loaf sat in a pan on the stove.

"I thought you'd be in thirty minutes ago," Kimberly said, sticking her lip out in an exaggerated pout. She wore a snug T-shirt and a tiny apron tied around a pair of jeans that looked like they were painted on. "I tried to leave the meat loaf in a little longer, but now it's burned and practically ruined."

"Nah. That's just how I like it," he reassured her, even though he knew he'd specifically said he'd come in at noon. "The extra char just gives it more flavor."

She turned to him, and her pout changed into a seductive grin. "You're sweet to say so. You've always been such a good guy. But I was hoping when you came in, you might be interested in a little something more than my meat loaf anyway." She took a step closer and threaded her arms around his neck, then grazed her lips along his throat. "Maybe I could take off everything except this apron, and we could start a little burnin' of our own."

Uh-oh. He'd been afraid this would happen. And he did not need this. Not today.

He'd lain awake most of the night before worrying about the ranch and all the things he needed to do and had barely made a dent in his list. With his dad out of town, all the responsibilities of Rivers Gulch, their family's ranch, fell to him, and he still had hours of work ahead of him. He'd skipped breakfast, and his stomach had been growling for the last hour. He just wanted to wash up, eat a good meal, drink about a gallon of iced tea, and get back to work.

Which was the whole reason he'd hired Kimberly Cox— even though he knew it was a bad idea and would probably come back to bite him in the ass. And that bite was about to happen.

"Listen, Kimmie." He tried to keep his tone light as he untangled himself from her arms. "I think you might've misunderstood my intentions when I hired you to do the housekeeping."

"Don't call me that." Her smile faltered, and she planted a hand on her hip as a shadow of doubt crossed her face. "We're not in high school anymore."

This was a fact he was well aware of.

If they *had* still been in high school, he and Kimberly would still be dating. And he would be oblivious to the fact that she was running around on him with Buster Cox, the guy she would eventually dump him for, then marry and raise three children with. Until Buster ran off last year with the rodeo queen from the Colorado State Fair, and

Kimberly had come sniffing around Logan's ranch. But he wasn't about to tangle with this woman again.

He remembered her angry tantrums, still had the scar on his right pec to show for one, and by the way her face was turning red, he figured he was about to get a repeat performance.

Kimberly's eyes narrowed, and her lips pinched together in a tight line. "I've been working all morning for you and spent the last several hours preparing this meal."

"And it looks delicious." He kept his voice even, placating her. "Really, I can't wait to eat it."

"Oh, so my meat loaf is good enough for you, but I'm not."

"I didn't say that. I'm just not interested in getting involved. With anyone. I was only hoping for a hot meal and some light vacuuming."

Pink rose to her cheeks as her eyes narrowed. "So you were just using me for my cooking and cleaning skills?"

He was tempted to say he hadn't actually seen any cooking or cleaning skills, but he kept his mouth shut. He might not be the smartest guy, but he wasn't a total fool. "I'm not trying to *use* you, Kimberly. I *hired* you." He offered her one of his most charming grins. "Why don't we just forget all this and sit down and have some of that delicious meat loaf? I'm starving."

An angry glint tightened her eyes as she picked up the meat loaf pan and held it over the sink. "This meat loaf?" She tipped the pan forward.

"Hold on there, Kimmie… I mean, Kimberly," he said, holding out his hands and taking a step toward her. "Let's not do anything crazy." *Shit. Wrong word.* He'd known it the second it slipped from his mouth.

"Crazy?" Her eyes widened, and steam might have shot out her ears. "I'll show you crazy, Logan Rivers."

"Please don't," he said softly, but it was too late.

She turned the pan upside down, and the meat loaf splattered into the sink in a greasy mess. "Do you want to eat it now?" She grabbed the bowl of mashed potatoes from the counter and dumped them on top of the meat loaf. "How about some potatoes to go with it?"

"Come on, Kim. I'm sorry." What the heck was he apologizing for? She was the one dumping his lunch into the sink.

"You're sorry? For what? For not wanting the meat loaf? Or not wanting me?" Her voice rose to a fevered pitch as she knocked the broom that had been leaning against the counter to the floor. It hit the hardwood with a crack, but she didn't seem to notice as her narrowed gaze roamed the rest of the kitchen. "How about a biscuit? Do you want one of those?" She plucked a biscuit from another bowl and chucked it toward him.

Not the biscuits.

It hit him square in the chest, leaving a circle of flour on his shirt. His stomach was growling, and he wished he would have caught it and stuffed it into his mouth. "I don't think this is working out, Kim," he said, backing up and raising his arms to deflect another hurled biscuit.

"Good, because I quit," she screamed at him before marching into the living room. She pulled her purse and jacket from the pegs by the door, knocking loose his hockey stick, which fell to the floor with a clatter. Leaving the stick on the floor, she slammed the door behind her and stomped down the porch steps.

Logan stuffed a biscuit in his mouth, then grabbed a fork

and tried to find a few palatable bites from the mess in the sink. What had he been thinking in hiring Kimberly Cox?

The household workings of River's Gulch had been turned upside down when his sister, Quinn, got married last summer and moved out. Not that Logan wasn't happy for her. He was. He'd been thrilled when Quinn's Prince Charming had ridden back into her life in an expensive convertible and brandishing a hockey stick. Well, maybe not thrilled—he'd been pretty miffed at Rockford James since he'd dumped Quinn for his professional hockey career, but the guy had proven himself. Logan was glad his little sister was getting her happily-ever-after. And he and his dad, Hamilton, had been doing fine as bachelors—if "fine" meant they were surviving on frozen pizzas and beanie weenies.

When his dad's brother had unexpected surgery and Ham got called to Montana to help out on his ranch, Logan had the bright idea to hire someone to help him by cooking a few meals and doing some light housekeeping. But the last two had been more interested in getting *into* his bed then getting the bed made. Well—last three now, counting Kimberly.

And three were enough for him. He didn't need the help that badly. He could go back to frozen meals and bologna sandwiches.

Harper swiped the last fry through some ketchup and popped it into her mouth. That had been the best burger and fries she'd had in months, and she'd eaten every bite. So had Rachel and little Josh.

Bryn strode up and gave them a nod of approval. "Can I get you all anything else?"

Harper leaned forward. "Got any specials on jobs today? That's what I really need."

Bryn leaned her hip against the counter, narrowing her eyes as if in assessment. "What kind of job are you looking for?"

Harper shrugged, trying not to shrink into her faded jean jacket or straighten her unruly hair. She was sure leaning her head against the seat of the bus hadn't done her already messy style any favors. "Something temporary. I'm only in town for a short time. But I'll do just about anything." *Except work with money.* She wanted to steer clear of any job that put her in charge of someone else's funds. She'd already shown she couldn't be trusted, and she had the embezzlement charges to prove it.

"Let me think about it." Bryn looked up, and her eyes widened.

Harper turned to see a woman marching angrily into the café. She flung herself onto a stool at the counter and motioned for the waitress. "Bryn, I'm madder than a het-up hornet's nest. I need a chocolate shake and an order of bacon-and-cheesy fries to go. And don't skimp on the bacon."

Bryn glanced to the cook behind the counter. He was in his midforties and wore a snug white cap over his shaved head. Given his hard, lean body and the anchor tattoo on one of his thickly muscled arms, Harper imagined him to be a surly sailor who had run his own galley.

A tiny grin threatened his otherwise gruff expression as he nodded to Bryn. "One 'furious female' special coming right up."

Bryn pressed her lips together to keep from laughing as she scooped vanilla ice cream into a silver shake mixing cup. "He's on it, Kimberly. What's got you so worked up today?"

"Not *what. Who.*" Her voice rose as fury flashed in her eyes. "And Logan Rivers is who. What an arrogant jerk. All I was trying to do was cook him a nice meal and offer him a little womanly comfort, and that bastard fired me."

"Fired you? Oh no. I'm so sorry."

"Not as sorry as he's gonna be. I dumped the amazing meal I'd cooked him into the sink. He's going to regret turning me down."

"Maybe he misunderstood your signals?"

"Hmph. Not hardly. I practically threw myself at the guy. I think my 'signals' were pretty clear." She dropped her head to the counter. "I'm so embarrassed."

Yikes. Harper tried to focus on her plate, but couldn't help eavesdropping on the conversation. Heck, it wasn't really eavesdropping. The woman was speaking loud enough for the whole café to hear.

"Order up," the chef called as he set the Styrofoam container on the counter.

"Thanks." The woman tossed down a ten-dollar bill, then took the container and to-go cup Bryn held out before flouncing from the café.

The waitress tucked the money into the register, then walked back over to check on Harper and Rachel. "If she thinks she's embarrassed now, wait till she gets home and realizes the whole café heard her holler that she tried to seduce Logan Rivers, and he turned her down."

Harper shook her head, all too familiar with how fast rumors could spread in a small town. "That guy sounds awful."

"He's not. He's really a great guy. I've known him forever. We went to school together."

"But he fired her. Just for making a pass at him."

Bryn chuckled. "Yeah, and she's the third one he's had to sack. He's a good man who's just looking for some temporary help with cooking and cleaning, but he's also hot as hell. These women keep showing up thinking they're applying for a spot in his bed, when he really just wants someone who can bake him a great pan of mac and cheese." She narrowed her eyes as she tapped her fingers against her chin. "Any chance you can cook?"

"Of course." She might not win any ribbons at the county fair, but she could manage a few recipes. "And I don't mind getting my hands dirty. I'm fine scrubbing floors and running a vacuum."

"If you're serious about looking for a job, it sounds like Logan could use someone—and right away. My shift ends in fifteen minutes. I can run you out to his place, if you're interested. Just don't make any passes at him or act like you're interested in *him*. Like *at all*."

"Yes, I'm very interested—in the job, not the guy. Don't worry. I've got enough problems of my own, and one of them is an extreme cash shortage. So I don't care how hot he is. I'm just looking for a job. The last thing I need, or want, is another man in my life."

CHAPTER 2

Fifteen minutes later, Harper followed Bryn outside to a battered blue sedan. She hiked her backpack onto her shoulder and pulled the edges of her jacket closer together as she fought the lump swelling in her throat. She'd just said goodbye to Rachel and Josh, and the little boy had given her a hug and whispered in her ear, "Don't worry. You can ask Santa to help you, and he'll make sure you find your boy in time for Christmas."

Harper wished she had the faith of the small child. Although at this point she'd take any help she could get, whether in the form of a Christmas miracle or a jolly fat guy in a red suit.

The waitress gingerly carried a metal lunch box and passed it to Harper before opening the passenger door. "Here, give me your backpack and you hold this, but be careful. There are fragile contents inside." The front seat was filled with a sack of dog food and a tote bag stuffed with paperwork. Bryn tossed both in the back and brushed off the seat, then put Harper's backpack on the floor.

Harper got into the car, holding the lunch box carefully as instructed, and noticed a few holes punched into the metal of the lid. "What kind of food are you eating that has to be handled so gently?" she asked as the waitress slid into the driver's seat and started the car. She jumped as the box rattled slightly in her hands. "Holy crud. And why does your lunch appear to be moving?"

"It's not my lunch." An impish grin crept across Bryn's face as she opened the clasp and carefully lifted the lid.

Harper peered inside and gasped at the adorable ball of fluff that was curled inside. "Is that a baby squirrel?"

Bryn's laugh filled the small car. "It is. Isn't she darling? My dog found her under a tree by our barn. I see coyotes around my farm all the time, and I'm pretty sure the mama squirrel was killed by one, so I've been taking care of this baby until she's old enough to transition back into the wild. I still have to feed her every four hours, so I bring her to work with me but leave her in the back office. And don't worry, I'm very careful about washing my hands before I help customers or spend time around the food."

"Good to know." The baby squirrel swished its small tail as it sniffed Harper's thumb. She let out a tiny coo as she ran her finger gingerly down its back. Her chest tightened for the enchanting little orphan. "It's so cute. And soft."

"I know. And she's a total snuggler. At home, she'll hang out in the pocket of my hoodie. It's ridiculously adorable."

A smile snuck across Harper's face as the squirrel nuzzled against her hand, and she wondered how she'd stumbled across this extraordinary woman who seemed to have a heart as big as the mountains of Colorado. Bryn rescued small animals and had not only fed three strangers but was also helping one of them find a job.

Maybe Harper's luck really was about to change.

Logan stretched his neck as he strode into the office set up inside the front corner of their large barn. The sizable space held a desk with a phone and a computer, a small bathroom, a mini-fridge, a coffeepot, and an old comfy couch his sister had been about to throw away. Even though Ham had been gone for several weeks, the office still smelled like his dad—the mingled scents of boot polish, Old Spice, and a trace of the sweet tobacco from the cigars his dad occasionally smoked. The office wasn't fancy, but that's what made it a good place to work midday when Logan didn't want to have to clean off his boots to go into the house.

A trio of kittens tumbled out of the gunnysack he'd tossed in the corner a few days before. The ranch always had a passel of barn cats roaming around, and it seemed like they had a new litter of kittens every four or five months. When his nephew, Max, had lived there, he was always chasing them around, coming up with names for all of them and trying to sneak them into the house as often as Ham was tossing them out.

The mama cat of this bunch was one of Max's favorites and probably the tamest cat on the ranch, since he was always petting her and carrying her around. And Quinn had often let her into the house during the day when Ham was out. She was a sweet, fluffy gray cat with a notch missing from her right ear, thanks to a tangle with a coyote, so Max had thought it fitting to name her Nacho. That kid's wit cracked him up.

Logan wouldn't admit it out loud, but he was a little partial to this bunch of kittens. That probably had something to do with the fact that Quinn and Max had moved out and Ham was gone. The little stinkers tended to keep Logan company, crawling over his feet and chewing on his boots whenever he worked in the office.

He snatched up his favorite, the black-and-white tabby, and rubbed his thumb behind her ears. They hadn't named the calico or the orange one, but he and Max had decided to call this one Tinkerbell. She had the most distinctive emerald-green eyes, with tinges of gold around the irises. Max had said they reminded him of the colors of Tinkerbell's dress and wings. Logan didn't know about that, but he had agreed the kitten had the spunk of the feisty little fairy.

The kitten had picked him more than he'd picked her, running to him whenever he entered the barn or crawling up the side of his pant leg to curl in his lap when he was at his desk. He'd always considered himself more of dog person, but he had a soft spot for this silly kitten.

He tucked her into the crook of his arm. "How's it going, Tink? You having any better day than I am?" He reached into the fridge for the carton of cream they usually kept there in case Quinn stopped by and wanted it for her coffee. But she wouldn't miss a little bit.

The mama cat and the other kittens came running as he poured some cream into the old pie plate sitting on the floor. The cats ate mostly scraps, but he'd been giving them cat food lately since he'd been eating so sparsely and didn't create many scraps. He set Tink next to the dish, then returned the cream to the fridge.

He considered making a pot of coffee. He had about twenty minutes to get a few emails answered before he needed to run another bale of hay out to the pasture. Before he could decide, an irritated whinny drew his attention to the back of the barn where he'd stalled one of the mares. She'd cut her leg on a piece of barbed wire, and he was keeping an eye on her while it healed.

He stepped out of the office, cooing as he walked toward the horse. "Hey now, what's going on there, Ginger? What's bothering you, girl?"

He lifted his head as he caught the faint scent of smoke. Heart pounding, he sprinted the rest of the way to the stall. Throwing open the gate, he swore as he saw the source of her agitation.

A lit cigarette dangled from the hand of a man lying in the hay in the corner of the stall.

Logan recognized his ranch hand, but couldn't tell if the guy was dead or passed out. If he wasn't dead yet, he soon would be, because Logan was going to kill him.

The boozy scent of alcohol filled the air, and Logan was surprised the fumes combined with the flame hadn't started the whole stall on fire. He kicked the butt from the man's hand, then stomped the ash out with the toe of his boot.

The man pulled his hand back as he groggily tried to sit up. "Hey, man, why are you kicking my hand?"

"Be thankful I'm not kicking your ass. Get up, Ted."

"All right." The ranch hand pushed unsteadily to his feet. He dusted stray bits of hay from his jeans. "Cool your jets, man."

Logan clenched his teeth as he pushed the other man out of the stall and slammed the gate closed behind him. He slowly let out his breath and loosened his jaw. This guy wasn't worth losing his temper over. Or losing any more of the ranch's money over. "I'm sick of your crap. You're fired."

"You can't do that, man. I was just taking a nap."

"I can do whatever I want. It's my ranch. Besides the fact that I don't pay you to *nap*, you were clearly passed out with a lit cigarette in your hand. You could've burned the whole barn down."

"It was an honest mistake." Ted stared at the ground, unable to meet Logan's eyes.

"Ya know, that's what you said last week when you failed to show up for work one day, and the week before when you showed up two hours late and smelled like a brewery. I told you then you had three strikes and you'd be out, and this is definitely a third strike. You have ten minutes to pack your crap and get off my property."

The ranch hand's sulking shoulders pulled back. "That's bullshit. You can't fire a guy right before Christmas. Besides, you need me."

"I need a hand I can trust. Not a hand who spends more time drinking than working."

"You're not gonna find another hand to help you feed all these cattle this winter."

"I'll make do."

Ted took a menacing step toward Logan, the heat of his anger almost palpable as it mixed with the stench of his alcohol-infused sweat. Fury flashed in his eyes as he curled his hands into fists.

Logan stood his ground, not even flinching as he stared evenly at the other man. "I don't think you want to go there, hoss."

The ranch hand held his gaze for another few seconds, then let his shoulders drop. "This isn't over, Rivers. You're gonna be sorry you canned me." He turned and stormed out of the barn.

Yeah. That's the second time I've heard that today. He was going to have work harder—and he'd be hungry and probably in sore need of a clean shirt—but Logan didn't think he'd end up being too sorry he'd fired either of his employees today.

He spent some time calming the horse and checking on her leg before he sauntered out of the barn to wait for the ranch hand. A rustic bunkhouse next to the barn was where they usually housed one or two guys, depending on the season. It was decent-sized with a couple of small bedrooms, a modest kitchen, and a sofa sleeper in the living area. They hired a college kid to spend the summer on the ranch when they had more work but usually only kept one guy on through the winter. Ted was a local, which was probably why Logan and Ham had given the guy a few breaks, but Logan was tired of Ted's crap and didn't have time for any more of his screw-ups.

He'd screwed enough up on his own.

Logan glanced down at his watch. The guy hadn't looked in the best shape, so Logan figured he could give him an extra five minutes. But he didn't want to give him enough time to trash the place. He was just getting ready to go after him when the bunkhouse door slammed open and Ted stormed out, two full duffel bags clutched in his hands. He lurched toward his truck.

"Whoa there," Logan said, approaching him in about the same manner he would a pissed-off rattler. "I can't let you drive in your condition. I'll give you a ride into town."

"I don't need your stupid ride. I'm fine."

Logan took a step closer, putting himself between Ted and the door of the pickup.

"Get outta my way." Ted dropped one of the duffel bags and tried to shove Logan to the side.

Logan stood his ground. He wasn't one to pick fights, but he could certainly hold his own if it came to one. He'd been playing hockey with the kids on the next ranch since all of them could skate, and the sport had made him no stranger to confrontation and throwing punches.

He wasn't looking for a fight with Ted, but he'd take the guy out if he had to because he sure as hell wasn't letting him get into his truck after he'd been drinking. Logan knew all too well the effect a single drunk driver could have on an entire family.

One had killed his mom when he'd been a kid.

"I don't want to hurt you," he told Ted, "but I'm not letting you get into that pickup."

Ted shoved him again. "What makes you think you can stop me? You're not my boss anymore." He took a wild swing, clipping Logan on the side of the jaw. The punch didn't have a lot of power behind it, but Ted was a strong guy and it still stung.

Taller by six inches, Logan grabbed him by the collar, hauling him up to get in his face. The guy reeked of booze and body odor, but Logan couldn't give him an inch or he'd take a mile. Before he had a chance to answer or deck the guy, they were distracted by a small blue car zipping down the ranch's driveway.

Logan dropped Ted's shirt and took a step back as they both watched the car pull in, then park about ten feet away. Two women got out, and Logan's heart slammed into his chest for the second time that day. He recognized the driver, but the other one took his breath away.

"Hey, Bryn," he said, trying to tear his eyes from the dark-haired passenger who was leaning casually against the side of the car and gazing around the ranch. She wasn't from around here—he could tell that much from looking at her. She wore sunglasses and a faded denim jacket, not warm enough for the winter weather of the Colorado mountains.

Most of the women around these parts either wore down parkas or Carhartt coats. But it wasn't just her clothes. Between the tight set of her jaw and the scuffed military boots she wore, she had a hard look about her, as though she'd come out swinging at anyone who even nudged her. He could have used her a minute ago with Ted.

"Hey, Logan." The waitress nodded to the other man. "Ted. Everything all right out here?"

"Fine and dandy," Logan said, rubbing his palm against his sore jaw. "Ted and I were just having a difference of opinion. But I think we're on the same page now. We've decided he's going to find another ranch to work for. Isn't that right, Ted?"

The other man snarled in return but was too taken with checking out the dark-haired woman to put much stock in Logan's comments.

Bryn raised an eyebrow as she walked toward Logan and gave him a warm hug. "Sounds like you're having trouble getting along with everybody today. I heard you lost your latest housekeeping help too."

"Wow. That gossip sure spread fast."

"Kimmie came into the diner. Said your arrangement didn't quite work out."

"You could say that." He wasn't interested in rekindling any old flames with his high-school sweetheart, but he also didn't want to fan any rumor-filled fires. Not that Bryn was much of a gossip. He'd known her since they were kids, and he trusted her. Still, he didn't want to bad-mouth Kimberly. "Let's just say we had irreconcilable differences."

Bryn grinned. "Like you wanted your food served on a plate, and instead she chucked it in the sink?"

He shook his head. "So you heard all the dirty details?"

"Oh yeah. The entire diner heard she offered herself for lunch, and you rejected her. Which launched your actual lunch into the sink."

Logan let out a sigh. *Great.* Just what he needed. He had enough messes he was dealing with—he didn't need some stupid small-town drama added to the mix.

Bryn nudged him in the side with her elbow. "Which is why I brought you a replacement. One who can cook *and* clean. And she's just looking for work—no drama." She took his hand and pulled him toward the car. "Logan, this is Harper Evans."

A replacement? He tried to imagine this woman in his kitchen, but his mind automatically went to her in that skimpy apron Kim had been wearing—and he wasn't imagining her tossing his lunch in the sink, but him tossing her into his bed.

Whoa. Where did that come from?

He was suddenly conscious of the dust covering his boots and the grease stain on the side of his jeans where he'd wiped his hand after working on the tractor engine that morning. He wore a black felt cowboy hat, but wanted to take it off and smooth his hair.

Cut it out, Rivers, he chided himself. *You're just introducing yourself, not asking her to the prom.*

"Nice to meet you." He held out his hand, suddenly feeling a little shy, but still wanting to touch her. *Shy?* What the hell was that about? He hadn't worried about his dang hair or felt shy or nervous around a woman in years. Maybe because he wasn't ever interested in starting things up with one.

But this one. Hell, she had him wanting to both duck his head and drive his hands through that mess of curly dark hair as he explored her mouth and the curves that denim jacket did nothing to hide.

Which was crazy. And not like him at all. He hadn't even met this woman, and he was already imagining her in his kitchen *and* in his bed. It's not like he didn't appreciate women. He did. Every once in a while. But nothing ever serious. His life had taught him to guard his heart in that department—that women didn't stay, and giving one his heart only ended in having it broken. It was easier to keep things light, easy, no complications. And this woman had *complicated* written all over her. He didn't want or need a woman muddling up his life right now—even one that looked this gorgeous.

"Good to meet you too." She took a step toward him, her chin out, her shoulders back, and looked him square in the eyes as she took his hand—not in a flirty way, but in an all-business, take-no-prisoners way. Her boots looked authentic, and he wondered if she'd been in the military.

He held her hand a beat too long, captivated by her eyes. They were the same bright emerald green as the kitten's, like *exactly* the same, right down to the flecks of gold. He'd never seen a woman with eyes that color, and he couldn't seem to look away.

"Where you from?" He tried to sound casual, treat her as a boss would while interviewing a prospective employee. But his skin felt tight, and his blood was pumping hot through his veins. *Pull it together, hoss. Just be cool.*

"Kansas."

"Been in town long?"

"Nope."

She wasn't needlessly chatty; he'd give her that. Still. He knew nothing about her. He couldn't hire her just because she was pretty and didn't talk his ear off. The job didn't require conversation anyway. What he needed was someone who could put a meal on the table and run a vacuum. "Bryn says you can cook?"

She nodded, still holding his gaze. "And clean. And do laundry."

He thought of the pile of clothes overflowing the hamper in his room. Apparently Kimberly had been more concerned with luring him into the bedroom than laundering the shirts piling up in there. "You know the job's only temporary?"

She nodded again. "Works for me."

She seemed perfect. And he really could use the help. But again, he didn't know this woman from Adam. He glanced down at Bryn. "How do you two know each other?"

"From the diner."

He lowered his voice, knowing the waitress and her heart for anything suffering. She was always bringing home wounded animals. "She another one of your strays, Bryn?"

The waitress shrugged, her lips curving into a grin. "Maybe. But she seems like good people, has a kind heart, and I think she deserves a chance." She smiled at Harper, who seemed to wince at the waitress's warm words.

Logan narrowed his eyes as if assessing her, which was really all for show since he knew he wanted her to stay. He wanted to talk to her, to get to know this mysterious woman. "Well, I've already sacked two people today, and I don't have it in me to let down another."

Bryn's smile grew. "So she can stay?"

"She can stay."

"Yay." She clapped her hands and turned to Harper. "You can stay."

A wry grin crossed the other woman's face. "Yes. I heard." She flattened her expression, rearranging her lips from smiling to solemn as she looked up at Logan. "Thank you. I appreciate the chance."

His shoulders dropped. He hadn't realized how much he wanted that smile turned on him—to feel the heat of it like the sun shining on his face. He swallowed, trying to stay on track. "When can you start?"

She shrugged. "How about now? It sounds like you didn't get much of a lunch." An impish grin pulled at the corners of her lips.

So she did have a sense of humor. Or at least a bit of a sarcastic streak. That was good. He put his hand over his gut as his stomach growled in response. "Now would be fine. I'll take you up to the house."

Bryn held up a fist to Harper, and they shared a smile as if they had some kind of inside joke. "Thanks, Logan," Bryn told him, then opened her car door.

"No problem. But can you do me a favor in return?" He angled his head toward Ted. "Can you take this guy back to town with you? He's been drinking, and I won't let him drive."

"Sure." She turned to Ted. "Toss your stuff in the back."

"I'll get your truck dropped off at your folks' house tomorrow," Logan told him.

"Whatever." Ted dumped his bags into the back of the car, then slumped into the front seat and slammed the door.

"Thanks, Bryn." He hoped he'd thank her later, hoped this worked out. He didn't have it in him to deal with another failed housekeeper.

"See you all later," Bryn said before getting in the car and speeding away, leaving Logan alone with the dark-haired stranger. A stranger he hoped knew how to fry an egg or cook up a mess of bacon. Heck, he was so hungry, he'd probably eat shoe leather if it was dipped in BBQ sauce.

He motioned to the house. "Come on in. I'll show you around."

Harper hoisted her backpack onto her shoulder and crossed the driveway. He tried not to watch the way her hips swayed as she walked up the porch steps, but he couldn't keep his eyes off her.

Cut it out. This is just business.

He'd made too many decisions and poor choices lately based on emotion or hasty assessments—including one that might cost him everything. After that stupid mistake, he'd vowed to slow down and think through his options, but he'd just done it again. He'd hired a woman he knew nothing about, with nothing to go on beyond the advice of a friend and the similarities her eyes had to those of his favorite cat.

He'd executed some idiot moves lately; he just hoped he hadn't made another one.

CHAPTER 3

As she walked up the porch steps, Harper didn't know if she'd just had a colossal stroke of luck or just landed herself in another gigantic pile of steaming poo. She didn't know any of these people, didn't normally trust folks much further than she could throw them, yet in the space of thirty minutes, she'd jumped in a car with a perky waitress and accepted a job keeping house for a hunky cowboy.

Bryn hadn't been exaggerating when she'd said Logan was hot. The man was sex on a stick—tall and lean, with muscled arms and eyes so blue that a girl could get lost in them and not find her way out for days. A girl, but not *this* girl. No way. She needed this job, and the one thing Bryn had made very clear was that the best way to keep it was through this man's stomach, not his pants.

It didn't matter that his chestnut-brown hair was a little too long—just the way she liked it—or that the way a lock of it fell across his forehead made her want to reach up and brush it back. It didn't matter that his smile had warmed her insides in a way that no man had since Michael. She wasn't here to mix it up with a cute cowboy—she was here to do a job, earn some money, and get her son back. She needed to stay focused on her objectives.

"Welcome to Rivers Gulch," Logan said as he opened the front door.

Harper took a step inside and gasped.

Logan let out a sigh as he looked around the room. "Yep."

The house was a ranch style, with an open living room and kitchen. A long hallway on the right led to what Harper assumed were the bedrooms. A huge fireplace took up most of one wall in the living room, and large, comfortable furniture surrounded a heavy, square coffee table. The open area was decorated in farmhouse style in shades of blue and white, with weathered gray wood accents. A long butcher-block counter separated the two rooms, and the kitchen seemed to be a mix of modern and antique, with one edge of the counter holding a gleaming KitchenAid mixer next to a vintage cake stand and an old crockery jar stuffed with utensils.

The living area was covered with thick, gray carpet but gave way to dark wooden floors in the kitchen, and a heavy oak table surrounded by chairs filled the back corner of the room. The design of the house was all about function, but Harper could see a woman's touch in the white antique pitcher filled with dried ruby-red roses and the wooden sign above the sink that read "Bless this home with love and laughter."

It was a good house, and Harper imagined there was a lot of love and laughter in these walls. It spoke of home. Or she assumed it normally did. Right now, it spoke of one pissed-off woman.

A giant glob of meat loaf and mashed potatoes had congealed in the kitchen sink, and biscuits lay scattered around the room as though they'd been fired from a cannon. A broken egg leaked off the edge of the counter, its shell clinging to the side of the cabinet where the rest of the yolk had dripped to the floor. A broom lay in the middle of the room, and some kind of dark, gooey substance was spread across the top of the counter. Harper could only assume it was the gravy meant for the mound of potatoes. And that was just the kitchen.

The living room was a mess as well. It looked as if it had been torn apart and then someone had forgotten to put it back together again. Between the piles of laundry and the downed curtains, it was a war zone of chaos, with the vacuum standing sentinel amid the destruction.

Harper gazed up at Logan as she planted a hand on her hip. "Either you seriously pissed that woman off, or you really are in dire need of a housekeeper."

He shook his head. "'Hell hath no fury...'"

"Like a scorned, horny housekeeper?"

He chuckled. "Yeah. Something like that."

She couldn't believe he was laughing. She wasn't known for throwing tantrums like this, but her mother certainly was. And if her mom had thrown this kind of fit, her dad would have lost his shit. She'd witnessed some serious knock-down, drag-out fights between her parents, but she'd never seen her dad good-naturedly laugh off one of her mom's stunts. Granted, her mom's exploits usually ended with court fines or jail time, but still. "You're being awfully calm about this," she told him.

"This kind of feels like the state of my life right now. Just another friggin' mess to clean up." He gazed around the room and chuckled again. "Besides, what else am I gonna do? The deed is done, so no use crying over spilled milk—or mashed potatoes, as the case may be."

She laughed with him. *Geez. What a disaster.*

He stepped between the strewn-about biscuits and picked up the fallen broom. Gripping the handle, he swung the end of it, connecting with a biscuit, and sent it sailing across the kitchen and into the overturned trash can. "Score."

"Impressive."

He whacked two more in, then let out a whoop. "Hat trick. And the crowd goes wild." He grinned at her. "If only I played this well on the actual ice. Granted, it's easier to score when there's no pesky goalie getting in the way."

She arched an eyebrow. "You play hockey?"

"A little. I played growing up and still get in a game now and then. I help coach a kids' minor team now."

Seriously? A cowboy who played hockey? *And* he coached kids? As if this guy weren't hot enough, his heat ratio just shot through the roof.

He jerked a thumb toward the window. "We've got a little pond between our ranch and the next one over. My sister and I started playing with the three brothers from that ranch about as soon as we were old enough to don skates. The oldest brother, Rock, went on to the NHL. He plays for the Colorado Summit."

"Rock? As in Rockford James? He's a legend on the ice. He's your next-door neighbor?"

It was his turn to arch an eyebrow at her. "You follow hockey? Now I'm the one impressed."

"Why? You think a girl can't follow sports?"

He held up his hands and chuckled again. "No, of course you can. My sister is a die-hard, balls-out fan. I just meant I was impressed that you had the good taste to like hockey. Not everyone follows the sport."

"I like it." She and Michael used to watch the games on television. Kansas didn't have a professional team, so they'd adopted the Summit as their team and had become huge fans. They'd even given Floyd a hockey stick and puck for Christmas when he was five, and he was always pushing it around the house and claiming he wanted to play some day. Unfortunately, they didn't have any kids' hockey leagues in the town where they lived. And it wouldn't have mattered if they did, since she couldn't afford for him to play anyway.

"I like it too. And I can probably score you an introduction to Rock. He's not just my neighbor; he's also my brother-in-law. He married my sister this past summer and built her a big house about a mile from here. Which is why I so desperately need the extra help. My dad and I were doing all right until my uncle had a heart attack a few weeks ago and my dad went to Montana to help run his ranch."

"Oh no. I hope he's okay."

"Thanks. He will be. He's a tough old coot. A lot like my dad. You know those old cowboys—tough as nails and don't let much get them down. Except bypass surgery. Apparently that'll knock you right out. But he'll be back on his feet soon, I'm sure. We're hoping my dad will be back in the next few weeks. Quinn—that's my sister—will kill him if he isn't home by Christmas."

Harper knew the feeling. It was her goal to make some money, earn enough for a couple of bus tickets and the next mortgage payment, and have Floyd back home by Christmas too. Until this last Thanksgiving, they'd never spent a single holiday apart. Hadn't spent more than a night apart before she'd been arrested.

A fist tightened around her heart. She was so close to her boy, finally in the same town, but she couldn't go to him, couldn't see him. She hadn't formed much of a plan beyond getting to Creedence, but she couldn't very well walk up to Judith's door and demand she give her son back. How would she take him home anyway? The town didn't seem that big. They could probably walk back to the bus station, but then what? How would she buy them tickets? They weren't going to get far on the two dollars she had left in her pocket.

She needed money.

That thought sobered her, and she bent to pick up the trash can. "I'll do my best to keep you fed until your dad gets back. And speaking of which, I'd better get to work if I'm going to earn my keep around here."

He swept the last few biscuits into a pile. "This mess is well beyond the call of duty. I'll help you clean it up."

"No way. I can get this. It won't be that big a deal once I start. And I'm sure you have more important things to do." She gestured out the front windows. "Ranch-type stuff."

He frowned. "Actually, I do. I'd been getting ready to answer some emails when I found Ted passed out in one of the horses' stalls. Now that he's gone, I'll need to run some extra hay out to the cattle. It might take me an hour or two. But I feel bad leaving you with this disaster right off the bat."

"Don't. Really. I'm fine. It looks worse than it is. I can get this cleaned up and figure out something to make for supper." She glanced at the clock on the stove. "Let's just plan on two hours. I'll have a meal ready and on the table then."

"That sounds great." He glanced around the house. "You need me to give you a tour? Show you around?"

She shook her head. "I can figure it out. I can certainly navigate my way around the kitchen, and I'll assume the room with the toilet is the bathroom."

He grinned. "Correct." He scribbled a number on the whiteboard that hung on the wall next to the refrigerator. "That's my cell. Call if you need me. Reception's sometimes spotty out here and Dad's old-fashioned, so we still have a house phone if you need to use it."

She waved him away. "I'll be fine. Go feed your cows. Let me worry about feeding you."

"Okay." He headed for the front door, then turned back, his expression sincere. "Thanks, Harper. I'm grateful for your help and really do appreciate this."

A lump formed in her throat so she couldn't speak. She waved him on instead, then turned away. It had been a long time since anyone had been grateful for her help. Except Floyd. He was an affectionate kid and quick to throw his arms around her waist in thanks for something she'd done for him. Thinking about a hug from her son wasn't doing anything to help the burn in her throat, so she focused on the mess instead.

Dropping her backpack, Harper shed her coat and pushed up the sleeves of her thermal shirt. She took a few minutes to look around the house and get her bearings, then pulled her hair up into a messy ponytail and got to work. Gathering the clothes from the living room, she started a load of laundry, then attacked the mess in the kitchen.

It only took her about half an hour to clean up most of the chaos. By that time, the washer had finished, and she'd rounded up all the towels and gotten a load of them running as well. Snooping around the kitchen, she found some chicken and a bag of potatoes. Thankfully, Kimberly hadn't tossed out the flour, so Harper had enough to dredge the chicken and make a fresh batch of biscuits.

She found a heavy cast-iron skillet and some oil to fry the chicken in, then peeled the potatoes as the chicken sizzled and popped on the stove. Her mom couldn't cook for crap, but her grandma was a master in the kitchen and had taught Harper how to bake and the basics of a few key recipes.

After Michael died, she and Floyd had moved in with her grandmother. Over the last few years under Nana's watchful eye, she'd gained more skill and confidence in the kitchen. The thought of her tiny, sweet grandmother had Harper choking up again.

Stop it. She didn't have time for tears or sentiment. She swallowed the pain, inhaled a deep breath, and pushed her shoulders back.

It had been nine months since Nana had died. Nine months in which Harper's life had fallen apart. Her grandmother had taken care of Floyd while Harper worked. But with no daycare, she'd had to stay home and lost her job. She'd tried to find something else, something she could do during the hours Floyd was in school, but jobs were scarce, and she couldn't find anything.

No job meant she couldn't keep up with the house payments, could barely keep food on the table. She'd sold everything she could part with, but it still wasn't enough. She was two months behind on the house payments with no future income in sight when her mom approached her to help with the accounting at the metal manufacturing company where she worked.

Normally, Harper wouldn't fall for one of her mom's schemes, but Brandy had sucked her in, assuring her this time was different. Harper was so desperate for the money that she let herself believe it. At first, the job seemed legit. Even though her mom had brought the books to her instead of her going in to an office. Harper was excellent at math, and it felt good to use her skills. Plus the hours worked with Floyd's schedule. But her mom was being too nice to her, too accommodating. That alone should have tipped her off. She should have known something was up, but she was so thankful for a paycheck again that she'd let her guard down and hadn't paid as much attention as she should have.

It was just a few changes at first—a few line items that her mom assured her were budgeting adjustments. But then the amounts got bigger, and there were more receipts for supplies purchased than outgoing products. It took her a few weeks, but Harper finally figured out what her mom was doing. What she was helping her mom to do.

She'd been planning to turn herself and her mom in. To throw herself at the mercy of the company's president and find a way to pay the money back. But she'd been too late.

They'd been arrested and charged with embezzlement before she had a chance to confess.

Harper hadn't realized her mom had been learning her technique, then making bigger changes back at the office and taking more money. But someone at the company noticed and traced the missing funds back to Brandy. Harper's paycheck hadn't changed, so she hadn't known the extent of what her mom was doing. That fact is what had kept her an accessory to the crime, instead of the main offender.

So she should have been grateful. At least that's what her court-assigned public defender told her. But she didn't feel grateful. She felt ashamed and foolish and angry at herself for falling for her mom's line of bull. And desolate for what she'd done to her life. She'd lost everything. Including her son.

She'd had no one left to turn to, except Michael's mother, Judith, the woman who blamed Harper for taking her son away.

Making that call to Judith Benning had been one of the hardest things Harper had ever done—harder than going to jail, than subjecting herself to a strip search, even worse than the horrifying moment when she'd sat in a cold room and had a pimply-faced guy who smelled like formaldehyde and stale salami hand her a photograph to identify Michael after the accident.

Nothing was worse than calling her already-disapproving mother-in-law and telling her she'd been arrested, then asking her to come get Floyd.

She could almost feel the guilt-laden judgment running down her spine like a slimy raw oyster slipping from its shell. But Judith had come. Right away. And she'd taken the boy without a moment's hesitation.

Now Harper just had to figure out a way to get him back.

Her mind raced with ideas as she scrubbed and vacuumed the house. She'd found cleaning supplies in the laundry room, and she tried to visualize her frustration disappearing with each surface she angrily wiped clean. It didn't take her long to have the living room and kitchen sparkling and smelling fresh again.

A small stereo hung from under the counter, and she'd turned it on earlier to clear the ghosts from the air. It had been set to an oldies station, and she found herself singing along to a favorite song as she set the table for Logan. She had the potatoes boiling, the chicken frying, the biscuits baking, and a pan of green beans ready to steam. All she had left was to mash the potatoes and stir up some gravy.

It felt good to be busy, to be doing honest work for an honest wage. Although, come to think of it, they hadn't exactly agreed on a wage. They hadn't even talked salary. She'd been so happy to get a job that didn't require her to work with anyone else's money—or admit she'd spent the last few months in jail—she hadn't even asked. She supposed they'd have to talk that through.

She lifted the crispy fried chicken onto a platter, then poured milk and flour into the drippings. As the gravy simmered, she drained the potatoes, then added butter and milk and mashed them until they were fluffy and lump-free. She scooped them into a bowl, dropped another pat of butter on top, and then seasoned them with salt and pepper. Nana had always told her to never be afraid to dash on a little extra pepper.

Another classic song came on, and she found her hips swaying as she stirred the gravy. Her favorite part of the chorus came up, and she belted out the lyrics.

"Wow, I didn't know I was going to get dinner *and* a show," a deep male voice said from behind her.

She shrieked and whipped the gravy-laden spoon into the air as she spun around. "Holy crap! You scared me."

Logan stood at the counter, looking down at the large dollop of gravy that had just landed on the front of his shirt. "I guess dinner's on me now."

"Wow. You are just the king of one-liners, aren't you?"

He grinned. "Not usually. But apparently tonight I'm on fire with them. I didn't mean to scare you. I just walked in like normal, but with the radio playing, you must not have heard me. The house looks awesome though. And whatever you're cooking smells amazing."

"Thanks." She scrunched her nose at the gravy sliding down his breast pocket as she handed him a paper towel. "Sorry about launching your supper at you."

"It's not the first time today someone has thrown a meal in my general direction," he said with a shrug.

She laughed. "Yeah, but I had planned on you eating this one. I spent the last two hours cooking and cleaning to impress my new boss and amaze him with my cooking prowess; then he walks in and I chuck gravy at him."

He dipped a finger in the gravy on his pocket, then licked it clean. His eyes widened. "Damn, that's good. Consider me impressed and amazed." He glanced around her to the counter. "How did you know fried chicken and mashed potatoes were my favorite meal?"

"To eat or to wear?"

"Come on now, I only wear meat loaf," he chided her good-naturedly. "And only when it's in season."

She laughed. He was cute *and* funny. She leaned a hip against the counter, a witty comeback on the tip of her tongue. *Wait.* She wasn't here to be witty or to be wooed by a cute cowboy. She was here to do a job, collect some cash and her boy, and get out of Dodge.

Pushing back from the counter, she straightened and smoothed the smile from her face. She could be pleasant, but *not* flirty. Bryn had warned her not to fall for Logan's obvious charms. But dang, she hadn't known he'd have so many. "Hope you brought your appetite. This will be ready in a few minutes. I just need to steam the green beans."

"Great. And I brought the appetite of Zeus. I haven't

eaten much today, so I'm starving, but I need to wash up, and I should probably change my shirt."

"I washed the stuff strewn across the living room and the rest of the shirts and jeans I found in the hamper in your room. They're all folded in a pile on the end of your bed. I found some ChapStick, a bolt, half a roll of butterscotch Life Savers, fourteen dollars, and some change in the pockets of those jeans. I left that all on your dresser."

His eyes widened. "Wow. That's great. Thanks. My sister always claimed finders keepers if she found cash in anybody's pocket when she did the laundry. And from what you've accomplished in the last few hours, you earned it. Especially those Life Savers."

Her stomach clenched, and she tightened her grip on the wooden spoon. "I wouldn't take money, or anything else, that wasn't mine. I'm not going to steal from you."

He shook his head and took a step toward her. "Harper, I didn't mean that. I wasn't accusing you of anything. I was just making a joke. And a bad one, apparently. I'm sorry."

She didn't know what to say, didn't how to respond. She wanted to brush off the remark, make it seem nonchalant, but his offhand comment had hit her in her core. And the worst part was, she didn't even have the right to act insulted. She *was* a thief.

"Let's just drop it, okay?" She needed to look at him though. Needed to assure him and say the words. "But you can trust me in your house. I'm not going to take anything from you."

He nodded, keeping his expression as solemn as hers. "I believe you."

"You'd better get washed up. These beans are almost ready."

He turned and headed down the hallway, and Harper let out the breath she hadn't realized she'd been holding.

———————————

Idiot. Logan chided himself for cramming his foot so far into his mouth. What had he been thinking? This morning, he'd fired a woman who was flirting with him, and tonight he was acting like some kind of Casanova. Well, like a nerdy version of Casanova. What was up with those dorky one-liners?

And he'd never meant to insinuate she would steal anything. Although someone seemed to have stolen the part of his brain that formed intelligent conversation. And she'd robbed him of his breath when he walked into the house and seen her shaking her groove thing as she belted out the words to the song on the radio. And she had a pretty great groove thing.

Her hair was piled on top of her head, but several tendrils had come free and were hanging loose along her bare neck. He'd stood and watched her for a moment before he spoke, imagining what it would be like to walk up behind her, slide his arms around her waist, and lay a soft kiss in the crook of her neck. He envisioned the way she would lean back into him, pressing her back into his chest as she let out a contented sigh.

It was also pretty easy to imagine Harper turning around and slugging him for making a pass at her. That woman had a fire simmering just under the surface, and he reckoned she wouldn't have any trouble putting him in his place. She tried to hide it—he could see her reining herself in at different times in their conversations—but he liked the occasional snark and sass she offered when she forgot to be so uptight and professional. He wanted to see more of that feistiness, and as a big brother to a spirited little sister, he knew what buttons to push to get that sass to appear. The only problem was that she had lots of different buttons he was interested in pushing. And most of them wouldn't be in a big brotherly fashion.

He stepped into his bedroom and temporarily forgot about her buttons as he took in the spotless room. Harper had made his bed, put away his boots, and straightened the books on his nightstand. The air smelled of Lemon Pledge with hints of laundry detergent from the stacks of fresh laundry folded on the edge of his bed. Neat vacuum tracks crisscrossed the carpet. The things Harper had found in his pocket made a tidy stack on the side of the dresser, which was now free of dust and also tidied.

His room hadn't been this clean in ages. And what a load off (literally) to have his shirts clean and folded. He'd been down to the last of them and hadn't had the energy at night to even fill the washing machine, and now Harper had done it for him.

He crossed to the Jack-and-Jill bathroom that adjoined his and Quinn's bedrooms. Although now that Q had moved out, he supposed it was just a Jack bathroom. It looked like Harper had spot cleaned this room too. The fixtures and mirrors sparkled, and the sink and vanity had been scrubbed and polished. Clean towels hung neatly from the rods, and the rugs had been vacuumed.

Shrugging out of his shirt, Logan quickly washed his hands and face, combed his hair, and applied another swipe of deodorant. His things had been neatly arranged on the side of the vanity, and at the last second, he grabbed a bottle of cologne and gave his neck a squirt before putting on a clean shirt.

He didn't want to think too much about that decision, but hey, she'd made an effort to make things nice for him, so the least he could do was not show up at the table smelling like a barn stall.

Smoothing down his cowlick, he walked back into the living room. The dining room table was set for one, and the platter of chicken and bowls of potatoes and green beans surrounded the lone plate. The buttery scent of biscuits wafted toward him, and his stomach let out a loud rumble. *Nice.*

Harper laughed as she carried over a small gravy boat brimming with pepper-flecked country gravy. "Sit down already. Before either the food gets cold or you wither away from starvation."

He gestured to the single place setting. "Aren't you eating with me?"

"No. I'll have something later."

"Don't be ridiculous. You're not the maid. You don't have to stand at the table and serve me. You've done your job just preparing this amazing feast. Please, sit with me and eat. I insist."

She shrugged. "I don't want to intrude."

"You're not intruding if I'm insisting." He knew he was going to do more than ask, so he walked around her—Lord, she smelled good, like vanilla and flowers—and pulled another plate from the cupboard. He got silverware from the drawer and put them all on the table in front of her. A glass of ice water sat on the counter, and since he already had a glass at his place, he assumed it was hers. He grabbed it and put it on the table as well, then pulled the chair out for her.

She shook her head. "You don't have to do that."

"I know." He wanted to say more, but couldn't seem to speak as she sat down on the chair in front of him and pulled her hair loose from the ponytail. His hands were so close, and they itched to touch the silky softness of the strands. But he didn't. Instead, he clenched his fingers into fists and pressed them to his legs as he sat down across from her.

"I'm sure I look a mess," she said, smoothing her hair. "Not that it matters. I mean, not that you'd notice. I was just planning to finish cleaning while you ate, so you know, you could eat in peace."

"I've eaten in peace every night since my dad and Quinn and Max have been gone, and frankly, I'm getting a little tired of my own company. I'm grateful to have someone else to talk to." He picked up his napkin and spread it across his lap. "So, tell me about you, Harper Evans. I want to hear all the dirty details. I already know every fact about everyone else in this small town. It'd be nice to hear some new stories. And you must be fairly new around here because everyone around these parts knows everyone else and we haven't met. So what brought you to our fair city of Creedence?"

CHAPTER 4

Geez. It was as if he'd asked her to divulge the secrets of national security, the way her face drained of color and she suddenly busied her hands by filling her plate with food.

"Just taking care of some business," she stammered. "Nothing too interesting to tell about me. Really, I'm pretty boring."

Logan arched an eyebrow. "I doubt that." He wanted to know everything about her. Where she grew up, her favorite kind of dessert, and how she liked to be kissed. Did she like to take things slow and easy, or hard and fast? Okay, he probably didn't know her well enough to ask her that. Heck, he didn't know anyone well enough to ask them that. But he wanted to get to know her. Wanted to hear her laugh. To make her laugh.

And he really wanted to know if she was already spoken for. Did she have a boyfriend? Was she married? She didn't wear a ring, but the skin around her finger seemed to be paler, as if she had worn one in the past. Was she divorced? He couldn't come right out and ask her any of that stuff. He needed to start with something easy.

He took a bite of chicken, then scooped a pile of potatoes onto his plate and smothered them with gravy. "This chicken is delicious. Where'd you learn to cook? From your mom?"

She snorted, then put a hand over her mouth. "Sorry. I almost spit some of that delicious gravy across the table."

"Wouldn't be the first time. But I don't get what's so funny."

"My mom couldn't cook her way out of a paper bag. She could barely boil water. Her idea of making breakfast was setting the cereal box on the table. My grandmother, my dad's mom, is the one who taught me to cook."

"She did a great job."

Harper shrugged. "I guess. Growing up, I was too busy rebelling against my dysfunctional family to pay much attention to my grandma, but I've learned a lot from her in the last few years."

"I can see you as a rebel—staying out past curfew, sneaking beer from the liquor cabinet, bringing home the tattooed guy that your parents would hate."

"Yeah," she mused. "You pretty much nailed it."

Hmm. From her expression, he reckoned he just got it all wrong. Although, did that mean she was a worse rebel, a real troublemaker, or had her comment been ironic and she'd really been a good girl who stayed home every night and focused on getting good grades? He wasn't sure, didn't know her well enough yet. He somehow had a feeling she could have gone either way.

"I can tell you, my childhood was nothing like this." She used the end of her chicken leg to point from the kitchen to the living room. "We moved from one crappy apartment to another every year or two. I went to ten different schools. I'll bet you've lived here your whole life. You probably took a bus to school and came home every afternoon to your mom baking chocolate chip cookies."

"Not quite. I have lived here my whole life, and I did ride a bus to school. You're right about that. But my mom never met us at the door with anything close to chocolate chip cookies. She despised living on the ranch—hated everything about it." *Especially me.* "She left when I was a kid and was killed the next year by a drunk driver."

"I'm sorry."

Logan shrugged and stared down at his plate. He couldn't look at her—was afraid she'd see the shame splashed across his face, the guilt of knowing he was the real reason his mother left. Why were they even talking about this? He didn't talk about his mom. Ever. Hell, he tried not to even think about her. The familiar knot in his chest tightened to a hard ball, and he realized he was clenching his teeth. He let out his breath. "It was a long time ago."

"Yeah, but something like that can stay with you and sometimes feel like it just happened yesterday."

He peered up at her and didn't see condemnation or scorn. In fact, she wasn't even looking at him. She was looking out the window behind him, staring at something he didn't think was actually even out there. "You sound like you know something about that feeling."

She glanced back at him, blinking her eyes as if trying to focus. "I guess I do. My husband was killed in an accident too. Motorcycle."

Well, that answered that question. But not the way he'd been expecting. "Dang. That's rough."

Her gaze dropped to her lap, and she picked at a loose thread on the seam of her sleeve. "Yeah. It was. Still is. Sometimes, I guess. He'd survived four years in the military and two deployments—he was a real hero—then lost his life doing something as trivial and stupid as going out for a gallon of milk."

"On a motorcycle?" Logan held up his hand. "Shit. That was insensitive. Sorry, I shouldn't have said that."

She shrugged. "It's true. I told you it was stupid." Leaning her head back, she pulled her hand through her hair. "Geez, how did we get on this depressing subject? I made all this great food, and this conversation is going to ruin your appetite."

"Not much could ruin this food for me," he said with a chuckle. "I'm ready to go in for seconds."

"Good. Let's focus on that. Or talk about something more exciting. Like what you want for Christmas this year, or why you kicked a wanton and willing woman out of your kitchen today." Her eyes, which moments ago had been shaded in sadness, now sparked with mischief.

"I didn't exactly kick her out."

"The meat-loaf mountain says otherwise."

"Touché." He lifted his shoulders. "I don't have anything against Kimmie… Kimberly, I mean. I just wasn't buying what she was selling."

"Why not? I mean, I saw her in the diner. She was pretty."

"Yeah, pretty angry. We have a history, dated back in high school until she dumped me for another guy. The one she married. All that stuff is in the past, stupid high-school bullshit. Except now she's going through a divorce and convinced me to hire her because she needed the money. Although I don't know if that was true or just a ploy. Whatever it was, I'm not interested in starting things back up with her. Fool me once, and all that business."

"And from the looks of things, she takes rejection well."

He laughed. "Honestly, it could have been worse. That woman has a mean streak a mile long."

Harper stood and reached to clear the dishes from the table. "Well, I can tell you I don't have much of a mean streak, and I'm terrible at holding a grudge. So I think your kitchen is safe in my hands."

"Good to know." He looked at her hands as she took the bowl in front of him and had a foolish longing to reach out and hold one, to twine his fingers with hers. Which was crazy. He hadn't held hands with a woman in...heck, he didn't know how long. But something in him wanted to touch this one, to pick up her hand and cradle it in his.

Damn, he was getting soft. He needed to snap out of it.

"Let me help you clear this stuff."

"I got it," she said. "This is what you're paying me for." She raised an eyebrow and cocked her head at him. "You *are* paying me for this, right? We never talked about money."

He chuckled. "Yes, I'm definitely paying you for the job. Do you want an hourly wage, or would you prefer a fixed rate for the week?"

"I'm not sure. What were you paying Kimberly?"

He told her the fixed amount he'd offered the other woman.

"But did she make chicken as good as mine?"

He grinned. He liked that she wanted to haggle. It made it more fun. "Nope. And she never did a single load of my laundry. In two hours, you've already surpassed her job performance."

She planted a hand on her hip. "And you haven't even tasted my peach cobbler."

He groaned. "Okay, I'll raise it by another hundred per week. But that cobbler better be worth it." Apparently he was confused about how this haggling thing worked. She hadn't even asked for more, and he was flinging money at her. It was the hip thing. He must be a sucker for a tough chick with curvy hips.

"You drive a hard bargain," she teased. "But I'll take it. And my cobbler is definitely worth it."

He chuckled again and tried not to think about how perfect her butt looked as she walked back into the kitchen.

Two hours later, Harper stood awkwardly by the front door, unsure if she should interrupt Logan to tell him good night. He'd taken her for a tour around the ranch after she'd finished cleaning the supper dishes, but then he'd gotten a call and closed himself in the home office. She'd busied herself by inventorying the kitchen and making a list of groceries they'd need for the next week, but it was already dark outside, and it seemed strange for her to hang out any longer.

She finally decided to write him a note, figuring that would be the best plan to avoid having him ask any tricky questions about where she was staying for the night or, even worse, offering to give her a ride somewhere.

She hadn't completely thought through her plans beyond getting to town, but she was resourceful and had been in worse spots. She figured she could find a church to sleep in or a twenty-four hour café where she could nurse a coffee for most of the night. But she hadn't planned on Creedence being such a small town and her all-night options being so limited.

As they'd toured the farm, she'd come up with a plan to sneak back after dark and slip into the office in the barn.

The room had been fairly warm, and she'd spied a space heater and a blanket and figured a night on that sofa seemed like a heck of a better plan than praying she could find a church to sneak into.

She'd just picked up a pen to write a note when Logan barreled out of the office. The pen flew from her hand as her body jumped, and she let out a tiny shriek of fright.

"Hey, sorry. I didn't mean to scare you," Logan said, grabbing his coat from one of the pegs by the front door. "I didn't know you were still here."

"I'm just finishing up."

"Well, I've got hockey practice in town. In fact, I'm running a few minutes late. But I'd be glad to drop you somewhere in town. Where are you staying?"

She waved away his offer as she shrugged into her jacket. "Oh, you don't need to bother. I've got my ride picking me up any minute now."

"You sure?"

"Yep. They just called." She hated the way the lie slipped so easily off her tongue.

Thankfully, Logan was distracted as he gathered his hockey equipment and didn't press her further. "All right then. You're welcome to wait inside until they arrive. I hate to run out on you, but I've got less than ten minutes to get to the rink and get my skates on."

"You'd better get going then," she said, handing him his hockey stick and following him out the door. "I was going to walk out to the road to meet my ride anyway. Stretch my legs. But I'll see you in the morning."

"See ya in the morning," he called as he tossed his equipment in the back of the truck and took off.

Whew. His hurried exit made Harper's plan a little easier, but she still made sure to walk all the way down the driveway before she doubled back and snuck into the barn. It smelled of hay and horses, a scent that was almost comforting.

Between the moon and the main yard light shining through the windows, she had enough light to cross the barn and slip through the door of the office. A bathroom with a toilet, a sink, and a small shower was tucked into the back of the room. She planned to hide in there until she was sure Logan had made it home and was finished with any nightly chores. A semiclean rug covered the floor, and she sank onto it behind the bathroom door. Maybe she should offer to clean the barn office in the next few days. Then she'd be sure it would be neat enough for her to sleep in.

For now, she was just happy to have somewhere warm and dry to spend the night. With her knees pulled to her chest, she tried to relax while still keeping an ear out for any signs of Logan's truck coming up the driveway. Getting caught in the bathroom would be awkward, but she could pass it off by claiming she'd needed to use it and hadn't wanted to bother him in the house. She'd learned that if she started spouting information about it being her "lady time," most men immediately wanted to change the subject. The topic might be embarrassing, but she'd used whatever it took to divert attention from Logan discovering her in his barn.

Leaning her head back against the wall, Harper closed her eyes, the tension in her shoulders finally easing. Her body was tired, and she was close to falling asleep when a soft shuffling sound came from the office, and her eyes popped open. Had Logan come back, and she hadn't heard his truck? Or was someone else on the farm with her?

Suddenly the empty barn—which seconds ago had seemed quiet and comforting—took on a sinister silence. Bending forward, she cocked her ear toward the door, straining to hear anything over the pounding of her heart.

She listened for several seconds, her hands gripping the edges of her backpack, her body tensed to run if she needed to, but she didn't hear anything else.

When she peered through the crack between the door and the wall, the office looked empty. Maybe it had been the horse she'd seen when she came in. Or maybe it was just the wind, or maybe it was the spirit of a long-dead ranch hand who still haunted the barn after hanging himself when his mail-order bride left him for another cowboy. *Or* maybe it was nothing more than her overactive imagination—which was evident in the fact that not only had she just imagined the barn as being haunted, but she'd also given the fictional ghost a backstory.

Regardless of what had made the noise, Harper didn't hear anything now. Letting out her breath, she relaxed her shoulders, then tensed again as the bathroom door creaked and opened the slightest bit toward her.

A plunger sat beside the toilet, and she grabbed it, brandishing it in one hand as she kept her eyes trained on the door. Not that a toilet plunger would do much good against a ghost, and her job would probably land in the toilet if she actually beaned her new employer with the thing, but still, it felt like something. At least she was ready to fight.

She clenched her hands tighter around the handle, her muscles taut, as the door opened another inch. Her eyes widened as her breath caught, her heart slamming against her chest.

The door moved a little more, and the creak was followed

by a soft mewling sound. Harper looked down and saw a black-and-white kitten peering around the edge of the doorframe.

She let out her breath with a relieved chuckle. "You little stinker. You scared the crap out of me," she told the kitten, who had come around the door and was inching its way toward her. She returned the plunger to its original spot and reached a hand out to the kitten. "Where did you come from, you little cutie?"

The kitten sniffed her hand, then daintily licked the end of her finger. Harper stroked her head a few times, and the tiny cat leaned into her palm as if relishing the petting. She lifted the kitten and cuddled it to her chest. "You are so much better than a crotchety, lovelorn cowboy ghost."

Another mewling sound came from behind the door, and two other kittens tumbled into the room. "Oh my gosh, there's more," she said out loud, delight filling her voice. She waited for the other kittens to approach and let her pet them before she scooped them into her lap. She couldn't think of a better distraction than a pile of kittens to keep her mind busy while she waited for Logan to return.

Logan's skates scraped the ice as he sailed around the rink, picking up the last of the scattered pucks. He'd agreed to coach the eight-year-old "mites" with his best friend and neighbor, Colt James, mainly because their nephew, Max, had wanted to play and Rockford had talked them into it.

Colt had convinced Max's teacher, Chloe Bishop, to coach with them when Madison Johnson, a girl in Max's class, had joined the team. Logan knew Colt had been interested in more than Chloe's coaching skills, and the two had formed their own team off the ice. Which was great. Logan was happy for his friend. Colt deserved to finally be happy, and Logan adored Chloe. She was a great person and a good addition to both the team and the neighboring ranch family unit that Colt and Logan shared.

He dropped the last puck in the bag and skated to the box. Practice had gone well tonight. It was fun to see the team really coming together. They were a great group of kids, and it was amazing what playing a sport could do for a child's confidence.

Hockey had been a saving grace for Logan. As a kid, it was the thing that had rescued him from falling into a crater of self-pity and loathing. Soaring around the ice didn't require reading or putting numbers in any particular order. In the rink, he was on an even level with the other kids, better than some in fact. The stigma of a learning disability didn't follow him onto the ice. Out here, he was one of the best. He could fly on his skates, and the stick felt natural in his hands.

In the rink, he didn't feel like "the dumb kid." He was a part of something, and he was one of the stars. He wasn't as good as the James brothers. It was obvious, even from the time they were little kids playing around on the pond, that Rockford and Colt had remarkable talent, but Logan and Mason, the middle James brother, still held their own. And the confidence Logan gained from hockey, not to mention the attention he received from the girls, was what had finally allowed him to step out of the learning disabled box he'd imprisoned himself inside.

Not that he was totally freed. He still had issues and

would always have the disability. And he still sometimes felt like that dumb guy in the room, especially over the last few weeks when he'd so royally screwed up, but hockey gave him a small reason to feel good about himself.

And ranching gave him another. He loved working the land and with the animals. Their horses didn't care if he could do math, and the cows never wanted him to read them a story. He never had to see the look of disappointment or failure in their eyes. Being outside and working the ranch had been his escape. He didn't have to be shy or timid around them.

Between hockey, working the ranch, and the friendship of the James brothers, he'd found self-assurance and could let go of that shy kid who always felt like the biggest idiot in the room. Most of the time. Until he made a bonehead move that put everything at risk.

And until he was around a gorgeous dark-haired woman who made his pulse race and his chest tighten. Then his shyness came roaring back and had him cracking stupid one-liners and acting like a dork.

He stepped off the ice and shut the door of the box behind him. With hockey, he knew what to do—skate, pass, shoot. In the rink, he felt comfortable. Around Harper Evans, he didn't have a clue.

Playing with the kittens had entertained Harper until she heard Logan's truck rumble back down the driveway and his bootheels on the porch steps leading into the house. She stayed hidden, venturing out into the office every thirty minutes or so to peer through the window. She could see the house and assumed if the lights inside went out, that meant Logan had likely gone to bed.

The house went dark a little after ten, and Harper felt comfortable leaving her hiding place. After the long day and the past night on the bus, it felt good to finally take her boots off and wiggle her toes. She'd given up her cell phone plan months ago and only had the cheap pay-as-you-go phone that used to belong to her grandmother, but it had an alarm clock, and she set it to go off at five, hoping that would give her enough time to get on her boots and sneak back out of the barn. Surely Logan didn't get up and start chores before five in the morning.

Leaving the rest of her clothes on, she curled up on the sofa, resting her head on a lumpy throw pillow with a pink pig embroidered on the front. A hearty wool blanket was folded over the back of the sofa, and she pulled it down and covered herself.

Now snug and cozy, she found the old couch comfortable in a sort of lumpy, broken-in kind of way. On one of her reconnaissance missions into the office, Harper had found the mama cat lounging in a pile of sacks in the corner of the office. The kittens had gone back to her, burrowing in beside their mother. The sight of them made Harper long for the warm body of her son cuddled against her, and she had to close her eyes to block out the vision of the feline family.

The insistent ringing of her phone's alarm woke Harper the next morning, and she struggled to sit up in the semidarkness, confused as to where she was. For a minute, she thought she was back in jail, and she fought against the panic rising in her chest as she tried to free herself from the scratchy wool blanket.

Everything's okay. This isn't a jail cell, she reassured herself as she finally sat up and turned off the phone's alarm. She looked down at her feet and couldn't help but grin at the pile of cats snuggled between her legs and the back of the sofa. The kittens curled around their mother, who raised her head and coolly regarded Harper.

"Sorry, didn't mean to bother you," she told the cat as she slipped out from under the blanket and pulled on her boots. She used the small bathroom to wash up, wistfully wishing she could strip down and use the shower. But she didn't want to take a chance of getting caught in the barn. Plus, it was freezing, and she couldn't imagine stripping anything off right now. Maybe she could sneak a shower in the house today, if Logan went in to town.

For now, she used the bare toiletries she had, swiping on some deodorant and brushing her teeth. There wasn't much she could about her hair beyond running a brush through it, pulling it up into a ponytail, and hoping for the best. She put on one of the other four shirts she had rolled in her backpack, then took a quick minute to apply a coat of mascara and a black stripe of eyeliner. She didn't usually wear much makeup—she'd only thrown in a single eyeshadow, one eyeliner pencil, and a tube of mascara—but she took the time to put a little on now, reasoning with herself that it made her appear more awake rather than contemplating too deeply whether it had something to do with looking nice for a cute cowboy.

Hating to disturb the kittens, Harper gently pushed them off the blanket, then carefully folded and arranged it back the way it had been the night before. Taking a quick glance around the office, she didn't see anything out of order.

She paused by the main door and pulled together the lapels of her coat as she braced herself for the cold. A tiny meow sounded, and she turned to see the black-and-white kitten had followed her through the barn. "Oh no. You crazy little cat," she said, bending to scoop the cat into her arms. She cuddled it against her neck, enjoying the steady, contented thrum of its purr, then turned and ran smack-dab into the chiseled, hard chest of Logan as he entered the barn.

He let out his breath in a whoosh but still reached out his arms to steady her. The heat of his palms warmed her arms, even through the fabric of her jacket. Or maybe it wasn't the heat from him, but the heat of her skin warming at his touch.

His eyes narrowed as he looked down at her. "What are you doing in here?"

CHAPTER 5

HARPER SWALLOWED. *WHAT AM I DOING IN HERE?*

It seemed like a perfectly reasonable question. And one she had been asking herself the past few months. *What am I doing in this life without Michael? What am I doing in this house without my grandmother? What am I doing getting mixed up in some stupid scheme with my mother? What am I doing in a jail cell?*

But this answer seemed simpler. At least the true answer she gave in her head. *I'm here to get my son.*

But that's not the answer she could give Logan. First off, because he didn't know anything about her son. Even though he'd given her the perfect segue the night before to tell him about Floyd, she couldn't do it.

She'd been let down so many times before—it took a lot to earn her trust—and even if Logan had pushed some—okay, *a lot*—of her feminine buttons, that didn't mean she was ready to share with him about Floyd. Besides, if she told him she was there to get her son, it would only lead to another more complicated discussion of why she'd lost him in the first place. And she sure as heck wasn't ready to admit to Logan that she'd just been sprung from the slammer. Even if she had only been in county lockup.

"Oh, um, sorry," she stammered, her brain spinning to come up with a logical explanation. She held up the small cat. "I saw a kitten and followed it in here." Yeah, that seemed reasonable. Who could resist a kitten?

"But how did you *get* here? Where's your car?"

"Oh, I don't have one. I had a friend drop me off."

"I didn't hear an engine."

"Yeah, I had her drop me at the end of the driveway. She was in a hurry, and I wanted the walk." She needed to move the conversation off her flimsy excuse for being there so early and magically arriving in a silent car. His brows were still drawn together, as if she'd told him she'd arrived by floo powder. She needed a distraction, and she had two things at her disposal, either act like a sex kitten or brandish the real kitten.

Since she had zero skills at the former, the choice was easily the latter. She held the small cat higher. "I saw this little bugger, and she was so cute, I had to pet her. Was I not supposed to come into the barn? I'm sorry if I overstepped. I'm just a sucker for a baby animal."

"No, it's fine you're in here. I didn't mean that. You just caught me off guard. I wasn't expecting to see anyone out here." He glanced down at the kitten in her hands, and his expression softened. "And yeah, I'm a sucker for that one too. Her name's Tinkerbell, and she's my favorite. When I met you yesterday, I thought your eyes reminded me of this kitten's. All cool green and gold."

She blinked. He'd noticed her eyes? Well, heck, what was she supposed to do with a comment like that? Changing the subject again seemed like her best option. "You were in a rush to get to practice last night, and I forgot to ask what time you wanted me this morning."

Crud. That wasn't the way she'd meant for that to come out. "I mean, wanted me to show up...to cook breakfast. And get started on the cleaning. It seems like ranchers usually get an early start."

A grin tugged at the corners of his mouth. "Not always

this early. But I'm glad you're here. I was trying to get a jump on things since I lost my ranch hand yesterday and will have to do double the chores."

"Anything I can do to help?"

He raised an eyebrow. "You've already done more than the last gal I hired. And I didn't put 'ranch hand' in your job description."

Geez. She hadn't done much beyond clean up and run a few loads of laundry. How bad had the last woman been if running the vacuum seemed that impressive? "First of all, you never gave me a job description." She still had the kitten clutched in one hand, so she planted the other one on her hip. "And second, I was under the impression you hired me to help ease the burden of your duties around this place. So that's what I'm here to do. I'm no stranger to hard work, and I plan to earn my wage, so if there's something I can do to help you this morning, let me do it."

He let out a sigh and scrubbed a hand across his jaw. "All right. There is something I could use a hand doing. I need to run a bunch of hay out to the cattle in the south pasture, and it's much easier with two people. If you can drive the truck, I'll push the bales off the back end. The hardest part is driving slow enough not to pitch me off the tailgate."

She chuckled. "That sounds easy enough—drive a truck around a field the same way my grandma used to steer down the highway. Got it. When do you want to start?"

"I haven't heard it put in terms exactly like that before, but that about sums it up." He laughed with her, then covered his stomach as it let out a growl. "I think breakfast is in order first though."

"Of course. I saw some sausage in the freezer, and we

had some biscuits left over from supper last night. I thought I'd make a pan of sausage gravy to go over them and scramble up some eggs. How does that sound?"

"Delicious. I've got a few chores I need to do now. Why don't you head on up to the house and get started, and I'll finish up my stuff and get the pickup loaded. Then we can eat and head out to the pasture after breakfast."

"Sounds good." She set the kitten on the ground, and it scampered toward the office.

"I started a pot of coffee, so help yourself."

"Coffee sounds great. Thanks." The man was tall and muscular and filled the space where he'd opened the door. She tried to squeeze around him, but got caught as the side of her hip and shoulder bumped against his. "Oh sorry."

"No, I'm sorry." He shifted to get out of her way, but she shifted in the same direction.

She shifted back, intensely aware of the way his leg brushed hers as he shifted again.

"Wanna dance?" he asked, raising his hand in a mock dance stance.

She wondered what he would do if she actually took his hands and led him into a slow dance or, better yet, grabbed his hands and started to salsa. Her mind filled with images of them facing off and each doing a moon walk or the Macarena. Although her dancing skills were more on par with doing the hokey-pokey or the chicken dance.

The absurdness of all the dancing ideas had her chuckling, and she stood still and pressed her hands to her sides. "As appealing as an early-morning dance-off sounds, I'm going to just stand here and let you pass."

"Good call." He grinned and sidestepped around her

and must have noticed the bulging backpack on her shoulder. "Geez, that's a big backpack. You moving in?"

If you only knew. "No. It's uh…not really a backpack. It's more like a big purse. I like to be prepared. I never know what I'm going to need."

"You're going to need a chiropractor if you keep lugging that heavy thing around."

She chuckled. He was funny, but she was ready to move the subject away from her backpack and why she was carrying around two weeks' worth of her belongings. "I'll see you up at the house then."

"Yep. I'll need about forty minutes. Will that give you enough time?"

Enough time to stop thinking about the funny things her stomach was doing every time he smiled at her or the way his muscular bicep felt as it brushed past hers? Doubtful. "Sure. Forty minutes should be fine."

Forty-two minutes later, Logan had finished his first round of morning chores and filled the back of the pickup with hay. He could smell the sausage as he opened the front door and hung his hat on the rack.

"Smells good in here," he said, brushing his hair off his forehead.

Harper came down the hall, her arms full of bedding. Her sleeves were pushed up, and loose strands of hair had escaped her ponytail and lay across her neck. Her cheeks were flushed a slight pink from exertion, and Logan's body responded with its own heat the instant he saw her.

What was it about this woman? He'd been in the same room while Kimberly had vacuumed and while the woman before that had fixed a four-course meal, but neither of them had affected him the way this one did as she walked toward him, blowing her bangs from her forehead.

"Thanks. If you want to wash up, I'll just get these sheets in the washing machine and then I can make you a plate." She breezed past him, leaving the slightest scent of vanilla and something floral in her wake.

"Sure." He crossed to the sink, tilting his body just the slightest to watch her walk into the laundry room on the other side of the kitchen. She turned and caught him looking right before she bent forward to load the washing machine.

Ah hell. He whipped his head away and focused on the sink as he quickly turned on the faucet. A skillet of gravy simmered on the stove next to a pan of scrambled eggs. But otherwise, the rest of the kitchen was clean. The fixtures and sink where he washed his hands gleamed from a recent scrubbing. The floors had been swept and mopped, and he figured she must be on her second load of laundry because the scent of laundry detergent hung in the air.

The coffeepot was full, but she'd already cleaned the cup he'd used that morning. He saw the red cup his dad typically used sitting on the counter, and it made him laugh that Harper had chosen that cup to drink from. It was a funny one Quinn had given him years ago and had an old man riding a tractor on the side with the caption "This is how I roll."

Logan grabbed a clean cup from the cabinet and filled it with coffee. He could tell from the smell she made it strong, just the way he liked it. "Thanks for making more coffee," he called toward the laundry room. "Want me to pour you another cup?"

"I'm good," she said, coming back into the kitchen. "Besides, I'm supposed to be serving you."

"That's not part of the deal. I didn't hire you to be wait-staff. You've already made this great meal. I can make my own dang plate." He filled his plate but noticed there was only one on the counter. "And I'm not real keen on eating it while you stand there and watch me."

"Oh sorry," she stammered, dropping the dish towel she'd picked up. "I can go clean another part of the house."

"Lord, woman, that's not what I meant." He set his plate on the table, cursing himself for coming off like such an idiot. "I wasn't trying to tell you to leave me alone. I guess I was rather clumsily inviting you to eat with me. But I apparently butchered the offer. Let me try again." He pulled out the chair next to him. "Harper, will you please join me for breakfast?"

She smiled. "How can I refuse such an articulate offer?" She pulled a plate from the cupboard and tipped a spoonful of eggs onto it.

"Exactly." Logan chuckled as he dropped into his chair, then took a bite of biscuit covered in sausage gravy and let out a groan. "Dang, that's good gravy." He sampled the eggs, noting the ribbons of melted cheddar running through them. "And these eggs are great too. Second meal in a row you've knocked out of the park."

"They're nothing special. Just a few eggs and some cheese." She kept her eyes trained on the table as she slid into the chair next to him, but he noticed the slightest trace of a smile, and it had his insides going soft.

He swallowed and dragged his gaze away from her mouth. "So to keep me from looking like an inarticulate fool again, can we just assume from now on that I'd like for you to join me and have us eat these nice meals you've prepared together—like at the same table, at the same time? Unless you don't want to, of course. I don't want to make you uncomfortable." Oh geez, why did his tongue keep tripping over his teeth? It was as if his brain and his mouth couldn't seem to get it together to express a logical thought.

"It's kind of making me uncomfortable right now watching you stumble through those last few statements." She shook her head and let out a soft chuckle. "How about I stop you now and just plan to set a place for myself to eat with you?"

"That'd be great." Logan stuffed another bite into his mouth to keep from saying anything more.

Ever since he woke up, his stomach had been flipping and flopping around like a hooked fish on the bank. It was something about her eyes, the way they flashed with humor one second, then went dark with mystery the next. And the way she moved had his hands itching to slide over her curves. She walked with purpose, a kind of tough-girl swagger, in her black boots and faded jacket, but she also had a softness to her, and he caught himself watching her when she wasn't looking and admiring the subtle sway of her hips as she worked.

Maybe his brain was stuck on the image of her the night before when he'd come in and caught her dancing and singing at the stove. She'd been so uninhibited, her body loose and relaxed. Free was the only way he could describe it, but it made him want to know more about *that* woman, the one who swayed and sang as she stirred not just the gravy, but also something in him.

She came across as friendly and professional, but still guarded, as though she held her cards pretty close to the vest. Which only made him want to peer behind the curtain to see what she was hiding. But it was more than that. Something in him had felt a spark when he'd met her, and he wanted to get to know her, to understand what made her tick. And yeah, he liked the idea of being able to win her over, to get her to let her guard down and to be the guy she felt that loose and comfortable with.

Which was crazy. Why should she trust him? They barely knew each other. And he didn't trust easily, especially when it was obvious a woman had something to hide. He could tell by the way her eyes slid to a far-off place when she didn't know he was watching her or the way she was so quick to change the subject or divert his attention when he asked her anything about herself. He might not be the smartest guy when it came to numbers and math, but he could read people, and he knew there was more to Harper Evans than she was letting on.

Her eyes narrowed just the slightest, and she tilted her head as she regarded him. He swore she was reading his mind. Which would not be a good thing, especially if she could see those thoughts he'd been having of her in his shower, with their boots and the rest of their clothes flung across the floor of his bedroom.

"Why don't you tell me more about how I can help with the hay this morning?"

"Yeah, sure." Good idea. He was thankful to be on more solid conversational ground and to have something to get his mind off ditching the cattle and carrying this woman into his bedroom. Using the placemat, his unused spoon, the napkin holder, and the salt and pepper shakers, he fashioned a semi-accurate map of the pastures and gates they'd pass through.

"The most important responsibility I have right now is keeping those cattle fed and alive through the winter," he told her. "We grow some crops and have a few side hustles as well, but our main livelihood comes from that herd. So I'll make sure they're fed and taken care of before I ever worry about putting a bite of food into my own mouth."

She nodded, her expression conveying the solemnness of his words. "I understand. I know what it's like to depend on a job for your livelihood, and I meant it when I said I'm willing to pitch in and help. I know this job is temporary, but I'm grateful to have it, and like I said, I'm not afraid of hard work. Just tell me what you need, and I'll get the job done."

He nodded. "You've proved that already." The more he talked to her, the more he liked this woman—liked her work ethic and her no-nonsense approach to getting things accomplished. It was obvious from what she'd done in the house this morning and the night before that she was a hard worker and good at getting multiple tasks done at the same time.

Yeah, okay, so there were a few things he liked about her other than just her work ethic—her feisty spirit, gorgeous green eyes, and the way she filled out her jeans came to mind—but he was choosing not to focus on those. Thinking about those things would only get him in trouble.

Harper might be gorgeous, and having her in his house stirred things inside him that hadn't been truly stirred in a very long time, but there was nothing he could do about it. She'd just reminded him the job was temporary, so she wouldn't be sticking around anyway. She'd probably be gone by Christmas, so no point starting something that would only last a few weeks. And in less than a day, she'd already proven her worth, and she was too valuable an asset for him to lose with one quick roll in the hay.

It was nuts that he was even considering the notion. He'd fired the last two women for wanting this exact thing, and here he was, imagining himself playing house with Harper and getting her naked and into his arms *and* his bed. And on the sofa. And in his shower.

"Do you want to go feed the cows now," she asked. "Or do I have time to wash up the breakfast dishes?"

"I've got a couple of calls to make," he told her. "Should take me about twenty minutes. Can you finish up and be ready to go by then?"

"Perfect."

Logan carried his plate to the sink, then refilled his coffee before crossing to the den. French doors separated the home office from the kitchen. He and Ham shared the room, using it for ranch business, and it had a masculine feel to it. The walls were painted a deep blue, and a tall gun case sat in one corner next to oak bookshelves filled with *Farmers' Almanacs*, agriculture reports, and old westerns. An aerial photo of the ranch hung from the wall, something Ham had bought from a traveling salesman when Logan and Quinn were kids.

A heavy wooden desk took up the center of the room, and Logan slid into the big leather chair behind it. He set his coffee on top of the safe next to the desk where they kept some cash and important ranch documents and then fired up the computer.

He answered a couple of emails, ordered some grain, and checked in with his dad. Swallowing the last dregs of his coffee, Logan headed back into the cleaned kitchen and found Harper folding a basket full of towels at the table.

"You ready to go?" he asked.

"Sure. I can finish these when we get back." She pulled her jacket off the hook by the door and shoved her arms through the sleeves.

Logan eyed the cloudy sky and the spits of snow floating in the air. "My truck's got a good heater, but I'm worried that jacket's not going to be enough to keep you warm." He tossed her the Carhartt coat he'd been wearing that morning. "Take this. It's got a sherpa lining. Should keep you good and toasty. And you're gonna need these." He handed her a pair of winter gloves.

She held the coat and gloves, not moving to put them on. "You don't have to loan me all your stuff. I'm sure I'll be fine. I'm pretty tough."

"You can be tough—and warm. I need you focused on driving, not on your shivering hands. I can't have you pitching me out the back of the truck with the hay bales." He offered her a grin, trying to make light of the situation.

"But what about you?"

"Oh, don't worry. We've got plenty of winter gear around here." He grabbed another coat from the hooks and pushed his hat on his head. A basket of hats, gloves, and scarves sat behind the door, and he rummaged through the contents, then pulled out a blue stocking cap. "You can take this as well. It was one of my sister's."

Harper had pulled on the coat and stuffed the gloves in the pocket. It was a little big, but it would do the job. And he liked seeing her in his jacket. She tugged the ponytail holder from her hair, then took the hat and pulled it on as well. The blue of the hat brought out the emerald in her eyes.

Since when did he notice how winter gear affected the color of *anyone's* eyes? Dang, he was getting soft. He held the front door for her, then led the way to the truck and opened the driver's side door. "I'll let you drive us out to the pasture so I can get the gates."

"Nice truck," she said, sliding past him and climbing into the cab.

He shrugged but was secretly pleased with the compliment. He loved that truck. He'd saved up for it for years, and it had been the first big purchase he'd made on his own, without the help of his dad.

He climbed into the other side as Harper held up the bag of marshmallows that had been sitting in the middle of the seat.

"Are these your afternoon snack?" she asked, her voice playful.

"Nah, those are for my girlfriend. She loves them."

"Oh, sorry." Her smile fell, and she set the marshmallows back on the seat.

He held back a chuckle as he leaned forward and tuned the radio to a popular station.

They listened to music and didn't talk much as they drove down the dirt road that led to the south pasture, but it wasn't an uncomfortable silence. The marshmallows seemingly forgotten, Harper was busy concentrating on the road, and he was busy trying *not* to concentrate on her.

Even though he sat on one side of the bench seat and she sat on the other, he was all too aware of her nearness and the way her body moved as the truck bounced over the ruts and washboard grooves in the road.

"I thought there would be more snow up here," Harper said, peering at the pasture as they approached. "We have a ton in Kansas, and it drifts up past our shoulders."

"We don't get as many drifts in the mountains because we have so many trees. And Colorado is famous for its sunshine. We can get dumped on with a huge storm, and then a few days later, the sun comes out and melts most of it away. That's why our snow usually looks so pristine and white."

"It's beautiful."

You're beautiful. The thought popped into his head before he could stop it. He didn't have the time or inclination to be paying any mind to what she looked like, but damn it, she *was* beautiful. Even in his too-big jacket with a stocking cap pulled down over her ears, she was gorgeous. The cold air had given her cheeks a hint of color, and her eyes were bright with wonder as she gazed over the clearing in the mountain.

The road was a little steep through this part, and they were almost to the gate when two deer leapt out from behind the trees and ran right in front of the truck.

CHAPTER 6

LOGAN SAW THE DEER, BUT IT WAS TOO LATE TO SHOUT a warning.

Harper hit the brakes, simultaneously shooting out her arm and pressing her palm to his chest in a mock-seat-belt move as they pitched forward.

The truck shuddered to a stop, narrowly missed the deer, and she turned to him, her eyes wide. Realizing her arm was still pinned across his chest, she snatched it back. "I'm so sorry. Are you okay?"

"Yeah. I'm fine. Are you?"

"I'm okay." Her knuckles were white as she used both hands to grip the steering wheel. She cringed as she glanced at his chest. "I can't believe I just pulled that mom move on you. I'm so embarrassed."

He laughed. "Don't worry about it. My mom used to do that move too."

She blinked, then shook her head. "Yeah. That's what I meant. Mine did as well. That must be where I learned it. Weird."

"Nah. I thought it was kind of sweet." He offered her a charming grin. "It's nice that you were trying to protect me."

Her lips curved into a smile, and a touch of mischief flashed in her eyes. "I wasn't trying to protect you. I was trying to protect that pretty dashboard. I'd feel awful if it got blood on it."

He chuckled. "Nice. And good thinking. I appreciate

you protecting the truck. But next time, just hit the deer. If you clip a big one, we make it last for several meals."

"Eww," she said, swatting him on the shoulder before inching the truck forward the last few feet to the gate.

Logan chuckled again as he climbed from the cab. "What? You don't know how to make roadkill stew? What kind of a cook are you?" He was still laughing as he opened the gate and waved her through. He never had this much fun with Ted.

He closed the gate and approached her window. They'd mapped out a plan, but he wanted to point out the route while she could see the pasture instead of imagining it as a napkin holder and a salt shaker.

She rolled down the window, and he leaned his head toward hers as he pointed out over the landscape. "You can kind of see the route we usually take. When you stop, I'll push the bail out, then bang on the side of the truck when I'm secure and you can keep going."

"Got it. I'll do my best not to pitch you over the side."

He tipped the brim of his hat and grinned. "I'd appreciate it."

Her gaze shifted to over his shoulder, and her eyes went wide. "Logan, watch out," she cried.

He turned to see a large black cow running toward him. Several cows were following in her wake. He stepped forward as the cow slowed to a stop in front of him. "Hey, darlin'. How's my girl?" he asked as the cow nudged his chest. The other cows had stopped a reasonable distance back, but they all knew they were about to be fed.

He stroked the small, white star-shaped patch on the cow's forehead, then turned to Harper. "Hey, will you pass me those marshmallows?"

A grin tugged at the corners of her lips as she handed the bag through the window. "I thought those were for your girlfriend."

"They are. This is Star. She's my best girl." He tore open a corner of the bag, then held out a handful of marshmallows to the cow. Her tongue pressed from between her lips and wrapped around the marshmallows, drawing them back into her mouth. "I've had her since she was born. She was a runt that nobody thought would live. I bucket fed her and practically slept in her stall, and I guess you could say we bonded. She'll even come when I whistle or call for her, or sometimes she'll just come running if she smells me."

"If she *smells* you?"

"Yeah. Cows have an amazing sense of smell. They can detect scents up to five miles away."

"No kidding."

"Cows are pretty smart. I don't think they get enough credit."

"I'll take your word for it."

He chuckled, then fed Star another handful of marshmallows before passing the bag back to Harper. "You can have some of those if you want. Star's a sweetheart. She'll share."

"Gosh, I think I'm good for now. But thanks for the offer. I'll keep them in mind as a possible food source if we have a zombie apocalypse or the end of the world is drawing near."

He laughed again, then gave the cow's head one more nuzzle before climbing into the back of the truck and shoving off a couple bales of hay. Crouching on the wheel well, he banged the side of the truck for Harper to drive forward. It took a little over an hour to distribute the hay, and

Logan was impressed with Harper's driving skills. The cattle knew they were being fed, and most of them plodded toward the feeding troughs or the truck as it drove through the pasture.

The work went much faster with the two of them operating together. And Harper was good at seeing what needed to be done and jumping in to help. He was going to have to leave Bryn an extra tip the next time he was in the diner. Her latest stray was proving to be a diamond in the rough.

When they finished, Harper went in the house to make lunch while Logan busied himself with more chores. She'd set two places this time, and her stomach gave a little flip at the small smile she saw on his face when he came in at noon and saw the table.

She needed to get a handle on that feeling though. This job was too important. More important than her ego and how pleased she felt that he wanted to eat his meals with her. Maybe he was just being nice, or maybe he hated to eat alone. Neither meant that he had any sort of feelings for her or was interested in her. And as blissful as him being interested in her would make her secret heart feel, that was the last thing she needed.

It felt as if they'd had a couple of flirty moments already that morning, and she needed to shut that business down. Logan needed to see her as the hired help only, not someone who was interested in him. And the best way to do that was through his stomach. She had to keep cooking delicious meals that would make him want to keep her around.

Although the pantry was getting paltry, and she'd had to get creative and use what she had to make their lunch. She'd put together a casserole with thick tomato sauce, lots of stringy melted cheese, and spaghetti noodles, and it had filled the house with the scent of garlic and tomato when she'd taken it from the oven.

The table held a basket of rolls, a bowl of salad, and the casserole. Logan peered curiously at it as she slid a square piece onto his plate. But he didn't hesitate as he scooped a bite onto his fork and into his mouth. He groaned his appreciation. "This is delicious. I don't think I've ever had a casserole with spaghetti noodles in it, but this is amazing."

She heaved a quick sigh of relief. "It was supposed to have elbow macaroni, but spaghetti was the only pasta you had. I was improvising."

He frowned. "Yeah. Sorry about that. It's been a while since I've made a run into town to pick up groceries. I've been so busy, I haven't had the time. And I really have no idea what we have or what we're out of."

"Funny you should say that." She pulled a folded sheet of paper from her back pocket. "I've been making a list of meal ideas and the groceries you need. I thought you could take a look at it and see if there's anything else you want to add."

"Good thinking." He stole another bite as he took the list, then raised his eyes to regard her over the top of the paper. "You know how to drive a stick?"

"Sure."

He lifted his chin. "There's an old blue pickup to the side of the barn. It's not much to look at, but it runs. Somebody offered it to me in trade for a tractor implement a couple of years ago. We don't use it much, but it comes in handy once in a while. You can take it to run into town to the grocery store." He passed her back the list without even reading it. "I trust you with this stuff. I'm sure you know better than me what we need."

Her heart leapt. If she had her own transportation, she could use it to find Floyd. "That works for me." She tried to keep the excitement out of her voice.

"The truck should have gas in it. And the keys are hanging on the hook by the front door. I think Dad labeled it the 'blue hunk of crap.'"

A grin tugged at the corners of her mouth as she nodded. "Blue hunk of crap. Got it."

Logan reached for his wallet, then pulled out a handful of twenties and set them on the table. "There's a couple hundred there. That should be enough to get us through the next several days. We'll get you added to the store account later so you can charge the groceries you need." He didn't actually say the words *if this works out*, but he might as well have. They both knew it's what he meant. "You have a cell phone?"

"Yeah, but it's a pay-as-you-go, so I only use it for emergencies." She didn't need to admit that it only had about five dollars of usage left on it.

He raised an eyebrow as she pulled the flip phone from her pocket. "Wow. A flip phone. Impressive. You're really going back to the future with that thing. Does it even get Wi-Fi, or do you just call Scotty and have him beam you up when you've learned all you can about our primitive civilization?"

She gave him a deadpan stare as heat flared to her cheeks. "Very funny. I'll have you know this phone belonged to my grandmother, so it's practically a family heirloom."

She knew he was teasing her, but the stupid, antiquated phone *was* embarrassing. Nana had used it for years and never had a problem with it, and as long as Harper kept feeding it money, the thing worked. And that's all that mattered. She needed a phone in case Floyd or Judith tried to reach her. And they'd made Floyd memorize the number to this phone in case he needed to call Nana. There was no way to let him know she had the phone now, but she'd recited the number on the numerous voicemails she'd left for Judith since she'd been released from county.

The woman hadn't returned a single call. In fact, Harper had only spoken to her a handful of times since she'd called her to come get Floyd, and Judith had never let her speak to her son. That was about to change. She had Judith's address, and thanks to Logan and the blue hunk of crap, she now had the means to get there.

"It does look pretty valuable," Logan said, still teasing her about the phone.

She shrugged off his ribbing. "Why spend money on all that newfangled stuff when this works just fine?"

He rolled his eyes and chuckled. "Now you sound like my dad. Does that thing even get text messages, or does it go directly to Life Alert?" He leaned off the side of his chair. "Help. I've fallen, and I can't get up. Or access Google."

She glared at him but said nothing.

He held up his hands. "Okay. Sorry. I'll quit teasing you about your granny phone." He ducked as she pitched a hunk of bread at his head. "For real now. I'll quit." He pulled his smart phone from his pocket. "What's your number? In case I need to get ahold of you?"

Her chest tightened. She didn't really give out her number.

But he *was* her employer, so it would seem weird if she didn't give it to him. She grudgingly told him the number and pushed down her trepidation as he entered it into his directory.

"All set," he said, pushing his phone back into his pocket. "Did you enter my number that I wrote down for you yesterday?"

She opened the phone and scrolled to Logan's contact information. She recited the number she'd entered.

A scowl replaced his good-natured smile. "Sorry, that's wrong. The last two numbers are switched around. It should be two eight, not eight two."

"Are you sure? That's what you wrote down on the white board." She didn't want to admit that she'd memorized the number as well as added it to her phone.

"I know. I probably did." He picked at a small scratch on his wrist, avoiding her eyes. "I do that on occasion. I mix up numbers and letters sometimes when I write. I must have been in a hurry."

He mixed up his numbers and letters? She recognized those symptoms and the shame that went with them. She'd been studying the learning disability ever since Floyd had been diagnosed with it the year before. She shrugged, trying to make Logan feel at ease as she corrected the number in her phone. "I can fix it. No big deal. My…um…friend… from school was dyslexic too, so I get it."

"I didn't say I was dyslexic," he snapped.

Oh-kay. She'd obviously hit a sore spot with him. "Sorry, I shouldn't have assumed. I wasn't trying to insult you."

He let out his breath. "No, I'm sorry. I shouldn't have snapped at you. It's just a touchy subject for me. I've struggled with it all my life, and I don't usually talk about it. My brain just mixes things up sometimes, but I'm not stupid."

"Of course not. I wasn't implying that. Dyslexia doesn't have anything to do with how smart you are. Some of the most creative and genius minds of our time suffered from it."

His brow knit together. "How do you know so much about it?"

She offered him an encouraging smile. "I told you. My friend. So really, I didn't mean to offend you. And I never thought you weren't smart. You're obviously running a very successful ranch, and I know that has to take a lot of hard work and good business sense."

A shadow of concern crossed his face like a cloud passing over the sun, and his lips formed a scowl. "Not always."

Crud. She was making this worse. She needed to ditch the shovel she was using to dig herself deeper and deeper into this hole. She nudged his hand with hers and fought to ignore the spark of desire that shot down her spine at touching his skin. "Although," she said slowly, "you have made some pretty sorry jokes today. That whole 'beam me up Scotty' thing was really pretty weak."

A grin tugged at the corners of his mouth. "Oh yeah?"

She nodded. "Yeah, and I don't know that I really trust your judgment now that I've seen your taste in women. Your marshmallow-munching girlfriend is kind of a cow."

He let out a laugh, and the sound of it had Harper's stomach doing that flip thing again. She stood and gathered the plates. "I'd better get this stuff cleaned up and let you get back to work."

He clapped his hands on the sides of his chair. "Yeah.

I've got a busy afternoon. But let me know if you need anything or have any trouble with Old Blue."

She wrinkled her forehead.

"The truck."

"Oh yeah. It's a little dull compared to the Ferrari I usually drive, but I'll manage."

He chuckled again and headed for the door. "Say, I need to drop Ted's truck off at his folks' house. Why don't we coordinate when we'll be in town so I can grab a ride back to the ranch with you?"

Dang. She'd hoped he'd be so caught up in his work at the ranch that he wouldn't notice how long she'd be gone. She'd need to rush at the grocery store if she wanted to sneak in some time to find Floyd. "That sounds good. I have a few things to do here before I go. What were you thinking?"

"I need to run over to the James ranch next door and talk to Colt. He's Rock's younger brother. I think I told you we coach the minor-league hockey team together—or we did until he got a fancy new job with the NHL. Now it's just me and my nephew's teacher, Chloe, who do most of the coaching. Then I wanted to check on some fencing I put up in the north pasture a couple of weeks ago. Should take me a couple of hours altogether. What do you say we meet at the diner around three o'clock? Will that give you enough time?"

"Sure. That works for me."

"Ted's folks live a few blocks from there. I'll drop off his truck, then walk down and grab a piece of pie while I wait."

"Sounds good." It actually sounded great. She quickly cleaned the lunch dishes and was running the vacuum in the living room when she saw his truck head down the driveway. She'd already pocketed the keys and the cash, so all she had to do was grab her jacket. It was still cold outside, and she was tempted to borrow Logan's coat again but decided against it. Even though the jacket was much warmer, and she loved the way it smelled—like a mixture of saddle leather and his cologne—she was all too familiar with how small towns worked. Showing up at the store wearing Logan's coat would surely start a few tongues wagging.

There would be enough speculation about why she was driving his truck, Harper thought as she climbed in and turned over the engine of the old truck. She'd have to make sure to mention to the cashier that she was the new hired help.

The engine rumbled to life, and she used the gearshift, which had been fitted with a black eight ball as the handle, to put the truck in gear. Her heart slammed into gear as well as she steered down the long driveway. After ten very long weeks, she was finally going to get to see her son.

CHAPTER 7

HARPER EASED THE TRUCK INTO A PARKING SPOT IN front of the grocery store. It had only taken about ten minutes to drive into town, so she figured she had an extra half hour or so to try to find Floyd.

The town of Creedence was small, consisting of only eight main streets that were each twelve to fifteen blocks long. A large brick courthouse served as the town center, with stores and offices filling the surrounding blocks.

Logan had told her the downtown area had undergone a major renovation and added gas streetlamps and given the buildings fresh paint. The whole area, with its cute storefronts and occasional picket fencing, seemed utterly charming. Christmas music could be heard on the streets, and garlands of holly and twinkling lights decorated the main square, giving it even more of a festive and quaint feel.

Bryn had given Harper a tour the day before, pointing out key places in town—like the bank, the courthouse, the sheriff's office, the library, and the best place to get her nails done—before driving her out to Rivers Gulch. Harper hoped to avoid going anywhere near the sheriff's office, and she hadn't had her nails done in years, but she had noted the location of the grade school and was relieved today that it was only a few blocks from the grocery store.

She left the truck in the parking lot in case Logan came into town early or on the off chance that someone mentioned seeing the blue pickup at the grocery store. Stuffing her hands in her pockets, she kept her chin up and walked with purpose toward the school. She'd learned long ago that the best way to *look* like she belonged somewhere was to *act* like she belonged there. True, this was a small town, and she was sure it was full of busybodies and nosy Nellies that recognized anything even remotely out of place, but she could do her best to act casual and like she fit in.

She could hear the excited shouts and laughter of kids on the playground before she turned the corner to the school. Her heart thundered in her chest. Would it really be this easy? Could her timing be coincidental enough that she'd catch him on the playground and he'd run right into her arms?

The thought of seeing him again had her stomach churning and her heart climbing into her throat. She was overjoyed, but would he be excited to see *her*? What if he was angry at her for getting arrested and leaving him behind? She'd tried to call him every day, but the few times she'd reached Judith, her mother-in-law had always made some excuse why Floyd couldn't come to the phone or convinced Harper it would upset him to talk to her.

Peering through the chain-link fence, she scanned the children's faces, searching for Floyd. Would he look different? *No, of course not.* It had only been a few months since she'd seen him. How much could an eight-year-old change? That was a dumb question. She'd seen him sprout an inch and outgrow a pair of shoes in what felt like a few weeks.

Her hands shook, her fingers freezing as she clung to the icy chain link. But she ignored the cold, her only focus on finding Floyd. The kids looked about the right age, but there was no way to know if this was even his class.

She fussed with the front of her jacket and smoothed her unwashed hair, suddenly conscious of the way she looked. Would Floyd be embarrassed by her? How would he react to some crazy woman standing at the fence outside the playground and shouting his name?

Suddenly, nothing about herself felt right, and her muscles jumped under her skin. Sweat broke out on her lower back, and she had an empty feeling in her stomach. Maybe she should leave—come back tomorrow after she'd showered and pulled herself together.

The idea of waiting so long and not getting to see him filled her with the same kind of remorse she'd experienced on the day of Michael's funeral—like a vise grip squeezing her heart, and she pressed a hand to her chest to ease the pain.

Then she saw him.

Her breath caught in her throat. *My baby.*

He wore a red hat and a black coat she'd never seen before. They both looked new, along with the snow boots on his feet. But she recognized his face. Of course she did— that beautiful smile was tattooed on her soul, and the vise grip eased, then transformed into a different kind of pain. A pain of longing as her arms ached to hold him, to hug him to her chest and breathe in the scent of his hair.

The sound of his laughter carried to her as he broke away from a group of kids and ran toward the jungle gym. Two boys followed, and they raced up the side of the structure.

Be careful, she wanted to shout. But she couldn't seem to speak. Her fingers tightened their grip on the fence as she tried to call his name, but nothing came out. She gasped in a breath of air but couldn't seem to swallow over the pain in the back of her throat.

She tried again. "Floyd." This time her voice worked, but the sound of it was lost in the sudden ringing of the school bell, indicating recess was over. The kids raced toward the door, and she pressed her face against the freezing chains of the fence. "Floyd!"

But it was too late. She'd missed him.

She bent forward, one hand still clutching the fence as all the air evaporated from her lungs. She'd missed her chance to talk to him, to let him know she was there. *Damn it!* She'd been so close. So close to seeing her boy, to touching him, to folding him into her arms.

This wouldn't be her only chance, she reminded herself. She was here, in Creedence. And now at least she knew for sure he was here too.

She checked the time on her phone. It had only taken her five minutes to walk to the school. Judith's house was only a few streets away. She still had time to walk there—to let Judith know she was in town and was coming back for Floyd. The older woman might have been able to keep her from talking to him on the phone, but Harper was here now, in person, and Judith couldn't keep her from her son. Surely she could understand that. She'd had a son too and knew the pain of not being able to see her boy.

Maybe Judith had changed, softened, and she'd invite her in and they could make a plan for when Harper could take Floyd back. She prayed for that as she hurried along the sidewalk.

She'd memorized Judith's address and had also paid close attention to the house numbers when Bryn had driven them down Maple Drive. Due to their limited finances and his deployments, she and Michael had never had the chance to visit Creedence. But he'd told her stories about the house he grew up in, and she knew it as soon as she saw it. He'd said their house had a huge tree in the front yard and told her how he used to crawl out his window and climb down the tree to sneak out when he was in high school.

She double-checked the numbers on the mailbox, just to be sure, but she didn't need to. This was it. She knew it. She could almost feel Michael here with her. She stood on the path leading up to the front door and imagined him growing up here, imagined him running through this same front door on his way to baseball practice or out to play with his friends.

It looked like a good house—a solid two-story painted yellow with a white wraparound front porch. Christmas lights had been strung along the front eaves, and an evergreen wreath wound with a festive red bow hung from the cheery navy-blue door.

Harper noticed a shiny, new kid-size bicycle leaning against the railing as she walked up the steps and rang the doorbell. Happiness for her son for having such a great bike warred with the green-eyed monster that reviled Judith for getting to be the one who bought it for him instead of her.

Harper took a deep breath and pushed her shoulders back as the door opened and she came face-to-face with Judith Benning, the grandmother of her child and the mother of the love of her life.

There wasn't a lot of love lost between the two women. They'd only met a handful of times—when Judith had come back to Kansas for Floyd's birth or a special occasion—but they had never gotten along very well. Judith had always been bitter about them eloping and not having a big wedding. And

Harper was sure it irked her that she'd kept her maiden name of Evans, even though they'd given their son, Floyd Michael Benning, the family name.

Judith had never thought Harper was good enough for Michael and had blamed her for making him stay in Kansas instead of coming home to Colorado. If she were honest, Judith probably blamed Harper for the accident too. Not that it was her fault, but he wouldn't have been there, wouldn't have been running that errand, if it weren't for Harper.

Or maybe Judith didn't blame her. But Harper still blamed herself.

It was apparent by the surprised, then pinched look on Judith's face that she hadn't expected Harper to be on her doorstep and didn't seem to like her any more now than she had the last time she'd seen her at Michael's funeral. "What are you doing here?" she sneered.

Harper clenched her hands into tight fists, the nails biting into her palms. She couldn't let this woman rile her. She needed to appear calm and friendly. *For Floyd.* "Hello, Judith. It's nice to see you."

"I'll bet." The woman narrowed her eyes at Harper. Her gaze traveled up and down Harper's body, seemingly taking in her shabby appearance.

Harper fought to keep her hands at her sides, struggling not to fuss with her hair or straighten her jacket.

Judith wrinkled her nose as if Harper smelled bad. "I heard you were out. I figured you'd show up here eventually." She gazed past her onto the street. "How did you get here? I thought you sold your car."

"I did." Her car had been one of the first things to go,

and selling it had almost covered an entire house payment. "I took a bus to Colorado."

"Classy."

"I'm here to get Floyd."

"Yeah? Are you going to take him back to Kansas with you on the bus?"

"Well, I wasn't planning to take him home today. I need to scrape together a little money first. But I've got a job."

"Here in Creedence? Doing what? Cleaning toilets?"

She tried not to wince. Judith's words hit too close to home. Her job entailed more than cleaning toilets, but she knew any attempt to explain that would just end up making it worse. Best to change the subject. "I just passed the school and saw Floyd on the playground."

Judith straightened, her eyes widening in alarm. "Did he see you?"

"No. The bell rang when I got there so I didn't have a chance to talk to him." As much as it pained her, she needed to appeal to this woman's good side. If she had one. At this point, Harper wasn't sure. "You must be doing a good job with him. He looked good. Happy."

"He is happy. He's doing well here. Now." Even though Judith was shorter than Harper, she still seemed to peer down her nose at her. "It took weeks for him to settle in after the trauma of you being arrested and him being taken into the custody of the state."

Harper rolled her eyes. "He wasn't taken into custody. He watched television and slept on the sofa in the social worker's office."

Judith raised an eyebrow. "Yeah, I'm sure he was having a great time watching cartoons after seeing his mom handcuffed by the cops and taken away in a police car, and then being taken away himself and not knowing what would happen to him. That wouldn't have been frightening at all."

Harper winced. She hated thinking about that night—knew that Floyd had to have been terrified. "I wasn't making light of it," she said, speaking through her teeth with forced restraint. This woman pushed all her buttons. "But that is in the past. And maybe if you would have let me speak to him on the phone, I would have been able to calm him down."

"I was the one who was finally able to calm him down. After I got him out of that town and brought him here."

Harper let out a slow breath. "And I appreciated that. Really. I can't thank you enough for all you've done for him the past few months. But I'm here now, and I'd like to see him and tell him I'm planning to take him home."

"Do you really think that's a good idea?"

"What do you mean? Of course it's a good idea. He's my son, and my heart is breaking with missing him. I just need a few weeks to make some money, and then I can take him home."

"Home? To where? That little hovel in Kansas? I went to the house to pick up some clothes and toys for Floyd, and I was appalled at the poverty and filth you were living in. There were dirty dishes in the sink, and the boy's bed hadn't even been made. Did he sleep on a bare mattress?"

"No. Of course not. That was just bad timing. His sheets were in the dryer, and we'd just finished eating when the police arrived, which is why the kitchen was a mess. I couldn't very well ask the officers to give me a few minutes to clean up the dishes before they arrested me."

The other woman crossed her arms over her thin chest.

She wore black dress slacks and a red sweater-and-cardigan twin set. Her only jewelry was a string of pearls around her neck and small ruby earrings.

Harper could imagine how her grandmother's small house looked to this woman, but it was home to her. And to Floyd. Nana had insisted on keeping things neat, and it felt as if every time Harper walked through the door, the house smelled like vanilla or cinnamon or a pot roast. The house might be old, and despite the mess the night she'd been taken into custody, the rooms had been scrubbed and polished and had all been filled with memories of laughter and comfort.

"We might not have a big, fancy house like this one, but we don't need one. We'll manage just fine. As long as we're together."

"Together on the streets? Or in a homeless shelter?" Judith gave her an impatient sneer. "Come on, Harper. Look at yourself. You have no money, no vehicle, and I'm assuming by the looks of your unkempt clothes and hair that you have no place to stay either. Where did you sleep last night? In the gutter?"

"No, of course not." She'd slept in a barn.

"It doesn't matter. You know what I'm saying. Have you even asked yourself what you *really* have to offer this child?"

Her words hit Harper like a punch to the gut. "He's my son. I love him."

"I know you do. But sometimes love isn't enough. Love doesn't pay the bills. As you've already learned. You couldn't support him without turning to illegal means. Think about Floyd for a minute. He's happy here. He's doing well in school, he's made friends, and he's even playing sports. Do you want to take that away from him? Rip him out of school and a home where's he's well fed and has a nice room and new clothes? You've already put him through the trauma of uprooting him from his home and school once. Do you really want to do that to him again? Just when he's doing so well? Who are you really thinking about? Him? Or yourself?"

Bile rose in Harper's throat, and she couldn't speak. Was Judith right? Had she only been thinking about herself?

"Seriously, Harper. What do you have to offer the boy? It doesn't appear that you can even take care of yourself. I was hoping you'd have it together before you showed up at my door, but it seems that once again you're only thinking of yourself and your needs." She pinched her lips together in a tight line. "I didn't want to have to do this now, but since you're here, I might as well tell you I'm filing for temporary custody of Floyd Michael."

The blood rushed to Harper's ears. *Filing for custody?*

"Y-Y-You can't do that. I'm his mother." But what kind of mother had she been lately? The empty feeling in her stomach from before switched to nausea, and she swallowed at the pain burning her throat as her stomach clenched and roiled.

"Normally that would be enough for you to get him back, but anyone can see you aren't really fit to raise him. Not in your current state. And you put him in jeopardy when you chose to bring a criminal into your home and let her be around your son."

"A criminal? You mean Brandy? She's his *grandmother*."

"She's also a felon. And currently serving a jail sentence. Which just goes to show you were raised in a life of crime, and illegal activities were modeled for you. That's not going to look good in court."

How could she argue with that? Her mother had been enmeshed in some sort of criminal activities for as long as she could remember. "My mom won't be around him now."

The other woman formed her mouth into a fake frown. "Only on visiting days, right?"

"I am *not* my mother."

Judith raised an eyebrow.

"I'm not. You can ask anyone."

"Anyone like who? Who do you have in your life that will stick up for you? Who's willing to testify on your behalf? Anyone who's willing to travel to Colorado? I'm assuming you don't have any real friends, or one of them would have bailed you out. So who's going to vouch for you in court here? Not even your own mother can testify."

Every word she said was like a nail to Harper's heart. She had no one. She used to have Michael and her grandmother. But now she couldn't think of a single person who would be willing to testify on her behalf. She'd burned bridges when she'd left her job, and being a single mom didn't leave her much time to make friends or go out.

"You might have had some leverage back in Kansas, but you're in my town now," Judith continued. "Everyone here knows me, including the county judge. He played golf with my husband for years. He's had dinner on numerous occasions in my home. I'm a deacon at my church and have served on the city council. People here know me, respect me.

"Who do you think they're going to choose to raise an impressionable young boy? His loving grandmother who is a pillar of her community and has the means to raise him or you, his jailbird mother who doesn't have a home or a car, or even a pot to piss in. All she has is a meager job and a prison record." Judith spat out the last words with venom that belied her outstanding pillar/loving grandmother status.

"You can't do this. You wouldn't. My son needs me. Think about Floyd."

"I am thinking about Floyd. And I *can* do this. I've already started the paperwork. I suggest you don't try to contact him. Like I said, he's doing well here. If you show up, you're only going to confuse him and hurt him all over again. If you really love him, you'll leave him alone and let him be happy." She stepped back and shut the door firmly in Harper's face.

Harper's shoulders slumped forward, and she weaved as she took a step back, reaching out to steady herself as she sagged against the porch railing.

Judith's words whirled through her head, and Harper had no defense. Everything the older woman had said was true.

I am worthless. And I have no one, not one single person, to stand up for me and say I'm a good mom. Or even say I'm a good person.

Was she a good mom? Sure, she loved her son, but she was sure Brandy loved her too, in her own demented way. Was love enough? The past six months had proven that love didn't put food on the table.

Harper took another step back and bumped into the bicycle. It fell to the porch with a crash, and she wanted to kick it, to stomp on it, to rip the handlebars off the frame and shove them down Judith's arrogant pearl-strung throat.

God, she *was* a terrible person. Who had these rage-filled thoughts of hurting another person? A person who was trying to do the best for her son?

She stumbled down the steps of the beautiful home. Nana's house was neat and filled with memories, but from the outside, it didn't compare to Judith's with its cheery Christmas decorations, two-car garage, and giant yard.

Judith said Floyd was happy here. He was doing well in school, making friends. Even playing sports. He'd asked to play soccer the summer before, but Harper hadn't had the money for him to even join a rec league.

Who was she kidding? No one was going to choose her instead of Judith and the life she offered.

What do I have to offer him? I have no home, no place to stay, and a temporary job fixing meals and cleaning toilets.

Harper staggered to the sidewalk, her shoulders heavy as if bearing the weight of loaded barbells. She didn't know what to do, had no one to turn to.

Fear and anger and rage churned inside her. She wanted to scream, to tear something in two, to hit someone. *I did this to myself. I gambled away my chance at being a good mom when I threw in with my own mother.*

Heat filled her body as if she was burning from the inside out, and all she wanted to do was escape, to run. She took a few steps forward, then stumbled midstride before catching herself and propelling her body forward. Her boots hit the concrete sidewalk as her legs pumped and she ran as hard as she could.

The scene with Judith, her terrible words, replayed in Harper's mind again and again, each condemning word pounding into her brain with every footfall. She made it two blocks before her lungs were burning and her body wanted to quit. But she didn't want to stop. Her chest tightened and her calves raged, but she was afraid if she stopped, she might break apart.

She ran another half block before her body gave out and she staggered to a stop, pressing her hand to her stomach where a stitch was splitting her side. She rolled her shoulders, violently rotating them as if the fabric of her clothes irritated her skin. The bitter taste of bile filled her mouth, and she spit on the ground, fighting another wave of nausea.

Stumbling on an uneven section of the sidewalk, she went down on one knee, cracking the bone onto the concrete and tearing the knee of her jeans. She rolled over on the ground, clutching her hurt knee to her stomach. Her body was spent and soaked with sweat, and she lay on the freezing concrete and felt the cold as it seeped through the thin layer of her jacket like water soaking into the sand after a wave has crashed on the beach.

Her mom had taken her to the beach once. It had been a big deal, a road trip to California for her ninth birthday, and her mom had promised to take her to Disneyland. But the first day they got there, they'd gone to the beach and she'd waded out into the water.

Her mom had laughed and encouraged her to run into the waves. She never warned her daughter about how cold the water would be or how fast and hard the waves smashed into the shore. Harper had run out, then realized she'd gone too far and had tried to turn back just as a huge wave crashed into her back, dragging her down and tumbling her over and over, the sand scraping her tender skin and the force of her fall snapping her wrist.

So instead of visiting Mickey Mouse or building sand-castles, Harper had spent her birthday in the emergency room getting fitted for a cast. Her arm had been broken along with something else—the blind trust she'd had in her mother.

Why hadn't Brandy warned her to be careful? Why had she still been lounging on her towel, flirting with some guy and laughing at her when Harper finally made it out of the surf and lurched across the hot sand, cradling her arm to her stomach? It wasn't until she held up her hand and her mom saw the funny bend to her wrist that she stopped laughing.

But something had changed that day. Some thread of trust that her mom would always watch out for her, would warn her of danger and be there to take care of her, was now broken. Brandy had always been flighty and cared mainly about herself and her own needs, but Harper had believed that if push came to shove, her mom would be there. That day, she'd been pushed and shoved. And Brandy had laughed.

That's the way she felt today, as if she'd been slammed by a monstrous wave, spinning and turning, her skin scraping against the sand and her bones cracking against the shore.

But instead of her losing that trust, she was afraid Floyd was the one who felt betrayed. And that hurt more than anything else.

She curled into a ball, shoving her hands into her pock-ets and hunching her shoulders. Her fingers grazed the folded stack of bills she'd shoved into her jacket before she'd left the house. Pushing herself up, she sat on the sidewalk and pulled the money that Logan had given her from her pocket.

A plan emerged as she gazed at the cash. There was close to two hundred dollars in her hand—not a lot—but when she combined it with the old blue truck she had the keys to, it was enough to get her and Floyd out of Colorado.

CHAPTER 8

HARPER STARED AT THE BILLS. COULD SHE REALLY TAKE Logan's money? And his truck? He'd said the truck wasn't important to him, but still. Grand theft auto, regardless of how ungrand the auto was, still held a much worse sentence than stealing a measly two hundred bucks.

And she'd be taking more than just his money and an old truck. She'd be taking his trust. For some reason, that mattered to her. It shouldn't—she'd only known the guy for one damn day. What did it matter what his opinion of her was?

But she knew it did. It mattered because he'd given her a chance. He'd trusted her and let her into his home when she felt like she'd failed everyone else in her life.

Maybe he would understand. She could write him a letter, explain about Floyd and how she needed the money, and swear she'd pay it back as soon as she was settled. Except where were they going to settle with only two hundred dollars? And how was she going to pay anything back when she had no job?

She let out a sigh and shoved the cash back into her pocket. She couldn't do it, couldn't take Logan's pickup or his money. She wasn't a criminal.

Oh wait, yes, she was. She'd just been released from county jail because she'd stolen money from her mom's employer. Even though she hadn't known what she was doing at the time, she had been a part of it. She *was* a criminal. But that wasn't who she wanted to be. She didn't want to hurt Logan. And she didn't want to break the tenuous relationship they'd formed. He made her laugh, and they talked and got along—like friends. And he was the first friend she'd had in years.

Although she'd never had a friend who sent heat shooting up her spine just by smiling at her, but that was beside the point. And thinking about that was not doing anything to help her current situation.

She had to stay focused on Floyd and what was best for him. She loved that kid so much. Was she really being selfish by wanting to keep him with her? Slumping forward, her shoulders caving in, she pressed her fist hard against her mouth as she fought not to break down and weep.

Stop it. She took a deep breath and pushed her shoulders back. She hadn't cried in jail. She wouldn't cry now. Those bitches in lockup had been a hell of a lot tougher than Judith Benning, and she hadn't let them tear her down. Why was she going to let some socialite from a small town defeat her?

Floyd was *her* son. She would do anything—go to the ends of the earth—for that kid. That's what made her a good mom. It wasn't money or a nice house. It was time spent teaching him to read and to throw a ball and playing hours and hours of Clue because it was his favorite game. It was being there when he was sick and being there when he needed her.

She *was* a good mom. *And* she was a fighter. She needed to pull it together. This wasn't her. When had she ever just lain down and taken it? When had she ever given up without a fight when something was important to her? And Floyd was the most important thing in the world to her.

Maybe she wasn't what was best for him right now. But

she could be. She just needed some time. Some time to get herself together. To make a little money, get them a place to stay, even if it was only temporary until she could get them back to Kansas.

She could do this. No matter how menial the work was, she did have a job, and she'd told Logan she wanted to be paid every Friday, so she'd have some money by the end of the week and would be able to find a place to stay.

She needed to rein in her emotions, think clearly, and make a plan. *And get up off the damn sidewalk.* She pushed to her feet and brushed the dirt from her pants. Taking a tentative step forward, she put a little pressure on her knee. It hurt, but she could walk.

Harper gave a panicked glance around her. Had anyone seen her fevered sprint away from Judith's house? That's all she needed—a witness to her crazed behavior.

Tucking her chin to her chest, she headed down the sidewalk. She still had time, but she'd need to stay focused and get the shopping done quickly. Ignoring the ache in her knee, she hurried back to the grocery store.

As she walked, she formulated a plan for what she needed to do to establish some stability. If Judith took her to court, she'd need to show she had a place to live and some income. Which meant she needed to keep this job, so no flirting with the boss.

She wouldn't be able to afford a place to stay until after she got her first paycheck, and even then it would be tight. She might be able to find a room to rent or a small cottage. They didn't need much, but she couldn't very well expect a judge to hand over her son if she was sleeping in a barn. If only she actually lived at Rivers Gulch.

Or…hmmm…a terrible but kind of brilliant idea came to her. What if she could *prove* she lived in a stable place without actually living there? All she'd need is a piece of mail addressed to her and delivered to the ranch. That couldn't be too hard.

The post office sat across the street from the grocery store. She waited for a car to pass, then hurried across the road and into the building. It would only take a few minutes to mail a letter. Except she didn't have a letter. Or a stamp. Or an envelope. Or the address of the ranch.

Think. She chewed her bottom lip as she glanced around the inside of the building.

"Can I help ya?" A tall, thin man with a pair of glasses perched on his balding head stood behind the counter.

"I need to mail a letter but don't have a stamp or an envelope."

"Ayup," he said and nodded to the self-service machine that sat against the wall.

Perfect. The machine had everything she needed. A small envelope cost a quarter, and a single stamp was forty-nine cents. Now all she needed was seventy-four cents and the ranch address.

Oh. She had it. She'd driven the answer into town. "I'll be right back," she called and hobbled quickly back across the street to where she'd parked the blue truck. Popping open the glove box, she rummaged through the papers inside until she found what she was searching for. *Ha.* She knew they'd keep the truck registration in here, and the address of the ranch was printed right on it.

On the floor of the truck sat a plastic console with two cup holders and a little storage compartment. The storage area held a box of matches, a packet of gum, three pens, assorted receipts, and some loose change.

She wouldn't take Logan's two hundred bucks, but she was desperate enough to borrow three quarters. She grabbed the coins and a pen and took the registration back to the post office.

The postman seemed unfazed by her return. Sticking the coins in the slot, she bought the supplies, then set them on the tall table next to the machine. She quickly stamped and addressed the envelope to herself, using the ranch's address. Should she just send the envelope or put something inside? A stack of red flyers for the Creedence Christmas Celebration sat on the table. She grabbed one, folded it, and stuck it in the envelope. Did she need to include any pertinent information on the flyer? Something to show she truly lived and worked there? Or should she write a note to herself to prove it was authentic correspondence? Maybe she should put her current employer's name on it and the date she was hired.

She wrote the word "Logan," then changed her mind and crossed it out. Her boss's name and a random date wouldn't mean anything. The envelope and the postmark were what mattered. She licked the envelope, sealed it, and held it out to the postman. "Will this still make it out in today's mail?"

"Ayup," he said, glancing at the envelope, then tossing it into a box on his desk.

"Thanks," she said over her shoulder as she raced back across the street.

Cheery holiday music played through the speakers of the market as she quickly moved up and down the aisles, searching for the things on her list and tossing them in the cart. She wasn't feeling cheery. Her emotions flipped from angry to frustrated to determined, and her jaw hurt from clenching her teeth. But at least she'd done something. She'd taken a step to help herself and her son.

Her phone suddenly vibrated in her pocket, and her heart leapt to her throat. Could it be Judith? Or Floyd? They were the only ones with this number. Maybe Judith had had a change of heart, or maybe Floyd *had* seen her at the school. Harper almost dropped the phone in her haste to extract it from her pocket, then cringed when she saw the screen.

She'd forgotten that one other person also had her number, and he was the one calling her now. What could Logan want? Was he checking up on her? She let the phone ring, not willing to waste the precious minutes left on the phone by answering. If it was important, he could send her a text.

She was starting to put the phone back in her pocket when it buzzed in her hand again. *Shoot.* Should she just answer it? With Judith's threat, Harper hated to waste even a second of the phone's remaining time in case she needed it to call an attorney or something.

That was laughable. She hadn't been able to afford an attorney when she was arrested, which was part of the reason she'd remained in jail so long, so where did she think she'd get the money to pay for one now?

The only way she had to make money was this job. So upsetting her boss by ignoring his calls probably wasn't the smartest move.

She flipped the phone open and held it to her ear. "Is this an emergency?" she snapped.

"Um, well, no," Logan stammered.

Oh my. The sound of his voice was deep and delicious and had heat melting down her spine like butter softening on a warm biscuit. Her knuckles turned white as she clutched the handle of the grocery cart and tried to even out her breathing. *Keep focused.*

"I was just calling because I realized I was out of toothpaste and was hoping you could grab me a tube while you're at the store. Are you still at the store?"

She blew her bangs off her forehead. "Yes, I'm still in the store, but toothpaste definitely does not constitute an emergency."

"Depends on who you ask. Four out of five dentists might disagree with you."

A grin threatened her mouth, but she pressed her lips together. She didn't have time for jokes. And was this really about toothpaste, or was he calling to see if she'd actually gone to the store or absconded with his money? Either way, the clock was ticking on her minutes. "Okay, toothpaste, got it. Any particular brand?"

"I don't know. My sister usually gets this stuff and stocks up. Since she moved out, all our stock is depleting. Just get what you normally use. Surprise me."

He made it sound as though she were the bartender and he was asking for a drink. Coming right up—one shot of fluoride and minty white freshness, on the rocks, shaken not stirred.

Geez. Her jokes were as bad as his. Apparently neither of them was cut out to be a comedian. She'd better keep focused on her day job. "Anything else? We're wasting my minutes." *Crud.* She hadn't meant to say that. She inhaled, then softened her tone. "I mean, if you need anything else, just text me. I'll be here another fifteen minutes or so."

"Sounds good. I'm getting ready to head into town. I'll see you at the diner in twenty."

"See you then. Bye." She snapped the phone shut, mentally calculating the cost of the call. They'd been on less than two minutes, so it couldn't have amounted to much. But she didn't have much to start with.

It only took another few minutes to finish grabbing the items on her list, including the toothpaste, and then she headed toward the only open register and got in line. The woman in front of her was eighty if she was a day, short and plump, with her thin lips pressed into a fierce wrinkled line.

A huge black bag sat in the top section of her cart. A small terrier poked its head out of the bag and rested its chin on the side of the cart. It was cute, but didn't look much friendlier than its owner, who was laying into the flustered cashier.

"I told you I got those three items out of the clearance bin marked fifty percent off and those six items out of the bin marked seventy-five percent off. These two cans were buy one, get one free, and I have coupons for every other item. I shouldn't be paying full price for anything." The woman crossed her arms and stared at the young girl, who didn't look older than fifteen or sixteen.

The green store apron hung on the teenager's thin frame, and she seemed to shrink under the older woman's gaze as her shoulders sagged inward. "I'm sorry, Mrs. Scary...er, oh my gosh, I mean Mrs. Perry. This is my first week, and I'm still getting the hang of the register." The girl's cheeks blazed pink as she focused on the groceries, picking up one item after another, then setting it back down.

The woman ignored the jab and peered over the teenager's shoulder. "Where's Martha? She's been checking me out for thirty years. She knows what she's doing."

"Martha's out for the next six weeks. She had surgery on her foot. It was a bunion, I think."

"Six weeks off *and* surgery? For a bunion? That's ridiculous. I've had a bunion for twenty years, and I've never taken a day off for it. My big toe is as crooked as a dirty politician, but do you hear me complaining about it? No. I just suck it up and get on with my day."

The girl gaped, her eyes wide as her mouth opened and closed.

"Martha just figures out the difference, then punches the new price into the register," the woman continued. "Didn't they teach you basic math in school? What are my tax dollars paying for?" The dog gave a tiny yip as if he agreed.

The girl swallowed and grabbed a calculator. She pushed her glasses up her nose as she studied it, then gave a baffled glance back at the register.

Harper couldn't take it anymore. She didn't normally butt into other people's crises, but these two obviously needed help. And if she didn't step in, they could be there all day. "Can I help? I'm pretty good with numbers." The cans were clearly marked with the regular price stickers, and she'd already done the calculations in her head.

The teenager's head popped up, and she eagerly nodded.

But the elderly woman wasn't so sure. She stared coolly at Harper. "Who are you?"

"I'm Harper. I work for Logan Rivers." Why did she bring up Logan's name? The idea was to stay anonymous and not cause any trouble for the man. She needed to get the focus back on the groceries. "And like I said, I'm good with math."

The woman narrowed her eyes, studying Harper, then gave a small nod. "The Rivers are good people. I trust Logan's judgment." She turned back to the cashier. "Give her the calculator."

The cashier thrust the calculator in her direction, but Harper waved it away. "I'm good." She pointed at the items on the conveyer belt. "The baked goods are regularly a dollar ninety-eight, but with the fifty percent off, they're ninety-nine cents each, so punch in ninety-nine cents and hit it three times. Those taco shells are normally two ninety-five but are now seventy-four cents with the discount." She continued with each sale item, figuring the price, then pausing as the cashier fervently hit the keys on the register. When she finished the sale items, Harper pointed at the last few things. "You can run the regular-price items through as they are, then scan the coupons, and the register will take off the correct amount."

"Thank you," the teenager mouthed, then finished scanning the items and conveyed the total to Mrs. Perry.

The older woman pulled a long, fat wallet from her bag. It was stuffed with cash, coupons, and what looked like every receipt she'd received since the Reagan administration. The leather was stretched and worn, and she pulled off the thick rubber band that held it closed. Thumbing through the papers inside, she retrieved a fifty-dollar bill and passed it to the clerk. "Wait. I've got the change."

Digging back into her bag, she produced a bloated coin purse and unsnapped the closure. As she pulled a wad of folded bills from the top to get to the change, one of the bills slipped off the counter and floated to the floor.

Harper stared at the money. It was another fifty-dollar bill, and the older woman hadn't noticed that it fell. All Harper would have to do was take a step forward and cover the bill with her foot, then retrieve it after the woman was gone. The older woman had so much cash stuffed throughout her purse that she'd never notice this bill was gone.

A person never knew with old ladies though. They could pinch the heck out of a penny and have stacks of cash stowed at the bank, or they could be on a fixed income and make the cash from their social security check last all month by buying day-old bread and expired taco shells from the bargain bin.

The woman wasn't paying the least bit of attention to Harper as she pointed to the bags of groceries. "I suppose you don't have anyone here to help me carry these to my car either. Who's supposed to take care of that? My dog?"

Harper thought of her own grandmother as she bent to retrieve the bill, then passed it to Mrs. Perry. "You dropped this, ma'am."

The woman turned and stared at the money in Harper's hand before reaching out and snatching it back like a bird seizing a worm from the ground. She glared at Harper as if she'd stolen the money instead of trying to give it back. "Thank you," she snapped.

"No problem," Harper answered. "And I can carry those bags out to your car." She nodded to her cart, then told the cashier, "It will just take me a minute. You can take the next person in line while I run this stuff out." She turned to the person who had come up in line behind her and was surprised to see Bryn, the waitress from the diner.

"Hey, Harper." Bryn was wearing a blue down parka

over her pink uniform, and her lips shone with a glossy pink shimmer as they curved into a smile. "Go ahead. I'll watch your stuff."

"Thanks. You can do yours while I'm gone." She glanced at the jar of olives and the two industrial-sized cans in the other woman's arms. One held peaches, and the other contained mayonnaise. "Although I'm a little nervous about what the heck kind of recipe you're buying those ingredients for."

Bryn laughed. "The owner of the diner is having a bad week and forgot to place an order for supplies. We were stocked up on most things, but she sent me to grab these." She juggled the items as she placed them on the belt. "Except for the olives. I think those are for her closing-time martini."

Harper smiled and loaded Mrs. Perry's bags into her cart. After the day she'd had, she could use a martini right about now. If only she weren't driving and martinis weren't so disgusting. She'd tried one of her mom's once, and it tasted like gasoline, with an olive. Whose idea was it to stick a weird, salty olive into a mixed drink anyway?

"I'll be right back." She gingerly held her hand out to let the dog sniff her before gripping the handle of the cart and following Mrs. Perry to her car.

She led Harper to a cherry-red Volkswagen Beetle convertible and opened the passenger door. "Just put them on the floor there. Romeo likes to ride in the front seat."

Harper assumed Romeo was the dog. Either that or Mrs. Perry was picking up her boyfriend on her way home. With this one, Harper couldn't be sure. "Fun car," she said, lifting the bags from the cart.

"I think so. I always wanted a convertible. But my husband thought they were too dangerous. So when he died, I went out and bought myself one. What do I have to be scared of?"

Harper shrugged and gingerly lifted the purse containing the dog and set it on the front seat.

"That was impressive back there," the older woman said. "What'd you say your name was again?"

"Harper. Harper Evans."

The elderly woman held out a wrinkled hand. "Nice to meet you, Harper Evans. I'm Etta Perry. You can call me Ms. Etta, or just Etta, or Mrs. Perry, or Mrs. Scary, if you want. I guess I prefer Etta, but I don't really give a fig what you call me, as long as you don't call me late for dinner."

"Nice to meet you too, Ms. Etta." Harper took her hand, and the other woman gave it an encouraging squeeze. The gesture and the woman's thin, papery skin reminded Harper so much of her grandmother that she had to swallow as an ache of loneliness burned her throat. She missed Nana so much.

Etta studied her face before letting go of her hand. "So do you always offer to help out feeble old ladies?"

"No." Harper peered around the parking lot. "Why? Do you see one around here who needs help?"

The woman's mouth curved into a grin. "Ha. You're a feisty one. I like that though. Too many women pander, and I've got no use for pandering. I'm too old for suck-ups."

"Me too." Harper finished loading the last bag and shut the door. "You're all set."

"Thank you, Harper." Etta still held her coin purse, and she hoisted it in the air. "May I pay you for your trouble?"

Harper shook her head. "It wasn't any trouble. I was glad

to help. I recently lost my grandmother, and I think you two would have made great friends." She didn't know why she just told Ms. Etta that. Harper wasn't usually much of a sharer—especially when it came to personal stuff in her life.

Etta let out a bark of laughter as she opened the driver's door. "I doubt that. I don't make a lot of friends."

"Well, you made one today. See you, Ms. Etta." Harper waved as she headed back into the store.

Bryn was unloading Harper's cart, and the cashier was just finishing running her items. "We saw you through the window and figured we'd get your stuff rung up so you wouldn't have to wait," the cashier told her.

"Oh thanks. You didn't have to do that."

"It's the least I could do. I can't thank you enough for helping me with old Mrs. Scary." She clapped a hand to her mouth. "Oh my-lanta. I did it again. It's a bad habit. I live down the street from her, and the kids on our block have always called her that."

Harper had a feeling more than just a few kids did. And Ms. Etta seemed to live up to, if not relish, the nickname. "It was no big deal. And she didn't seem so bad. I thought she was funny."

Bryn rubbed a hand across Harper's back as she crossed behind her and started bagging the groceries. "You continually surprise me, Harper. From the outside, you seem tough, but every time I've been around you, I've witnessed you doing something nice for someone else. I think you might be a softie on the inside."

Every time she'd been around her? She'd been in the waitress's company exactly two times. Harper wasn't sure that constituted much of an "every time" instance.

The cashier gave her the total, saving Harper from having to answer Bryn. Not that she knew what to say to her comment anyway. The waitress might have seen her do a couple of nice things, but they didn't negate the truly terrible things Harper had done when she'd risked her freedom and abandoned her son. If Bryn knew what kind of person she really was, she'd run fast and far away from Harper.

But for now, the waitress was the only semifriend she had in this town. Well, besides her semifriendship with Logan and her recent acquaintance with a cantankerous widow. And as long as she was tallying, there was a feisty kitten back at the ranch who held her in pretty high regard. So, by her recent standards, she was actually doing all right in the semifriend department. It was the most semifriendships she'd had in a long time.

Harper paid the bill, and Bryn fell in step with her as they left the store. The lot was empty except for the blue pickup. "Where's your car?"

"I walked over," Bryn said, shifting her bags so she could pull a hot-pink stocking cap from her pocket.

"I'm heading to the diner now to meet Logan. I'll give you a lift."

"Thanks." Bryn followed her to the truck. "Sweet ride."

"It's one of the ranch trucks. Logan loaned it to me so I could come into town and get some groceries."

"Things must be going pretty well with him," the waitress commented. "If you're driving one of the farm trucks, he must not have fired you yet. And by the looks of this food, it seems like you're feeding him pretty well. Thank goodness you really can cook. Otherwise, we both would have been in hot water."

"So far, so good," Harper said, loading the bags onto the seat. "Thanks again for recommending me for the job. I think it's really working out."

"I'm glad. For both of you. Logan's a good guy, and he needs a hand right now. You haven't been tempted to get up to any housekeeping hanky-panky, have you?"

Housekeeping hanky-panky? Did Bryn think she was up to no good with the housekeeping job? Did she think she would steal from Logan? She turned to gape at the waitress.

But Bryn was wearing a playful smile, and she waggled her eyebrows. "He is pretty dang cute. It's easy to imagine playing house with him."

Oh. *That* kind of hanky-panky.

Harper's cheeks warmed. "Is he cute? I hadn't noticed." She tried to keep a straight face, but her lips tugged up in a grin. "Just get in the truck."

CHAPTER 9

THE TWO WOMEN WERE STILL LAUGHING AND JOKING around when they walked into the diner five minutes later. Harper liked the waitress and had even agreed to get together for coffee with her later in the week. It had been ages since anyone had invited her out for a coffee, and the invitation somehow made her feel like a real person again, not just a number in the county system or the empty husk she'd been feeling like since Nana died.

She kept a pretty hard shell around herself, but Bryn was breaking through the cracks, and it felt good to have another woman to talk to. Not that she had told her any of her real problems. Or about Floyd. She didn't trust her that much yet. She didn't trust *anyone* that much.

The waitress might be sweet and fun, but Harper knew when it came down to it, the only one she could truly rely on was herself. But it did feel good to laugh.

Her laughter caught in her throat as she glimpsed Logan sitting at the counter. His hat sat on the stool next to him, and his chestnut hair was mussed. He was looking out the window, a pensive expression on his face as he pushed the remaining crumbs around on his plate.

"Hey, Logan," Bryn called out as they walked toward him. "Look who I found at the market."

Harper had no choice but to follow in the waitress's wake. She'd carried in the giant can of peaches and held it awkwardly against her stomach. Logan turned his head toward them, and his lips curved into a grin as his gaze bobbed from Bryn to her.

She swallowed. *Holy hot hunk of cowboy.* What a grin that man had. Her stomach dropped like an elevator whose cable had just snapped.

Her tongue was tied in all kinds of knots, and her mouth was suddenly so dry, she wasn't sure she could speak. "Hi," she finally managed.

"Hey," he answered, glancing down at the industrial-size can in her hands. "Nice peaches."

Her eyes widened, and he let out a chuckle. "I guess you weren't kidding about that peach cobbler. But how much are you planning to make?"

She smiled, her face heating. *Geez.* What was happening to her? She wasn't normally affected by a man just because he was good-looking. But something about Logan had her body heating and her skin flushing every time she was around him. "This isn't for us. It's for the diner. I was just helping Bryn," she answered, her words coming too fast.

He grinned. "I figured. But I couldn't pass up a chance to tease a woman carrying a giant can of peaches. It was too easy."

Bryn moved behind the counter, setting down her bags and taking off her hat and jacket. She smoothed her hair as she approached Logan. "So, it sounds like everything is going great out at the Gulch. I told you my girl was a good bet."

Harper swallowed again, but this time for a different reason. Bryn's words touched her. She hadn't considered herself anyone's idea of a good bet in a very long time. Now both Bryn and Logan had taken a chance on her, and she didn't want to let either of them down.

Logan tilted his head, narrowing his eyes and appraising Harper as if she were a prized calf. "I gotta give you it to you, Bryn. You were right about this one. She's doing a great job. In fact, I was hoping I'd see you today so I could tell you thanks. I owe you one."

Bryn chuckled. "You owe me several. But who's counting, right?"

"Apparently you are."

Harper smiled with them, but she hated the twinge of jealousy that snaked through her at their easy camaraderie. Of course they could tease and joke. Bryn had said they'd known each other since high school. Harper pushed down the yucky feelings and tried to get in on the joke. "Hello. You know I'm standing right here. And still holding a colossally heavy can of peaches."

"Oh shoot. Sorry." Logan jumped up and took the can from her, then set it on the counter.

It hadn't really been that heavy, but the chivalrous way he'd leapt to his feet to take it from her had her stomach doing those crazy flips again. Now that she didn't have the can, she had nothing to hold, and she suddenly couldn't figure out what to do with her hands. "Well, we should probably go. Since we've got groceries in the truck and all."

"Good point." He picked up his hat and gave Bryn a wink. "Thanks again. I really do owe you one."

"Don't worry. I know where to find you when it's time to collect." Bryn waved as they headed toward the door. "Catch you all later. And Harper, don't forget about getting that coffee."

Harper smiled and waved, but couldn't seem to breathe because Logan had opened the door for her, then put his hand on her back to guide her around a family with five kids hustling in from the cold. She knew he was just being nice and the gesture meant nothing to him, but the heat of his hand seemed to burn through her thin jacket.

"I want mac and cheese," one of the younger kids yelled as he jostled past his brother and shoved into her legs.

If her brain hadn't been so muddled from dealing with Logan's touch, she might have been steadier on her feet when the kid ran into her. Instead, she stumbled backward and right into Logan's chest. His hands must have automatically come up to catch her, but all she felt was her back against his muscled chest and her body wrapped in his strong arms. She was just the right height so the underside of her breasts rested in the crooks of his elbows, and her nipples tightened with unexpected arousal. Her breasts hadn't been touched on *any* side in so long that she wasn't sure they still worked. But apparently they did, because they were standing at attention and begging for more.

Down, girls. This wasn't sexual. She wasn't falling *for* him. She just fell *into* him. *Yeah, right,* they seemed to answer. Oh geez, she was really losing it when her boobs started talking to her.

Logan held on to her until the rowdy bunch had passed, and then she put her hands on top of his to push herself away. All the other touching had been through their clothes, but touching his hand, his skin was different. It all happened so fast, really just a few seconds, but every moment of contact was ingrained on her mind, seared into her body.

She sucked in a breath as they stepped outside, the cold air filling her lungs. The temperature seemed to have dropped ten degrees since they'd gone into the diner. Either that, or the air just seemed colder because her body had heated to furnace level.

"You okay?" Logan asked, his hand still on her back.

"Yeah, of course," she said, striding toward the truck. "Sorry about that. I didn't mean to fall all over you." Oh geez, why did she say that? She needed to shut her trap. She pressed her lips together and reached for the door handle of the truck.

But Logan beat her to it, his hand already there as he pulled open the door and held it for her to climb in. Thank goodness the groceries were partially in the way and gave her something to focus on as she rearranged them to give her more space to sit.

"Looks like you got some good stuff," Logan said as he got in and started the truck.

Thank goodness he was ignoring her stupid comment and moving on. "Yeah, I picked up some essentials you were out of and should have enough meals planned to get through the end of the week."

"Great." He surveyed the shopping bags before pulling out onto the road. "Did you have enough money?"

The warm fuzzy feelings of being pressed to his chest dissipated like steam in the air. Why did he go right to asking about the money? Was he still thinking about her falling against him, or was he not affected by that at all? Was his question innocent, or did he see the number of bags and suspect she took some of the cash?

"Yes, I had plenty, but I owe you a dollar because I had to buy an envelope and a stamp," she answered as she held out the remaining cash. "Here's the rest of your change."

He shrugged. "Keep it."

"What? No. It's yours."

"It's yours now. You earned it."

"By doing what? A run to the grocery store?" She surveyed the cash in her hand. "I don't think picking up some hamburger and a tube of toothpaste constitutes this much of a tip."

"How much is left?"

"Twenty-six bucks and some change."

Logan slowed the truck and pulled into the parking lot of the convenience store. He nodded to the door as he parked. "How about this? Why don't you take the leftover money and go inside and buy a card or whatever you do to add more minutes to that silly phone."

Her heart leapt at the thought, but she still felt awkward taking his money. "I couldn't."

"Sure you can. Look, I'm your employer, and there may be times I need to get ahold of you. Like if we have another domestic emergency."

"Like if you run out of shampoo?"

"Possibly. I take personal hygiene pretty seriously." He offered her a teasing grin, but butterflies careened through her stomach as she imagined him soaping up his muscular pecs in the shower. She was also reminded of the fact that her hair was going on its third day without being washed. She needed to figure out a way to take a shower.

She looked down at the money in her hand, then back at him, deliberating if it was worth it to keep arguing. His features were set, and really, her losing this argument would still end up as a win because she'd have more minutes on her phone. "Fine," she said. "I'll be right back."

Logan inhaled a deep breath as he watched Harper through the window of the convenience store. Damn, but the woman was beautiful.

And the heck of it was that she didn't seem to realize it or use it to her advantage. She hadn't flirted with him or used her feminine wiles to get anything out of him. In fact, he practically had to twist her arm to get her to take even the smallest things from him, like borrowing his truck or accepting money for her phone.

He liked the way they got along, and it surprised him how comfortable he already felt around her. They talked easily, and she had been a little playful, but as soon as things turned flirty, she seemed to shut it down, keeping them on the friend level.

If that's all she was offering, he'd take it. Hell, he could use a friend right about now.

And it wasn't like there was any point in starting anything up with her. She'd already said she wasn't staying. She was just trying to earn enough money to leave. Which was how things went in his life. Don't know why he was expecting anything different this time.

Maybe because this time it felt different. *She* felt different. Like there might actually be a chance for something there.

Shut it down.

He knew not to get his hopes up—not to expect too much. Harper was gorgeous and smart and had his blood running hot, but there was no chance of a future with her. She was going to leave. Just as every woman he'd cared about had. Evidently a dumb cowboy who couldn't figure out the correct order of numbers and had trouble reading wasn't worth sticking around for.

And apparently it wasn't just women. It seemed like everyone in his life had left him lately. Between Quinn and Max moving out, his dad taking off, and him firing his hired hand, he felt pretty alone.

With Harper there, it was nice to have someone else around to converse with and to have the smell of food baking in the house. But it wasn't just having a warm body and someone to talk to. It was more than that. It had to be. Otherwise, he should have been happy to have Kimmie there. She'd been offering food *and* company, in the kitchen and anywhere else he wanted it. But he didn't want it, not with her.

And it wasn't like that anyway. He knew where to find female company if he wanted it. This was different. He just liked being around this woman. She made him feel good about himself, even though he didn't deserve it. He couldn't believe the crap about his learning disability had come up that morning. He never talked about that. In fact, he tried to pretend it didn't exist. But when he'd admitted his struggles with dyslexia, she hadn't made him feel stupid, even though he knew he was. The mess he'd made of the finances at the farm proved it.

But Harper didn't seem fazed. He didn't think she'd even blinked. Was that what made her different? Made her seem special? No, because his heart had been slamming against his chest from the minute he met her.

He studied her through the glass. Her hips curved as she leaned against the counter waiting for the cashier to ring her up. She reached up and collected the mass of dark hair cascading down her back, then twisted it into some kind of knot on top of her head. The move seemed natural to her, as though she'd done it a hundred times, but there was something so fluid, so graceful about the way her fingers twisted and shaped her hair. .

Graceful didn't seem like an adjective normally used to describe her. Tough, snarky, and a little standoffish were better descriptions. So what was it about this guarded woman with her military boots and a shade of suspicion behind her gorgeous green eyes that was making him get all sentimental and causing him to sweat every time she got too close to him? When she'd fallen back against him as they left the diner, his arms had automatically gone around her, and he hadn't wanted to let go.

A truck pulled up not far from him, drawing his attention away from the dark-haired woman. His jaw clenched as he recognized the man getting out of the passenger side.

The convenience store was on the edge of town and shared a parking lot with The Keg, a dive bar where the locals hung out. The truck had parked between the two businesses, and Logan sighed as he watched his former hired hand amble into the bar. It pissed him off that he'd lost his only help because the man couldn't get a handle on his alcohol addiction.

He had no real interest in talking to the guy, but he should probably let Ted know he'd dropped his truck off at his parents'. He wasn't sure where Ted was staying, but he might eventually need his pickup.

Logan climbed out of the truck as Harper was coming through the convenience store door. He pointed next door.

"I need to take care of something. You can wait in the truck. I'll be back in a minute."

The woeful twang of a sad country song played from the jukebox as Logan stepped into the dimly lit bar. It smelled like stale beer, popcorn, and the sawdust sprinkled across the floor. He scanned the room, surprised at how many people were already there in the middle of the afternoon. But he guessed it was five o'clock somewhere.

He didn't see Ted, but spied a familiar face at the bar and crossed the room to clap the back of the man as he slid onto the stool next to him. "Hey, Zane. I didn't know you were back in town."

The other man's shoulders tensed, then relaxed as he looked sideways, and his scowl eased a bit. "Hey, Rivers. I wasn't planning to be, but apparently the old man needed a hand."

"I heard about Birch's heart attack." Birch Taylor had a well-earned reputation as the town drunk and was known for picking fights and getting into a few scrapes with the law. His son was often either the one getting him out of those scrapes or the one at the other end of his fists. "How's he doing?"

Zane shrugged. "He's out of the hospital and ornery as ever. But at least we know now that he *has* a heart. I've never been sure before." He turned to Logan and offered the merest ghost of a grin, which was akin to a full-on burst of laughter from anyone else. The broody cowboy didn't show much in the way of emotion, and this was about the closest he got to actually cracking a joke.

Although Logan guessed Zane had a right to be broody, having grown up in a small town with his father the butt of any number of jokes. Zane was a year ahead of Logan in school, but they'd had some classes together, and Zane had played hockey on the high school team with him and the James brothers. Zane had always played defense so he didn't do a lot of scoring but he was big and had a mean scowl that scared most players away before he even had to touch them.

He gave off a dangerous vibe, but Logan had never seen him get into a fight or raise a hand to anyone. Hamilton had known Birch for years and had a soft spot for his kid, so Zane had spent quite a few summers working as a hand on the ranch, and he had a gift with horses and animals. For a big guy, he was surprisingly gentle with animals. Quinn had teased him about being able to talk to animals and called him Dr. Dolittle. But only once.

It was just Zane and his dad, and the money he earned on the ranch back then went to pay their rent. He'd also saved enough to buy an old pickup, and it wasn't a week after he'd graduated that he packed it up and left town. But not before getting caught in a public argument with his father and the wrong end of a broken beer bottle that ended with twelve stitches and a trip to the ER.

Zane had always been a good-lookin' kid, and he'd grown into a handsome guy. Except for the long, jagged scar that ran from under the corner of his eye down across the edge of his cheek. A parting gift from his father that night and the final straw that had Zane leaving town.

He'd been back a few times and stopped by the ranch, but Logan hadn't seen him in a couple of years. "What have you been up to? I heard you were working a horse ranch in Montana."

Zane nodded. "Yeah, it was a good gig. I might go back. For now, I told Dad I'd stay through the holidays."

"Good to see you. You'll have to come out to the ranch. We've—" Before he could finish his sentence, pain exploded in his cheek as Logan was sucker punched to the side of his face.

CHAPTER 10

LOGAN REELED BACK, AND HIS HAT FLEW OFF AS HE WAS shoved against the bar. Adrenaline spiked through him as he rose to his feet, his fists already raised. He felt Zane stand behind him as he glared at his former ranch hand. "You'd better back off, Ted. You might have gotten in one punch, but you won't get another."

"Oh yeah? What are you going to do about it? You already took my job and any pride I had left." Ted's voice slurred as he spat out the words.

"I didn't *take* your job. You lost it when you showed up to work drunk."

"So what are you doing here?" He nodded to Zane. "You're settin' the bar pretty low if you're considering this guy for my replacement."

"You need to watch your mouth, Ted." It was taking all Logan had to keep himself in check and not drive his fist into the other man's smug face. "I dropped your truck off at your folks so why don't you go on home now."

"You gonna make me?" He took a step forward and raised his hands to shove Logan, but before he could, a dark-haired woman slipped between them and planted her hands on Ted's chest.

"Ted? Is that you? I was hoping I'd find you here. My cousin said you were a looker, but she failed to describe just how handsome you are in person," Harper said.

At least Logan thought it was Harper. Although she

didn't look, or act, or sound like the Harper he'd just spent the last few days with. This Harper was sultry and seductive as she dipped her head and pouted her lips. Her hip jutted out as she firmly lodged herself between the two men, and Logan noticed the top button of her shirt had been undone. The flash of skin visible almost had him undone.

She was having the same effect on Ted, who had dropped his clenched fists and was staring hazy-eyed down at Harper's chest. "Huh? Who's your cousin?"

"You all went to school together, and she told me to look you up when I came to town. Can I buy you a drink?" Even her voice was different, lower and with a hint of a southern accent.

"Sure, honey," Ted slurred to Harper, then looked back at Logan. "We're not done here, Rivers. But don't worry, you'll get what's coming to you." He slung an arm around Harper's shoulder, and she led him across the room.

The anger Logan felt for getting sucker punched was nothing compared to the fury building in his chest at the sight of that man's hand on Harper's shoulder. How dare he touch her? He took a step forward but stopped as Zane's hand clamped firmly on his shoulder.

"She went to all that effort to break up the fight," Zane said. "Don't screw up her gesture by starting it over."

"You're right." Logan blew out a breath as he turned back to the bar and slammed his fist into the padded barstool. "But I still want to deck the guy. Or at least break the hand he's using to touch her."

"Understood. Who is she?"

"My new housekeeper."

Zane raised an eyebrow. "Mrs. Decker comes in once

a month and cleans our house, but she's never looked like that. I swear she was old even when I was a kid."

"It's temporary. Just through the holidays until my dad gets back." Logan shook his head. "I haven't told him that I fired Ted. Even though I know he would have done the same thing, he's not gonna be happy about it."

"What'd the guy do?"

"Besides show up drunk to work? I found him passed out in one of the horse stalls with a lit cigarette."

"With the horse in it?"

Logan nodded.

Zane's eyes widened, and his mouth tightened into a hard line. "He could have set the whole barn on fire, killed himself and the horse. I don't blame you for firing him. I would have kicked his ass off the ranch too. After I clocked him for putting the animal at risk."

"I almost did."

Zane leaned back against the bar. "Alcohol ain't never caused nothing but trouble in my life. I'm telling you, no good ever comes from getting drunk."

"Agreed. But if that's how you think, what are you doing here having a drink before you've even had supper?"

"First of all, I'm having a drink of soda. And second, I'm here doing what I've been doing since I was eight years old."

As if on cue, Birch Taylor stumbled out of the men's room and headed toward Zane. He lifted his voice and belted out an old Waylon Jennings song.

Zane's jaw tensed, but his face remained expressionless as he let out a weary sigh. "I'm taking care of my dad."

Before Logan could reply, Harper appeared at his back and took his arm. "Let's get out of here."

"Where's Ted?"

"I left him leaning against the jukebox trying to pick a song. The asshole thinks I'm going to dance with him."

Zane nodded toward the door. "Get out of here. We'll continue this entertaining reunion another time."

Logan followed Harper out the door. The cold air felt good against his heated skin.

"I'll drive," Harper said, heading for the driver's side of the truck. "You need to take care of that eye. It's starting to swell."

He passed her the keys. Having grown up with a strong-willed sister, he recognized the determined look in Harper's eye and figured it wasn't worth arguing with her. And it didn't matter to him who drove them home.

"Let me see it," she said, leaning toward him as he climbed into the truck.

He tilted his head to let her examine his eye, but wasn't prepared for the zing of heat that shot through him as her fingers lightly skimmed his forehead.

"It's a little swollen, but no blood." Harper reached into one of the grocery sacks and passed him a bag of frozen corn. "Here. Put this on it."

Logan pressed the cold bag to his face, more to appease her than out of concern for the swelling. "I'm all right. I've been hit much harder than this. The only reason he got one in was because he sucker punched me from behind."

She nodded. "I know. I followed you in and saw him hit you. It was a cheap shot. Asswipe."

"So you saw a big drunk guy punch me and thought you'd step in between us?" He was trying to keep his pride out of it, but she'd dinged it a pretty good one. "Because why? You didn't think I could take him? I was handling it, you know. I didn't need you to defend me."

"I wasn't defending. I was diverting. Jerks like that have tiny Neanderthal brains. They just need something else to focus on." She shifted gears as the truck sped up. "And I had no doubt you could take him, but I just went to all the trouble to buy these nice groceries, and I didn't want them to spoil while I bailed you out of jail."

She offered him a small, impish grin, and his puffed-up arrogant pride deflated as he let out a laugh. "So, really it wasn't even about me, huh? You put yourself in harm's way because of the groceries?"

She shrugged. "I found some nice pork chops. I didn't want to see them go to waste."

Later that night, Harper pulled her jacket around her as she hurried down the driveway. It was starting to snow and the flakes danced in the air, reflecting the moonlight as they swirled to the ground. Normally, she would have stopped to appreciate the beauty of the snow, but tonight all she could think about was the dip in temperature and how cold it was going to be sleeping in the barn.

Logan still thought she was staying with a friend and had again offered her a ride back to town, but she'd brushed him off and assured him it was fine for her "friend" to pick her up. He did question why she had to walk out to the highway instead of them pulling up to the house, but Harper kept her focus on wiping down the counter and mumbled something about stretching her legs and the friend being kind of a jerk like that. What did it matter if she bad-mouthed her? She was a fake friend anyway.

They'd had a good meal. She'd fried the pork chops and mashed some potatoes. It was nice having a stocked pantry, and Logan had raved about her gravy.

She liked talking to him. Although she did more listening than talking. He had fun stories to tell about him and his sister growing up on the ranch. She hoped she'd get a chance to meet Quinn. And Max. That little kid sounded adorable. Logan said he was eight, and she couldn't help but wonder if he knew Floyd, or if they were in the same class, or if they were friends.

She still hadn't told Logan about her son. She'd talked about growing up and had shared a little about her close relationship with her grandmother. But for the first time in a long time, she'd met someone who didn't know anything about her past, who didn't have any preconceived notions about her because they'd heard stories about her crazy mom.

Logan didn't know anything about her, and she liked the freedom of getting to be anyone she wanted to be. She wasn't bogged down by her criminal record or being looked at through the screen of being a poor widow or the bad mom who abandoned her kid when she got sent to jail. She could just be herself, and it felt nice.

She was only going to be here for a few weeks, a month tops, and then she'd never see Logan again. What was wrong with pretending her life was normal and she was an ordinary woman who happened to make excellent gravy?

He seemed to like being around her. He listened when she talked and laughed at her snarky jokes. She'd set the table and bowed her head when he'd blessed the meal. She didn't want to think too hard about the fact that it felt like they were a married couple sitting down to a typical supper. That it felt a little like they were playing house.

But if they really were married, she'd have been able to kiss him and touch him. And she'd be tucked against him in bed right now, running her hands over his hard, muscled body instead of freezing her ass off as she scurried away from the house.

She rounded the corner of the driveway and figured she'd gone far enough. If for some reason, Logan had happened to watch her leave, she should be out of his line of sight. She ducked behind one of the evergreen trees lining the driveway, then doubled back and snuck into the barn. Logan must have used the space heaters while he worked in the office earlier that night because the room still held a cozy warmth.

She sat on the floor and played with the kittens to pass the time until she saw the lights go out in the main house. Even then, she waited another thirty minutes before her chest eased and she felt she was in the clear.

Since she had stuck only the essentials into her backpack when she'd left, she had travel-size shampoo and conditioner and a razor, but not soap or shaving cream. Using the moonlight shining through the window and the dim light from her phone, she searched the bathroom and came up with a sliver of bar soap from the sink and what passed for a clean towel. The only towels under the sink were hand towels, but they'd get the job done. She'd dried herself with paper towels while she'd been at county, so this was a step up.

Pulling back the shower curtain, Harper peered into the

small, shadowy shower and wondered when it had last been used. It smelled dusty, and she squinted into the dark as she searched for dead bugs or spiders. Dammit, why was she thinking about spiders?

She'd stood up to a six-foot drunken bully this afternoon without a second thought, but the idea of stepping into the shower with a spider, or three, gave her the willies. Holding up her phone, she tried to peer into the corners, but it was too dark. She hated to turn on the light, but maybe she could just do it for one second, just to check for spiders or cobwebs.

If she shut the door, surely the light wouldn't be that noticeable. Except that the only light switch was on the wall outside the bathroom, so she wouldn't be able to completely shut the door. *Double damn it.*

Okay, she could do this. She put the supplies on the small shelf in the shower and stripped out of her clothes. Cringing, she reached her hand partway into the shower, then snatched it back.

Come on, Harper. It's not like a spider can kill you. Unless it was a brown recluse... Then it could. *Triple damn.* She couldn't do it. She had to turn on the light. Just for a second.

She closed the door as far as she could while still reaching her arm through. Her fingers touched the switch, and with her other hand, she held the shower curtain open as far as she could so she'd be able to see every corner in the quick moment she turned on the light.

The bathroom was small, but she still must have looked like a crazy, naked woman as she stretched out the shower curtain with one hand and reached her other hand through the door. But she couldn't dwell on that. Or the fact that with the door almost shut like this, the bathroom was super dark. And creepy.

But spiders creeped her out more. She took a deep breath, preparing to search the shower as fast as she could, then flipped the switch.

Holy shit! The switch turned on both the bathroom light *and* the office light! She immediately flipped the switch back down and crouched on the floor. She wasn't sure why the hell she was on the floor. It wasn't as if someone was shooting at her, but dropping to the floor was always the first thing characters did in movies, and it felt like the right thing to do. Except that she was naked, so nothing felt right.

She grabbed the tiny towel and held it up to cover herself as she gingerly stepped into the office and peered out the window toward the house. No lights had come on. The house still looked quiet. If Logan was already in bed, or even in the bathroom, he wouldn't have seen the quick burst of light.

After waiting a beat, she tiptoed back to the bathroom. The good news was she hadn't seen any spiders scurrying across the tiled shower. The bad news was she was going to have to leave the bathroom door and most of the shower curtain open if she wanted to be able to see to take a shower. There was no way she could manage it in the pitch-blackness that would result if she shut the door.

In the time she'd been in jail, she'd learned to shower efficiently and could wash her hair, soap her body, and shave her underarms in less than five minutes. And that was with lukewarm water and mediocre pressure. Even though the room was dark and creepy and conditions were less than ideal, she figured she could manage it here in less than four—as long as the water was hot.

Leaving the door open to let as much moonlight in as possible, she pulled back the curtain and turned the shower valve. It took a few seconds, but the water was hot and the pressure was good. She stepped in and let out a sigh as the warm water flowed over her body.

Logan couldn't sleep. He'd tossed and turned and smashed his fist into the pillow to change its shape, but nothing helped. It wasn't the bed. No, the sheets were clean and crisp, thanks to Harper. But the idea that she'd been in his room and *making* his bed had him imagining her *in* his bed. And his imagination was running wild with images of her arching into him and of him pressing his lips to her skin as he explored every inch of her curvy body. Images that were doing nothing to help him sleep.

His brain wouldn't seem to turn off. And switching his thoughts to the ranch didn't help either. He was stuck between contemplating how many ways his dyslexia had screwed up the ranch's finances and fantasizing about a woman with whom he had no chance of a future because she'd already told him she hoped to be gone by Christmas.

Maybe he could ponder what an idiot he was in general. He let out a frustrated sigh as he threw back the covers and got out of the bed. Standing at the window, he surveyed the ranch in the moonlight. Soft flurries of snow floated through the air and all seemed quiet, which should have settled that uneasy feeling in his gut. But nothing felt easy tonight.

His gaze traveled over the landscape of the ranch buildings, and a small flicker of light in the barn caught his eye.

Squinting, he searched the windows, trying to see it again. There. In the office. He swore he saw the slightest glimmer of light. But only for a second, and then it was gone.

He rubbed his eyes. Maybe the moonlight was playing tricks on them. This wasn't the first restless night he'd had lately, and he *was* exhausted. And he'd already deduced that his imagination was running on overdrive. He was starting to turn away and head back to bed when the overhead light in the barn office blinked on. *What the hell?*

It went off again as fast as it had come on. But there was no way he was imagining things this time. Someone was out there! And there was only one person who would be sneaking around his ranch in the middle of the night. Ted!

The hired hand had threatened to come back, to make him pay. And Logan wouldn't put it past the spiteful jerk to try to start a real fire this time or burn the whole barn down.

No way was Logan going to let that happen. He sprinted through the house and skidded into the den, avoiding turning on any lights to keep from alerting Ted that he was on to him.

Thankfully, the keypad lock on the gun safe was back lit. He quickly punched in the code and swung open the door. He wasn't about to face a belligerent drunk sneaking around his barn without being armed. He grabbed a shotgun and some shells, then hurried to the foyer to cram his feet into his boots and jerk on a coat before slipping quietly out the front door.

The moonlight was all Logan had to see by as he carefully entered the barn, but he'd grown up here and knew every inch of this barn by heart. The light had come from the office, but Ted could be anywhere by now.

Logan cocked his head, straining to hear the slightest noise, and was surprised to hear water running through the pipes. Why would the water be running? That idiot was probably so drunk, he had to stop to take a piss in the middle of his vandalizing mission. That would be just Logan's luck to catch an intruder with his pants down and his junk in his hand.

Or Ted could have turned on the water to flood the office just to cause malicious harm.

Logan's heart slammed in his chest, and he could feel the adrenaline shooting through his veins as he made his way to the office. He checked behind him, furtively glancing around the dimly lit barn to make sure Ted wasn't hiding in one of the stalls, waiting to get the jump on him.

The hair rose on his neck as he carefully opened the office door and heard the water in the shower suddenly turn off. Someone was definitely in there!

He flipped on the light and pointed the gun toward the open bathroom door. "Hold it right there, assho—!" His words faded as he took in the naked dark-haired woman he'd just caught stepping out of the shower and reaching for a towel.

CHAPTER 11

HARPER SHRIEKED, AND HER EYES WIDENED AS SHE SAW the gun. She raised her hands over her head while squinting at the bright light. "Don't shoot! It's just me."

"Harper?" Logan croaked. "What the hell are you doing out here? And why are you naked?" His voice cracked on the word *naked*.

"Because I was taking a shower." She said that as if it made perfect sense, and he was the slow one. "Are you gonna shoot me?"

"Shit. No. Sorry." What was wrong with him? He unloaded the gun and set it on the sofa, dropping the shells into his pocket as he turned his back. He'd been staring at her like a deer frozen in the headlights. And she had some damn fine headlights. "I thought you were Ted. Well, I obviously didn't think *you* were Ted, but I thought Ted was out here. He threatened me this afternoon, and I thought he'd come back to cause trouble." He could hear her scrambling to pull her clothes on.

"I'm dressed. You can turn around."

She'd pulled her jeans up, but her head was tilted down as she buttoned her shirt. Her wet hair was dripping onto the front of the shirt, and she apparently hadn't taken time to fully dry off or put on a bra because the soaked white fabric of the shirt was practically see-through as it clung to her full breasts. *Holy hell!* The sight of her hardened nipples erect through the cloth was almost more erotic than seeing her naked. Well, maybe. It was a toss-up. Either way, his brain couldn't seem to connect with his mouth.

She looked up and caught him staring at her breasts, but instead of covering herself, she planted her hands on her hips and pushed back her shoulders as if daring him to look. Cocking an eyebrow, she nailed him with a steely stare. "First time you've seen a pair?"

"Yeah..." He nodded, then shook his head, trying to break his stupor. "Wait... I mean no. Of course not. They're just so...perfect. I mean...you're so perfect... Hell...I don't know what I mean. I can't think with you standing there practically naked."

Could he be any more of an idiot? He turned his head as he shrugged out of his jacket and passed it to her. "Here. Put this on. Please. You've got to be freezing."

"What about you? If I take your jacket, you'll be the one who's practically naked. Where the hell are your clothes?"

Shit. He looked down at himself, realizing for the first time that he'd run out of his house in only his boxer briefs and boots. He'd been in such a hurry to catch Ted, he hadn't bothered to put on his pants. "Don't worry about me. I'm not cold. The heat of my severe humiliation is keeping me plenty warm." In fact, his skin seemed to be on fire. His body was heating from the inside, and he was sure it wasn't all due to embarrassment.

"What do you have to be humiliated about? I'm the one that just got caught naked in your barn."

"Lord, can we please stop saying the word 'naked.'" He kept his eyes fixed on the office wall and tried to think of baseball stats or hockey stats or any kind of stats that would help keep *his* hockey stick from rising to the occasion. It was already making claims that it was ready to get in the game. And the thin boxer briefs wouldn't do much to disguise that fact. "I was already in bed. But I couldn't sleep, so I got up and saw the light come on in the office."

"Damn. I was hoping you wouldn't see that," she mumbled.

"I'll bet." He was hoping she hadn't seen the way catching her in the shower was affecting him. He picked the gun back up and held it in front of himself. "Let's go in the house and get you some dry clothes." *Or take those back off again.* "And then you can tell me what the hell is going on."

He hazarded a look her direction and was thankful she'd pulled his coat on and was cramming her feet into her boots. Her backpack was open on the floor, and she tossed the few things she had on the bathroom counter into it and stood.

She let out a long breath. "After you."

The gentleman in him couldn't accept that, so he swept his hand toward the door. Plus, he'd rather follow her than risk having her get another look at his eager player trying to step up to the plate. Hopefully, the freezing walk to the house would calm it the hell down.

Inside the house, he leaned the gun against the wall. "Give me a minute to put on some pants, then I'll find you a towel and some dry clothes." He strode down the hall and into his bedroom. Dropping onto the bed, he jerked his boots off and tossed them on the floor, then grabbed his jeans and tugged them on. A stack of clean T-shirts sat on the edge of his dresser, thanks to Harper, and he grabbed the top one and pulled it over his head.

He grabbed another T-shirt, this one of a dark material instead of white—he groaned as the image of her breasts outlined in the wet shirt popped into his mind again—then rummaged through his dresser and found a pair of sweatpants.

He carried them out to the living room where Harper was sitting on the edge of a dining room chair. She'd taken off his coat and set it on the table.

She patted the jacket. "My hair is still dripping, and I didn't want your coat to get any wetter."

This time, he kept his eyes trained on her face. "Don't worry about it. It gets wet all the time." He handed her the clothes and nodded toward the hallway. "Here. Take these. And there are some dry towels in the bathroom. I'll wait while you get dressed."

Her bravado didn't seemed to have diminished as she stood and took the offered clothes. "Thank you" was all she said before walking away, the loose shoelaces of her boots dragging behind her.

He swallowed as he sank into the chair and dropped his head onto his coat. Lord have mercy, the fabric smelled like her shampoo. He groaned. What the hell was going on? Why was she taking a shower in his barn? Was she homeless? He'd been so enamored with her, so glad to have someone to talk to—yeah, okay, it was more than that—but had he been so blinded by her beauty and quirky personality that he hadn't taken the time to figure out anything about her?

No, that couldn't be true. He *did* know things about her. He knew she was from Kansas and had been living with her grandmother. *Nana*. And that Nana had recently passed away, and Harper was having a hard time dealing with her death. She hadn't told him that part, but he'd gathered it from the way her eyes had swelled with tears and she'd turned her head away when she'd been telling a story about her grandmother.

He knew that Harper liked ketchup on her scrambled eggs and drank her coffee black. He knew that her favorite color was purple, and she was a Chiefs fan. But apparently knowing how someone took their eggs and what football team they followed didn't mean crap when it came to really knowing who they were.

The bathroom door opened, and Harper stepped out. Her hair was still wet, but not sopping, and it hung in loose waves around her shoulders. Damn, even with wet hair, no makeup, and baggy clothes, she was gorgeous. Her feet were bare, and she'd rolled the waistband of the too-big sweats over several times. It was obvious she still didn't have a bra on, but not as obvious-in-your-face as it had been before. Aw hell, now he was thinking of her breasts in his face. Damn, he was a pig.

He cleared his throat. "You ready to tell me what's going on?"

She shrugged. "How about something hot first?"

His eyes widened.

She planted a fist on her hip. "I mean something hot…to drink. How about I make us some tea?"

Of course that's what she meant. What else would she have been saying? *How about we strip down and make out a little before I tell you why I was naked in your barn at eleven o'clock at night?* Yeah, that seemed plausible, dude.

He needed to get his mind out of the gutter and focus. "Some tea would be good." *And toss a shot of whiskey in mine.* On second thought, he was having enough trouble keeping a clear head. He didn't need to add booze to the mix.

He watched her walk into the kitchen and pull the tea

bags and two mugs from the cupboard. She heated water in the microwave and poured it over the prepared tea bags, then carried the steaming mugs to the table. "Okay. Enough stalling. Tell me what's going on, Harper. Why were you showering in my barn? Are you homeless?"

"No, not exactly." She took a sip of tea as she regarded him over her mug. "It's complicated."

It always is. "Try me."

"I'd rather not."

He leveled a cool stare at her.

"Okay. Let's just say that I have business in Creedence and came to town to take care of it. When I got here, I didn't exactly have a place to stay so I thought I'd couch surf in your barn until I got paid on Friday and could stay at a hotel or rent a room in town. It's really not that big a deal."

"Then why didn't you just ask me if you could sleep there, or in the house, instead of sneaking around like a criminal?"

She winced. "I wasn't acting like a criminal. I didn't steal anything. I told you I wouldn't take anything from you."

Except a couple years off his life when she'd scared the hell out of him in the barn. And a little bit of his pride when he'd confronted her while wearing only his boots and a snug pair of boxer briefs. "I didn't think you took anything. But why didn't you just ask to stay?"

"Because I like you. You've been good to me. And besides Bryn, you're the only friend I've got in this town, and I could use some friends right now. So I didn't want you to know I didn't have a place to sleep because I didn't want you to look at me the way you're looking at me now."

He lowered his gaze. "I don't think less of you. I feel sorry for you."

"That's just as bad. I don't need you to feel sorry for me. I'm not a damsel in distress. Or a street urchin. I have a home. I told you, my grandmother left me her house back in Kansas. I'm just in between jobs and had business in Colorado and didn't want to waste money on a hotel."

What she was saying made sense. Mostly. She had told him about her grandmother leaving her the house. "This town is barely bigger than a postage stamp. What kind of business could you possibly have in Creedence?"

She glanced down at her hands and picked at a loose cuticle on her thumb. "Again, I'd rather not say. It's personal."

"Is it illegal?"

Her head shot up, and she glared at him. "No. It's *not* illegal. It's family stuff."

"You have family that lives in Creedence?"

She shrugged. "Sort of."

"Then why didn't you stay with them?"

"I told you…"

"It's complicated. Yeah, I get it." He took a sip of tea as he studied her and tried to figure out what to do. She hadn't technically done anything all that bad. She hadn't lied about sleeping in the barn. She'd just omitted telling him about it.

But so what if she'd slept out there? She hadn't hurt anyone. Except herself. He'd slept on that sofa in the office and knew it was hell on a person's back.

He didn't like all the guarded information about her family and what she was doing in Creedence, but it wasn't really any of his business. He was her employer. She didn't need to tell him everything—or anything, really—about her personal life.

"So what are you going to do?" she asked, her fingers

tightening on her mug and her voice edged with that tough tinge she got when she thought he was insulting her or looking down at her.

What *was* he going to do about it? It seemed to come down to one of two decisions—kick her out or let her stay. And the thought of her leaving in a few weeks was already killing him. He wasn't ready to kick her out of his life yet. He needed her. And not just to cook and clean.

But it was too late at night, and he was too tired to be thinking about that. Thoughts of her had stolen too much of his sleep lately.

He covered his mouth as a yawn snuck up on him. "Look, it's late, and we both need some sleep. I'm not thrilled with what you did, but it's done and there's no point in looking back. You're doing a great job with the meals, and knowing you're here and taking care of the house stuff has taken a load off my already burdened shoulders." He gazed into his empty cup as if the leaves might tell him what to do. "Plus, I like you. I like hanging out with you and eating our meals together. And I could use a friend right now too." He raised his eyes to meet hers. "I'd like you to stay."

Her fingers loosened on her mug as the tension in her shoulders relaxed just the slightest. "Thank you. I'd like that too."

Their gazes locked and held. It was hard to gauge what she was feeling, but they seemed to be communicating with more than words. Her free hand was on the table next to his, and he was tempted to touch her fingers, even just the slightest brush to offer…what? Friendship? Support of her bad situation?

His pinkie was so close that all he'd have to do was barely stretch it to the side and it would touch hers. But what if she took that the wrong way? He *had* just seen her naked. But he sure as heck didn't want her to think that was the reason he wanted her to stay. *But wasn't that part of it?*

He pulled his hand away and clapped it to his thigh as he pressed up from his chair. "You can sleep in Quinn's room tonight, and we'll talk some more in the morning. We'll figure something out. Maybe I can give you an advance on this week's pay—just enough to get you someplace to stay."

"That would be great." She stood as well and reached to pick up the mugs.

The scent of her shampoo filled the air as she stood, and he wanted to pull her to him and bury his head in the silky dark waves. Yeah, he needed to go to bed. And now. Not that he would be doing much sleeping, knowing she was in the room down the hall. "Just leave them. We can get them in the morning."

She curled her fingers into her palms and pressed a hand to either side of her thighs. "Good night then."

"Good night."

She turned to head down the hallway toward Quinn's room, then stopped and pivoted back around. "Thanks, Logan. You're a good man. And a good friend."

Emotion swelled in his throat. Harper didn't seem the kind to give out compliments easily. Her words meant something to him.

And at least he was good at something.

Harper had been up early, determined to prove to Logan that he'd made the right decision to keep her on.

By the time he stumbled out to the kitchen for coffee, she had a complete spread ready of eggs, bacon, fruit, and waffles. She'd even heated the syrup.

His hair was tousled and his eyes were a little blurry, but he still looked hot as hell, and she couldn't help but imagine how things could have gone differently the night before. Yes, he could have fired her and kicked her out on her sofa-surfing ass. Or she could have snuck into his room and crawled into bed with him.

She'd seen the way he'd looked at her after catching her in the shower. His eyes had held the hunger of a starving man staring at a perfectly prepared steak. And Lord help her, she wanted to be that cut of meat. The gun he'd been holding had about given her a heart attack, but after he'd put it down, she'd half hoped he'd become so overcome with desire after catching her naked that he'd stride forward and take her in his arms. Then take her on the floor. Then the sofa.

Nice fantasy, but if that had happened, she probably wouldn't be standing in the kitchen flipping a waffle onto a plate. Logan had made it clear he didn't want complications. He wanted someone he could trust to take care of his house—not take care of him.

Although he had been giving off mixed signals. One minute he was all business; then the next his voice was all breathy as he told her he wanted her to stay. And it didn't sound like he meant stay to sweep the floors but to stay with him. His hand had been next to hers on the table, and she swore at one point that he was going to hold her hand.

She'd almost come undone when he'd asked her to stay. If he had taken her hand, she would have crawled into his lap and kissed him until their clothes fell off.

"How'd ya sleep?" he asked, his voice all deep and morning-husky-sounding, making her wonder not for the first time what it would be like to wake up next to him.

He poured a cup of coffee, then leaned back against the counter and closed his eyes as he took a sip.

Seriously? The man made drinking coffee look sexy.

"Great. Thanks again for letting me stay in your sister's room." She hadn't really slept well. Not at first. She'd lain awake worrying that she'd blown it with the only chance she had at making enough money to get her son back. And thinking about the fact that a smokin'-hot cowboy was in bed only a few steps down the hall hadn't helped either.

"She wasn't using it," he mumbled around the slice of crisp bacon he'd just stuffed in his mouth. "Great bacon, by the way."

A smile tugged at her mouth. "Thanks," she answered, as pleased as if he'd complimented her personality. She handed him the plated waffle. "Warm syrup is on the table. I'll get you some eggs."

"Thanks." He snatched another piece of bacon, then took the plate and his coffee to the table and dropped into a chair. "Give me till I'm a half a cup in, and then I'll be ready for more civilized conversation than grunting about the bacon."

"You're fine," she said, secretly aware of the double entendre. The man *was* fine. Even straight out of bed with a dark smudge of whiskers on his cheeks.

She scooped some eggs onto a couple of plates and joined him at the table, giving him the space he needed. She didn't want to do anything to make him regret letting her stay.

She'd barely made a dent in her meal when he scraped the remaining syrup from his plate with his last bite of waffle and stuffed it in his mouth. He leaned back in his chair and patted his stomach. "That was delicious. I haven't had a waffle in a long time. Thank you."

"Yeah. Of course." She stared at her plate and pushed a pile of eggs from one side to the other. Breakfast had gone well, but she needed to remind him of her worth and give him more reasons to keep her around. "I already put a roast in the slow cooker this morning so we'll have pulled pork sandwiches for lunch. Then I was planning to make lasagna this afternoon to have for supper. Does that sound okay?"

"That sounds great. Amazing. I haven't had homemade lasagna in months." He finished the last swallow of his coffee and offered her a grin that did those funny things to her stomach. "Okay. I'm human again."

"You want me to get you another cup?" She rose partway out of her chair, but he waved her back down.

"No, I'm good. And if I want more, I can get my own dang coffee. But I could use your help with something else. You up for helping me feed the cows again this morning after breakfast?"

"Sure. Give me fifteen minutes to clean the breakfast dishes, and I'll be glad to help." She meant it. She wasn't just trying to appear useful this time. She really did enjoy helping him with the cattle. Maybe she'd been a pioneer woman in a past life. Or maybe she just liked spending time with him. Watching him toss hay bales around was a nice perk too. And if it made her appear more useful, it was a win, win, win.

It took them a couple of hours to take care of the cows,

but Harper loved it. She liked the work and liked talking to and joking around with Logan. He seemed to have gotten over being mad about her staying in the barn, because he was acting like his normal charming self again, teasing her and goofing off with Star. Harper had gotten out of the truck this morning and been formally introduced to the cow. She'd fed Star a marshmallow and stroked the soft white tuft of fur on the cow's forehead. And she'd only half believed it when Logan told her he'd once saddled the beast and ridden her.

Apparently riding a cow is *not* a thing. Now she knew. Not unless it was being done in a rodeo and on a bull, but that was something else entirely.

As much as he joked around with her, he taught her things too. He explained about the different grasses and how they rotated the cattle to different parts of their ranch to take advantage of the best grazing. And he told her how playing hockey had made him a better rancher and vice versa. Both things had contributed to his work ethic, and the more he did each one, the better he got at them. Both ranching and hockey could be cold and brutal and hard, and he'd had to learn to dig deep and rely on his passion for both to get him out of bed in the morning to do chores or get to practice. Learning to work as a team helped him on the ice and at the ranch when he worked alongside other men to round up cattle or move them to different pastures.

She'd never imagined how the two parts of his life, hockey and being a cowboy, could overlap and blend together in so many ways. But listening to him talk, it was obvious he'd found his self-confidence and his strength of character on the land and in the ice arena. He didn't brag or boast about either, but his knowledge and commitment to both shined through as he spoke.

He educated her on how the cattle part of the ranch worked as well, telling her how they purchased calves and raised them to later sell and what a good acquisition price was and how much they hoped to sell for.

At one point, she'd asked a question about how he kept it all straight. His expression had darkened, and he'd alluded to a stupid mistake he'd made that year. He didn't tell her what it was, but she'd seen the same expression when he'd been talking about his dyslexia, so she had a feeling the mistake had been due to the disability. She wished he could hear himself talk though. The man was far from stupid. He might have trouble with reading and writing numbers, but he was crazy smart about raising cattle and how the market worked.

Harper was still driving when they got back to the ranch, and Logan had her pull over in front of the barn.

"I had an idea last night," he told her as they got out of the truck. "I want to show you something." He led her across the yard to the small bunkhouse where Ted had been living. "We usually have our hired man live here, but due to a lack of intelligence on his part, the place has recently been vacated. I figured since you've been taking on the roles of housekeeper, cook, *and* hired hand, the place should be yours."

Harper's heart leapt in her chest. Was he offering her a place to live?

"Now don't get too excited. It's nothing fancy. But I'm sure with your miraculous cleaning skills, you could whip it into shape in no time. And I could help."

She shook her head. This seemed too good to be true.

There had to be a catch. If he let her live here, did that mean he wouldn't pay her? "I appreciate the offer. And I don't care what kind of shape it's in," she told him. Heck, she'd spent the last few months in a jail cell and the last few nights in a barn. Being picky was not a luxury she could afford. But this place had to be out of her meager budget. Maybe she could haggle down the price or barter for another service. She could offer to cut his hair or wash his truck or his tractor or whatever he needed washed. "I'm a little worried about the rent. I've got some expenses, and I can't afford to have too much taken out of my pay. How much would you charge me?"

He pulled his head back. "Charge you? I wouldn't charge you anything. The place comes with the job."

"Comes with the job? You mean I wouldn't pay *any* rent? At all?" She couldn't believe it. She didn't know what to say. It was as if he knew the most important thing she needed to get her son back and was offering it to her with no strings attached.

"Nope. No rent at all. It doesn't cost me anything beyond basic utilities. But like I said, it's nothing fancy—think summer camp meets rustic cabin with the ghosts of some old cowhands."

She didn't care if it was fancy. She didn't need fancy; she just needed a place to live. And she couldn't beat the price. A few ghosts didn't scare her, and neither did hard work. She could do magic with some cleaners and a little elbow grease. As long as it was warm and had a bed for Floyd, that's all that mattered. And seriously, how bad could it be?

Logan pushed open the door and they both stepped back, struck by the overwhelming scent of spoiled milk and decay.

"Holy crap. What is that smell?" He covered his nose with his sleeve as he walked into the living area.

Okay. So it was pretty bad. Harper stepped in behind him and surveyed the room. But it had potential.

An overstuffed tan sofa and coffee table faced a fireplace with a television mounted over the mantel. A faded brown leather recliner sat next to the sofa, its seat layered with old newspapers and sports magazines. Pizza boxes, fast-food trash, take-out containers, and empty beer bottles littered every surface. Harper picked her way gingerly through the room, stopping to peer down at a smutty magazine that lay across the corner of the coffee table. It was open to the centerfold and had a naked woman seductively perched on a motorcycle. Well, not entirely naked. She was strapped into a pair of biker chaps. Harper nodded to the magazine. "Classy guy."

She made her way into the kitchen where the smell was the worst. Rotten food covered the counter, and the refrigerator had been left open. Its contents were meager but still gave off a ripe odor. Knowing what she did about Ted, she assumed the ranch hand left it that way on purpose. Along with the half-empty milk jug he'd dumped in the sink.

"This place is disgusting." Logan shook his head as he came into the kitchen and peered over her shoulder at the mess. "I had no idea he'd left it like this. I'm really sorry. I thought this would be perfect."

Harper could see beyond the trash and filth. She knew the place could be cute and homey with a little work. Okay, a lot of work. But she'd never been afraid of hard work or getting her hands dirty. And the payoff would be worth it.

She could make the bunkhouse a home, could show

Judith—and the court, if it came to that—she had a place to live, a house to bring Floyd home to. At least for now. Until she could make enough money to get them back to Kansas.

Harper had never been one to succumb to emotion. She mostly thought crying was a waste of energy and never helped anything anyway, but now, having Logan give her this gift had tears welling in her eyes. As she blinked them back, the emotion burning her throat, her body hummed with elation, and she didn't know how to express to him how happy he'd made her.

Her mind might not know, but her body did. She turned and threw her arms around him, burying her face in his neck. "Thank you so much. It's perfect."

CHAPTER 12

HARPER INHALED LOGAN'S SCENT BEFORE SHE HAD time to think about what she was doing. He smelled so good, like a woodsy aftershave and laundry detergent. His chest was hard, and her gratitude transformed as a spark of desire shot up her spine, and she had the sudden urge to climb him like a tree.

But that tree had just offered her a precious gift, and she couldn't blow it now. She started to pull back, already feeling awkward about the spontaneous display of affection, but his arms had come up to encircle her waist, and his strong hands splayed against her back and pulled her closer.

It had been a long time since she'd been in the arms of a man, and her control slipped as she melted into him, letting out the softest of sighs as she savored the feeling of being wrapped in his arms.

She pressed her cheek to his shoulder and tightened her grip on his neck, holding on to him for just a beat, just one delicious moment.

But that moment, combined with an impulsive need for this man, could ruin everything. And she couldn't let that happen. Not when he'd just offered her a home.

She swallowed and let go, stepping away and turning back to the kitchen.

He cleared his throat and pushed the refrigerator door closed. "Yeah. Of course. Although I don't know how you can think this is perfect. It seems like a disgusting mess."

"A mess that can easily be cleaned up." She walked through the kitchen and peered into the first bedroom. "Maybe not *easily*, but you'd be amazed what a little spit and polish will do for the place," she said, quoting one of Nana's favorite sayings.

Logan stepped into the first bedroom, wrinkling his nose at the rumpled bedsheets and another dirty magazine laying open on top of the nightstand. He pinched the corner of the magazine between his fingers to close the offensive pages. "Spit and polish. And a blowtorch. Geez-a-Pete, this is embarrassing. I should have checked the place out before I brought you in here."

"No way. Then you might have changed your mind." Or changed his idea of offering it to her free of charge.

He opened the next door in the hallway. "This second bedroom isn't too bad. It doesn't look like he even used it, except to store a couple boxes of stuff. It's small, but it has a twin bed and a dresser and a desk if you wanted to use it like an office or something."

Harper peered around his shoulder and tried to quell the excitement building in her chest. This room would be perfect to fix up for Floyd. She'd thought the place only had one bedroom, and she would have gladly slept on the sofa and willingly given the room to Floyd, but this was even better. She couldn't believe this stroke of luck. The bunkhouse could change everything. Which meant she couldn't do anything to mess this job up.

Logan waved his hand through the air. "This room isn't disgusting, but it's pretty dusty. You can stay in the house again tonight, and I can get somebody in here to clean the place up for you."

"What? Like a cleaning lady?"

"Yeah."

She raised an eyebrow and planted a fist on her curvy hip. "You realize I *am* your cleaning lady?"

"Well, yeah, I guess. I mean, I don't really think of you like that." His cheeks colored with a tinge of pink. "But this is beyond anything I would expect you to do."

"No. Really. I mean it, Logan." She touched his arm. "This is beyond perfect. And it looks worse than it is. Get a mop and bucket in here and a little disinfectant, or maybe a lot of disinfectant and some bleach, and I'll have the place sparkling in no time."

He shook his head. "If anyone can do it, you can. But I do feel bad. I thought I was offering you something great, but it turns out I should probably pay you to live here."

She grinned impishly. "Okay." She laughed, glad to have them back to joking around and not swimming in sexual tension. "I'm just teasing. I'm thrilled with the place. All I need is some rubber gloves and a couple of hours to work. You'll be amazed at what I can accomplish even in an hour." Her fingers itched to get started. "I'd love to dig in now. If that's okay with you. I don't want to take time away from the main house."

"It's fine. I can't imagine what you have left to clean in the house. It seem like you've already scrubbed it from top to bottom."

"Oh, there's always more to clean."

"I've got some boxes in the barn, and I can grab some garbage bags and help you clear the trash out of the place."

"You don't have to."

"Yeah, I do. I couldn't live with myself if I didn't. I don't want you having to deal with his raunchy crap."

She grinned, pleased that he was trying to protect her fragile innocence. "I can handle a dirty magazine or two."

"But you shouldn't have to. Plus, I'm scared of what other craziness we might find in here. Who knows what else this guy was into? He might have a dead raccoon in the freezer."

"Geez, I hope so. Then I won't have to make lasagna for dinner. Ever since we almost ran over those deer, I've been brushing up on my roadkill recipes, and I think I've found one for raccoon stew."

"Nice. Sounds delicious." He chuckled, then shook his head. "Ugh, I just can't believe he left it like this."

"I can. The guy doesn't appear to have a lot of class. And he seems bent on getting back at you for firing him, whether it's through a sucker punch to the face or leaving food to spoil in the kitchen."

"That's what I'm afraid of. I can handle the mess, and even the sock to the eye, as long as he doesn't try to mess with the ranch. Or with you."

Her face warmed at the emotion in his words. "With me? Why would he try to mess with me?"

"You did stand him up for that dance and left him high and dry after offering to buy him a drink."

She waved her hand. "Oh gosh. That guy was so drunk, he won't even remember that happened. And I'm sure he won't remember me."

Logan caught her eye, holding her captive in his gaze. "You're pretty hard to forget."

Oh my. And he was making it pretty hard not to throw herself into his arms and beg him to strip her bare. Although the idea of getting naked in this place the way it looked now had her cringing, even if it was with the hot cowboy.

He looked around the room, almost as if reading her mind. "I'll go get those garbage bags."

———————

An hour and a half later, they were still working. *But Harper was right*, Logan thought as he finished cleaning the mirror in the bathroom. They had made a significant dent in the place.

They'd worked together to clear out the trash, filling several bags with rotten food and empty beer bottles. She'd brought cleaning supplies over from the house and spent most of her time working in the kitchen and living room while he attacked the main bedroom and the bathroom. Harper said she'd work on the second bedroom later, so Logan had just moved Ted's junk out and closed the door.

Most of Logan's job had been throwing stuff away, including the sheets and the old bedspread that had been on Ted's bed. He couldn't stomach Harper sleeping in the same bedding that animal had slept in. Hell, he would have burned the mattress, if they had any way for him to get a new one out here tonight.

Thankfully, his sister was good at stocking things, and they had several comforters, mattress pads, and sets of sheets in the house that Harper could use.

After ridding the bedroom of everything except the bed, dresser, and nightstand, Logan stripped down to his under-shirt and donned a pair of rubber gloves to tackle the bath-room. Harper had assured him she could do it, but the place was worse than a truck-stop john, and he couldn't put her through the agony of cleaning it.

The bathroom wasn't big—just a toilet, a sink, and the shower—and he'd sprayed everything with either Scrubbing Bubbles or Clorox cleaner, then swept and scoured every surface until it shined.

"Wow," Harper said, poking her head into the bathroom. "I thought I was gonna need a hazmat suit to tackle this room. But it looks amazing. You do great work."

He shrugged. The room did look pretty good. "I'm used to mucking out stalls, so it didn't bother me. But I've had pigs that kept their pens neater than this guy. And don't worry. I used a lot of bleach."

"Me too."

He followed her back to the kitchen and couldn't believe the transformation. She'd washed and scrubbed the counters and sinks, and every surface gleamed. And she must have brought a candle down from the house, because the air smelled like pumpkin spice mixed with soap and cleaning solutions.

"It looks great in here," he said, marveling at the change.

She'd stripped the dingy curtains, and they lay in a pile on the counter. "I'll wash and rehang the curtains this afternoon, and I need to do more in the kitchen, but we made a great start. I dusted and straightened the living room. Now I just need to mop and vacuum the floors this afternoon, and then I can move in."

"Great. Let's do it now. I can run the vacuum if you want to mop."

"Aren't you hungry?"

He shrugged. "I'm getting there. But we're so close, I'd rather knock this out, then go back to the house and shower. I'll be able to enjoy my lunch more if I know we've got this ready for you."

Her eyes widened. "Thank you. That's really nice. You've done so much for me. I don't know how to repay you."

"The pulled pork you're making me for lunch is payment enough. And that roadkill stew you mentioned sounded pretty tempting."

She rubbed her stomach and swatted him with a kitchen towel as she laughed. "Oh yeah, it's got to be delicious. And a payment well worth the labor of an hour spent hosing down that disgusting bathroom."

He liked to hear her laugh, especially that one, the loud bawdy laugh she used when he'd really amused her. But he was serious about this, and he wanted her to know how glad he was to help. He grabbed the end of the towel and used it to pull her a step closer. "Honestly, Harper, I wanted to help. And you've done plenty for me too." He lowered his tone as he looked into her eyes. "I think we make a good team."

"We do," she whispered, then looked away as if his words embarrassed her. "But you are paying me, so you'd better kick my butt in gear to get this floor swept and mopped." She let go of the towel and kept her focus trained on reaching for the broom.

He let out his breath. He had plenty of ideas about her butt, but none of them involved kicking it. And he *was* paying her, which was one more reason he shouldn't be thinking about her butt. But damn, she had a great one.

Time to get his mind on something else. Like cleaning the old potato chips out of this couch. He plugged in the vacuum and pushed it toward the sofa.

An old radio sat on top of the refrigerator, and Harper had it set to a station that played classic rock. Logan had just pulled the suction hose from the vacuum cleaner when one of his favorite songs came on. "Hey, turn this up. I love this song," he told Harper, who was sweeping the floor next to the fridge.

"Me too." She reached up and cranked the volume, then used the end of the broom as a microphone to belt out the opening lyrics. Her voice was gravelly and raw, and even though she was joking around, she still harmonized perfectly with the band.

He chuckled as he used the vacuum hose to play an awesome air-guitar riff, then joined in the chorus with her. Except he made his voice extra deep and twangy as he imitated the lead singer. She broke into laughter, holding her stomach as she doubled over.

The song ended, and she turned down the radio and leaned against the counter, trying to catch her breath. "Wow, if this ranching thing doesn't work out for you, we could form a band. I think we're almost ready to take it out on the road."

"I could see that. We could call our band the Cleanup Crew. I think you're on to something."

"I think you're a dork."

"A dork? Or a rock star? I've been accused of both."

She raised an eyebrow. "I'll bet not very often. I can't imagine many people would accuse you of being a dork."

"That's because they don't all get to see my awesome air-guitar-vacuum-hose skills. I only make rare appearances."

She clutched her hands to her heart and made her voice go dreamy. "Then I must be one of the lucky ones. Can I have your autograph?"

"I'll consider it." He offered her one of his most charming grins. "But you'll have to give me yours too. You've got some pretty great pipes. You were showing me up with those vocals."

She tossed a kitchen towel at him. "Get back to work, rock star."

He chuckled as he switched on the vacuum.

The smell of barbecued pork met him as he walked down the hallway and into the kitchen. They'd finished cleaning the bunkhouse and come back to clean up and shower off the grime before lunch. He'd thought he'd been pretty quick in the shower, but Harper had beat him and was already back in the kitchen putting together sandwiches.

She was still barefoot, and the sight of her wearing snug jeans and a light-blue Henley top that hugged her perfect breasts had him hungry for more than pulled pork. Her hair was still damp, and the scent of her shampoo hung in the air as he slid in next to her.

"Anything I can do to help?" he asked, trying to control the urge to touch the soft waves in her hair. Her neck was exposed as the collar of her shirt dipped into a vee, and he wanted to follow the vee as he tipped his head and laid a trail of warm kisses along her throat and down her chest.

"I've just about got it. I'd planned to make something more substantial like scalloped potatoes this morning but got caught up in cleaning the bunkhouse. Hope potato chips work."

"Chips are great." *You're great.* Oh man, he needed to pull it together. He was going full-on nuclear with his crush on this woman—one minute wanting to set her up on the counter and wrap her legs around him as he stripped off her shirt, the next thinking sappy sentiments.

He liked to watch her work. Her movements were quick and efficient. She opened thick potato buns and buttered both sides, then set them on a cookie sheet and put them in the oven under the broiler. Setting the timer for two minutes, she turned back and dumped chips on each of their plates.

"You want water or iced tea?" she asked.

"Water, but I'll get it." The kitchen normally seemed good-sized, but not when he was sharing it with her. It seemed small and tight as they tried to maneuver around each other. He filled the glasses with ice and water. She'd had water with every meal so far, so he assumed she'd want it again.

He shut the fridge and accidentally bumped his hip against hers. "Sorry."

She turned back, and their elbows bumped. "Nope, I'm sorry." She tried to turn to one side to get around him as he turned the same way.

"Wanna dance?" he asked, laughing as he held his arms out.

"Only if you want your feet smashed. I'm a terrible dancer."

"I doubt you're terrible at anything."

She reared her head back. "Why would you say that? I'm quite terrible at many, many things."

He shrugged, acutely aware of how close they were still standing. "I don't know. From where I'm sitting, you can cook and clean better than my grandma, which sounds like a dig, but is actually high praise. You're gorgeous without trying, smart as a whip, and funny as hell. You can drive a stick, and I haven't seen anything you're afraid of yet, including that giant spider we saw in the bunkhouse that you fearlessly stomped on."

She stared up at him and for once didn't seem to have a response. Her eyes were big and round, and the light in the kitchen caught the gold flecks buried in the green. Her cheeks were flushed, and a smudge of flour dusted the top of one.

"You've got a little flour on your face," he said, reaching up to wipe it from her cheek.

She stilled as his thumb brushed the edge of her mouth, and her lips parted as she inhaled a soft breath. He held his hand right above her face, barely caressing her skin.

"You're wrong you know," she whispered. "I might seem brave, but I'm afraid right now."

"Don't be." His voice was low and husky as he whispered back. He pressed his hand to her face, cupping her cheek and dipping his head.

"I'm afraid of all these feelings I have." She licked her lips, and he almost came undone.

He wanted to crush her mouth with his—to kiss her, to taste her. "Me too." He leaned lower, closing the gap between their bodies as his lips hovered above hers. His heart pounded so hard against his chest that he was surprised she couldn't hear it.

She tilted her head, just the slightest movement, but it brought her closer still.

Heat shot through his veins, and his fingers tingled with need. He wanted to haul her against his chest and take her mouth. But she'd just said she was afraid, so he knew he needed to take it slow. He brushed her lips with his, barely grazing her mouth and earning another soft gasp.

Taking it slow was important, but it was also killing him—the anticipation of finally tasting her, of feeling her pressed against him.

He couldn't do it—couldn't wait another second. His right hand was still holding her cheek as he leaned in and took her mouth, crushing her lips with his.

CHAPTER 13

THE KISS—WHICH STARTED SO SOFTLY—DEEPENED with hunger as Logan pulled her closer. Harper's lips were soft and pliant, and she gave back every bit of the passion he was pouring into her.

Bringing his other hand up, he slid it along her neck and wound his fingers into her hair, finally able to touch the silky strands. She gripped his shoulders, clutching the fabric of his shirt as she arched in to him.

She moaned softly against his lips. He was ready to lift her onto the counter and tear her shirt open when the oven timer suddenly went off, its shrill beeping filling the room. She pulled away, blinking and shaking her head as if waking up from a trance.

"Oh my gosh. The buns," she said, opening the oven and reaching for the hot pads. A cloud of steam poured from the oven, but it didn't compare to the warmth filling his chest from the intensity of the kiss he'd just shared with Harper.

She was focused on pulling the pan from the oven, and he was just standing there trying to recover from the best kiss of his life. Damn, that woman had an amazing mouth.

"Do you want to put the glasses on the table? I'll have these sandwiches ready in a minute." She transferred the buns to the plates and filled them with pulled pork.

Screw the sandwiches. He didn't give a fig about lunch. He wanted to get back to kissing her. Her mouth had been delicious, but he'd only grazed the surface of the places where he wanted to kiss her.

It seemed the moment had been lost.

Even though her lips were still swollen from the kiss, her focus was on getting lunch on the table. She'd had everything else ready, so he followed her lead and carried the glasses to the table, then sat down across from her.

"Dig in," she said, busying herself with the jar of barbecue sauce and avoiding his eyes.

He took a bite of the sandwich and groaned. The combination of warm, buttery bread with the pork slathered in sweet, tangy sauce was incredible. "This is outstanding."

A smile tugged at the corners of her lips. "Thank you. It's all about heating the buns."

"I do enjoy warm buns," he teased, trying to get her to laugh.

She grinned and shook her head. A small victory, but it seemed to have broken the awkwardness, and she was able to look at him again.

They settled into eating and talked about what else needed to be done in the bunkhouse, and he told her some of the other chores he had to take care of that afternoon. She planned to do some laundry and clean out the fridge. Apparently she'd found a butter tub of something moldy and mysterious in the back of the refrigerator and planned to scrub the whole thing down.

Eating sloppy barbecue and talking about moldy mystery food took away the tension of having to talk about the kiss, but that didn't mean Logan could stop thinking about it.

They finished eating, and he helped her clear the dishes, this time relishing the moments he bumped or brushed against her. She seemed intent on cleaning up, but he just wanted to get back to the kissing part.

She finished washing the dishes and stood next to the counter drying her hands, then folding the towel and hanging it neatly on the handle of the stove.

He stepped in behind her and brushed her hair from her neck. A shiver ran through her as he leaned closer to her ear. "Harper..." he started, then was interrupted by the dinging of his cell phone signaling he'd received a text.

Dang. What was up with them getting interrupted by dinging, beeping, blasted timing devices?

The text was from Colt. Logan had promised to come over for a couple of hours to help his neighbor work on a tractor engine that had been giving him trouble. "Damn. That's from Colt. I gotta go. I forgot I told him I'd help him out this afternoon. I was supposed to be there ten minutes ago."

Harper turned to face him, pressing her hand flat against his chest as she looked up at him. "Logan, as scared as I am about what I'm feeling for you, the thing I'm the most afraid of is losing this job."

He sighed. "But I'm not—"

She reached up and pressed her fingers to his lips. "You'd better go. You're already late. I'll see you later." She dropped her hand and strode down the hall, leaving him standing in the kitchen. Alone.

So that was that.

———————————

Logan spent a few hours helping Colt, then put in another hour working in the barn office, but his thoughts kept drifting to the house, and he couldn't seem to stay away. He told himself he was just thirsty, but he knew he was thirsting for something more than a hot drink. He was craving a little more time with the gorgeous woman who was filling his thoughts.

She'd shut him down after the kiss, and that was fine, for now. But he still wanted to see her. He tried to convince himself she was simply fun to be around, but he knew it was something more. He was falling harder than a bucket of rain in a downpour, and he couldn't seem to get his mind off her.

The kittens were racing around the yard, tumbling over his boots as he crossed to the house. He stepped over Nacho, the mama cat, as she lay in a patch of sun on the front porch. Opening the front door, he walked into the house and inhaled the scents of cinnamon, vanilla, and fruit. "Mmmm, peaches."

Harper looked up from where she was folding a stack of towels on the sofa. She cocked an eyebrow. "Did you just call me Peaches?"

He chuckled. "I will if it'll score me a piece of whatever you've got baking in here."

"I told you I make a fantastic peach cobbler."

He was starting to think everything about this woman was fantastic. "I had no doubt."

The sound of an engine drew his attention, and he swore as he saw the pickup towing a small silver horse trailer pull down his driveway and stop in front of the barn.

"What's wrong?" Harper asked, getting up to stand next to him and look out the window.

"Oh, nothing. I just forgot I had to see a man about a horse today."

She offered him an impish grin. "Isn't that code for taking a leak?"

"In most cases, yes. But today it's the real deal. This guy, Gus, has a horse he's bringing by. Gus is a friend of my dad's and lives about twenty miles up the pass. He was having trouble with the horse and sold her to me for a song."

"She must not be much of a horse then. I've heard you sing."

He chuckled as he shrugged back into his coat, thankful he hadn't taken off his boots. "You're hilarious. That peach cobbler better be amazing to make up for that zinger."

"It will be." She craned her neck to see around him. "Can I come out and see the horse?"

"Sure."

She grabbed a coat and followed him out as another truck pulled down the driveway. She'd worn his coat a couple of times today, and he liked the way she looked in it. Something about her being kept warm and protected by something of his made him feel good.

"Heck, it's like Grand Central Station around here today." But he recognized the pickup and waved as the tall cowboy stepped out.

"Hey, Zane," Logan called. "What brings you out this way?"

Zane reached back into his truck, pulled out Logan's hat, and passed it to him. "Thought you might want this," he said. "It fell behind the bar when Ted hit you last night."

"Thanks. I appreciate it—the hat, not the humiliating reminder that I got sucker punched in the face." He'd given the hat up as gone, but had mourned the loss of it. It was a great hat. One of his favorites. Which had only pissed him off more that Ted had caused him to lose it.

He dropped the hat on Harper's head, then leaned in close to her ear. "Hold this for me, would ya, Peaches?"

She chuckled. *Thank goodness.* He figured he might be taking his life in his hands with that comment, but teasing her and drawing out that playful grin she sometimes got was well worth the risk.

And that grin had just curved her lips. "Sure, Cowboy."

A quick yip drew Logan's attention back to the cab of Zane's truck where a black-and-white dog sat up in the seat. It looked to be a cross between a border collie and an Australian shepherd. "Hey, good-lookin' dog you got there. What's its name?"

Zane shrugged. "I don't know. She's not my dog."

"Then why is she riding around in your truck with you?"

"Because every time I open the door, she jumps in." He shook his head. "She was hanging around the alley behind my dad's house, and I made the mistake of giving her some food."

Logan reached a hand toward the dog who sniffed it, then gave his palm a friendly lick. One of her ears folded forward while the other stood up straight, and when the dog opened her mouth to pant, her lips seemed to curve into a smile. Almost as if she understood what Zane had said and was grinning at her own cleverness. "She seems sweet."

"Yeah, that's what I get for tossing a few scraps to a stray. Now she thinks my house is her home and that she gets to run my life."

"Strays have a way of doing that." Logan scratched the dog under the chin, then glanced toward Harper, thinking she'd want in on petting the pup, but her gaze was trained on the ground, her mouth stretched into a tight line.

"What's with the trailer?" Zane asked, drawing their attention from the subject of the dog as he eyed the man trying to back the trailer closer to the corral.

"Picked up a horse from this guy, Gus. He's a friend of Ham's, so I got her for a steal. Guy says she's green broke, but for the deal he gave me, I kind of doubt it. Still, I figured I could work on truly breaking her myself this winter, then most likely sell her this spring. I seem to recall you've got a gift when it comes to horses. You wanna take a look at her?"

A gift with horses was an understatement. Zane connected with the beautiful beasts like no one Logan had ever met before. It was like they looked into his eyes and saw something there, something that made them trust him. It was the real deal—almost like a mystical connection. Zane was a true horse whisperer.

Logan wondered if the abuse Zane had suffered at the hands of his father had contributed to his gift with animals. As if he was hypersensitive to their needs and feelings or saw things in them that others might miss. He also had the patience of a saint. Whatever it was, Logan had seen it happen time and time again, the utter and complete trust a horse that might have been given up on had with Zane.

"Sure. I'll take a look." Zane followed Logan over to the trailer where the other man was opening the back gate. Logan introduced the men, and they shook hands and exchanged pleasantries.

Zane peered into the trailer at the sorrel-colored quarter horse. "She's a feisty one."

Great. Another feisty female. Just what Logan needed.

The horse was not happy about being in the trailer, but she was less happy about trying to get out. She stamped and kicked and huffed every time Gus or Logan tried to get close to her.

"She's just nervous from the ride over," Gus explained. "You know our ranch is close to twenty miles from here, and it wasn't a peaceful ride."

Logan knew Gus was just making excuses for the horse so he wouldn't change his mind and back out of their deal. The horse did seem a little crazed, but he'd dealt with crazy before.

"You can stop trying to sell me on the horse, Gus. I'm not gonna back out of our deal. But I do have to be able to get her out of the danged trailer."

Zane stepped forward. "Mind if I take a crack at it?"

"Be my guest."

Zane opened the side door at the front of the trailer and spoke softly to the horse. He cautiously climbed in, holding out his hand as he continued to offer quiet assurances.

The horse reared back, throwing her head and sending spittle and slobber flying as she pulled against the lead rope holding her to the front end of the trailer. She let out a whinny, then a huff, but her wild eyes seemed to settle a little as she stared at Zane. He spent a few more minutes talking to her in hushed tones, then released the lead and gently guided her backward.

Logan and Harper stood together as they watched Zane work his magic. Harper seemed fascinated and moved closer to get a better view.

The horse's back feet caught on the edge of the trailer as she tried to step out. She stumbled and spooked, fighting the lead. Releasing another anxious whinny, she reared back, kicking and bucking right toward Harper.

Logan reacted on instinct. He stepped in front of Harper, wrapping his arms around her to shield her as he pushed her out of the way.

Zane grabbed the horse's halter and worked to settle her again.

Harper gripped the front of Logan's jacket, her breath coming in hard gasps.

"You okay?" he asked, not quite ready to let her go as his own heart pounded against his chest.

After a few seconds, she nodded. "I'm okay. But oh my Lord, horses are much bigger in person than they look on television. I thought she was going to trample me."

"That would be terrible, seeing as how we haven't even had the peach cobbler yet. I'd feel awful eating it if you'd just been killed in a freak horse-trampling accident."

"I'll bet you would. But you'd still eat it." She grinned, but he noticed she didn't let him go either.

"Well, of course. It's peach cobbler."

She chuckled, then pushed away from his chest. "With all this talk about the cobbler, I think I'd better go check on it. Bring Zane in when you're done, and I'll dish some up for both of you. It's best when it's warm with a scoop of vanilla ice cream."

A lot of things were best when they were warm, and he was warming again just watching her walk back to the house. She still wore his cowboy hat and looked cute as hell. Except they were going to have to find her some cowboy boots. He needed to get her out of those combat boots—and while he was at it, out of those jeans too. But for now, he had to focus on this horse.

He strode back to Zane and Gus. The men worked

together to get the horse into the corral, then Logan settled up with Gus, and he closed up the trailer and drove off.

Zane was perched on top of the corral fence, his hat pushed back as he watched the horse run. Logan climbed up and sat next to him. "You did great work with the horse. That was impressive the way you got her out of the trailer and calmed her down after she stumbled."

"It was no big deal," Zane said, chewing on a piece of straw. "She was just scared."

"It *was* a big deal. You've got a gift with horses and with all animals. I've seen it."

Zane tossed the straw and gazed around the corral. "I forgot how beautiful this ranch is. I loved spending my summers here as a kid. It feels good to be back."

"How'd you like to be back on a more full-time basis?"

Zane cocked an eyebrow. "You offering me a job?"

"You in the market for one?"

He shrugged. "I could be."

"I could sure use the help. With Dad gone and the unfortunate circumstances surrounding my last hired hand, I'm down to me and Harper trying to run the ranch. I just told her she could stay in the bunkhouse, so I can't offer you housing, but I could offer you a full-time wage."

"I don't need housing. It's better for me to be at home with my dad in the evening anyway." Zane stared out across the mountain range. "I don't know how long I'll stick around. But I promised Dad I'd be here until after the new year anyway."

"That works for me."

Zane shrugged again. "Sure. Why not? I might as well be doing something useful. When do you want me to start?"

"Is now too soon?"

Zane offered Logan a side-eye.

"Sorry. I know it's soon, but I'm coaching a kid's hockey team and need to be in town tonight. I was gonna run a load of hay out to the cattle in the north pasture before I left, but if you could do it, it would sure ease up my evening." The two men had done the task together many times, and Logan had full faith in Zane's abilities to get the job done.

"Sure. I've got some time. I can run it out now, then I'll be back in the morning."

"Great. I'll help you load your truck."

Later that night, Harper caught herself humming a Christmas carol as she shook a pillow into a clean case and dropped it on the bed. Logan had told her she could use any of the extra bedding in the linen closet, and she'd chosen a purple comforter and a matching set of sheets covered with lilacs. The slightly feminine style made her think the bedding had either been Quinn's or was used in the guest room. But Harper liked the purple, and lilacs were among her favorite flowers. Even though Christmas was right around the corner and snow was swirling in the air outside her door, the flowers made her think of spring and new beginnings.

Could this thing with Logan be a new beginning for her?

How could it be if she hadn't even told him about Floyd? How could she consider starting any kind of anything when she hadn't even told him about the most important part of her life? But telling him about Floyd would mean having to tell him about everything, including the embezzlement charges. It didn't matter that she'd only been in the county jail or that her sentence had only lasted a short time or that she'd unknowingly committed a crime in an attempt to save her and her son. In the eyes of the law and of society, she was a criminal. And she wasn't ready for Logan to look at her like an ex-con and a thief.

For the first time in years, she was feeling something for another man. After Michael died, she'd thought that part of her had died too. Her heart had been shattered into a trillion pieces, broken so brutally she wasn't sure it would ever beat again. But it had sure been beating earlier that afternoon when Logan had pulled her into his arms and pressed his lips to hers. It had been thumping so hard, she was surprised it didn't leave a bruise.

Logan had kissed her—*kissed* her. She still couldn't believe it had happened. But it had, and her heart had shown up, pounding against her chest as if it wanted out.

What was she doing? Her sole purpose for being here was to get Floyd and get out of Dodge, not to get involved with a smart-mouthed cowboy, no matter how hot that cowboy was or how delicious his mouth tasted.

Harper knew she couldn't have it both ways. Logan wasn't looking for something serious; he'd made that clear by firing the last two women who'd tried to pin him down. And she wasn't looking for anything at all. Even if she were, she had her son to think about, so she wouldn't get involved with anyone if she didn't think it could *become* serious.

That's part of why she hadn't bothered dating yet, because she didn't want to put Floyd through having and losing another man in his life. Well, that and because she hadn't found anyone she had wanted to date. In fact, she'd thought those parts of her—the parts that yearned for a man's touch, that got tingly and tightened at the brush of a man's skin—had broken along with her heart. But they seemed to be working now. When she was around Logan, all her parts were tingling and tightening and yearning as if they'd been doused in flames and were calling out for water.

She needed her life to be simple. Needed to get her crap in order and get her boy back. She did not need the complications of a man—no matter how tall, dark, and handsome a man he was.

This job was supposed to be simple—cook a few meals, do some dusting and a few loads of laundry, and collect her paycheck. But it had her head spinning and her heart crashing into her chest just from thinking about Logan. And now the kiss complicated things even further. Especially because she *loved* the kiss. She'd felt it all the way from her toes to her tingly parts, and she hadn't wanted it to stop. She wanted Logan's hands on every part of her body, wanted to feel him touch her, claim her.

She'd been lost in the essence of him, every one of her senses taking in the way his strong hands held her back, the soft rumbling sound in the back of his throat as he deepened the kiss, the way he smelled like soap and aftershave and tasted like toothpaste. Even now, she could still smell a hint of his aftershave on the front of her shirt.

If the oven timer hadn't gone off, she's not sure what would have happened, how far things would have gone. She was so immersed in the moment, so spellbound in his kiss that if he'd carried her to his bedroom, or heck, if he'd lifted her to the counter, she would have complied. She'd been like putty in his hands.

Gah. She did *not* want to be putty in anyone's hands. Putty signified she could be molded or shaped by someone else's impression of her, that she could be controlled. And she was done with that, done letting other people control how she felt, how she acted, what she thought. She sank down onto the bed, her shoulders slumping forward. Except that wasn't true. Because even now, at this moment, she was letting someone else control her. She was letting Michael's mother dictate how and if she got a chance to be with her son.

Everything she was doing right now was under the control of Judith Benning: the job, making the bed, cleaning the bunkhouse, creating a home for her son, even denying herself the carnal attraction to a man—and holy hell, she was feeling all kinds of carnal thoughts toward Logan, thoughts involving teeth and biting and tearing clothes.

She flopped back on the bed and covered her face with the pillow, letting out a scream into the lilac design. It didn't matter if she had the pillow or not. Logan was gone for the night, so she was alone on the ranch. The only ones who would hear her scream would be the kittens, the cows, and the horse who'd tried to trample her that afternoon.

Rolling over, Harper pressed her face harder into the pillow and screamed again. Screamed out all her frustration and fury at the unfairness and the anguish of the whole situation.

Stop. I need to stop feeling sorry for myself and do something about it. She sat up and pushed her hair from her damp forehead. Geez, she was so mad, she was sweating. But mad didn't get her anywhere. And if her mom had taught her one thing—besides how to embezzle money from a large corporation—it was that life wasn't fair.

Judith might be in control, for now, but that didn't mean Harper had to lie down and take it. She could still fight. And no one was going to do that for her. There was only one person left in this world that she could truly trust and count on to stand up and fight her battles, and that was herself.

She'd trusted her mom, but Brandy had betrayed her.

She'd trusted Michael and her grandmother, but they had both died and left her behind.

The only one left was herself. She needed to quit rolling over and screaming into pillows, and instead draw out her weapons and scream a battle cry. She grabbed the pillow and threw it against the wall.

She might have made a few mistakes—okay, a lot of mistakes—but she wasn't giving up, wasn't going down without a fight. Or without her son.

She pulled out her cell phone and called Judith.

CHAPTER 14

HARPER HELD HER BREATH AS SHE LISTENED TO THE phone ring. Once. Twice. Three times. Four. Then the machine answered, and Judith's nasally voice instructed her to leave a message.

Harper snapped the phone closed. She wasn't ready to leave a message. She'd been ready to bite the woman's head off and demand that Judith let her have her son back. *Damn.* Her shoulders sank inward. Maybe it was best that Michael's mother hadn't answered. She didn't seem like the type to take too well to having her head bitten off.

No, she seemed calm and educated. Well, Harper couldn't compete with that—not unless she wanted to wait four years while she ran out and got a quick college degree—but she could appeal to the older woman's logic. And her ego.

Judith wanted her to jump through hoops for Floyd. So Harper needed to quit floundering and start asking "how high?" She'd claimed Harper didn't have a home or an income or a way to support Floyd. So she needed to show the woman she did. That she was working on it.

Harper opened the phone again and typed a text message to Judith that read: I've found a nice place to live and am working hard to create a home for Floyd. She already had a home. It was back in Kansas. But until she had enough money to get them back there, she needed Judith to believe she was trying to make a home here. I'd like to see my son.

Even for a visit. I could come there, or you could bring him here. Please. I miss him. She pressed Send.

She paced the floor of the tidy living area, strategizing reasons to take the truck into town so she could see her son. Surely Judith would agree to let her visit. The woman had to have a heart. Even if it was buried under a layer of ice, it had to be in there somewhere.

If the chance miracle happened and Judith did soften and agree to let Floyd visit the ranch, Harper would have to tell Logan. But she'd cross that bridge when she came to it. She wasn't planning to keep her son a secret forever. She would eventually tell Logan.

But she knew telling him would inevitably be the end of the relationship, or whatever it was they were doing. *Relationship* seemed too strong a word—maybe *rapport* was better. Whatever they had, it would come to a screaming halt when Logan found out she was a criminal who had spent time in jail and lost her son in the process.

It didn't matter. The most important thing was Floyd. And getting to see him and hug him to her chest. Her arms ached to hold him, to wrap him up and tell him how much she loved him.

Her phone dinged, and she pressed it to her mouth, afraid to look. She took a deep breath, snapped the phone open, and then let out a heart-wrenching moan.

> I appreciate your efforts, but we have to put Floyd first. He is happy where he is, and seeing you will only bring up all the past hurts and feelings of betrayal and abandonment. I know you want to see him, but you have to put

his needs first. Floyd is happy. Do you really
want to mess that up?

Judith included a picture of Floyd sitting on a sofa—
Harper assumed it was in Judith's house—and laughing as
he held a controller to a video-game system. Harper soaked
in every detail of the picture, her heart aching to hear her
son's laughter.

He did look happy. And she'd never be able to give him
any kind of gaming system or the kind of home she could
see visible in the background of the photo. But what did that
matter? Plenty of kids grew up without a PlayStation and in
less-than-perfect houses, and they adjusted fine. Granted,
they probably didn't have ex-cons for mothers, but still.

This was just one setback. It just meant she needed to
work harder to prove to Judith that being with his mother
was the best thing for Floyd. *Or*...the demon side of her
conscience piped up...it meant that she just needed to
forget asking permission and go take back her son.

But how? It's not like she could march into the school
and take him. There's no way the school would allow that.
And Judith had made it clear she wasn't going to let Harper
into her house.

But what if she didn't wait to be invited? What if she
waited until she knew Floyd was home, then barged
through the door? She might get to see her boy for a few
minutes, but then knowing Judith, she'd have her arrested
for trespassing.

No, Harper needed to be smart, to be patient, and to
play Judith's game. She was back to jumping through hoops,
but she'd do it. She'd do whatever it took.

She stripped down to her thermal shirt and undies and climbed between the fresh, clean sheets. It was still early, but she'd borrowed a paperback thriller she'd been wanting to read and hoped it would take her mind off her problems. Settling against the pillows, she tried to focus on the book, but her mind kept wandering as she thought about Judith's text. What if Michael's mother was right and she was only thinking of herself? Was she really just being selfish? *Would* Floyd be better off—happier—if she left him with Judith and quietly disappeared from his life?

Logan stepped out of the locker room and waited by the bleachers as the rest of the kids straggled out. Hockey practice had gone well tonight. Colt and Chloe had both been there, so they'd been able to separate the kids into groups and work on individual drills. He glanced across the arena to where the two of them were huddled on the bleachers, their heads bent together as they studied a clipboard.

Logan smiled as he sank onto the bleachers next to them, happy for his two friends and the relationship they'd found with each other. "What are you two working on?"

Chloe wore a soft, blue knitted beanie over her mass of blond curls, and she smiled over at him. "We were just working on the lines. I'm thinking of changing a couple of kids on the blue and red lines." She had convinced him and Colt to name the offensive and defensive lines with colors instead of numbers so none of the kids felt like they were on a lesser team.

The teacher in her was always thinking of things like that—ways to boost the kids' morale and keep them engaged.

"Sounds good to me."

"You're awfully agreeable tonight." Colt gave Logan's shoulder a nudge. "In fact, you've been in an exceptionally good mood the last few times I've seen you. So who is she?"

Logan feigned innocence. "I don't know what you're talking about." Although of course he did, and he knew his innocent act wasn't fooling his best friend.

"Yeah, sure. That grin and your all-around good mood wouldn't have anything to do with a certain woman you can't stop talking about, would it? A woman who's been cooking you supper and whose name sounds like a musical instrument and rhymes with Tarper."

"*Tarper*? Seriously? That's not even a word."

"Sure it is. It's someone who lays out a tarp. Look it up. And you're avoiding the question."

Logan shrugged. "Yeah, okay. I may have been spending a little time thinking about Harper. But wait till you meet her. She's pretty great."

"She must be," Colt said. "I haven't seen you all googly-eyed and falling for a woman in…well, ever."

"That's because I don't get googly-eyed." Logan's brows knit together. "And I never said I was falling for her."

"You never said you weren't."

Logan's shoulders slumped forward, and he let out a sigh, tired of this game. "Look, you know I don't do relationships. The women in my life don't tend to stick around, and this one isn't planning to either. She's already said she'll be gone by Christmas, so it's a nonstarter. We just have fun together, and I like being around her."

"Don't listen to this lunkhead," Chloe said, giving Colt one of her teacher stares. "Personally, I think it's great you found someone you can tolerate to help you out. I wasn't sure after the last few. I was afraid I was going to have to come out and cook for you. And if you like this woman, you don't have to turn it into a big thing about whether she's going to stay or leave. Just enjoy each other's company. It doesn't have to be forever. It can just be nice for now."

Chloe made a lot of sense, but Logan's gut had already turned sour. He didn't know what he was thinking, imagining some kind of future with Harper. He never should have kissed her. It had only made things worse, made him want something he could never have.

Logan shrugged. "Whatever. It's no big deal. I appreciate the support, Chloe, but in my experience, you can't count on women to stick." He nodded to the boy walking toward them—a boy they all knew was currently living with his grandmother because his mom had abandoned him. "Case in point."

The boy smiled shyly as he approached Logan. "Hey, Coach."

"Hey, Floyd. How's it going? You did great in practice tonight."

"Thanks. I'm having a little trouble with my stick though." He held up his hockey stick. "Think you can help me? I can't get the tape on the end right." The end of his stick was a wadded ball of tape. "My grandma tried, but I don't thinks she's very good at this kind of thing. She said it made her hands all sticky."

"Sure, bud." Logan patted the bench next to him, then held out his hand for the stick. "Have a seat, and let me take a look at it."

The boy handed him the stick and plopped down next

to him. Logan stripped the sticky, black misshapen ball of tape from the end of the stick, then dug through his hockey bag and found a fresh roll of white tape. "I like to use white tape because it doesn't mark up your gloves. Is that okay?"

Floyd nodded. "Yeah. I think that black stuff was just some tape my grandma found in the garage."

Logan agreed. "I like to put one nice, clean strip at the top, then let the tape dangle a few feet and give it a couple of quick spins." He wrapped a neat strip around the end, then spun the roll while the tape dangled. "That's gonna make your tape curl up like a rope, and that's what will give you a good grip for your top hand." He wound the curled tape a few inches down the end of the stick. "You want to wind it down like a spiral so it's like you're getting finger grooves in there, then wind the tape back up to the top. And make sure it's nice and tight." Circling the handle, he neatly wound the tape back up the stick, covering the rows of curled tape. "Then the trick to getting a good knob is to just use half the piece of tape at a time. Then you're not wasting the roll." He ripped the tape down the center and twisted it around the end several times, then wrapped the stick with the other side of the piece. "You want a nice knob on the end so if you drop your stick, you can pick it up easier off the ice without having to take off your gloves."

Floyd was watching as he listened intently to Logan's instructions. "You're good at this."

Logan shrugged and wrapped the end with a fresh piece of tape to seal off the knob. "I've been doing it a long time. And this is how the pros do it. I have a good friend who plays for the NHL, and this is how he taught us."

"He did? That's cool."

"I think you've met him. It's Max's dad, Rock."

"Oh yeah. He covers the penalty box during the games once in a while. And sometimes he cusses at the ref."

Logan chuckled. "Yeah. He shouldn't do that. But he's a good guy most of the time."

"Yeah. Max is lucky." The boy stared at the top of his shoe. "I don't have a dad anymore. I did, but he died."

Logan's hand stilled on the end of the stick. "I'm sorry. That's a tough break for a kid. I know what it's like. My mom died when I was a kid too."

Floyd lifted his head and squinted at Logan. "Yeah?"

"Yeah. And it was hard."

The boy let out a soft sigh, and his shoulders slumped. "I miss him."

"I'm sure you do."

"Sometimes I miss him so much, I feel like my chest is going to break in half. Did that ever happen to you?"

Logan swallowed. It was happening to him right now. His heart was breaking for this kid. "Yeah, it did. It sometimes still does. That's pretty normal."

Floyd looked out over the ice. "I wish he could see me play hockey. He gave me a stick and a puck for Christmas when I was little. My grandma says he's always watching me play, like from heaven, ya know. Do you think that's true?"

Logan couldn't speak because of the ball of emotion clogging his throat. He nodded instead, then swallowed. "Yeah. I do, buddy. I think that's absolutely true."

"Cool." Floyd shifted his gaze to the hockey stick. "That looks way better than when my grandma did it."

Logan chuckled. "Thanks. And this is what coaches are for. You let me know if you need help with any of your other equipment, or if you just want to talk. About your dad, or whatever."

"Thanks, Coach." A smile beamed from the boy's face as he looked up, and Logan felt like a superhero.

Floyd hopped up from the bleachers just as his grandmother, Judith, walked toward them. She put a hand on the boy's shoulder. "Hey, honey, why don't you go get your hockey bag, and we'll stop for ice cream on the way home."

"Okay." He turned to wave to Logan before running off. "See ya, Coach."

Judith smiled as she watched him go, then turned to Logan. "I saw you helping him with the tape business on the stick. I'm afraid I made a mess of it. Thank you for fixing it."

"No problem. And I was happy to help. Let me know if he needs anything else. That's what we're here for."

"That's kind of you. I did want to ask how you think he's doing. He seems to really be taking to the team."

"Oh yeah. He's a great kid."

"He's had a rough time. You know his dad—my son, Michael—died years ago, and his good-for-nothing mother has been serving time in jail." She shook her head in disgust. "I don't know how my Michael ever let himself get involved with a woman like that. I tell you, she cared more about herself than she did Floyd. And she was too lazy to get a job and resorted to criminal activity instead of taking care of her son."

Fury churned in Logan's gut. How could a mother abandon her own kid? Especially a kid like Floyd? He was smart and funny. He had a good heart and was generous to a fault. Logan had seen him share his snacks numerous times, and Floyd was the first to help another kid who had fallen on the ice or needed an extra hand or someone to partner with for a drill.

This was Floyd's first year playing hockey, but he was already showing great skill at skating and was adept with stickhandling and moving the puck. He was easily one of the best kids on the team, yet he still listened to direction and never hogged the puck. Logan and Colt had grown up with and passed on to their team the philosophy that good players scored, but great players passed. And Floyd often passed the puck, even to Maddie, the lone girl on their team.

"I'm sorry to hear that, Miss Judith. No kid deserves that. And like I said, Floyd's a terrific kid and a great addition to the team. You must be a good influence on him."

"Thank you." She smiled and puffed out her chest, reminding him of a peacock they'd once had and the way it had strutted around the ranch.

Logan didn't know Judith well. They'd occasionally crossed paths at church, so he knew who she was, like people in small towns knew of each other. But she seemed like a nice enough lady, and she appeared to really care for her grandson.

"We'll see you at the next practice." Judith waved, then walked to where Floyd was waiting with his bag by the door.

Logan turned to Chloe, who was Floyd's teacher as well. "I feel so bad for that kid. Is it as rough for him as Judith makes it sound?"

"It's not good. Floyd's a sweetheart, but he's been having some trouble lately. He keeps saying his mom should be out of jail now, and he's expecting her to come get him, but she hasn't shown up. And from what he says, I don't think she's had any contact with him since she was arrested."

Logan's chest tightened, memories surfacing of missing his own mother and the all-too-familiar feelings of abandonment, of being left behind. But Floyd was a great kid. He didn't have a learning disability that took over his family's life with extra tutoring and studying and spending hours working on exercises and trying to read the same books over and over again. She may have thought she was hiding it, but Logan could hear the frustration and exhaustion in his mom's voice every time she had to sit with him to help him read. "Maybe some women aren't cut out to be mothers."

Chloe tilted her head. "Maybe. But his mom couldn't have been that bad if she raised such a sweet kid. Or else his grandma had a lot of influence in his life. I can tell he loves Mrs. Benning, but he's really missing his mom. I think he's struggling with the fact she hasn't tried to contact him at all."

Anger and frustration swirled in Logan's gut. He felt for the kid, and he pledged to spend more time with him at practice, just to give him a little extra attention and show him other people cared about him.

They finished getting the rest of the kids off, then Logan headed home. He spent the drive thinking about Floyd and mired in memories of his own mother who had abandoned him. He knew what the kid was feeling, and old hurts surfaced that he'd thought he'd laid to rest a long time ago. Old hurts that festered and stung like a fresh scab he'd picked.

Which was why he didn't let himself get involved with women. It wasn't worth the pain of them leaving you. And they did leave. They always left.

So what was he doing letting himself get swept up in something with Harper? She'd made no secret of the fact she was eventually leaving, so why even bother spending more time with her?

A good question. One he didn't have a good answer for.

The house was dark when he got home, and he didn't bother with the lights as he headed to the kitchen. The scent of peaches and cinnamon hung in the air, but his gut was a mess of queasy and upset. The thought of eating anything made his stomach roil.

He tossed back some antacids and drank a glass of water. Digging the chalky tablets out of his back teeth with his tongue, he leaned against the counter and determined to spend the better part of the next day in the barn or outside. Maybe he'd even take lunch in town at the diner. There was no point in pursuing this thing with Harper, so why make it worse on himself by spending any more time with her?

The decision made, he strode down the hall to get ready for bed. Restless, he wandered through his room as he brushed his teeth. From his window, he could see a faint light burning across the yard in the bunkhouse. What was she doing over there? Was she already in bed?

It was cold, and a light snow was falling. Maybe he should go over and check on her. Just in case she needed something, like maybe another blanket. Or another body to crawl in bed with her to keep her warm.

For someone who'd just vowed to keep his distance from the woman tomorrow, it hadn't taken him long to renege on that promise tonight.

He picked up his phone. Maybe he'd just call her. Or send a text. There didn't seem to be a lot of harm in a simple text.

No. Hold strong. He tossed the phone on the bed and walked away.

CHAPTER 15

A SHIVER RAN DOWN HARPER'S BACK, AND SHE SNAPPED the book she was reading shut. Why had she thought it would be a good idea to read a suspense novel about a woman stranded on a ranch?

What was that? The hair on her arms rose as she swore she heard a noise outside the bunkhouse. She slid further under the covers, sure it was just her imagination.

Nope. There it was again. She was sure of it this time. There was something outside.

It sounded like something—or someone—had bumped or scraped the front of the house. Visions of a serial killer scratching his hand along the siding filled Harper's mind.

But why would a serial killer be on the ranch? That didn't make any sense. Not that serial killers made sense in the first place, but one being on this ranch did seem unlikely. It was probably the cats, except that it sounded too big to be a kitten. It might be a coyote or a raccoon.

She knew one thing. She wasn't going to figure out what it was by hiding beneath the covers. Slipping from the bed, she snuck into the living room, leaving the lights off so she could see outside. Tiptoeing toward the door, she caught her breath as a shadow passed the window.

Holy crap. That wasn't a cat. Or a raccoon.

It could be that rat bastard Ted coming back for revenge. Or, more than likely, he was drunk and had forgotten he didn't live here anymore. Glancing around the room, she searched for a weapon.

They'd taken almost everything out of the room in their earlier attempts at cleaning up. The kitchen counters were practically bare as well. Except for the toaster, the coffee maker, and a crock filled with a meager number of utensils. So, unless she was going to offer him a slice of toast or a cup of Joe, those were out. And she didn't think she could inflict much damage with a pancake turner.

But she had seen a cast-iron skillet in the oven. It would have to do in a pinch. She tiptoed across the hardwood floor, carefully eased open the oven, and pulled out the skillet.

Creeping back across the room, she peered out the front window. She couldn't see who was in front of the door, but she could see a large shadow on the ground.

The shadow wasn't moving. Maybe the light was playing tricks on her, and the shadow was from one of the chairs in front of the bunkhouse. She could be getting herself psyched out over a piece of porch furniture.

Only one way to find out. She put one hand on the doorknob and raised the skillet above her head with the other. Her heart pounded against her chest, but knowing what the heck was really out there had to be better than standing in here and imagining the worst. Serial killer or drunken farmhand, either way, they were about to get a frying pan to the face.

She yanked open the door and let out a primal yell. "Get out of here!"

Holy crap!

A man really *was* standing outside her door. Not a piece of furniture, but a tall man whose face was shadowed by a cowboy hat. Her scream must have startled him because he stumbled back and threw his hands in the air as if in surrender. "It's just me, Logan."

"Logan?" Harper squinted into the darkness as she lowered the skillet.

"Yes. Logan. The guy who lives in that big house across the driveway."

"Holy smokes. You scared the crud out of me."

"*You* scared the crud out of me."

"I thought you were a serial killer. Or Ted."

"A serial killer? What would a serial killer be doing out here? And if I *were* a serial killer, what were you planning to do with that skillet?"

"Whack you in the head with it, of course."

He offered her an impish grin. "I wasn't sure. Maybe you were going to offer to fry me some bacon. You do make great bacon."

"Hey, don't dis my weapon of choice. We cleaned this place out so well, there weren't a lot of options left for defensive maneuvers. It was this or the toaster."

He lifted one shoulder. "Then I'd say you made the only logical choice."

"What are you doing out here anyway? Besides scaring ten years off my life." She pressed a hand to her chest, suddenly acutely aware that she wasn't wearing a bra. In fact, she wasn't wearing much of anything. Thank goodness her thermal shirt covered her butt, but just barely.

"I was checking on the animals and thought I'd check on you too. You know, as long as I was out."

"I feel so special getting lumped in with a pig and a cow."

His voice lowered and took on a flirty tone. "I was lumping you in with the kittens."

Oh my. A hard rush of desire tore down her spine, and her nipples tightened when he'd said *kittens*. Dang, that man could make anything sound sexy. His eyes had just dropped to her chest, and from the look of hunger that filled them, she was pretty sure he'd figured out her braless status. "So why didn't you just knock?"

"I didn't want to bother you."

"You just said you wanted to check on me."

"I know. I did. But I also didn't want to bother you."

A gust of cold air blew across her legs, and she shivered as she took a step back. "So, are you coming in, or what? It's freezing out there, and I don't think my landlord wants me heating the whole outside."

Logan tilted his head as if studying her. Apparently, he wasn't very good at hiding his emotions, because she watched them all play across his face. His eyes, which had gone dark and flirty, changed to wary and suspicious. That wasn't good. Why would he be suspicious of her?

Maybe he thought she was offering him more than a piece of toast. Heck, maybe she was. She might not be saying the words, but her body was calling out to his. Her breasts were aching and full and craving the feel of his large hands, and it was taking everything she had not to squirm from the tingles tightening there.

His expression changed once more to resolve as he shook his head. "Nah. I didn't want to intrude. I just wanted to make sure you were okay and warm enough. I mean, that you had enough blankets."

What should have been a relief at him not hitting on her—and hence her getting to keep her job—felt more like a letdown. "I'm okay. And I took an extra blanket from the house, so I'm plenty warm. Or I *was*." *Oops*. Her body must have felt that rejection and turned it into a little snark.

She'd better get herself in check and remember why the last woman had lost this job.

"Oh yeah, well, I'll let you get back to bed." He took a step back, then another forward again. "Oh, and I also wanted to tell you that I'm taking lunch in town tomorrow. At the diner. And I plan to get an early start, so you don't have to worry about me for breakfast either. I'll just grab some coffee and a leftover biscuit or something. So you can sleep in, if you want."

She jerked her head back. "Sleep in? You don't pay me to sleep in." *Uh-oh.* She needed to get this conversation back on track. Logan wasn't a cute cowboy stopping by for a flirty booty call. He was her employer, and the only lifeline she had to getting Floyd back. She needed to tread carefully. And to remind him why he needed her. "I'll make sure the coffee is on when you get up, and I can fry an egg to stick in that biscuit. Then I'll spend the morning working on cleaning the house and taking care of laundry. I'm planning to do a pot roast with brown gravy and mashed potatoes for supper. And I was going to make my grandma's recipe for yeast rolls. Does that sound good?"

His expression softened. "That sounds great. What would I do without you?"

Let's not find out, she thought as she said good night and shut the door.

What an idiot.

Logan couldn't believe Harper had caught him lurking outside her front door. Well, not exactly lurking. He'd been getting ready to knock. He'd just been working up to it for a good five minutes. No wonder she'd been freaked out.

Then *he'd* been freaked out. He hadn't expected her to answer the door brandishing a skillet, and he dang sure hadn't expected her to be bare-legged, wearing nothing but a thermal shirt. A shirt that hugged her curves and clung to her full breasts. The hem of the shirt barely covered her ass, and it took an enormous amount of willpower not to press her against the door and kiss her thoroughly as he explored every inch of skin that shirt covered.

Her dark hair was down and had that messy-sexy look as it curled around her shoulders, and he imagined the way it would look spread across his pillows.

She set something off inside him, something that made him want to flirt with her, to win her over with his charm and coax that sexy smile onto her face. He'd earned it with that kitten comment, but then she'd caught him dropping his gaze to her chest. The thin white shirt only emphasized the curves of her ample breasts, and her rigid nipples told him she either liked the flirting or she was freezing. Either way, he appreciated the view, and his mouth went dry at the thought of sucking one of the tight, hardened nubs into his mouth.

Then she'd made that "landlord" crack, and reality had crashed into him. He was her boss. What the hell was he doing showing up at her doorstep after dark? He'd said he was checking on the animals, but he hadn't checked anything. He'd made a beeline for her front door, then stood there like a doofus trying to get up the courage to knock.

This woman was getting to him, and it had to stop. He'd made the right decision in telling her he wouldn't be around for breakfast or lunch. He hoped she'd stay in bed, and he could avoid seeing her at all tomorrow, but danged if she didn't offer to still get up and make him coffee. And a breakfast sandwich.

He stomped through the house and into his bedroom, trying to avoid looking out the window. He stripped down to his boxer briefs and snuck one glance as he slid into bed. The bunkhouse was dark. She must have gone to sleep.

Now if only he could do the same.

The next day, Logan kept his pledge and spent most of the day either in the barn or the pasture. At least his body did. His mind kept sneaking into the house and trying to imagine what Harper was doing.

Zane had shown up early, and they'd taken a truckload of hay out to the cattle. Although Logan appreciated the other man's strength and strong work ethic, he missed the laughing and joking around from when he'd done the task with Harper. Zane was congenial and cracked the occasional dry joke, but for the most part, he was the silent, contemplative type and didn't talk much. But Logan hadn't hired him to chat. He'd hired him to help take care of his herd. And that's what he'd been doing. And then some. Zane had spent an hour working with the new horse, then taken the tractor and transported huge, round hay bales out to different areas of the pastures.

Which gave Logan more time to moon over the woman folding laundry in his living room. He'd had lunch at the diner, but he couldn't avoid the house forever, he thought as he gathered the day's mail and carried it back to the house. But he could shut himself in the den and spent the latter part of the afternoon getting some work done. Except that he hadn't exactly shut himself in. The door was still partially open, and he was acutely aware of Harper's presence moving around the house.

He couldn't seem to focus as he used the letter opener to slice open the stack of envelopes. Was she singing Christmas carols? Or maybe that was the radio.

He absently pulled the letters from the envelopes—bill, bill, junk, church bulletin, junk...*wait*. What was this? He unfolded the red sheet of paper. It was a flyer for the Creedence Christmas Celebration, but why did it have his name written at the top, then crossed off? Who would send him this?

He reached for the envelope and turned it over just as a knock sounded at the door and Harper poked her head in.

"Hey, it's starting to snow, and I thought I'd make some hot chocolate. Could I bring you a cup?" The smile on her face turned to alarm when she saw the letter clutched in his hand. "Is that my mail?"

He looked down at the envelope and realized it was clearly addressed to Harper Evans. "Oh shit. Sorry. I was just opening the stack and didn't realize it was addressed to you."

She twisted her hands together in front of her. "Yeah, I was going to tell you I was expecting something. I just thought I'd be the one to grab the mail." She held out her hand, but wouldn't look him directly in the eyes. "Can I have it, please?"

"Oh sure. Of course. I'm so sorry I opened it." He passed her the flyer and the envelope.

She took the papers and folded them together, then stuffed them in the back pocket of her jeans. "It's no problem."

"Harper?"

"Yeah."

She still wouldn't look at him, and he had a pretty good idea of what was going on now. "I noticed my name was on the top of that flyer. Were you going to invite me to go to the Christmas Celebration with you?"

Her eyes widened, then she slowly nodded. "Yep. I sure was. That's exactly why I mailed this flyer here." She took a step back as if trying to slink out of the room. "But then I got too embarrassed. It was a dumb idea anyway. Let's just forget about it."

"Wait. I don't think it's such a dumb idea."

She stopped, her hand on the doorknob. "You don't?"

"No. In fact, I think it's a great idea. I wasn't sure if I was going to go this year, since my dad's not around. He's the one who likes us to make an appearance. Which is weird, because he's this gruff ol' cowboy, yet he participates in the Reindeer Roundup and the Holly-Jolly Huckleberry Pie-eating contest every year." Logan shook his head, surprised at the twinge of melancholy he felt over his father missing the celebration, and at how much he was missing his dad. "Anyway, I figured I'd skip it because I didn't want to go solo, but it might be fun for us to go together. Especially since you've never been."

"Oh-kay. That sounds good. And it does look like a fun event."

"It is. It's a little hokey, but it has booths and games, and they have a live band and a little dancing."

"I thought you said you don't dance."

"I said I wasn't much good at it, but I can still cut a *small* rug. Not like a full-size carpet or anything, more like a little throw rug or a welcome mat."

A grin curved her lips. "I get the idea. And I would love to go together."

"Great. It's a date."

Her eyes widened again.

"I mean, not a *date*-date," he backpedaled. "But like an 'I'll put the date on my calendar' date...thing...kind of deal." *Oh geez.* He was making it worse. Why had he even suggested they go together? By the way she was backing out of the room again, the idea was obviously making her uncomfortable.

Before she could say anything more, she jumped as a horn sounded from a car that had driven up to the house.

"Who's here?" he asked, rising from the desk chair. He wasn't expecting anyone.

Harper leaned back to peer through the office door, and the color drained from her face.

CHAPTER 16

THE AIR RUSHED FROM HARPER'S LUNGS, AND IT TOOK
everything she had not to run to the door. She'd only caught
sight of the two people walking up the porch steps from the
corner of her eye, but she knew it was a woman and a child.

It had to be Judith and Floyd.

Michael's mother must have gotten her message and
changed her mind. Harper pressed her fists against her sides,
fighting the urge to smooth her hair. "I'll get the door," she
said, trying to keep the tremble out of her voice.

She took deliberate steps, doing her best to act calm as
she approached the door, a hundred things she wanted to
say to her son crashing around in her head. She couldn't
even think about what she was going to tell Logan. But it
didn't matter. All that mattered now was seeing her boy.
She'd figured out what to say to Logan later.

The tall cowboy had followed her from the office. Why
wouldn't he? This was his house. There was no reason to
imagine that someone would be at the door for her.

Taking a deep breath, she felt as if she was walking
through molasses as she crossed the room. But before she
reached the door, it was flung open and the woman and
child walked into the house.

Harper took a staggering step back as her heart sank—as if
it had literally dropped from her chest and fallen onto the floor.

It wasn't Judith and Floyd.

It was a boy and a woman, and the boy was around Floyd's

age, but he wasn't Floyd. This boy had blond spiky hair and small, round glasses and hugged a stack of books to his chest. The woman with him was tall and gorgeous, her long blond hair curling around her shoulders and her smile radiant as she flashed it at Logan.

A thousand emotions flowed through Harper as she gripped the back of the sofa to keep her knees from giving way. Most were in line with sorrow and anguish and grief at missing her child, but she also felt a twinge of jealousy as she watched this woman stride confidently through the room and throw her arms around Logan.

"Hey, Lo," the woman said. "You're quite the talk of the town. I heard you fired Ted, and Kimmie is telling anyone who will listen that you practically threw her out of your house for not starching your shirts correctly."

"That's hilarious," he said. "Since she never starched my shirts at all. I don't think she got around to doing a single load of laundry while she was here."

If it hadn't have been for the shock of thinking it was Floyd at the door, Harper would have realized sooner that the woman was Logan's sister, Quinn, with his nephew, Max. She'd seen pictures of them in the house. She swallowed the lump of disappointment that had formed in her throat.

"I figured," Quinn said.

He motioned to Harper. "Quinn, this is Harper Evans." He paused as if not sure how to introduce her.

Harper smiled and held out her hand. "I'm the new Kimmie. Except that I have already done the laundry."

Quinn laughed and shook Harper's hand, then gazed around the room. "It's nice to meet you. Bryn told me she'd found a replacement for Logan's latest housekeeper fiasco. And the house looks great."

"Kimmie's not even in the ballpark of what Harper's done since she's been here. And she can cook fried chicken to rival Grandma Rivers."

Quinn raised an eyebrow. "That's high praise." She gestured to the boy who had spread out on the sofa and already had his head inside a large book with dinosaurs on the cover. "This is my son, Max. Max, say hello to Harper."

He looked up, a friendly smile on his face. "Hello, Harper. Did you know that some dinosaurs had tails that were over forty-five feet long, and some of their skulls were as big as a car?"

"I did know that, yes. Did you know that all dinosaurs laid eggs?" Harper countered.

"Yes." He pushed his glasses up his nose and grinned at her as if realizing he might have just found a worthy adversary. "Did you know that some dinosaur eggs were as big as basketballs?"

"I may have heard that." Harper narrowed her eyes. "Did you know there was a dinosaur who had fifteen horns?"

"Yes. I'm quite an expert on all things dinosaur."

"I can tell. Very impressive. I can see I've got more studying to do. Next time I see you, I'll try to bring something stronger to the table."

He grinned. "I look forward to the challenge."

Harper liked this kid. He was smart and talked like an adult. Floyd loved dinosaurs too, which is where she'd gotten the few trivia facts she'd shared. But now she'd have to google some better data for the next time she saw Max. If there would be a next time. She wasn't planning to stick around here forever. Who knew if she'd even see this kid again? But maybe she could look up a fact or two, just in case.

"I just stopped by because I needed to pick up the Christmas cookie cutters. Max and I are going to make sugar cookies with Rock's mom this afternoon." She tapped her son's shoulder. "Why don't you go grab the cookie cutters? They're in the bottom drawer by the oven."

Max closed his book and rolled his eyes at his mother. "I remember. I did grow up here, ya know."

Quinn offered Harper an amused grin. "My son is an old man trapped in a boy's body. Some days I think he's eight going on eighty-eight."

"I can hear you," Max said from the kitchen where he was digging through the drawer. He pulled out a Ziploc bag of cookie cutters and held them up. "Found them." He grabbed another bag. "I'm bringing the dinosaur ones too. We can make Christmas dinosaur cookies, can't we, Mom?"

"I can't imagine *not* making Christmas dinosaur cookies, son," Quinn told him, her face breaking into an affectionate grin.

Seeing the mother-and-son interaction was sweet, but it also tore at Harper's heart. It had been her and Floyd's tradition to make cookies as well, and they always made Nana's recipe for peanut butter blossoms. Last year they'd made them *with* Nana, which had made the tradition even more memorable and special.

Maybe she could try Judith again and see if she'd be interested in the three of them making cookies together. It pricked at her pride to keep begging for scraps from the woman who was basically keeping her son from her, but she'd do whatever it took to get him back. Even if it meant begging for time with Floyd and sharing their tradition.

"I think I saw some sprinkles in the pantry," Harper told Quinn, trying to get her mind off the situation with her son. "Do you want those as well?"

Quinn waved her hand. "No thanks. I've got more than enough sprinkles and icing tubes and glittery sugar. We made gingerbread houses last week, so I'm stocked up on festive frosting and Christmas candies for the whole year."

Harper took a step toward the kitchen. "Can I get you all something to drink or eat?"

Quinn shook her head. "No, we can't stay. Vivi is expecting us."

"You sure?" Logan asked. "Harper makes some mean peach cobbler."

Quinn raised an eyebrow at her brother. "A mean peach cobbler *and* fried chicken as good as Grandma's? Seems like you hit the jackpot with this one." She grinned and turned her gaze back to Harper. "Thank you for the lovely offer, but we really can't stay. Although I'd love to stop by another time for coffee and some girl chat. I need to get to know the woman who can recite dinosaur trivia and has my brother gushing over her home cooking."

"Gushing might be a bit of stretch, but he hasn't gone hungry yet." Harper liked Quinn and the way she good-naturedly razzed her brother. "And I would love to have coffee with you. Stop over anytime." That felt a little awkward…inviting Quinn to the house she grew up in and had only moved out of a few months prior.

The other woman didn't seem to mind the comment. "It's a date then."

Gosh, Harper suddenly felt quite popular. That's two "dates" she'd been offered in one day. Although the idea of coffee with Quinn didn't have her pulse racing and her palms sweating like the thought of going to the Christmas Celebration with Logan.

Quinn motioned to Max. "Come on, buddy. Grab your books. We need to get over to Grandma Vivi's." She gave Logan another hug, then gestured to the living area. "It's no wonder you've been gloomy lately. This place has zero Christmas cheer. I mean, it's clean, but you haven't put out a single decoration. You don't even have a tree up yet. And Christmas is right around the corner."

Logan shrugged. "I haven't been *gloomy*. I'm not Eeyore."

Quinn raised an eyebrow, but let the comparison drop. "All I know is that if Dad makes it home for Christmas, he'll be pretty disappointed to walk in and find the house bare of any Christmas spirit. You need to at least put out Grandma's holiday candy dish, and you'd better have a tin of Almond Roca on hand."

"All right. All right. I hear you." Changing the subject, Logan held out his hand to his nephew for a high five. "See you at practice, dude. You better bring me a dinosaur Christmas cookie."

Max grinned. "I will. I'll bring one for Harper too."

Aww. That kid was melting Harper's heart. At least that's what she was attributing the pain in her chest to. Instead of pinning it on the real emotions of grief and longing for Floyd and the hard pangs of jealousy at seeing the mother and son together. She wished she and Quinn really could be friends—like normal people. It would be fun to sit down for coffee and chat while Max and Floyd had a playdate and shared dinosaur stories.

But that wasn't going to happen. Not once this family

found out she'd just been released from jail. It didn't matter, she tried to console herself, because by that time, she'd have found a way to get Floyd back and they'd be home in Kansas where they belonged.

Quinn and Max waved their goodbyes, and Logan shut the door behind them, then turned and studied the room. "Quinn's right. I should get out the decorations and put up a tree." He offered Harper a sidelong glance. "Any chance I could talk you into helping me get one?"

She blinked, surprised by Logan's invitation to share in his holiday tradition. A tentative smile curved her lips as the idea sank in. "Yeah, sure. That sounds like fun." And it did sound fun. If she couldn't be with Floyd, at least she could help another family make sure their holiday turned out great. "But like Quinn said, Christmas is only a few days away. Do you think the store will have any trees left? How picky are you? The selection might be a little sparse."

"*Store?* Why would I go to a store for a tree? I've got a whole mountain of them behind the house to choose from."

Harper peered through the window. "You mean you just go out and cut one down, then bring it in the house? Like a Christmas lumberjack?"

Logan chuckled. "I've never thought about it like that, but yeah, I guess. Haven't you ever gone into the mountains and picked out your own Christmas tree?"

"No, I have not. I'm from Kansas, remember. We don't have any mountains to tromp through with our trusty axes."

"Well then, I think you are in for a treat. Maybe not the tromping part, but picking your own tree is kind of fun. We do it every year. And by *we*, I mean Dad and I follow along while Quinn and Max study and evaluate every single tree we pass on the mountain until they find the exact one they deem 'perfect' for that year. Then we cut it down and bring it back."

"So maybe *you've* never picked out your own Christmas tree either."

He grinned. "You know, you're right. I don't think I ever have been the one who actually picked the tree."

"Then it sounds like it's about time you did."

"Yeah, I guess it is." He tilted his head to look out the front window. "We'd better go now because it's gonna be dark soon. And it'll be cold when we lose the sun, so we'll need to bundle up. Do you want to go change into some warmer clothes?"

She had on jeans, a navy-blue thermal, and a pair of faded black Converse sneakers. "I can change into my boots, but I don't really have anything much warmer."

"Hold on," he said and hurried down the hall to his room. He was back a minute later with a burgundy Creedence High Hockey sweatshirt in his hand. "Here, try this."

She took the offered sweatshirt and pulled it over her head. It was warm and roomy and smelled like Logan. It made her want to wrap her arms around herself, cuddle into the sweatshirt, and pretend it was Logan she was cuddling into.

"Why don't you go get your boots," he said, oblivious to her snuggling fantasy. "I'll grab a sweatshirt and a couple of things and meet you in the barn in ten."

Ten minutes later, Harper poked her head into the barn where Logan was fitting a toboggan sled to the back of an ATV.

"We're taking this to get the tree?" she asked, crossing to the four-wheeler.

"Yeah, how did you think we were going to get up the mountain?"

"I guess I thought we'd be hiking up."

"The best trees are higher up. We can get there quicker with the four-wheeler."

She gestured to the toboggan, a worried expression wrinkling her forehead. "Am I supposed to ride on that thing? Does it have a seat belt? Or some kind of safety harness?"

He chuckled. "No, this is for the tree. Unless you really *want* to ride on it. But I thought you'd rather ride the quad with me."

"Yes. I'm choosing that option."

He finished attaching the sled, then reached into the open storage box on the back of the quad and pulled out a red scarf. "I figured you'd need this."

She'd already put on his extra coat and grabbed the stocking cap and gloves that she'd almost begun to think of as hers. "Thanks." She reached for the scarf, but he'd already lifted it in his hands, and she stilled as she let him wrap it around her neck.

His fingers skimmed her throat as he twisted the ends, then tucked them into the front of her coat. "There. That should help keep your face warm." His expression softened. "You look good in red."

She hoped so, since she had a feeling that's the color her cheeks were turning. Red wasn't a color she usually chose for herself, preferring to wear mostly black and the darker shades that camouflaged or slimmed her curvy figure. Every once in a while she'd add a pop of color, but it was usually blue, or a little pink or purple. Red seemed too daring, too racy, too dangerous. And she'd had enough danger in her life the last few months. Boring black was fine with her, especially if it meant her life could be calm and ordinary.

Logan shut the storage box, climbed onto the ATV, and patted the seat.

She climbed on behind him. Nothing about wrapping herself around this man's back to ride up into the mountains together seemed calm or ordinary. Her pulse was pounding, and she wasn't sure where to put her hands. The inside of her thighs warmed as they straddled Logan's, and she was glad he couldn't see the nerves she was sure were written all over her face.

He turned the key and the engine rumbled to life, sending another set of tingles through her already trembling legs. "Hold on," he told her as he grabbed her hands and wrapped them around his stomach.

The ATV lurched forward, and she had no other choice. She held on.

Logan was a skilled driver and obviously familiar with the terrain. He steered the four-wheeler up a path behind the house, and Harper held on as the ATV crisscrossed up the mountain.

Dusk was settling in, and a slight breeze blew the snow from the trees, filling the air with tiny ice crystals and giving the mountain a magical feel. Logan veered off the path and deftly weaved between the trees, then stopped and cut the engine in a small wooded area.

The section had several smaller trees and a clear space where the view opened up on the valley below. The setting was breathtaking, and with the bits of snow shimmering like diamonds in the air, Harper felt as if they were inside a giant snow globe.

Logan pointed to a grouping of trees as they climbed off the four-wheeler. "We usually find something in this area. The trees are younger so they're a little smaller. And we have to be careful, because they always look smaller out here than when we actually try to fit them into the house. One year we brought home a huge monster that Quinn was sure would fit and ended up having to cut three feet off the bottom of the stump."

"Oh no."

He shrugged. "It was okay. Dad and I knew it wouldn't fit, but it was Max's first year picking, and he'd worked so hard to find the perfect one that we didn't want to disappoint the kid, so we made it work."

"That was nice of you."

"I'm a fairly nice guy, when I want to be." He offered her a teasing wink as he opened the storage box. "We always bring up some hot chocolate. It's kind of a tradition." He held up a small thermos and two blue tin cups. "You want some?"

"Yes, please. I don't want to mess with the tradition."

He set the cups on the edge of the fender and poured cocoa into each, then reached back into the storage box and brought out a small bottle of peppermint schnapps. "You want yours leaded or unleaded?"

"Leaded, please." She rubbed her gloved hands briskly over her arms and stamped her feet as she watched him pour a splash of schnapps into each cup and swirl it around.

He passed her a cup, then held his up for a toast. "To your first Christmas-tree-cutting adventure."

She clinked her cup to his and took a small sip. The drink was hot and rich, and the alcohol warmed her chest. She took another swallow. "That's good."

He grinned and drained his cup, then pulled a saw from the storage box. "You ever used a bow saw?"

She shook her head.

"Well, you're about to because you're going to help cut this tree down."

She peered over the storage box lid. "Geez, you're like Santa Claus and his bag with this storage box. What else are you going to pull out of this thing?"

"You never know what kind of tricks I've got up my sleeve," he said with a chuckle, then pointed to the section of trees. "You'd better go over there and start searching for a tree."

She took the last swallow of her cocoa and passed the cup back to him before turning to the trees. A sense of giddiness filled her chest. She wasn't sure if it was due to the magic of the forest, the surreal feeling of being here with Logan, or the booze. But whatever it was, she wanted to laugh and play in the snow and throw her arms around the beautiful trees.

A giggle bubbled in her chest at what Logan would think if she actually hugged a tree. Better just to point to the one she thought looked good. Her steps were light as they wandered among the trees. "How do you pick? They all look so beautiful."

"Sometimes the tree picks you. I think you'll know it when you see it."

They stepped between two trees, and Harper caught her breath. "That's it." She pointed to a full evergreen that stood about six feet tall. Its sides were symmetrical, and the boughs were full and lush and bent almost to the ground. "It's perfect."

Logan studied the tree. "I think you're right. This looks like a pretty good one. It's a Douglas fir, so its needles are nice and thick, and it'll smell great in the house. I think it's an excellent choice."

"But how am I supposed to cut this thing down?" She dropped to her knees and lifted the lowest bough to peer at the trunk, then gasped at the three pairs of chocolate-brown eyes that stared back at her. "Oh, Logan, come down here. You've got to see this."

He crouched next to her and peered under the branch at the three small bunnies cuddled together against the trunk. "Those are mountain cottontail. Looks like a mama and a couple of kits."

"Oh my gosh, they're so cute."

"They are. But they'll move when you stick the saw in there."

She gasped. "I'm not sticking the saw in there."

"Then how are you going to cut down this tree?"

"I'm not. I'll pick another tree." She dropped the branch. "I'm not going to be responsible for kicking a mama and her babies out of their home in the middle of winter. I'm not a monster."

He chuckled. "Okay. You'd better pick another one then."

She stood shakily to her feet. Apparently a little peppermint schnapps went a long way on an empty stomach.

Logan caught her arm as she swayed into him. "Whoa there. You all right?"

She stared up at him, need and desire swirling in her

chest as she thought how easy it would be to press her lips to his, to pull him down in the snow and climb on top of him. Or lie under him.

The alcohol urged her on, seductively whispering to her to kiss him.

CHAPTER 17

IT WOULD BE SO EASY. *DO IT*, THE SCHNAPPS INSISTED.

"I'm fine," Harper whispered, leaning closer and staring at Logan's mouth. She parted her lips in anticipation, then…a loud hiccup bubbled out of her. *Oh. My. Gosh.* She pressed her hand to her mouth, her eyes widening as she tried to hold in a burst of embarrassed laughter.

Logan's face broke into a grin, and he laughed with her. "Maybe you should have gone with the *un*leaded cocoa."

"Maybe I shouldn't have drunk spiked cocoa on an empty stomach."

"Maybe I shouldn't be trusting you with an ax."

Maybe I shouldn't be trusting you with my heart.

The thought popped into her head, and she sent up a silent thank-you that she hadn't blurted the words aloud. But they were true. She was falling for this man. And she didn't do "falling." She did "running" and "avoiding" and "locking" her heart up tight. So what was she doing in the middle of the forest fantasizing about kissing him in their own private wintry snow globe?

It had to be the alcohol. It was making her soft. *Yeah, right.* Well, that was her story, and she was sticking to it. But she needed to get her brain off thinking about his lips and how strong his arms looked holding that ax and how they would feel wrapped around her. *Crud.* She was doing it again. *Dang that peppermint schnapps.*

She turned her head and peered around, anything to

avoid looking at his chiseled jaw and his amused blue eyes. Her gaze lit on another tree, and she pointed to it. "How about that one?"

Logan followed her finger and examined the tree. "This one looks pretty good." He took a few steps toward it and crouched down to look at its trunk. "And no family of bunnies living underneath it."

Harper walked around it, but she shook her head when she spied a bird's nest tucked into its branches. "Nope. This one won't work either. It's got a nest in it."

Logan stepped behind her and peered over her shoulder. "I don't know if a bird's living in it now. It looks empty."

"But they might come back to it and find their home is gone."

Damn. Why did everything have to be a reminder of the situation with her son? Even the simple act of cutting down a Christmas tree.

She glanced around at the other trees. "Maybe we need to find a different kind of tree. These Douglas firs are gorgeous, but the animals seem to really like them too."

A grin tugged at the corners of his mouth. "Okay, no more Doug firs. So, you're looking for an uglier tree?"

"Not necessarily uglier, but maybe one not as pretty. Like with the branches more spread apart so we know that an animal would be less likely to be living in it."

Logan chuckled as he strode through the snow and stopped at a homely-looking tree that wasn't quite as tall as him. "How about this semipathetic creature? Its needles are sparse, and the branches have plenty of space between them so you can clearly see no woodland creatures are living in its boughs. It's a ponderosa pine, otherwise commonly referred to as a Charlie Brown Christmas tree."

His tone was sarcastic, but Harper loved it. "It's awful. And perfect. It looks like it needs a good home. Let's take it."

"Wait. I was just kidding." He gestured around the forested area. "You have a zillion other gorgeous trees to choose from. You don't need to pick this one just because you feel sorry for it."

She offered him an impish grin. "Oh, but I *didn't* pick it. *You* did. I'm just agreeing with your excellent choice."

"What? No, *I* didn't pick it." He paused and scrubbed a hand over his face. "Aw hell. I guess I did pick it. But I'm amending my choice. I'm electing to choose *any* other tree in this forest."

"No take backs." She laughed as she nudged his arm. "You already picked. And I think it's a fine choice."

"I think you've had too much to drink."

"Maybe you haven't had enough," she teased.

"I don't know if there *is* enough drink to make this sad tree look good."

Harper chuckled again and held out her hand. "Pass me the saw."

Because the tree wasn't very big, the trunk wasn't too tough to saw through. Logan only helped with the last bit. They shook the snow off, then dragged the tree back to the quad, where he secured it to the toboggan, strapping it in with some rope and a bungee cord.

He brushed the snow from his pants as he stood and offered her a roguish grin. "You ready to head back, or should we have another hot cocoa cocktail before we go?"

Harper shook her head and peered down at the tree. "I think we've made enough cocoa-cocktail-induced decisions for the day. We'd better head back."

The sun had gone down, and the forest had an ethereal quality as they made their way down the mountain and through the trees. Harper laid her head on Logan's back and let out a contented sigh. A tingling warmth filled her body, and she was pretty sure it didn't have anything to do with the schnapps.

Two hours later, they had the tree up and a slew of decorations dispersed around the room. Harper had helped Logan carry several Christmas boxes up from the basement, and then she'd put together sandwiches while he had fit the tree into the stand and strung it with lights.

They ate while they decorated the room and the tree, laughing as Logan told stories of past holidays and shared the meaning behind different ornaments and decorations.

Harper loved listening to him talk, loved the way his face lit up as he shared some crazy thing he and his sister had done with their dad or with the James brothers next door. She heard him say many times that his dad was a rough, gruff cowboy, but listening to Logan tell the story about the year Ham drove them all the way to Denver to see a special display of lights at the zoo and the time he filled in as a shepherd in the church play when the original shepherd came down with the flu told her the older cowboy might not be quite that tough. Especially when it came to his kids. It was obvious in the way Logan talked about his dad that he respected and admired him.

Harper shared a few stories from when she was growing up, but she mostly listened, content to hear Logan talk.

Every time he laughed, it sent a funny shiver of heat coursing through her.

Yeah, she could fool herself into thinking she didn't do "falling," but she was definitely doing a slow sink.

"Well, we did it," he said, placing the star on top of the tree. "This is the last one."

"And no woodland creatures were harmed in the making of this tree," Harper teased, coming in from the kitchen with two mugs of cocoa in her hands. "Sorry, it's unleaded," she said, handing him a mug, and they grinned like fools at each other as they each took a sip.

"It's still good."

"It's my grandmother's recipe." Harper sighed, a wistful smile curving her lips. "She would have loved all of this. I thought fixing her cocoa might make it feel like she was here with us in spirit." Her grin turned sheepish. "Although after the goofy way I acted this afternoon, I've probably had enough 'spirits' for the day."

Logan laughed and set his cup on the coffee table. "You ready to light the tree?"

"Ready," she said, placing her cup next to his and standing back as Logan plugged in the lights. The room lit with the cheery glow of the twinkling lights, and Harper's chest warmed as if the glow came from inside her.

Logan walked back to stand next to her, their shoulders not quite touching as they looked at the tree together.

"I love the star on top," she told him. "Some people like to put an angel on the tree, but I've always preferred the star."

"Yeah? Why's that?"

"I don't know. I guess I think of the star as a promise

of something amazing ahead. Like the star the wise men follow in the Christmas story. They don't question it, they don't second-guess it, they just believe. And it led them to everything they would ever need. They didn't have to earn it or even deserve it. They just had to follow the star, and the promise would be fulfilled." The lights on the tree blurred and transformed to tiny twinkling stars as she blinked back the tears filling her eyes.

"Sorry. I love the Christmas star the most, but I think stars in general are amazing. They're so far away, and we shouldn't even be able to see them, but we can. I think each one is like a little miracle, and maybe they shine so brightly because they hold so many of our wishes."

She shook her head. "Gosh, that sounded so dorky. I sometimes think sappy stuff like this, but I don't often say it out loud. I didn't mean to get all gushy."

"It's not gushy at all." Logan gazed up at the star. "We always put the star on last, but I don't know that I've ever really thought about what it represents. But I like what you said, that the star is a promise of something amazing ahead."

They were standing shoulder to shoulder and not looking at each other, but she still felt as though they were seeing each other. As though here in the glow of a hundred tiny, sparkling lights, they were each giving the other a small piece of themselves, holding it out to see if the other would take it and cherish it, or refuse it with scorn.

"I guess I've always thought stars represented whatever it was that you wanted," he said. "Like your deepest desire. You know, you reach for the stars like you're going for something you really want." The back of his hand grazed hers, and his pinkie finger twined around hers. "We've always used the stars to guide us. The night sky was the original GPS. If you're ever lost or can't find your way, you can use the stars to lead you home."

His words were doing nothing to quell the emotion building in her throat. She'd always loved the Christmas star, loved what it represented, but she didn't think she'd ever said her feelings about it out loud. Or maybe she had.

Her son loved everything to do with space and the stars. She'd hoped to get him a telescope for Christmas this year. He loved to learn about the stars and the planets. One morning at breakfast, he'd told her he wanted to be an astronaut, to fly into space and be among the stars.

Harper remembered smiling and asking him why—and having her heart shatter into a million pieces when he said it was so he could be with his dad.

Thinking about Michael and Floyd and all she'd lost had pain piercing her heart. She missed them both so much. So much that she couldn't see the right path to take or the correct choices she was supposed to make. She needed a star right now—needed something to guide her, to lead her to her deepest desire. She felt more lost than she'd ever been.

She stared into the lights of the tree and prayed for guidance and wisdom and for something to give her hope to hold on to. The ache in her chest felt as if it might turn her inside out and swallow her whole.

She started to tighten her hand into a fist and realized her fingers were now completely entwined with Logan's. A surge of warmth had flowed through her a few seconds ago when his pinkie had gently looped around hers, but when had she taken his hand? And why was she squeezing it now as if he were the lifeline she'd been looking to cling to?

A sob threatened her throat, and she let go of his hand. She didn't want to *cling* to anyone. She'd been down that road before, hanging on to other people, holding to the idea that they would save her. But there was no one to save her now. Not Michael, not her grandmother, and not the tall cowboy standing next to her.

The only one who could save her, and her boy, was her. The only one she could truly count on to come through for her was herself.

She swallowed and took a step back. "I should probably go. It's been a long day, and I'm sure you need to get to bed." She picked up their mugs and wiped a smear of hot chocolate from the coffee table with the back of her little finger.

Logan blinked and cleared his throat. "Yeah. Sure. Of course." He grabbed the lid to the box of decorations and fit it neatly on top. "Um, before you go, I have something for you."

"For me?"

"Yeah. I mean, it's no big deal. I just thought it would, you know, help." He turned away, avoiding her eyes, then hurried down the hall toward his bedroom. "I'll be right back."

Help? What did he have for her that he thought would help? What did that even mean? Did he feel sorry for her?

A few seconds later, he returned, carrying an envelope and a small brown bag with the name of the local coffee shop printed on the side.

He'd gotten her some coffee? Interesting choice. And he was right, caffeine almost always did offer her a little help. But he could have just left that on the counter next to the coffeepot.

"Here," he said, holding the items out to her. "It's not wrapped or anything fancy, but I thought you'd appreciate it."

She took the envelope. It was plain white, not the kind you'd give someone a card in, and it wasn't sealed. Turning it over, she lifted the flap and smiled. It was a check. A paycheck.

"I know we said I'd pay you every Friday, but I figured you could use what you'd earned so far, in case you want to get some groceries for yourself or whatever. I mean, you're welcome to eat anything here. I just know the refrigerator over there was bare, and I figured there were probably other things you might need."

Yes, there were other things. She didn't care about buying groceries—she could go without having food in the bunkhouse—but this money would go a long way toward setting things up to get Floyd back. She could actually buy some things to show she was making a home for him.

"Thank you, Logan. Really. This helps a lot."

He passed her the bag. "This should help too."

She peered inside. What the heck? It wasn't coffee. Her brow furrowed as she pulled out an electronic device. It looked like a small tablet and was about the size of a paperback novel.

"It's a Kindle Fire thingamajig. You can read books on it and stuff. It's like a little computer."

She passed it back to him. "I know what a Kindle is, and it's 'like' a little too much. I can't accept this."

He held up his hands, refusing to take it back. "It's no big deal. I didn't go out and buy it or anything. Quinn gave it to me for Christmas last year, and I've never used it. She said she loaded it with some books, and I know how you like to read, and I just figured you would use it way more than I would. Or have. Plus, you can get the internet on it and do all kinds of other things besides just read. I already set it up for you with Wi-Fi and a username and a password. I put them on a Post-it on the back."

She turned the Kindle over, and a grin tugged at the corners of her mouth as she read the note. He'd written the Wi-Fi code, then set her username as "HarperEvans" and her password as "Peaches1."

His face broke into an impish grin. "I thought you'd like that."

She shook her head. "I do like it. I love it. But it's still too much."

"Okay, then don't take it. For now. We can just say you're *borrowing* it." He fake-coughed out the word *forever*.

She narrowed her eyes at him.

"Seriously. You can borrow it, if that makes you feel better." He turned his head to the side. "You just don't ever have to give it back."

She really could use a way to access the internet. She'd missed being able to google and look up information.

"And I have an Amazon Prime account that's in there. Sometimes it's hard to get stuff in a small town, so you can use it to get free delivery out here."

She hadn't thought about using Amazon. That tiny tidbit was the final tipping point. She could order what she needed and not have to find ways to borrow Logan's truck. "Okay. I'll take it. But I'm just borrowing it."

"Yep. Just borrow it." He grinned. "But keep in mind you don't ever have to return it."

"Thank you. Really, this is great. This whole night has been amazing." It had been great, except for the one missing component that constantly overshadowed every moment in her current life. Floyd wasn't here. Just thinking about decorating for Christmas without her son made her stomach queasy. Had he and Judith decorated her tree together? Had he made Christmas cookies with *her* instead?

Judging just from Judith's front porch, Harper was sure her house was decorated to the hilt inside. She probably even had one of those Christmas villages set up—the kind with little shops and houses that get added to every year.

Harper didn't even *have* a house this year. If Floyd was with her, what would they decorate? She thought of the boxes of decorations in her grandmother's attic. They should be home in Kansas, drinking hot chocolate and putting Floyd's homemade ornaments on a tree they'd dragged home from a grocery store lot.

If only her grandma hadn't died. If only she hadn't listened to her mom. If only she hadn't gone to jail. But all of those things had happened, and she couldn't go backwards.

Logan touched her arm, concern creasing his brow. "Hey, you okay?"

Harper shook off the memories. No use worrying about spilled milk or, in this case, embezzled cash. "I'm fine."

"Your eyes just got really sad. Where'd you go?"

She shook her head and pasted on what she hoped didn't seem like too fake of a smile. "Nowhere. Sorry. Just took a quick trip down memory lane."

He nodded. "Sorry. I'm sure all this Christmas stuff brings up a lot of memories of your grandma." He rubbed his hand over her shoulder.

It would be so easy to step in to him, to slide her arms around his waist. He was offering something. Whether it was just a hug or something more, it was there. And her body yearned to accept it, just to take the physical touch of another person. Although she wasn't sure a hug was where it would end with Logan. The contact might be just the beginning. But it could be the end of her job. And she couldn't risk that. No, for now, she needed to keep her eye on the prize, and that was getting Floyd back. Although even one embrace with Logan would have been quite a prize.

"I'd better go." She took a step back, letting his hand fall from her shoulder. "Thank you again. For everything. This has been a great night. The tree, the cocoa, the gift." She turned and headed for her coat, her legs heavy as she pushed down the regret building in her chest at walking away from what might have been with him. But one night wouldn't have been worth the potential cost.

Are you sure? her inner vixen asked, already pouting at another missed chance to wrap herself around the handsome cowboy. *It's not too late to turn around.*

But it was too late. She needed to stay focused on what was important—what really mattered. It was fun doing holiday things with Logan, but the thing she wanted most for Christmas was to spend it with her son. And to have him back with her.

She hugged the coffee-shop bag to her chest as she hurried through the cold to the bunkhouse. Thanks to Logan's generous "gift," she could use her bank's mobile app to deposit her check tonight, then finally be able to use her debit card for something besides scraping the ice off a windshield.

A tiny measure of what felt like hope bloomed in her chest as she thought about what she could do with the money. She hadn't bought a single Christmas present. Not yet. She hummed a carol as she let herself into the bunkhouse. She had some shopping to do.

The next day, Harper found herself back at the counter of the Creedence Café, sitting on the same stool where she'd sat the day she arrived.

Logan had told her he'd be gone for the morning and early afternoon, and she'd asked to borrow the pickup again to run some errands. By errands, she meant trying to see Floyd. The night before had filled her with anguish as she longed to see her little boy. Even getting to see his face would help.

But apparently, it wasn't meant to be. Not this morning at least. Her errands hadn't gone quite as she'd hoped. She'd parked downtown and taken off on foot, trying to catch Floyd on the playground as she'd done before. But the schoolyard had been empty. It was a cold and snowy morning, which made Harper wonder if they had kept the kids in that day due to the cold.

The lights glowed from inside the school, and she was tempted to go inside and wander the halls, just to try to get a glimpse of him. But strangers wandering the halls of an elementary school didn't go over very well, and she wasn't sure making a scene at the school would be best for Floyd.

Head down, hands stuffed in her pockets, she'd walked to Judith's house, hoping to get another chance to talk to her, to reason with the woman and try at the very least to arrange a time when she could see her son. But no one had answered when she'd rang the bell.

Feeling dejected, she'd meandered through downtown, looking in the shop windows and wallowing in a pity party for one. But a display in the department store had caught her eye, and she'd gone in and made a purchase that had brightened her spirits. The shop window had declared "Aim for the Stars This Holiday Season" and been filled with space-themed gifts.

She'd found a purple and blue comforter set depicting the Milky Way and a poster with a full moon that read "I love you to the moon and back." She'd grabbed both, plus a night-light that shined a variety of constellations onto the ceiling and an inexpensive hanging mobile of the solar system. As she carried the things to the register, she passed an endcap that had a display of educational toys. She couldn't believe it when she saw a box holding a small tele-scope on the shelf.

It was more than she should be spending, but when she'd picked it up and spied the half-off clearance sticker on the box, she knew she had to have it. She'd left the store with a renewed spring in her step, and after dropping her purchases in the truck, she'd decided to really splurge and get a cheeseburger at the diner.

The lunch hour was busy, and Bryn was hopping from table to table, but she still managed to stop at the counter and catch up for a few minutes. Harper was surprised to see Rachel, the woman she'd met the day she arrived, wearing a pink waitress uniform and serving coffee.

Bryn offered Harper a sheepish grin when she asked

about Rachel. "I couldn't help it. I felt so bad for her and Josh. They're staying with me, just until she gets back on her feet and figures out what she wants to do."

"And you got her a job at the diner?"

"She's just filling in during the holiday rush."

Harper arched an eyebrow at her new friend. "Are you sure you're not related to Santa Claus? You seem to be giving a lot of people just what they need this Christmas."

Bryn shrugged. "Maybe. I can't seem to stop myself. When I see someone in need, I just have to jump in and help."

The cheeseburger had been delicious, and Harper left Bryn an extra tip. Not that she could spare the extra five dollars, but Bryn deserved it. She'd done so much for others, for her. Harper wouldn't have the money to even cover the soda she'd just drunk if it weren't for the generous waitress.

She stopped at the store on her way back to the ranch and grabbed a couple of groceries, then spent a few hours setting up the space-themed decorations in the small bedroom in the bunkhouse. She borrowed a blue twin sheet set from the house and found some tacks to hang the poster and the mobile. There had been several rolls of wrapping paper in the boxes she and Logan had brought up the night before, so she cut a small piece to wrap the telescope and then set it on the small nightstand next to the bed.

The room looked great when she finished. Now she just needed the boy here to offer it to.

By midafternoon, Logan had finished his errands and was back at the ranch. He'd been screwing around on the computer and pushing papers around on his desk for the last thirty minutes, trying to ignore thoughts of the woman working in the next room. He'd already come up with several reasons to go into the kitchen and at least two things that he needed from his bedroom, but he knew they were all just excuses to be in the same room as Harper.

In frustration, he swiped a stack of paper off his desk, and his dark mood settled with the pages that fluttered to the floor.

He'd got up that morning thinking the Christmas decorations would make him happy and bring to mind all the fun they'd had the day before, but all the festive trimmings had done was remind him he would most likely be alone on the holiday. Christmas was getting closer, and Harper had said she'd be gone by then.

She'd made no indication that her plans had changed or that she was even interested in staying. So why did he keep hoping she'd come to him with plans to stay?

His mood had been dark all day, and he once again spent the morning admonishing himself for letting his feelings get in the way of his good sense. He'd lived this time and time again. Women acting like they cared and then leaving anyway. Why did he expect Harper to be any different? Especially when she'd already told him she planned to leave. It wasn't a new revelation she was going to spring on him. She'd said it right from the start.

But he'd let his heart hope anyway. "Let" might be the wrong term. He hadn't "let" any of these feelings happen. They'd come over him like a five-thousand-ton freight train speeding down the tracks. He couldn't stop them if he tried.

And he had tried. Had tried to convince himself that

Harper Evans was no one special. That she was just a woman who happened to make really great country gravy. But he knew it was more than that. Knew it the minute she stepped out of Bryn's car and flashed him that tentative smile that held both warmness and defiance. It was a smile that said it didn't matter if he hired her or not.

That had been attraction. And it was easy to understand why he was attracted to her—her body was a lush playground of curves, and that mess of dark curly hair was the stuff fantasies were made of. But he'd been attracted to women before, and they hadn't affected him like she did. It was more than the way she looked.

It was the way she made him feel, the way she listened and understood him, yet didn't accept his bullshit, and the way she challenged him when she thought he was wrong. He'd shared his biggest weakness with her, and she'd shrugged it off as if it didn't matter—didn't matter that it took him longer to read something or that he mixed up numbers and had to concentrate to do simple math problems that she could figure out in a split second.

Harper Evans *was* someone special. He could deny it until the cows came home, but he knew it was true. Knew it in the way his heart skipped a beat when she smiled at him or the way his stomach dropped when her fingers brushed his skin.

He knew she wasn't perfect. And knew she was hiding something from him—could tell there was something going on with her in the way she sometimes couldn't meet his eyes or the deft way she subtly changed the subject and lobbed the conversation back to him when he asked anything too personal. There was more to Harper than she was letting on, and he imagined it probably wasn't all good.

But in his heart, he was sure she was a good person. He'd bet his last dollar on that fact. He'd seen her goofing off with Max and laughing with Bryn. He'd watched her when they were around Zane and had never caught her staring at his scar or treating the wounded man any differently. He'd witnessed her tireless work ethic but also seen her goofy fun side and knew she could sling sarcasm and jokes with the best of them.

"Hey, sorry to bother you." Harper poked her head into the office. She glanced down at the papers scattered across the floor but didn't comment on them. "I was going to make some hot tea. Thought I'd check to see if you wanted a cup, or a snack, or something?"

He couldn't answer right away because his mouth had gone dry at the sight of her. She had on jeans and a faded blue flannel shirt that made her eyes seem more teal than green today. Her shirt was untucked but still hugged her curves, and she had her hair pulled up into that messy knot thing she did that had loose tendrils falling over her bare neck.

His heart thundered in his chest, and it was a wonder she couldn't hear it beating from across the room. He wanted something all right. But it wasn't a snack or a cup of hot tea. It was her hot body pressed against his.

He was fooling himself if he thought there wasn't something happening here. Something more than just attraction. This was deeper, fiercer, more intense than anything he'd ever felt for another woman. Which meant it was going to hurt a hell of a lot worse when she left.

He tore his gaze from her and returned it to his computer. "No, I'm good. Thanks."

A pounding knock sounded from the front door, and Harper turned and waved whoever was knocking in. "It's Zane," she told Logan.

He got up from his desk and followed her into the living room where Zane had just come in and was shaking the snow off his hat.

"Sorry to bother you," Zane said. "But the snow is really coming down, and the National Weather Service just issued a winter storm warning." He passed Logan his phone, the screen open to the AccuWeather forecast app.

Logan checked the screen, then peered through the front window. "Dang. It's gotten worse just in the last half hour." Another reason not to get involved with this woman. He was so distracted by her that he wasn't paying attention to the weather, and ranchers were *always* supposed to be paying attention to the weather. "We should get out there and try to bring the cattle in before it gets any worse."

"That's what I was thinking. I figured we should try to get 'em all moved into that west pasture closer to the ranch before the worst of the storm hits."

"My thoughts exactly. It's more protected and has plenty of tree cover. Plus, we'll know where they are and can get them fed and watered easier if the storm lingers." He passed the phone back to Zane and reached for his jacket. "All hands on deck. Let's take the quads and then go in a circular pattern and drive them all back."

Harper grabbed his other coat and pulled a stocking hat over her hair.

Logan paused as he jerked on his gloves. "Where are you going?"

"You said all hands on deck, and I can drive a quad. So

I'm going with you." She didn't phrase it as a question but as a statement of fact.

He didn't have time to argue. And she'd proven herself before. "Okay, but it's gonna get pretty rough out there. You don't have to come with us."

She paused to give him a potent stare. "I'm from Kansas. A little snow doesn't scare me."

The weather app had shown signs of a formidable storm, and he had several hundred head of cattle to round up and get closer to the ranch. And he couldn't afford to lose a single one.

So she might not be afraid, but this snow scared the hell out of him.

CHAPTER 18

LOGAN STOOD UP ON THE QUAD AND TRIED TO PEER across the field. The snow had worsened just in the time it had taken the three of them to get outfitted in winter gear and ride the four-wheelers out to the farthest pasture. It was coming down in thick, wet flakes and had already accumulated several inches.

They'd made a plan for Zane to take the left flank and Harper the right. Logan would stay in the center and pick up the slack where he was needed. The cattle were used to being herded between pastures and cooperated fairly well with only a few stragglers, and they made good time moving the herd from the north pasture into the west.

Zane pulled up to Logan as he was shutting the gate. "I just got a text from Trudy," he said, referring to the bartender at his dad's favorite dive. "She said my dad left the bar over an hour ago, but he hasn't made it home. She's been calling him to check, and he isn't answering."

"You better git on then and go find him."

"I hate to leave you like this, but I'm also a little worried that my old man is passed out in a snowbank somewhere freezin' his nuts off."

Logan waved away Zane's concerns. He could use the extra hand, but there was no question what came first when it came to family. And Harper had been doing a great job. She acted like she'd been born on a four-wheeler and didn't have any trouble taking direction and getting the cattle moved. "Don't worry about it. We already got most of the herd. Harper can help me clear what's left of the south pasture."

Zane squinted through the snow. "You sure?"

"Yeah, I'm sure. Go save your dad's nuts."

"Thanks, brother. I'll run an extra bale of hay out to the herd before I go, then be back in the morning to help you get 'em fed." He tipped his hat to Harper and roared back toward the barn.

Logan gunned the engine and pulled alongside Harper's rig. "Zane's got to go check on his dad. You good helping me finish up what's left of the herd in the south pasture?"

She nodded, as he knew she would. The woman had spunk, and he hadn't seen her back down from a challenge yet. "Let's go."

He led, and they bypassed the road and made their way across the field. A large group of cattle were huddled together, which made it easier for the two of them to move them back to the closer pasture. As they led them in, Logan saw that Zane had moved in not one, but three giant round bales of hay.

The snow was getting thicker, and it was becoming harder to see. Harper pulled up next to him and shouted through the wind. "Did we get them all?"

He'd counted the ones they'd brought down from the north pasture and verified the number with Zane so he knew they needed to find another eighty head in the south pasture. But the group they'd just brought in only had fifty.

He shook his head. "No. We're still missing about thirty head. Including Star."

"The storm's getting worse."

He didn't care how bad the storm was. He wasn't losing a single head. And he sure as hell wasn't losing thirty. He couldn't afford to. "You can head back to the house. I'm not leaving them out there."

She tucked her chin to her chest. "I'm staying if you're staying. Let's go find them."

They headed back across the field, slower this time because the visibility had gotten worse. He yelled Star's name as they rode into the pasture, but he couldn't see a single other cow. In one direction was a stream, so they might find the stragglers near the water. The mountain rose on the other side of the pasture, and it was dotted with trees. The cows might have headed that way for protection from the storm.

Logan figured the trees were a better bet. He steered the quad that direction and heard Harper fall in behind him. He drove along the edge of the trees, straining to see through the white curtain of snow as he tried not to panic.

Increasing his speed, he plowed through the snow. His head was screaming at him to slow down. He knew he was pushing the quad to go too fast for these conditions, but he had to find the cattle. He stood up in the seat and shouted for Star again.

The front wheels of the ATV hit a patch of ice, and the quad spun out, completing a full circle before it tipped over as it slid into a ditch next to a tree.

Logan was pitched off and landed in the snow three feet from the overturned quad.

Harper cut the engine and jumped off her ATV. She ran to his side, falling into the snow next to him. "Oh my gosh, Logan. Are you okay?"

"Yeah, I'm fine," he muttered, sitting up in the snow. "Thankfully, I landed in a snowbank and wasn't thrown into that tree. I'm pretty sure only my pride and my ass are bruised."

"Well, your ass deserves it. You were driving way too fast for these conditions."

He knew she was right, but her harsh words still rankled. "I know. And I'm the one who landed ass-over-teakettle in the snow." He avoided looking at her as he pushed up and tested his weight on his legs. He seemed to be fine, but the ATV wasn't. Its front wheel was wedged under the tree's limbs. "Give me a hand, would ya? Let's try to get it free."

They pulled and pushed at the quad, trying to work it loose, but it was good and stuck, and Logan finally waved at Harper to give up. "Forget it. We're not getting it out of this ditch today. I'll have to ride with you, and we'll come back and tow it out after the storm is over."

He climbed onto her quad and she got on behind him, pushing her body snug against his. It was most likely for warmth, but the feel of her legs wrapped on either side of him sent a swirl of heat through his gut. If he weren't so damn worried about his cattle, he might enjoy this a little more. But right now, all he could think about was finding the rest of the herd.

The wind was picking up, and the snow was swirling around them as he started the engine. Harper leaned forward and yelled into his ear. "I think we need to go back. This is too dangerous."

"I can't," he yelled back. "I can't leave the cattle out here." His voice was edged with panic, but he didn't know what else to do.

"This is crazy. We can't see more than a few feet in front of us. The cows aren't stupid. They'll find protection or huddle together. I'm sure they'll be fine."

He turned in the seat so he could see her face. "I *have* to find them. I'm sorry you got dragged into this, but I have no choice. I literally can't afford to lose even one. I have to keep looking."

She narrowed her eyes, studying his face, then nodded her head. "Okay, let's keep looking. But at some point we need to head back and get warmed up. Your clothes are soaked. You won't do anyone any good if you catch pneumonia." She offered him a tiny grin. "And I can't get paid if you freeze to death."

He knew she was right. And he appreciated her efforts at trying to make him smile, but he didn't have any humor in him at the moment. All he could think about was how disappointed his dad was going to be and how he was going to let down his whole family if he lost the cattle and any of them died.

Turning back around, he bent his head against the wind, put the quad into gear, and inched forward. They spent another thirty minutes searching the trees and the side of the mountain before Logan admitted defeat and agreed to head back to the barn. But he planned to drop Harper off and change into a pair of dry coveralls, then resume the search.

He wasn't ready to give up entirely. And he hadn't checked the area on the other side of the pasture. An old cattle run fed into the far section, and there were a lot of trees where the cattle might have taken cover.

The back of his throat ached, and his stomach churned with nausea at the thought of losing the cattle. His shoulders were hunched forward, and he was focused on the road ahead as he drove back toward the ranch.

Harper pounded on his shoulder and pointed toward the pasture. "Logan, look! It's Star!"

He peered up, his heart in his throat as he prayed Harper was right.

And sure as heck, she was. He couldn't believe it. Coming from the other side, down through the cattle run, was his favorite bovine. And she was leading the rest of the herd toward the west pasture. Whether she heard him calling or smelled the fresh hay Zane had put out, he wasn't sure, but he could not have been happier to see that dang cow.

He let out a whoop and sped toward the gate. Hopping off the quad, he pulled open the gate. Star lumbered toward him, and he counted all thirty of the missing cows plodding in her wake. He threw his arms around the cow's neck, relief flooding through him. "You did it, Star. You brought the herd home. I'm bringing you an entire bag of marshmallows tomorrow."

He released the cow, and she fell in step with the last stragglers as they trudged through the gate. After shutting it behind them, he turned back to where Harper was standing next to the quad, and took two steps forward and pulled her into his arms.

"We got 'em," he whooped as he lifted her off her feet and swung her around. She laughed and cheered with him. "Thank God we got 'em. And thank Star, the freakin' wonder cow." He set Harper down and peered into her smiling face. "And thank *you*. Thanks for stickin' with me and not giving up."

Flakes of snow clung to her long, dark eyelashes, and her

cheeks were pink from the cold. But the grin she wore told Logan she was just as happy as he was that they'd found the cattle. Her smile lit up her face, and he was struck by how insanely beautiful she was. He impulsively leaned down and pressed a kiss to her lips.

It was a quick kiss that took them both by surprise.

Harper's eyes were wide when he pulled back, but her lips had been soft and pliant. And she hadn't pulled away.

His heart thundered in his chest—he knew it was a bad idea—but he dipped his head and kissed her again. This one slow and more deliberate than the last, and her lips parted with a soft sigh. A hot rush of desire surged through his veins, and he pulled her closer.

She melted in to him, giving back the passion he offered. Well, melted in to him as well as she could in the bulky coat and gloves.

A shiver ran through her, and he wasn't sure if it was from the kiss or the blizzard raging around them. He pulled away and rubbed his hands briskly over her arms. "You're freezing. We need to get back and get you out of these wet clothes. I mean…get you warm."

A grin pulled at the corners of her just-kissed lips. "I'm getting pretty warm now." Her voice was soft, and she said the words with a touch of flirtation, but her gaze was sultry as it met his—heated and full of promise.

Yeah, he was going back to his original statement. They needed to get back and get her out of those clothes. All of them. And as soon as possible.

"Come on," he said, climbing onto the quad. She got on behind him, but this time it felt different when she pressed against his back and wrapped her arms around his waist. She tucked her head between his shoulders and used his back to protect her from the snow as he sped toward the barn.

Zane had left the main door open, so Logan pulled into the barn and parked the quad. Harper climbed off and stamped her feet as she waited for him. Her jeans were soaked and crusted with ice, and her feet had to be freezing in those stupid boots.

He pressed a hand to her back. "Let's get inside."

She rubbed her hands together, but instead of heading for the open barn door, she hurried to the office in the corner. "Just a second. I want to check on the kittens."

He followed her into the office and could hear the kittens mewling.

Harper was lifting them from where they'd been cuddled together in the folds of the blanket on the sofa. "Their little bodies are freezing, and they're yowling like they're starving. I don't see the mama cat anywhere. But I can't believe she'd leave them like this."

Logan had a hard time believing it too. "Maybe she got caught out in the storm." Or she got caught by another animal. They were always losing barn cats to coyotes or to cars traveling too fast down the highway. But Nacho had been around a long time, and she seemed too smart for that.

"We've got to take them into the house." Harper had all three clutched in her arms as she hurried through the barn.

The snow hit them hard in the face as they left the barn, and Logan stopped to pull the big barn door shut behind them. Several inches had accumulated and they trudged through it, heading toward the soft glow of the house.

A sinking feeling coursed through his chest as the yard light blinked out and the house went dark.

With the loss of electricity, the ranch was blanketed in silence, the only sound the whoosh of the wind and the soft swish of their boots in the snow.

"I'll make a fire," he said as they stepped through the door of the house. It was warm inside, but that wouldn't last long without the heat coming from the furnace.

Harper stamped her feet, then headed for the kitchen. "I'll feed the kittens."

"I think Quinn left a little kitten chow in the pantry. You can put some in a pie tin and pour some table cream over it," Logan told her as he shed his coat and gloves and knelt in front of the fireplace. He stacked wood and kindling in the grate and got the fire going before taking off his boots and setting them by the hearth to dry.

Harper took off her gloves and scarf and gingerly set the three cats on the floor. She followed his instructions, and the kittens climbed over each other trying to get to the pie tin when she put it down beside them. A stack of his clean shirts was on the counter, and she grabbed a sweatshirt from the top of the pile. "You okay if I use this?"

"Sure." He thought she meant for her, but instead she wadded it up and put it on the floor close to the kittens to give them a warm space to crawl into after they'd eaten.

The fire crackled and spit as he walked toward her. "Okay, now that you've taken care of the animals, it's time to take care of you."

"Me?" She swallowed. "I'm doing fine."

"You're freezing, and you've got to be soaked to the skin. We need to get you out of those wet clothes."

The same impish grin curved her lips from before, and a frisson of heat shot up his spine. Her gloves lay on the counter, and her hands shook as she tried to unzip the coat. He wasn't sure if that was from the cold or from his suggestion.

"Here, let me help." He pulled the zipper of the coat down, and she shrugged out of it, then wrapped her arms around herself. "Normally, I'd suggest a long, steamy shower, but I don't know how long the hot water will last, so we should probably just use the fire to get you warm." He grabbed a blanket from the back of the sofa as he led her to the fireplace.

Easing her onto the hearth, he set the blanket next to her, then untied her boots. He gently slid them off and rubbed her stocking feet between his hands. They were like icicles, but surprisingly, the boots had kept her feet pretty dry.

With the electricity out and the storm blowing outside, Logan felt cocooned in their own space, as if nothing else existed outside their circle of firelight. As though the rest of the world had faded into the darkness, and nothing else mattered except the two of them.

Harper must have felt the same. Her customary snark was absent. In fact, she wasn't saying much at all. At least not with her mouth. But her willingness to let him lead her to the fireplace and peel off layers of her clothing spoke volumes. Her body was speaking to his, telling him she wanted—needed—this as much as he did.

She still wore the stocking cap, but her hair was soaked and dripping onto her shirt. He tugged the hat off and smoothed his hands over her head, twisting his fingers through the damp locks. The scent of her shampoo filled the air, and he wanted to bury his face in the velvety strands.

Her eyes were soft as she looked up at him, trusting, without a trace of her usual wariness. She was so beautiful.

He knew he should stop—should quit touching her—but even the slightest graze of his hands on her skin was making him feverish with need. And he didn't want to stop.

He didn't want to think and deliberate if this was the right thing to do or if this was a terrible decision. He just wanted to touch her, to feel her against him. All his senses seemed to have left him, and he didn't care what being with her would mean or do to him later. He didn't want to ponder where things would go or how long this would last.

All he cared about was right now, this moment, and this woman whose stunning green eyes seemed to dance and glitter in the light of the fire.

His hands rested on her shoulders. "Your shirt is soaked," he whispered, unable to find his voice.

Her voice was husky and sent need surging through him as she said, "Then take it off."

He swallowed, suddenly feeling nervous and shy. She'd given him permission to take off her shirt, and his hands trembled as he lowered them and fumbled with the top button.

Her gaze held his, but he had to look away, had to focus on the task although he was dangerously close to giving up and just ripping her shirt open.

He eased the next button through the hole, and his mouth went dry as the fabric fell back, revealing a black lacy bra, the color stark against the creamy skin of her chest. He wanted to dip his head and kiss the luscious slopes of her breasts, which were barely contained in the bra.

He flicked open another button, then couldn't help himself as he ran his thumb over the top lacy edge of the bra. Her breasts were lush and ample, and it took all he had not to pull the cups down and fill his hands with their weight.

Another button. Another. Then the last one that let the shirt fall completely open. He caught the slight inhale of her breath as he ran the backs of his fingers up the center of her stomach, then along the top of one breast before reaching her neck, then across to where he eased one side of the shirt off her shoulder.

His breath hitched as he gazed at her bare skin, then threaded his fingers through her hair. She tilted her head, just the slightest, giving him access to her neck.

This was it. Harper was here, baring herself to him, and all he had to do was lean down and take his fill of her. This was the moment to stop. Before things went too far.

Hell, her shirt was open, and he'd already skimmed the edges of her bra. It seemed as though things were already progressing into the "far" category. But he could still stop. He could still save himself from jumping completely in, save himself from drowning—in her.

Because if he did this, there would be no going back. Once he gave in, once he tasted her, grazed her skin with his lips, he would only want more.

He flicked his gaze to her, studying her face for a sign. All he saw were her sultry, hooded eyes as she looked up at him from under her lashes. The air around them seemed thick with excitement and uncertainty. Then her full lips quivered and parted, and he was lost.

CHAPTER 19

HARPER HELD HER BREATH, EVERY NERVE IN HER BODY tingling as Logan stared down at her, carnal hunger evident in his gaze. She knew he was debating his next step and looking to her for reassurance that taking that step was okay.

She had no idea if it was. Her head told her to slow down, to think about the consequences of what she was doing. But her body screamed *Screw the consequences*. She could worry about those another night.

His eyes looked into hers with such feeling, and she was a slave to his desires. She'd made it her life dictum to not trust anyone, yet she trusted Logan to lead her to the fireplace, to slowly and deliberately undress her.

Her whole body had been alert as she'd stood still and let him undo each button. Each time his fingers brushed her skin, she'd wanted to melt, and she thought she'd die if he stopped. She wanted to weep at the delicious torture of his fingers skimming the edge of her bra.

After Michael had died, she'd put away her few lacy bra and panty sets. She'd swapped them out for more sensible cotton styles, not caring what she wore since no one ever got to see her underwear anyway. But when she'd been in county, she'd only been allowed to wear a plain white bra and panties. Her jailers had controlled everything she did, down to her underwear.

When she was released, she hated the sight of her plain bras, so she'd dug through her drawers until she unearthed the lacy things. Even if no one saw them, even if no one knew she wore them but her, it gave her a sense of freedom, of control, to put on one of the prettier versions.

But tonight, someone else *was* seeing them, and she'd secretly thrilled at the look of desire in his eyes when he'd peeled back her shirt and discovered the sexy black bra. A spark of heat tightened her nipples each time his hand brushed over the lace or across the top of her breast.

Everything in her ached for him, wanted him, and a shiver of arousal coursed through her. She wanted him to kiss her, to touch her, to *everything* her.

Desire had awakened in every inch of her body. It had been there, sparking just below the surface, since the first moment she'd seen him. But she'd pressed it down, kept it in check, dismissed it as nerves.

Now her nerves were alive and buzzing and not about to be dismissed. What might have started as a spark was now a wildfire of desire. A fire that couldn't be tamped down or put out, even by the blizzard raging outside the windows.

The situation felt out of control, but Logan was giving her the power to decide what happened next. He was asking her with his eyes, but he wasn't pushing her. He was giving her a choice, and that gave her the control she so desperately needed.

He was also what she desperately needed. Everything about tonight felt good. Okay, so she was terrified and freezing and anxious about what would happen tomorrow. But right now, in this moment, standing half naked before him, with his hand on the bare skin of her shoulder and his eyes seeking permission to kiss her, this felt good. He felt good.

She couldn't speak, couldn't articulate the words, but

she lifted her chin and arched into him, saying yes in every silent way she could think of.

He must have understood because he leaned down, his breath a whispered caress against her skin as he moved a wisp of her hair from her neck before pressing a kiss to her shoulder. His whiskers scraped her sensitive skin as he laid another tender kiss on her throat and another on the soft spot just below her ear.

He raised his hands to her neck and cupped her cheeks in his palm, holding her face as his gaze traveled from her eyes to her mouth. Dipping his head, he traced his thumb over her bottom lip, his mouth hovering over hers, barely grazing her skin.

They were so close, and the need in her so strong that she sucked in a breath as if the motion might pull him closer.

He leaned in the slightest bit, the anticipation sending waves of heat coursing through her veins. Then he finally, *thank you, Lord*, finally closed the distance and pressed his lips to hers.

His kiss was deep and demanding, and she was instantly overwhelmed, consumed by the first touch of his tongue against hers. He slanted his lips against hers, tasting deeply, thoroughly. She moaned into his mouth, tilting her head as she invited him deeper.

His hands left her face, gliding down her neck and over her shoulders. Her breasts were tight and heavy, yearning for his touch, as his kisses sent a slow surge of warmth through her body. She moaned again as he moved one hand down and curled it around her breast. Sliding his thumb inside the cup, he grazed the tight, tingling nub of her nipple.

Her breasts ached with need and want, desperate for the

attention they'd been lacking over the last several years. She let out a quivering sigh and sent a silent thank-you to whoever had invented the front-fastening bra as Logan popped open the snap and brushed the cups to the sides.

He dipped his head and sent another shiver of desire through her as the scruff of his whiskered cheek scraped the hardened tip of her nipple. His breath was warm as his tongue circled the nub, then sucked it between his lips.

Filling his hands with her breasts, he lavished them with attention, massaging and kneading, kissing and licking and sampling their tender tips. Scorching need seared through her each time he drew a sensitive nub between his lips.

He eased his hands down, skimming her waist, then reached for the top snap of her jeans. They were soaked and clung to her legs, but she barely felt the cold. Every part of her body was hot with want and need. But as much as she wanted him, if she did this, there would be no going back.

She put her hands on top of his, and he froze.

"What's wrong?" His voice was breathless and hoarse.

"Nothing's wrong. Exactly. I'm just scared, I guess. This could change everything."

He nodded. "I get it. I'm scared too. I like you, Harper. I mean, I *really* like you. You're funny and smart, and you just seem to get me. Plus, you're sexy as hell." He raised his hand and cupped the side of her cheek, tilting her head to look up at him. "I know I'm saying it wrong. I don't know how to tell you all the ways you affect me and all the things you mean to me, but I want this. I want you."

"I want you too. Like I want you with everything in me. But I don't want to screw this up. With you or with the job. I work for you, remember?"

"Screw the job. This doesn't change that if you don't want it to."

"Are you sure?"

"Yes. I don't care about that. I care about you."

"I care about you too. But it's been a long time since I've been here, and I don't want to mess it up. I really like you, Logan, and my body is aching for you to touch me, but I *need* this job."

His voice was husky as he dipped his head and spoke into her ear. "I need you."

That was it. She was lost. "Then take me," she answered. "I'm yours."

One hand slid around her waist and pulled her against him as his other hand cupped the back of her neck, holding her head as his mouth slanted against hers. His kisses were deep, passionate, demanding surrender, but promising pleasure.

He let go of her just long enough to drag his shirt over his head, and she caught her breath at his beautifully sculpted body. His shoulders were broad, and the physical labor of ranch work had his body lean and strong. With his defined abs and powerful arms, the glow of the firelight turned him into a muscular god, and all she wanted to do was touch him. She couldn't get enough.

Trailing his lips down her throat, her chest, her stomach, he sank to his knees in front of her and set to finishing what he'd started when he'd first reached for the snap of her jeans. The soft whisper of the zipper sent a shiver coursing to the tight bundle of nerves at the center of her legs. A shiver that turned into an onslaught of sensation as he drew her jeans down her legs and pressed his mouth against her stomach, laying a row of hot kisses along the waistband of her lacy panties.

He pushed her jeans further down, and she willingly stepped out of them and kicked them aside. Her legs trembled as anticipation thrummed through her, and she could feel her pulse beating wildly in her throat as he kissed the top of her thigh, then pressed his lips to the triangle of lace at the juncture of her legs.

Her breath caught in a gasp of pleasure. His breath was warm. She could feel the heat of it through the thin fabric, along with the abrasive scratch of his whiskered chin, and she couldn't hold back the shiver that passed through her body. He pulled back, and her knees almost gave way from wanting his touch.

"Stay here," he told her, rising to his feet. "Don't move. I'll be right back."

"Wait? What?" She struggled to catch her breath, but he was already gone. She heard his footsteps hurrying down the hall. *Really?*

"Hold that thought," he yelled from the vicinity of his bedroom. "I'm coming right back."

Seconds later, he appeared, his arms laden with the pillows and blankets from his bed. "This should make you a little more comfortable. And a lot warmer."

She was already warm enough, her body was on fire, but the pillows would certainly make the floor more comfortable, and she had a feeling they'd be sleeping there tonight as well.

He dropped everything on the floor in front of the fire. Including a box of condoms.

Oh.

He caught her eye and gave her a sheepish shrug as she looked up from the box. "Just thought we should be prepared. In case things went that direction."

"Good thinking." She offered him a sultry smile. "I'm glad you brought the whole box."

He chuckled. "Damn, but I do like you, woman."

"I like you too. But I'd like you better if you resumed where you left off and got back to the business of kissing me."

He laughed again and grabbed her hands, bringing her down onto the blankets with him. Pulling over the pillows, he eased her head onto them, and she gazed up, awed by the sight of him. His chestnut hair was tousled, and she should have been afraid. It had been so long since she'd done this. Not just *this*, although it had been a long time for that too, but so long since she'd trusted someone enough to give herself over to him.

But Logan was smiling and looking down at her as if she were the exact Christmas gift he'd wished for. As if she were the thing he wanted above all else.

That look was a little daunting. She didn't feel worthy of that kind of praise, but if he were imagining her as a gift, she was ready to be unwrapped. As if he could read her mind, he slid his hands inside her shirt and pushed it back from her shoulders. She shrugged out of it and the straps of her unfastened bra and pushed them to the side of the blanket, then lay back on the pillows.

He shimmied out of his jeans, then lay down next to her and skimmed the back of his fingers over her cheeks. "God, you're beautiful," he said, his voice a gravelly whisper. He ran his hand through her hair, fanning it out on the pillow. "I've never met anyone like you."

She started to fire back a snarky comment, but he pressed his finger to her lips.

"Don't. Just take the compliment." He ran the tip of his finger over her parted lips, then leaned down and replaced his finger with his mouth.

She didn't know how to take a compliment anymore. It felt like it had been so long since anyone had given her a sincere one. She didn't know what to say, and he apparently didn't need her to say anything. So instead, she showed him how she felt by kissing him back with all the passion and fervor she could muster.

Their legs were tangled as if they couldn't get close enough. He shifted as they kissed, and his body rose above hers, the firelight casting shadows over his muscled chest and arms.

A moan escaped her lips as she relished the feel of a man's weight on top of her, a feeling she hadn't realized how much she'd missed. He was warm and solid, and she arched in to him, desperate to feel more of him. His hips ground against hers, and the sensations thrummed between her legs where the slightest friction made her light-headed.

It might have been a long time since she'd felt like this, but her body reacted with an instinct that came from deep inside her. She shifted against him, craving more of the tantalizing friction.

He kissed her mouth, her neck, her chest as his hands roamed over her body, discovering what she liked and what made her moan and sigh and arch with need.

Clutching his shoulders, she ran her fingers over his muscled arms as she kissed him back, her body needy and frantic to touch, to taste, to learn every part of him. She kissed the soft spot below his ear, and a low growl escaped his throat. She loved knowing she could affect him like this.

He reared back, pulling away, and she tried to catch her breath as she watched him scramble for the box of condoms, tear one open, cover himself, then settle back between her legs.

"You okay?" he asked, brushing the wisps of hair from her forehead.

She nodded, unable to speak. Gazing into his eyes, she felt something she hadn't in such a long time. No matter how hard she tried to fight it, she was obviously falling for the guy. She felt those crazy, nauseous, roller-coaster feelings in her stomach every time she was around him.

But this was different.

This was a feeling of trust, of handing over control, of giving herself to another person and believing he wouldn't destroy her. Trust was not something she gave lightly, but looking into Logan's eyes and seeing her feelings reflected there made her think maybe this was a man she could finally let go with, that she could finally let herself believe in someone again.

He bent to lay the softest kiss on her lips as his hips stirred against her. Then she couldn't think anymore, couldn't process any semblance of thoughts. She could only feel, and move, and react to the rhythm he set. She gripped his shoulders, holding on as the sensations scorched through her, pulsing in the deepest part of her.

He'd barely set the pace, but she was already climbing, every muscle tense, as pleasure radiated through her, electrifying every nerve. Her body hummed with tension as the sensations ricocheted through her.

Her senses were so deliciously heightened that every caress sent another hot current of desire to her core. Circling, spinning, tumbling, soaring, she succumbed to the pleasure with a gasp as shudders rocked through her body.

Logan kissed her, catching her gasps in his mouth as if taking in her very essence, while his strong arms held her tightly against him. She'd never felt anything like this—this intensity that quaked through her in a frenzied rush. All she could do was hold on, helpless against the fierce tremors that reeled through her body. His muscles tautened, and a low growl hummed against her lips as he rocked with her, matching her release.

A blizzard of emotion whirled through her, rivaling the storm that raged outside the windows, and she didn't know how to hold it all in. It was all too much—the feelings, the sensations, the stress of trying to do everything on her own, coupled with the closeness she'd allowed herself with this man. Gripping his shoulders, she held on as a sob escaped her throat.

He didn't even flinch, just held her tighter, and that one reaction was all it took for the floodgates to release. For the first time in months, she let herself cry. And not cry like a few tears escaped her eyes, but cry like shoulders-shaking sobbing into his neck.

They held each other, their bodies connected in the most intimate way as she clung to him and wept. When she'd cried herself out, he released his grip and eased down next to her.

Pulling her close against him, he pressed a tender kiss to her forehead. "You okay?"

"Yes."

"You want to talk about it?"

"No." She let out a shaky breath. "That was just intense.

Like toe-curling amazingly intense. I guess I've been bottling up a lot of emotion, and…I don't know… That's never happened to me before. Apparently my body chose that moment to let it out. Sorry."

"Don't be sorry. I felt it too." He brushed his fingers lightly over her shoulder. "Anything I can do?"

A smile tugged at the corner of her mouth, and she pulled back slightly to look up at him. "You already did *more* than enough."

He let out a soft chuckle. "Oh darlin', I was only getting warmed up. I can always do more."

Her eyes widened along with her grin. "More? I can't imagine topping that."

He rolled over and dragged her under him. "That sounds like you're throwing down a challenge, Peaches."

Her nipples tightened in anticipation, and she wrapped one of her legs around his muscled calf. "Maybe I am."

His lips curved into a seductive grin. "Challenge accepted."

A giggle bubbled up in her, and she marveled at the range of emotions this night had torn from her. Then his lips slanted across her mouth, and she couldn't think at all.

Hours later, they lay together, their bodies spent and curled into each other for warmth. Sated and happy, Harper snuggled into Logan's shoulder. He'd just put another log on the fire, and it snapped and crackled and sent tiny sparks into the air. The snow still swirled and spun in flurries outside the window.

"The storm sounds like it's gotten worse," Harper said, running her fingers lightly along his chest. "I'm glad we got all the cattle in when we did."

Logan blew out his breath, and his shoulders tightened. "You have no idea."

She tilted her head to look up at him and was surprised to see the furrow of his brow. "You got a little panicked out there. Did you really mean it when you said you couldn't afford to lose even one cow?"

"Damn right I did."

"I didn't realize that a ranch depended so much on the loss or gain of one animal."

He let out a heavy sigh. "Normally, it doesn't. But Dad was immersed in all this stuff with his brother, and I was in charge of buying the calves this year." He paused, and she waited, knowing there was more to the story but feeling that if she said anything, he wouldn't go on. "You know how I told you I mix up numbers and letters sometimes."

"Yeah."

"Well, I must have really blown it when I got all those calves. I don't know what happened, but I checked the market report a couple of weeks ago, and whatever I did, however I must have mixed up the numbers, I screwed myself out of about twenty thousand dollars. And that's if I sell every single one of them for the price beef was going for that week *and* they all come in at seven hundred pounds or more. If they don't, or if I messed something else up, it will affect how many calves we can buy for spring and could ruin our entire year's income."

"Oh no."

"Oh yes. Another Logan screwup. Just one more reason

why you can't trust my idiot brain to make decisions." He pushed up to a sitting position, the muscles of his back and shoulders tight and tense. "It was such a stupid mistake. And I feel like an idiot for not catching it sooner."

"But you caught it now. I'm sure your dad's glad about that."

"You haven't met Hamilton Rivers. He doesn't get glad about much of anything. He's an old-school cowboy, tough as nails, and he doesn't suffer fools." Logan let out a bitter laugh. "Which is why I haven't told him about it." He dropped his head to his chest. "Because I'm too ashamed."

Her heart broke for him. She'd known from their last conversation that his dyslexia bothered him, but the shame he felt obviously went deeper than she'd imagined. "I'm sure your dad will understand. Haven't you struggled with this kind of stuff your whole life?"

"Yeah, I have."

"But it's not your fault. It's just a learning glitch."

"It's not a glitch. It's a 'disability.'" He said the word as if it left a bad taste in his mouth. "That means something is wrong with me. And everyone knows it. My dad knows it, my sister knows it—we *all* know it because it's the reason my mom walked out and left us."

Harper sucked in her breath. That couldn't be true. "I thought you said your mom died in a car accident, that she was hit by a drunk driver."

His shoulders slumped forward. "She was. But she'd already left, gone back to Denver, because of me. Because of this stupid disability. She couldn't take it. Couldn't abide by the fact that she'd created this stupid child. I was the firstborn son. I was supposed to be perfect—the golden boy—not a moron who couldn't learn to read until the third grade."

"That couldn't be the reason. No mother thinks of her child like that."

"My mother did. I don't think she was cut out for ranch life in the first place, and she'd never really seemed happy, not like other moms who baked cookies and volunteered at school and laughed and played with their kids. She might have been okay if it was just the ranch stuff, because I think she really did love my dad. He wasn't so gruff back then. But then she had me to deal with, and all the extra work added to her already unhappy life. Exercises and tutoring and hours spent reading the same sentences over and over again."

"But she was your mom. I'm sure she didn't mind."

"Oh, I'm *sure* she did. I know she did." He stared into the fire as if he could see the past in the flames. "A kid knows. I could feel it in the way her body tensed when I got a sentence wrong and in the way she sighed when Dad told her we needed to work on my exercises. It was as if he was handing down homework assignments to both of us. My mom never liked being told what to do. And then she gets saddled with this stupid son who gives her no choice, who has a disability that rules her life, who makes her sit in a chair and listen to him make the same mistakes again and again."

"That can't be true."

"It was. I'd hear her fighting with my dad, and nine times out of ten, the fight had something to do with me. Or to do with the extra money we were spending on a tutor and the slew of reading specialists and speech-language pathologists. After one of those fights, she'd get even more frustrated with me and tell me I just needed to try harder. Which usually backfired on both of us, because it only made me more discouraged and unable to concentrate. Then I'd end up mad and either give up or throw the stupid book I was failing to read across the room."

"I'm so sorry that happened to you. But dyslexia is not something that is your *fault*. In fact, a lot of times it's hereditary, so you may even have gotten it from your mom's side of the family."

"Somehow, I don't think her knowing that would have helped anything."

"No. You're right. Probably not. But what I'm trying to say is that your mom leaving was not your fault either. That was a choice she made."

"Because of me." He turned back to her, his gaze intense as the muscles in his shoulders stiffened. "Don't you get it, Harper? She left because her son was stupid. Because I didn't measure up to the ideal child she'd imagined she'd have."

Tears burned her eyes, and she wrapped her arms around his neck. "No, that's not true."

"It is true, but I appreciate you saying otherwise." His voice was husky and raw, and he slid his arms around her and pulled her tightly against him.

They stayed like that for a minute, holding each other, and her heart broke for the child in this man who blamed himself for his mom walking out on his family. She pressed against him, telling him with her body the things she didn't know how to say.

He laid her back against the pillows and brushed away the lone tear that had escaped her eye. His smile was playful as he looked down at her. "Don't cry, darlin'. I thought you were a pretty tough chick, but it turns out you're kind of a softie."

She had a feeling this was what he did, deflected the attention away from his learning disorder with his charm and wit. But she wasn't going to be deflected.

Now was the time. She needed to tell him about Floyd. Tell him she was a mom, and that she had a son who suffered from dyslexia. And that it didn't change the way she saw him or affect his worth in her eyes. "Logan, I need to tell you something."

CHAPTER 20

"Don't." Logan pressed his fingers to Harper's lips. "Don't tell me anything. I've heard it all. *It's not your fault. It's just a learning disorder.* None of that matters or makes me feel like less of an idiot."

"I don't think you're an idiot," she said against his fingers. "That's not what I was going to say."

"Please, Harper. I mean it. Don't say anything else." His brows knit together, and the pain was evident in his eyes. "I shouldn't have told you all that stuff about my mom and the cattle and the stupid dyslexia shit. Geez. I hate even saying the word. Just talking about it makes me feel stupid and like less of a man because my idiotic brain doesn't work right."

She glanced down at his chest. "Logan, you are more than enough of a man. And I think every part of you works right. In fact, it all works exceptionally well."

A grin tugged at the corners of his lips. "Yeah?"

"Yeah." She smiled as she stroked a finger down his arm. He needed this, needed to know she didn't think him unworthy or dumb. There would be time to tell him about Floyd later. It's not like her son, or her mom status, was going anywhere.

Right now, in this moment, the most important thing she could do for Logan was to prove to him that the dyslexia didn't matter, that it didn't make him less. Of anything.

"Logan, you *are* smart. And thoughtful and kind. You're skilled at both ranching *and* hockey, and I know playing hockey takes great aptitude. You have to have a sense of the game as you judge the actions of yourself, the puck, and the other players while still following what's happening around you and planning ahead for the next several moves to get the puck down the ice. You have to know where your players are to pass to as well as where your opponents are who are trying to stop you.

"All that takes talent as well as a razor-sharp focus to be able to play and pass and shoot while keeping from going off-sides or icing the puck. Plus, working with a team takes intellect and comprehension to figure out lines and plays and keep your head and your body cool under pressure. And you have to be intelligent to run this ranch—to grow crops, to buy and sell cattle, and keep track of the hundred and one other things you do. I know you made a mistake, but that could have happened to anyone. That doesn't make you an idiot."

His eyes had started to soften, but now they narrowed.

Uh-oh. He apparently didn't want to hear about the mistake again. She switched back to telling him all the great things she saw in him. "You're a good man. I've seen that in the short time I've known you. And it didn't take me long to figure it out. You give back to the community by coaching hockey to little kids, and you took a chance on a woman you didn't know to offer her a job and a leg up when no one else would." Shoot. She didn't want to think about the job any more than he wanted to think about his disability.

She ran her gaze slowly down his chest, then offered him a seductive smile. "And you're sexy as hell."

He laughed, then leaned down and slanted his mouth against hers in a kiss that turned urgent as he slid his hands up her torso and cupped her bare breast.

There will be time to talk later, she thought as she gave in to the feel of his hands roaming over her skin.

Harper blinked as the morning sun streamed through the window. Her body was stiff and achy from lying on the floor. And from other things. But those aches were good.

She was alone and still naked, but warm under the pile of blankets. A chorus of soft mewls sounded, and she looked down to see the kittens as they tumbled over the crease of the top blanket in an effort to get closer to her. Reaching out her hand, she stroked their soft fur and pulled them against her. "Good morning, cuties. I'll bet you're hungry."

So was she. The clock on the wall told her it was almost seven, and the scent of freshly brewed coffee hung in the air. The light above the sink was on, and she was thankful to see the power was back. "Logan?" she called out to what felt like an empty house.

No answer. The snow had stopped, and he had probably already gone out to start his morning chores. She stood and padded to the window, wrapping the blanket around her as she went. Logan's truck was gone, so she guessed he was feeding the cattle.

She looked around for her clothes, which appeared to be strewn across the room. Her jeans were still damp, so she threw them in the dryer, then fed the kittens and put them outside while she swigged a few gulps of coffee. She pulled on one of Logan's sweatshirts from the stack of laundry she'd done the day before, then stuffed her feet into her boots and hurried across the driveway to the bunkhouse.

She needed a hot shower and clean clothes before she made breakfast.

It took her less than twenty minutes to get her body showered, her teeth brushed, and a fresh set of clothes on. Except that she only had one pair of jeans, and they were in the dryer. She took a quick peek out the window and still didn't see Logan's truck, so she wrapped a towel around her waist and ran back to the farmhouse.

She'd let the kittens outside when she'd left, and they were now curled together in a patch of sunlight on the porch. She paused to scoop them up and bring them inside. The mama cat should have appeared by now, and Harper imagined the worst—that either the storm or another animal had gotten her.

"Don't worry, little kits, I've got you," she told the kittens as she cuddled them under her chin. She might not be able to be a mom to Floyd right now, but she could pour a little of her mom energy into these kittens. Who knew what would happen to them once she went back to Kansas? But she couldn't think about that now.

She toed off her boots and padded to the kitchen in her bare feet. The towel wouldn't stay knotted, so she dropped it on the chair, then stopped in the kitchen to pull out the skillet and start the bacon.

The dryer buzzed, and she hurried into the laundry room to grab her jeans. Pulling them on as she walked back to the kitchen, she had one leg in when the front door opened and Logan strode through.

She froze, her jeans halfway up one leg and her other leg bare. *This is awkward.* But also convenient if he was coming in and hoping to pick up where they'd left off the night before. Just seeing his long, lean body encased in jeans and boots had her engine revving, and she offered him a small flirty grin. "Um…hi."

"Oh, uh, hi. I thought we'd have…" He paused, and she was ready to chuck the jeans and cross the room to climb him like a tree, but her flirty smile fell as he finished the sentence with "…breakfast."

"Oh gosh, yeah, of course." *Shit.* What was she thinking? She *was* the housekeeper. Why wouldn't he expect food to be on the table when he came in from doing his chores? That was her job. And the way she'd wanted it. *Right?*

A hot flush heated her cheeks as she stuffed her other leg into her jeans and quickly zipped them up. Avoiding his eyes, she hurried into the kitchen and grabbed the eggs from the refrigerator. "I've already got the bacon going, and I sliced some fruit. I'll have some eggs fried up for you in a few minutes."

"Harper," he said, his brow furrowed as he took a step toward her. "I thought this is what you said you wanted. For nothing to change."

"No, it is. You're right. It totally is." She couldn't look at him. This *is* what she'd said she wanted. But just because she wanted to keep her job didn't mean she wanted the other stuff—the stuff that had happened in the dark in front of the fireplace the night before—to stop. Or did she?

Or did *he*? Maybe he was only interested in a one-night fling, and this was his way of getting them back on the boss-employee track. It would be easier to blame it on her than to admit he'd made a mistake and let things go too far between them.

But that hadn't seemed to be the tune he was whistling the night before. He'd acted like he'd wanted something more.

She kept her gaze focused on the bowl as she cracked

eggs into it. "Last night was crazy—the blizzard, the power outage, rescuing the cows. We just got caught up in the madness of the night, and things got carried away. But we both knew it was a one-time thing, and it'll never happen again."

His brow furrowed in confusion, and she could have sworn she saw a hurt expression cross his face. Or maybe that's just what she wanted to see.

Before he could say anything else or clear up the confusion, the sound of boot steps on the porch had him turning to open the door. A gust of cold air blew through the room as the new hired hand stepped in and stomped his boots on the rug in front of the door.

Zane tipped his hat to Harper before taking it off and hanging it and his coat on an empty hook behind the door. "I'm much obliged to you feeding me breakfast, Harper. I didn't have time to grab anything this morning, and that bacon sure smells good."

Logan offered her a small shrug, but she could tell he didn't want to embarrass the other man.

"Absolutely. I was just frying up the eggs now. You want two or three?" She could roll with this and act like Logan had already mentioned it. Plus, she liked Zane and didn't want him to feel uncomfortable. Besides, there was more than enough food, and it wouldn't take but a minute more to cook a few extra eggs. She was just thankful she had her pants on when Zane had walked through the door.

"Two's fine," he said, as he headed down the hall toward the bathroom. "I'm just gonna wash up." His glance veered to the mess of blankets and two pillows spread on the floor in front of the fireplace, but he quickly averted his gaze and didn't comment.

Harper focused on getting breakfast on the table and was glad the conversation turned to the blizzard and what had to be done with the cattle. It sounded like the town had taken a few hits with downed trees from the storm, but the power had been restored there as well. One of the great things about Colorado was that it could snow like hell one day, then be sunny the next. The air was still cold today, but at least the brunt of the storm was over and the sun was shining.

The men ate quickly, both anxious to get back to work. Logan told her they had already fed the cattle and were going to be working in the barn that morning. "Zane's going to spend some more time with the new horse. He's already making great progress with her. I may have bought her, but the dang thing couldn't care less about me. Yet she comes running toward Zane like he's got sugar in his pocket." Logan turned toward the other man. "Is that the trick? *Do* you have sugar in your pocket?"

Zane shrugged, his expression and tone neutral as he quipped, "Nah, I just have a naturally sweet disposition."

The three of them stared at each other, holding a beat before they all burst into laughter. Even Zane, who normally didn't offer much more than a soft chuckle, showed his teeth as he laughed with them.

It warmed Harper more than any blanket could to feel like the tough cowboy trusted her enough to let her in on the joke and to let down his guard enough to laugh with her. These people—this ranch—was starting to feel like a home, and she directed her focus to wiping down the counter as she fought the sudden burn of emotion in her throat.

"I was going to make cinnamon rolls this morning," she

told them as they zipped back into their coats and donned their hats. "Why don't you come back in around ten thirty? I'll have warm rolls and a fresh pot of hot coffee for you."

"Sounds good," Zane said as he pushed through the door.

"Breakfast was great," Logan said, right on the other man's heels. Before closing the door, he turned back and gave her a wink, a grin tugging at the corners of his lips. "Thanks, Peaches."

With a laugh, she threw the dishcloth toward him. But he'd already pulled the door shut, and she could hear his boots thumping down the steps. Heading for the kitchen, she dove into getting the dishes done and the rolls started, thankful Logan was back to teasing her again. While the rolls baked, she straightened the living room, clearing up the bedding and putting the pillows back on the sofa.

With festive Christmas carols playing on the radio, she mopped the snow from the hardwood floors and ran the vacuum. The heavenly scent of cinnamon and bread filled the house, and she'd just finished frosting the rolls when Logan and Zane stomped back in.

"Those smell incredible," Logan said, heading for the sink to wash his hands.

She stood at the counter, and he walked behind her, not touching her, but she felt his presence as clearly as if he had. He stood at the sink, smelling like hay and soap and the subtle hints of his aftershave, and she wanted to wrap her arms around his middle and lay her head against his back. She might have if Zane hadn't been in the room.

The other man was a great buffer to keep them from talking about what had happened the night before, and she half wondered if Logan had planned that on purpose. He hadn't brought Zane into the house for a meal before. Granted, the guy had only been working for him for a few days, so she hadn't had time to observe their routine. And Ted had been fired before she'd started work. Maybe feeding the hired hand was normal.

If so, she'd need to stock up on more groceries. Which would give her the perfect excuse to take the truck into town and provide her with another chance to try to see Floyd. She now knew what time his recess happened, so maybe she could catch him on the playground and at least talk to him through the fence. She just wanted to hear his voice and tell him how much she'd missed him.

An ache settled in her chest as she tried to stay focused on what the men were talking about. Zane wasn't much of a talker, but he listened attentively and occasionally added to the conversation. They seemed to spend a lot of time conferring about the cattle and discussing the weather. Which made sense since it was their livelihood, but it felt as though they'd already covered this ground. Maybe they were uncomfortable with her listening in.

She'd just started to clear the table when Logan's cell phone rang.

He pulled it from his pocket and pressed it to his ear. "Rivers here." He paused. "Hey, Gus, what's up?" Another pause. "You don't say."

Harper stacked the plates but stopped as Logan put a hand on her arm and motioned for her to sit back down.

"Well, that clears up our mystery. She's one of our farm cats and just had a litter of kittens. We noticed she was gone after the storm but figured she got taken by the blizzard or another animal." He paused again. "Yup. You too. Thanks for letting us know."

He disconnected the call and dropped the phone back into his shirt pocket. "Well, that was Gus. You know, the fellow that came by the other day to drop off the horse?"

"Yeah." Harper was sitting on the edge of her seat, reluctant to hear what the caller had said. She could tell by the frown on Logan's face that the news wasn't good.

"Apparently Nacho, that mama cat, must have gone into his trailer the other day while we were dinkin' around with the horse. He said she ran out when he got home and unloaded the trailer. 'Bout scared the devil out of him, he said. He tried to catch her, but she ran off. He's been keeping an eye out for her, but he hasn't seen her again and figured he'd call just to let us know, in case we noticed she was gone."

"We noticed," Harper said, surprised by the sting in her throat. "Her babies noticed. Now they have to grow up without their mother."

Logan shook his head. "It's a dang shame. I'm sorry, Harper. I know you love those little rascals." His palm was still on her arm, and he slid it down to cover her hand as he offered her an encouraging smile. "We'll just have to find homes for them. How about you? Want a kitten? I know you're partial to Tink. You want to keep her?"

"I can't take a kitten. I won't be here long enough to take care of her."

His smile fell as he pulled his hand away from hers. "That's right. You're leaving." He stared at the table as he scratched at a dab of dried frosting. "But maybe you could stay. For the kittens."

The lump in her throat burned hotter. Had he just asked her to stay, as in stay with him, or did he only mean he wanted her to stay longer to take care of the kittens and the house and cook his meals?

And how could she leave the three small orphaned cats? How could she leave him?

She gave a start as another ringtone sounded. This time it chimed from the front pocket of her jeans. Digging it free, her heart leapt in hopes that it was Floyd. Or even Judith. Maybe she'd had a change of heart and was calling to set up a time for Harper to visit.

Her soaring spirits sank as she finally freed the phone and saw her new friend's name listed on the caller ID. She flipped open the phone and pressed it to her ear. "Hey, Bryn." She almost smiled as she noticed the way Zane's ears pricked up at the mention of the perky waitress's name, but the alarm in the other woman's voice kept her smile at bay. "Slow down. What's wrong?"

"Everything," the waitress wailed. "And I'm so mad at Otis, I could spit. I'm in trouble over here, Harper, and I don't know who else to call. Can you come over now? Just for a few hours? I really need your help."

"Okay, take a breath. And hang on." She lowered the phone and turned to Logan. "It's Bryn, and she's upset. I can't tell if she's scared or crying or just really mad, but she said she needs my help. Can you spare me for a few hours so I can go over there now?"

He nodded. "Yeah, sure. What's going on?"

She shrugged as she lifted the phone. "I'll be right there, Bryn. Are you sure you're okay? Do you need me to call someone? Is anyone hurt?"

"Not yet. But there's about to be. Just get here." Harper heard her yell; then the phone went dead.

"What happened?" Zane asked, pushing up from his chair. "Is she hurt?"

"I don't think so," Harper answered, heading for her coat. "But she was pretty upset. I heard her yelling at someone, then the phone went dead." She stopped and turned to Logan. "Crud. Can I borrow the truck? And can you tell me where she lives?"

"I'll drive," Zane said, already across the room and reaching for his jacket. He shoved his arms in the sleeves as he pushed out the door and rushed down the steps.

Harper followed, and Logan was right on her heels. "I'm coming too," he said as he shoved the last bite of cinnamon roll in his mouth.

They made it to Bryn's farm in record time, taking the turns in the road a little too fast, but Harper felt safe cocooned in the truck between the two men. The waitress only lived a few miles down the road on a small farm where she'd lived with her grandfather. Logan had told Harper that Bryn's grandfather had died the year before, leaving the run-down but still functioning farm to his only granddaughter.

Pulling up the drive, Harper took in the faded-yellow two-story farmhouse. It had a wide front porch, and a festive green wreath hung from the door. A few strands of Christmas lights had been wrapped around the porch railings, and handfuls of evergreen boughs wrapped in glittering red ribbon adorned the white clapboard shutters.

The farmyard held a large barn flanked by corrals. Chickens roamed in the fenced-in section of a chicken coop, and what looked like a garden area sat to the right of the house. It was quaint and charming, but Harper had a feeling the layer of snow helped to give that impression.

Zane pulled the truck to a stop and was out of the cab practically before the engine had a chance to die. Harper and Logan clamored out of the truck and followed him up the steps, hitting the porch as he knocked on the front door.

A loud crash sounded from inside the house, followed by shriek. Zane's shoulders tensed and he reached for the doorknob, ready to break his way in, but the door flew open before his hand reached the knob.

Harper gasped. "Oh my-lanta. What happened to you?"

Bryn stood in the doorway, her clothes in disarray and her hair poking up in sticky clumps. Globs of red and orange muck dotted the front of her pink waitress uniform, and the red goo was spread through her hair. The front of her bangs stood up in one spiky blob as if she'd pushed her hair back with a sticky hand and it had stuck that way. Harper was pretty sure there was a cherry stuck in there as well.

Bryn's hands and wrists also held traces of the goop, and she was missing a shoe. Her face was as red as the cherry mixture, and her hands were clenched in fists at her sides. "Thank God you're here. I was just about to get out the ax. One of us is going down, and it's not going to be me."

"What the hell happened?" Zane asked.

"I stayed up all night making fifteen pies for the church bazaar and left them cooling on the counter while I went in to cover the breakfast shift at the diner. The latch has been sticking on my front door, and I must not have got it completely closed, because Otis found his way in and either ate or destroyed every single one."

"Who the hell is Otis?" Harper asked, wondering how one person could devour fifteen pies.

As if in answer to her question, a loud bleat came from inside the house, and Bryn pushed the door back to reveal a black-and-white billy goat standing in the center of her dining room table.

CHAPTER 21

HARPER CLASPED A HAND OVER HER MOUTH. "HOLY shit! There's a goat on your table."

"Yes, I know," Bryn fumed. "A goat that's about to get murdered."

They peered into the house. The kitchen counters and floors were littered with the remains of what looked like cherry, peach, and apple pies. The table was askew, and two of the chairs were knocked over. Small red footprints dotted the floor, and a long smear of cherry pie filling streaked across the kitchen tile.

"It looks like someone was already murdered in here." Zane took a cautious step inside, glancing around as if assessing the situation. "You got a rope?"

Harper and Logan followed him in, carefully stepping between the splotches of pie filling.

Bryn pointed to the lead rope on the counter. "I tried that already. Then I tried luring him outside with more pie, but apparently he's full. Fifteen pies must be his limit. I've been chasing him around the house for twenty minutes. I've caught him a couple of times, but the ornery bastard keeps slipping out of my grasp." She looked down at her uniform. "Which accounts for why I'm wearing at least three of the dang pies."

"I got this." Zane picked up the rope and gingerly approached the table, cooing to the goat in soothing tones. "What's his name again?"

"Otis. My granddad named him after his brother who he said was as ornery and stubborn as an old goat, but I can't imagine my great-uncle being as cantankerous and willful as this animal has proven to be."

"Hey now, Otis." Zane kept his voice soft and calm, but cocked an eyebrow at Bryn when a frightened whine sounded from underneath the table. "You got more than one pie-eating goat?"

"No. That's my dog, Lucky. He's scared to death," Bryn explained. "He's been hiding under the table since I got home."

"Poor dog," Harper said, peering under the table to see a medium-size yellow dog hunkered next to the legs of a chair.

"What do you want me to do?" Logan asked Zane, stepping toward the back end of the table.

"Nothing," Zane answered, holding the gaze of the goat. "Just stay back. I've almost got him." He took another cautious step forward, gently holding out one hand while keeping the circled loop of the rope loosely in the other and continuing to quietly coax the animal toward him.

Like an old dog that knows its master, the goat stepped forward and dipped his head to let Zane scratch him between his ears. The cowboy chatted amicably with the goat as he carefully eased the rope around its neck, then slowly cinched it. The animal didn't seem to mind as Zane led it off the table and walked it toward the front door. "Where do you want him?" he asked Bryn.

She raised an eyebrow at Zane. "At the bottom of the lake right now. But I'd probably regret that decision tomorrow. You can just put him in the barn. In that first stall. He'll probably get out again, but he knows where to show up if he wants to be fed."

Zane nodded. "I can't imagine he's going to be hungry any time soon."

"No, I suppose not." She sagged against the kitchen counter. "Zane, you are seriously my hero. Thank you."

He dipped his head, a blush creeping up his neck. "It was nothing. And not the first time I've had to deal with an old goat." He opened the door for the animal. "I'll grab my tools from my truck after I put him up, then come back and fix this door."

"You're a saint," Bryn called after him as he led the goat onto the porch. After the door closed, she crouched next to the table. "You can come out now, boy. Come on, sweetheart."

The dog's nose appeared first, just the end of it poking out from under the edge of the table. He sniffed the air, as if checking to make sure the screwball goat was really gone. Then he limped out from his hiding spot and hobbled toward Bryn. She opened her arms and cuddled the dog to her chest.

"It looks like he's hurt," Harper said. "He's limping."

"He was hurt a long time ago. He's fine now. Well, except for being traumatized by the crazy durn goat." Bryn pulled back so Harper could see the dog's body.

She gasped as she realized the dog only had three legs.

"He was hit by a car and left for dead," Bryn explained.

"Another one of Bryn's strays," Logan said.

That's what he'd said about her the first day Harper had met him. That she was another one of Bryn's strays. Now, she knew what he meant.

Logan leaned down and touched Bryn's shoulder. "Why

don't you go take a shower and wash the gunk out of your hair, and we'll start cleaning up down here."

"Oh no. I've got too much work to do. And I can't leave you with this mess."

"If you saw what a mess you were right now, you wouldn't be arguing with me." Logan chuckled. "You have a cherry stuck in your bangs."

"I'm sure you'll feel better if you take a shower and put on some clean clothes. And we'll be fine," Harper assured her. "We're used to cleaning up messes together." She offered Logan a knowing grin.

"Yeah, this is nothing compared to the disgusting disaster that Ted left in the bunkhouse. You go on now and get changed. We'll have this picked up in no time."

Bryn nodded and headed down the hall to what Harper assumed was her bedroom.

Searching the pantry, Harper found a mop, some paper towels, cleaning supplies, and a box of trash bags. Logan found the kitchen stereo and tuned it to a classic country station. The twangs of guitars and soulful crooning filled the air as they worked together to throw away the remains of the destroyed pies and wipe down the counters. Harper filled the sink with the empty pie pans and hot sudsy water as Logan mopped the sticky mess from the floor.

After putting the mop away, Logan found a dish towel and stood beside her, drying each pan as she washed and rinsed it. They didn't talk much, but she was aware of his every movement, feeling the heat of his body next to her as he dried the dishes and softy hummed along with the music.

She was washing the last dish when Logan reached his hand into the water. "If you give me the washcloth, I'll wipe off the rest of the counters." His fingers brushed the back of her hand as he searched for the cloth, and a dart of heat raced down her back as she remembered the way his hand had brushed over her bare skin the night before.

His thumb skimmed her wrist as he dipped his head to her neck. She closed her eyes, already anticipating the soft scrape of his whiskers against her throat.

He pulled back as they heard Bryn's steps coming down the hall.

"Wow. It looks great in here," she said, gazing around the room as she walked into the kitchen. "This is amazing. I can't believe you got this cleaned up so fast."

"We're a good team," Logan said, offering Harper a wink. "What else can we do to help?"

Bryn chewed on her bottom lip. "I hate to ask, since you've already done so much, but what I'm really hoping is that I can talk Harper into sticking around and helping me bake another fifteen pies."

"When do you need them finished by?" Harper asked.

"Tonight."

"Tonight?"

"Yeah, I've got to have them to the church by five."

"Then we'd better get to work." Harper peered up at Logan. "Are you okay if I stay?"

"Of course," he said. "I'll stay too."

"You?" Bryn asked. "You're going to stay and help me make pies?"

"Sure. Why not?"

"I don't know if I have an apron that fits you," Bryn teased.

"You better look for one for me too," Zane said as he walked through the front door. "I'm staying too."

Bryn shook her head. "I can't believe it. Thank you. But you guys really don't have to do this."

Zane arched an eyebrow. "You think you and Harper can make fifteen pies and have them delivered in four hours by yourselves?"

"I figured we could dang well try." Bryn studied the broody cowboy. "Have you ever made a pie before?"

"No. But I've also never delivered a baby before, and I'm pretty sure I could if I had to. Besides, how hard can it be?"

Bryn let out a surprised laugh. "Well, it's a heck of a lot easier than delivering a baby."

Zane shrugged, his rugged jaw set in the same surly expression he usually wore. "I've helped deliver calves and foals, and it's the same basic anatomy. And I've baked a cake and made cookies, so I'm assuming the fundamentals are similar. You and Harper can do the heavy lifting, and Logan and I can be your grunts. Just tell us what to do."

Bryn arched an eyebrow. "You're serious?"

"As a heart attack."

"Even if I make you wear an apron?"

"I wouldn't have it any other way."

A collection of aprons hung from a hook next to the pantry, and Bryn rifled through them and pulled out the frilliest one. It was pink and teal with a hot-pink ruffle and a giant glittery cupcake on the front. She held the armholes up as she offered the cowboy a challenging stare.

He held her gaze, his mouth set in a hard line as he accepted her dare. He took off his hat and hung it on the coatrack, then stepped into the apron and turned for Bryn to tie it around his waist.

Harper had been watching the exchange, and the tension

between the other couple was as thick as the pie filling that had earlier been strewn around the room. She stood a little behind Logan and clutched the back of his shirt, holding her breath as Bryn took a step closer to Zane and picked up the apron ties. It was obvious by the slight tremor in her hands that as bold as Bryn was acting, she was a little unnerved by tying a bow around the lean waist of the handsome cowboy.

Logan turned and winked at Harper. That small gesture told her he was picking up the same tension between the other two, and he must have approved. "Hey, that's the apron I was going to choose," he said.

Zane turned his head slowly, his eyes narrowed in a death stare as he glared at Logan. He lowered his voice. "Tough shit. There's only one man in this room who's badass enough to wear a glittery cupcake on his chest."

Logan took a menacing step forward. "We'll see about that. Bryn, you got any more glitter in that stack?"

Bryn pressed her lips together to keep from laughing as she rifled through the assortment of aprons. "No glitter. Best I've got is dancing chickens or"—she paused as she dug through and pulled out another choice—"purple pansies." The apron was lavender and yellow with an array of pansies covering the bodice and a cranberry silk flower pinned to the top corner.

Logan held Zane's unwavering glare, not backing down, as he held out his hand. "I've gotta go with the pansies. That pink posy on the front is the clincher." He pulled it over his head, and Harper hustled forward to tie the strings around his waist.

He planted a hand on his hip and glowered at Zane. "Who's the badass now?"

Zane pressed his lips tighter together and shook his head, trying to hold back his grin. But he couldn't do it, and a hard laugh burst from his lips. He bent forward, holding his stomach as gales of laughter poured from him.

They all busted out, joining in the raucous laughter, giggling and hooting. Harper let out a snort of uncontrollable hilarity when Logan held out his arm and the two badass cowboys in their frilly aprons linked elbows and did a high-stepping circle followed by a do-si-do. Then Logan let go and looped his arms through Harper's and swirled her around as Zane followed suit with Bryn.

The little dog yipped and tried to jump on Bryn and Zane as if it wanted in on the dance, and Bryn let go of Zane and lifted the dog into her arms.

Zane shrugged. "Damn, you know you're a terrible dancer when your partner replaces you with a three-legged dog."

"This dog might not have four legs, but he's got soul," Bryn teased as she swirled around with the dog.

Logan chuckled and patted Zane sympathetically on the shoulder.

Harper doubled over, holding her stomach as she tried to catch her breath. This was a new feeling for her—this rowdy laughter and camaraderie with a group of friends. But she was having fun. Heck, it was so fun just to feel like she had friends. And she couldn't remember the last time her stomach had hurt this much from laughing. It was good. This was good.

Bryn put the dog down and headed to the sink to wash her hands. "Enough with the dance party. We need to get to work."

"Yes, ma'am," Logan said. "Just tell us what to do."

Harper chose the apron with the dancing chickens and pulled it over her head as the waitress laid out an assembly line of instructions. Bryn and Harper would be in charge of mixing the dough while Zane and Logan greased and floured the pans. Then the men would roll out the crusts while the women put together the filling. They made a plan to do five at a time, starting with the apple, then moving on to the cherry and peach.

"What are you going to do with all these pies?" Zane asked as he picked up a stick of butter.

"Sell them," Bryn said. "I spent weeks this summer and fall collecting and canning this fruit from the trees on our property. I sold pies last year at the church's Christmas bazaar and made just enough to cover the yearly taxes due for this farmhouse. That was my plan for this year too."

"Why don't I just buy the pies that the goat ate, and you can tell the church you sold out?" Zane reached for his wallet.

The other three stopped what they were doing to look at the cowboy.

Bryn blinked, her voice soft as she asked, "You would do that? Buy all fifteen pies?"

Zane shrugged, a scowl forming on his lips as a pink tinge colored his cheeks. "Yeah, why not? If it helps you out. And saves you the stress of having to remake them all."

She swallowed. "Thank you. That's really nice. And unexpected. But I can't take your money."

His scowl deepened. "What's wrong with my money?"

"Nothing. It's not that. It's just that most of the pies were preordered, so people have already paid for them and are expecting to pick them up tonight."

The tension in his shoulders eased. "Gotcha. Well, we'd better get to work then. But you can put my name on one if you have any left at the end of the night. I'll take it home to Birch. My dad will lose his mind over a home-baked pie."

The group spent the next three hours mixing, measuring, rolling, and baking. They finished with thirty minutes to spare. Standing in the kitchen, they gazed at the rows of gorgeous pies packed neatly in shallow tubs. Bryn had done lattice tops on most of them, but had used cookie cutters on the extra crust and added small touches like stars and Christmas trees to the tops before they were baked. The pies looked like festive works of art.

Zane offered to drop Logan and Harper at River's Gulch, then come back and drive Bryn and the pies into the church and help her get set up.

"That would be so great," Bryn said. "But you've already done so much."

He shook his head. "I haven't done anything. I'm glad to do it. You get cleaned up. I'll be back for you in ten minutes, and we'll load the truck."

"Just keep the dang goat out of the house until he gets back," Logan instructed as he leaned down to give Bryn a hug.

The waitress laughed, then let go of Logan and pulled Harper into a hug. "Thanks so much. You all saved me today."

Harper was covered in flour, and her skin was sticky with sugar and fruit filling, but her insides were warm with joy. It felt so good to be considered a help instead of a burden. "It was nothing. I had fun." They said their goodbyes, and she and Logan followed Zane out to the truck.

Harper had said it was nothing to help Bryn. But that wasn't true. It wasn't nothing. It was everything.

Logan followed Harper into the house. The faint scent of cinnamon hung in the air, and the kittens mewled and tumbled out to greet them as they hung up their coats.

He picked one up and cuddled it to his chest. "Darned if I'm not getting used to having these furry little things around the house." They weren't the only things he was getting used to having around the house, he thought as he watched Harper stroll into the kitchen and pour some cream into a dish for the kittens.

She'd told him earlier that morning that they'd only gotten carried away in the storm and that what happened the night before couldn't happen again. But her opposition didn't quite match the expression in her eyes.

He'd *never* said it was a mistake, and he *wanted* it to happen again. And again. He wanted her. He knew it didn't make sense, knew she was going to leave—hell, she'd reminded him of that fact that very morning—but at this moment, gazing at her generous curves as she moved through his kitchen, he didn't care about that.

He didn't care about anything except getting his hands on her and that luscious body beneath him. He'd think about her leaving later. Or maybe he wouldn't think about it at all. Denial wasn't just a river in Egypt. It was also flowing through him right now.

Harper turned to him, her smile easy, and his heart flipped over in his chest.

"Are you hungry?" she asked. "Do you want something to eat?"

"Yeah, I am hungry, but not for something to eat." He eased up behind her and slid his hands around her waist. "I'm hungry for you." Her hair was still pulled up, and he bent to brush his lips against the side of her ear. "I thought I had a handle on this, but I can't seem to get enough of you."

She didn't answer, but he saw her pulse quicken in her throat. He pressed his lips to the spot, then laid a trail of kisses down the smooth slope of her neck, savoring the taste of her skin.

Her breath seemed to cease completely.

She turned in his arms and pressed her forehead to his. "I thought we agreed this couldn't happen again," she whispered.

"I never agreed to that. I *want* this to happen." He grazed her lips with a soft kiss. "Again. And again." He pulled back and looked into her eyes. "But if you don't want this…" He held her gaze as his hand slid down her side, over her hip, then slipped between her legs. "Tell me to stop."

She inhaled a sharp intake of breath, but didn't say anything. Her eyes stayed locked on his as he slowly moved his hand, stroking and massaging. Sucking her bottom lip under her teeth, she pressed into him, a soft moan escaping her as she rocked against his palm.

"Tell me to stop, Harper. You have to stop it, because Lord help me, I can't do it on my own. I can't stop thinking about you, about last night. But not just last night. About every moment I've spent with you. You make me laugh. You challenge me. And you make me want to be a better version of myself to live up to the way you look at me."

Her breath came out in a harsh gasp. "I'm nothing. You deserve more than someone like me."

"I don't *deserve* you. But I want you. With every part of my soul."

His hand was still between her legs. He'd stopped moving, but he held her cupped in his palm. "Tell me now if you don't want me, Harper. Tell me to stop."

CHAPTER 22

"I CAN'T, DAMN YOU. I DON'T WANT YOU TO STOP." HARPER buried her face in Logan's neck and arched her chest against him. "Don't ever stop," she said breathlessly into his skin as she writhed against his hand, then moaned as he resumed stroking her.

He'd never been so captivated by another woman's pleasure, but once she said yes, she held nothing back.

She took his breath away. He was a slave to the sensations moving through her, and he couldn't get enough. He wanted to please her, to hear her moan against his neck, to feel her fingers tighten against his back.

He lifted her onto the counter and pushed her shirt up and pulled her bra down, freeing her full breasts and cupping one in his palm. He rubbed his thumb across one tightened nipple, and heat surged through him at the tiny moan his touch elicited. Dipping his head, he circled the same nipple with his tongue, drawing out the anticipation, knowing his breath was warm against her sensitive skin.

From the corner of his eye, he could see her hands. Her knuckles were white from clutching the counter, and she clenched the fingers of one hand into her palm as he slowly drew the nub of her nipple between his lips, alternately licking and sucking. Her breath caught as he scraped the sensitive tip with his teeth before moving to the other breast and showing it the same attention.

He stopped, pulled back, skimming a stare over her lush

curves. He wanted to see her. He locked his gaze with those gorgeous green eyes. "You are so beautiful. I have to stop just to look at you."

She looked so damn sexy with her hair messy from his hands and her shirt pushed up, exposing her breasts. He wanted to strip the rest of the clothes from her body, but he was enjoying this view way too much. He planned to remember this moment, to memorize every inch of her skin, to capture the picture of her like this in his mind's eye so he could remember it forever.

He loved having her only half-undressed, knowing that he'd been thinking about what was under her clothes all day—hell, all week—and now he got to slowly peel them away, baring one section at a time.

She offered him a slow, seductive grin, almost as if she could read his mind. Then she gripped the hem of her shirt, pulled it over her head, and dropped it to the floor.

He reached down and flicked free the button of her jeans and slowly eased the zipper down. He felt the quiver of pleasure ripple through her as his thumb skimmed over the top edge of her lace panties, and then he slid his hand inside.

Her fingers clutched his shoulders as she pushed against his hand, her body pleading for more. He gave in to her, demand coursing through him as the tempo of his stroking increased.

He kissed her—had to—had to capture that gorgeous mouth. She kissed him back, so deeply she stole the air from his lungs. Greedily, he swallowed her blissful moans and soft whimpers of pleasure as she surrendered to the tremor that rose, then quaked through her.

A growl ripped from his throat as she first clung to him,

then dropped her head back and drew a ragged breath. He wanted to be gentle, but passion overwhelmed him and he pulled her legs around him, twining them around his waist as he lifted her off the counter and carried her to his bed.

———————

Hours later, Harper woke, her body sated and still sleepy as she snuggled naked against Logan's chest. Her legs were tangled with his, and she felt his deep inhale of breath as he stirred and ran his hand in a slow caress up her back.

"Dang, I really fell asleep," he said, his voice groggy as he dragged his hand through his hair.

"I must have worn you out," she teased.

She heard his soft laugh. "Not hardly." He rolled over and bent to kiss her, but his eye caught something over her shoulder. "Shit! Is that what time it is?" He scrambled out of bed and searched the floor for his pants.

Harper raised her head to peer blearily at the clock. "I'm going to guess the clock is keeping accurate time, yes."

"I'm supposed to be at hockey practice in fifteen minutes."

"Oh shoot. I didn't know you had to be somewhere. Can't you skip it? Just this once?" She admired the view of his rippling abs as he pulled a clean T-shirt over his head. "Can't you play hooky tonight instead of hockey?" She grinned at her own joke.

"No, I can't. Not that I don't want to." He leaned down and pressed a kiss to her lips. "But I can't. I told Colt I'd be there." His eyes widened, and he smacked a hand to his forehead. "Shit."

"You said that already." She sat up in bed, dragging the sheets with her as she leaned against the headboard.

"No. This time it's serious. I'm in charge of the... Shit, shit, shit." He kicked the blanket that had fallen off the bed across the floor. "Where the hell are my pants?"

"What? You're in charge of the shit, shit, shit? Slow down and tell me what's wrong. Maybe I can help."

He stopped and let out his breath. "I'm in charge of bringing two dozen cupcakes to practice tonight."

"Oh, that's easy. I actually *can* help with that."

"You can?"

"Sure. There's a cake mix and a container of white frosting in the pantry. I can make them and bring them down to the ice arena."

He sank onto the edge of the bed. "You'd do that? For me?"

"Yes, of course. Well, for you. And the kids. Is chocolate okay?"

"Chocolate is awesome. And we wouldn't need them until after practice, which gives you at least an hour and a half."

"Easy. I'll have them there by seven."

He kissed her again. "Dang, but I do like you, Harper Evans."

She grinned as he bounced off the bed and grabbed a pair of clean socks from his drawer. "I like you too. And Logan..."

"Yeah?"

"Your pants are on the floor in the living room by the sofa."

He offered her a devilish grin as he must have just remembered shucking the pants in their feverish rush to the bedroom. "Yes, they are." He took two strides back to her and dove his hand into her hair as he leaned down to ravage her mouth. A low growl sounded in the back of his throat as he dragged himself away. "To be continued…" he said, racing out the door and down the hallway.

"See you at seven." She could hear him shimmying into his jeans and the two soft whooshes of his feet sliding into his boots.

"Save some of the frosting," he called.

"Already planning on it," she called back, an impish grin covering her face as she leaned back against the headboard and listened to the front door close behind him.

It took her twenty minutes to get dressed, mix the batter, and put the cupcakes in the oven. She set the timer, then dropped to the floor to play with the kittens. Tinkerbell got away from her and raced into Logan's office.

"Get back here, you little sneak," Harper called as she followed the kitten into the den. It had found a paper clip on the floor and was batting it around with its paw. That could hurt if someone stepped on it just right in their bare feet. Harper picked up the paper clip and tossed it onto a stack of papers on the desk.

The top page caught her eye. It was Logan's notes on the upcoming sale of the cattle. The printout of the market report stuck up from behind his notes.

As much as she tried to stay away from any kind of monetary equation, the lure of a good math problem was too much for her. Besides, it wouldn't hurt to just take a quick look at his calculations. He had said that he'd hoped he'd made a mistake.

Easing onto the edge of the desk chair, she pulled the

top page toward her and studied his figures. It took her a few minutes to familiarize herself with how the reports worked and to follow his train of thought in his notes, but she got the idea that cattle were sold by the pound and that Logan had about three hundred head on his ranch.

Grabbing a fresh sheet of paper, she started from scratch, trying to duplicate his thought process, yet still decipher where he might have made a mistake.

Her heart leapt when she saw it. It was so simple, yet changed so much. He'd transposed two numbers, changing the price per pound from a dollar fifty-four to a dollar forty-five. It was such a tiny mistake, only nine cents difference. But nine cents difference in a seven-hundred-pound cow equaled sixty-three dollars a head, and when she multiplied that by three hundred head of cattle, it came out to nineteen thousand dollars!

This was Logan's error. It was perfectly clear to her. But his brain could have twisted the numbers again and again, making the error impossible for him to find. If he wasn't so stubborn and embarrassed about his learning disability, he could have asked his sister, or her, to look over his figures or talked it through out loud, and they could found the error and saved him the worry and anguish he'd been going through.

She had to tell him. This would make his night. She pulled out her phone and scrolled to his number. He was still in practice, and she was sure he wouldn't answer, but she could leave a message and he'd get it as soon as he got off the ice.

She could barely contain her excitement as she waited for the beep. "Logan, hi, I know you're still in practice,

WISH UPON A COWBOY

but I couldn't wait to tell you that I found the error you've been looking for with the cattle. And you're not really out twenty thousand dollars. I know I shouldn't have been in your office, but I followed the kitten in here and saw your calculations on your desk, and don't be mad, but I just took a quick peek to see if I could spot the issue. And I found it! It was in the price per pound. You switched two numbers around. The beef price is really a dollar fifty-four per pound, not a dollar forty-five like you'd written. That nine cents difference equals almost twenty thousand dollars. I'll show you when we get home, but I had to call and leave you this message. I'm so, so happy for you. Okay, can't wait to see you. We'll celebrate with the leftover frosting. Bye."

She snapped her phone shut, a grin splitting her face. He was going to be thrilled. And she had been the one to figure it out. Her math skills had done something good. They'd helped someone instead of being responsible for swindling them out of their profit.

The timer sounded, and she practically danced her way to the kitchen to check the cupcakes. She took them from the oven and set them on a wire rack for five minutes, then stuck them in the fridge for another five so they'd be cool enough to frost.

She mixed the carton of white frosting with half a container of whipped topping, then scooped the mixture into a Ziploc bag. Cutting the corner off the bag, she piped the whipped frosting onto the chocolate cupcakes, then stuck a mini Oreo in the center of each to resemble a hockey puck. It was the best she could do in the limited amount of time.

After giving the frosting another five minutes to set, she packed the cupcakes into a covered nine-by-thirteen pan and snapped on the lid. She glanced up at the clock and saw she had fifteen minutes to get the cupcakes to practice. Perfect.

Checking her reflection in the mirror by the door, Harper smoothed her hair and wiped the stray mascara smudges from under her eyes. It had been quite a day, but she didn't look half bad. Her hair was clean and in surprisingly good shape for being in a ponytail half the day and smooshed on the pillow when she'd fallen asleep with Logan. Running around the kitchen had put a little color in her cheeks—at least that's what she was contributing the color too. It could also be from a raucous afternoon in bed and the excitement of sharing some great news with a guy she couldn't wait to see again.

That thought should have scared the hell out of her. But tonight, she felt invincible, as though things were actually going her way for once. Besides all the great stuff going on with Logan, she had a job she enjoyed and a roof over her head—a temporary one, but it was a home. And she had a place for her son to sleep.

As she pulled on her coat, she made the decision that she was going to tell Logan about Floyd *tonight*. No more secrets. She'd tell him about her son and Michael, and how she'd tried to save her home and got sucked into the scam with her mom and ended up in jail. She wasn't a victim; she didn't want him feeling sorry for her. She would take responsibility for her part of the embezzlement charges, own up to what she'd done. But Logan had made mistakes too. And she knew in her heart he'd forgive her. He had to.

This was her night. She could feel it. After falling so far off the rails for so many months, her life felt like it was finally back on track. She felt happy, and she dared to hope for the first time in a long time.

She was going over to Judith's after she dropped off the cupcakes. This time she wasn't taking no for an answer. She wanted to see her boy. And she wasn't going to let anyone stand in her way.

She picked up the red scarf. A few days ago, she'd thought she didn't need any more red in her life, but maybe it was exactly what she did need. Not any more danger—she'd had enough of that in that last few months—but maybe a little more risk, a little more daring. Maybe the answer wasn't to calmly play along with Judith, but instead to boldly stare her down and tell her she was ready to take back her son.

She wrapped the scarf around her neck, picked up the cupcakes, and pushed back her shoulders. She was armed with a full heart and a pan of perfectly frosted cupcakes.

I got this. Bring it on, world.

Harper's bravado faltered as she approached the doors of the ice arena. She knew small towns were a hotbed for rumors and speculation. There were probably already reports of a strange woman working at Rivers Gulch. She'd need to play it cool with Logan, let him take the lead on how he wanted to act in public. He'd been fun and flirty with her all afternoon, but that was just in front of Bryn and Zane, and they were friends.

This was different. This was the community.

So she'd be cool. She could do that. She shook out the tension in her shoulders and pushed through the doors.

The arena was chilly and filled with the sounds of kids laughing and the sharp scrapes of skates on the ice. Her gaze traveled around the room, over the faces of parents and the excited heads of the kids on the team as she searched for Logan.

But her heart stopped when her gaze landed on a familiar face—a face she knew better than her own.

Floyd.

CHAPTER 23

HARPER'S SON WAS STANDING TWENTY FEET IN FRONT of her. All she had to do was call his name, walk toward him, and sweep him into her arms. But her throat had closed up, and her feet were frozen to the floor. She couldn't move.

What if he didn't want to see her? What if he was angry with her for abandoning him? She'd thought her heart had broken when they'd taken him away from her the night she was arrested, but if he didn't want to see her now, it would shatter. That would break her.

She thought she had it all together—like everything was going so well—but now the curtain had been lifted, and she could see she didn't have anything together. Yeah, she had a job and a place to live, but her job was as a temporary housekeeper, and she lived in a bunkhouse, a place normally inhabited by sweaty cowboys.

Floyd looked good. His hair had recently been trimmed, and he wore new clothes she'd never seen. He had on a nice ski jacket and expensive tennis shoes, brands she could never afford, and he held a hockey stick and was laughing with two other boys on the team. *On the team?* She just realized Floyd was here because he was on a hockey team. He was playing hockey. Just as Michael had always dreamed he would.

Emotion burned her throat, and tears pricked her eyes. Harper pressed her lips together to keep from sobbing.

What was wrong with her? She'd dreamed of this day—

had spent the last two months wishing and praying for this day to come—and now she couldn't move.

"Floyd?" Her voice was hoarse as she croaked out his name. She said it again as she took a tentative step toward him. "Floyd?"

There was no way he could have heard her. But somehow, some way, some instinct must have had him turning his head, and his eyes widened as his face lit with joy. "Mom!"

Joy. He was glad to see her.

"Floyd," she said again as relief flooded through her. Her knees gave way, and she sank to the floor as her son ran toward her. A quiver ran through her whole body, and her hands were shaking so badly, the cupcakes slipped from them. The lid popped off, and two of the cakes tumbled out as the pan skidded across the floor. Her heart thrummed against her chest as she opened her arms.

Floyd fell into her lap, crashing into her body and almost knocking her over as he threw his arms around her neck. "Mom. Mom. Mom. You're finally here."

Tears spilled down her cheeks, and she sobbed into his precious, sweet neck. He smelled like sweaty boy and some foreign shampoo, but underneath that, he smelled like Floyd, like her child. "I'm here, Baby. Mama's here."

She pulled his head back and kissed his face, one side, then the other. His cheeks were wet and salty. He was crying too. "Let me look at you," she said, her voice trembling as she took in every one of his features.

He raised his hands to her cheeks, holding her face as well, just the way he'd done since he was a toddler. A grin split his face, and she noticed the gap on the side and the new tooth pushing through. "You lost a tooth."

He nodded as he lifted his lip to give her a better view. "It was already loose, but it got knocked out by another kid's stick at hockey practice. It bled and everything. But the tooth fairy gave me five dollars for it, so she must have felt bad about the blood."

"Five dollars?" Harper's heart swelled, taking up all the space in her chest, and she feared her body might split apart, not able to hold all the love she felt for this priceless child.

"Yeah, and I wasn't expecting her to come at all 'cause last time I lost a tooth we were in Kansas, and I wasn't sure if she would be able to find me in Colorado. But she did." The smile on his face fell, replaced by a frown. "How come the tooth fairy could find me here, but you couldn't? I've been waiting for you to come and get me."

Her heart, which seconds ago had been full to bursting, shattered into tiny shards of glass. "I'm sorry, Baby. I got here as soon as I could."

His small voice trembled, and tears filled his beautiful blue eyes—Michael's eyes. "I missed you so much, Mom. I prayed for you every night. But you never called me or anything. Didn't you miss me?"

"I missed you with every ounce of my soul. I missed you so much sometimes I thought my heart would stop beating, it hurt so much."

"Then why didn't you come get me? Why didn't you even try to talk to me?"

"Harper?" A strangled voice spoke her name, and her head jerked up to see Logan staring down at her, a pained expression clouding his face.

She'd thought it had already splintered into a million

slivers, but seeing that hurt and the look of anguish in Logan's eyes had her heart crumbling to dust.

But she couldn't deal with Logan right now, or the few other boys and parents from the team standing around them, including Judith, who stood at Logan's elbow and glared down at her. Not with Floyd in her lap asking why she hadn't tried to reach him, when she knew that she'd tried to call every single day.

Judith had been the one who hadn't let her talk to him, who'd convinced her that he was busy or he was at school or that her call would only upset him. Judith was the one who had kept them from speaking. And now that woman stood above her, her lips pinched in an expression that combined anger with fear that Harper had finally broken through her barricades and found her son.

Harper held Floyd to her, wanting to tell him she'd tried, that she'd called him every day, but that look of fear on Judith's face kept her from opening her mouth. Did she really want to taint this relationship her son had with his grandma? He'd already lost so much. Could she really take this away from him too?

Judith might have been a cow to her, but she had been good to Floyd. She'd taken him in on a moment's notice and had given him everything. It was obvious Floyd was doing well.

She kissed the top of her son's head, then took his face in her hands and tried to convey everything she felt without knowing exactly how to express it. "I wanted to. I wanted to call you every day, but it wasn't possible."

"Because they don't let you have phones in jail?" he asked. A sharp gasp sounded from one of the bystanders standing around them, but Harper didn't look up to see who it was.

If Logan didn't seem hurt and confused enough that she had a kid, his head had to be spinning now that he'd just learned an ex-con had been frying him bacon and scrambling his eggs.

"I know it's hard to understand," Harper continued. "But I left Kansas as soon as I got out and had enough money to buy a bus ticket to get here. I've been doing everything I can to make it so that we can be together."

"All right, that's enough," Judith said, stepping forward and reaching for Floyd. Her voice was probably shriller than she'd meant it to be, and her eyes had a bit of a wild cornered animal look to them. "It's getting late, and we need to get home. Tell your mother good night, Floyd."

His arms gripped her neck. "No. I don't want to go."

"You don't have to," Harper told him.

"Yes, he does. This isn't the time or the place to do this." Judith's voice was firm, and she clamped a hand on Floyd's shoulder. "And you don't want to make promises you can't keep."

"No," Floyd cried, clutching his mother.

"Judith, can't we talk about this?" Harper said, trying not to turn this into any more of a scene than it already was. She could hear the desperation in her voice, but now that she had her boy in her arms, she didn't want to let him go.

Maybe she didn't have to. Maybe she could just take him and run. It wasn't kidnapping if she was the mother. Except that she didn't technically have a vehicle—unless she stole Logan's old truck—so they really would have to run. And she hated running, so they wouldn't make it very far.

Judith aimed her next words at the group of onlookers. "Don't you people have homes to get to? There's nothing to see here." Most of them took the hint, and their kids, and turned to leave as Judith spun back to her grandson. "Come on now, Floyd. You're making a scene. It's time to go." Her tone was stern, commanding, and the boy slid out of Harper's lap and took his grandmother's hand.

"No, wait." Harper tried to reach for her son, but her hands missed his coat, and she fell forward, her hands striking the concrete floor of the arena. Frosting from the spilled cupcakes splattered across the floor, grazing the side of her hand as she tried to scramble to her feet.

Pain swirled through her, from her bruised hands and her battered heart, and she couldn't seem to get her feet under her. Stumbling, she pitched forward, falling against Judith and taking them both down in a heap.

"Help!" Judith screamed. "This woman is attacking me."

"I'm not attacking you. I tripped," Harper explained, trying to untangle herself from the other woman.

"Get off me," shrieked Judith, flailing her arms.

"Harper, get off the woman." Logan's voice instructed from behind her.

"Is there a problem here?" another deep male voice said from behind her as a hand gripped her arm.

"No, we're fine," Harper said, jerking her arm away and landing her elbow right in the chest of whoever had grabbed her.

She heard an *oof*, then the hand seized her again, this time with more force as its owner hauled her to her feet. She tried to pull away and turned to see the man holding her was a cop.

"Why don't you come with me, ma'am?" he asked, but it wasn't meant as a question.

"Mike, thank God," Judith said, collapsing on the floor with a melodramatic flare. "Arrest this woman. She assaulted me. And she's a felon. She's barely out of prison."

"It wasn't prison," Harper said, trying to explain. "It was just county, and I wasn't assaulting her. It was an accident. I tripped."

"She didn't trip. She purposely tried to harm me so she could kidnap this boy."

"That boy is my son," Harper cried, but the scowl on the officer's face told her he was taking the word of the local pillar of the community over some stranger in town with a criminal record who he'd just pulled off said pillar.

The cop, whose name tag read Officer Michael Russo, had a firm grip on Harper's arm, while another one of the parents helped Judith to her feet. "Are you okay there, Mrs. Benning? You hurt?"

Judith cradled her arm. "I think she broke my arm. I heard a crack. You've got to arrest her."

"Are you saying you want to press charges?" Mike asked.

"Yes, get her out of here."

"Mom?" Floyd spoke for the first time. He'd been huddled next to Judith, but now he rushed forward and threw his arms around Harper's waist. "Don't go, Mom."

"We're gonna need to go down to the station and get this straightened out."

"Straightened out? I didn't do anything. I tripped," Harper stammered, attempting to explain to the cop while also trying to soothe her son.

"This woman says you attacked her. And I could make

a case that you assaulted me." He leaned forward and said quietly into her ear, "You don't really want to make me cuff you in front of all these people, and your son, do you?"

The last thing Harper wanted to do was traumatize Floyd more by having him see her taken away in handcuffs. Again.

"Fine, I'll go." She leaned down and stroked her son's head. "Floyd, honey, it's okay. I need to go with this nice policeman, but I will be back."

"When?"

"I don't know, but soon." She didn't know how long they could hold her, and she didn't want to make another promise she couldn't keep. "It won't be like last time."

"No, Mom, please. Don't go." Floyd clung to her waist, breaking another piece off her already shattered heart.

"I have to go, honey. I'm sorry." Harper choked out the words, emotion burning her throat.

Floyd pulled back, his face changing from hurt to anger. "Fine. Go then," he yelled, his voice reminding her of the angry tantrums he'd thrown after his father had died. "I don't want you here anyway." He turned and flung himself into Judith's waiting arms.

"Come on, Floyd. It will be all right," Judith said, lifting her nose in a smug manner as she aimed a glare at Harper. "Grandma's here."

Harper couldn't bear another second. "Get me out of here," she instructed the cop, who led her through the front door to his patrol car. They'd almost made it to the vehicle when they were stopped by a familiar voice.

"Wait, Mike. Can I have a minute?"

Harper dropped her chin to her chest, unable to face Logan too.

"Sure," the officer said. He'd just opened the back door. "You're not gonna run off, are you?" he asked her.

She shook her head. "Where am I gonna go? I just left my whole world in that ice arena."

He dropped her arm and stepped back a few feet so she could talk to Logan. Except that she didn't want to talk to him. She didn't even want to see him. She couldn't take the look of disappointment and torment on his face.

"What the hell is going on, Harper?" he asked, his tone low, his expression a cross between anger, shock, and dismay. "You have a son?"

"I wanted to tell you. But I couldn't."

"Why couldn't you tell me about Floyd? He's a great kid." He scrubbed his hand across his jaw. "I can't believe you're the one who left him."

He used her son's name like he knew him. "How do you know Floyd?"

"He's on my hockey team. I've been his coach for months. I've talked to the kid. And to his grandmother. I know how heartbroken he's been over his mother abandoning him. Do you have any idea what you've put this kid through?"

She jerked her head back. "How dare you say that to me? You don't know me."

"You know, you're right. I don't." Logan let out a heavy sigh as if the act of breathing itself was a burden. "I thought I did. But I can't make sense of how the woman I thought I knew could abandon her child."

"I meant you don't know the whole situation. And I didn't *abandon* my child." Although she had, but not willingly. "I was arrested."

He shook his head. "You still left. You don't know what

that does to a kid." He slammed his fist against his chest as his voice and his anger rose. "I know what that's like. I know how it feels to have your mom walk out on you. To not matter enough to have her stay and fight for you."

"Screw you, Logan. Whatever you think you know, whatever Judith told you, isn't even close to the truth. That woman skews everything to suit her needs."

"Maybe I don't know the truth," he spat back, "but that's only because you never told me. And now you made me look like an idiot in front of half the town."

"Oh, poor you. I just left my son bawling in there and have to go back to the one place I swore I would never return to."

"I can't believe you were in prison."

"It wasn't prison. It was county lockup, and I was only there a few months. It was for embezzlement charges. It's not like I murdered anyone. And I've been trying to make it better, trying to get my son back. That's why I told you I needed this job. And why I was so grateful for the place to live."

He narrowed his eyes and blew out another breath. "Geezus. You're an ex-con, and you've practically been living in my house." His voice lowered as he shook his head in disbelief. "In my bed."

His words stung as if he'd slapped her across the face. He was acting and saying everything exactly as she'd feared he would when he found out. "Not anymore. I'll find someplace else to stay."

She had nowhere else to stay, not even a car to sleep in. It was probably for the best she was going to jail tonight. A holding cell would at least have a bed. And she wasn't sure she even deserved that. She'd tried so hard to make everything right, to deserve to have Floyd back with her, but she'd screwed everything up, again. And now she'd hurt the two people she cared most about in the world.

She let out a trembling breath. "I'm sorry."

"That's not good enough."

She knew that. She knew it wasn't good enough for Logan, and it wasn't good enough for Floyd. He'd said her apology wasn't good enough—but all she'd heard was that *she* wasn't good enough.

"I know," she whispered, then turned away and sank into the back seat of the patrol car. She slammed the door shut and buried her head against her knees.

My son deserves better than me. And so do you.

CHAPTER 24

THE NEXT MORNING, LOGAN SHOVED A PIECE OF TOAST in his mouth. He'd had a restless night, tossing and turning because he couldn't get thoughts of Harper out of his mind. One minute, he was ready to forgive her and talking himself into getting out of bed and heading down to the police station to get her, and the next, he was mad as sin and didn't care if he ever saw her again.

In the light of day, after a rough night's sleep, he was no closer to knowing what to do. His heart and head were locked in a vicious battle, and his stomach was now jumping in the fray because it was sorely missing Harper's home-cooked breakfast.

But he couldn't forgive her and take her back just because she made a good breakfast. She'd deceived him. And worse than that, she'd turned out to be just the kind of woman he swore he'd never get taken in by again. His biggest fear was being left by a woman who claimed she loved him, and now he'd fallen for one who'd abandoned her child. How could he count on her staying with him if she didn't even stay for her own son?

Logan swore as the trio of kittens tumbled across his feet, another reminder of kids who'd been deserted by their mother. It wasn't the kittens' fault though. And now he felt like a shit for swearing at the baby cats. He poured some food into a saucer and set it on the floor.

He needed to get outside, do something constructive

with his hands, anything to get his mind off Harper. But the clock was ticking, and he knew he had a decision to make.

He'd known Mike a long time. The cop had called him an hour ago to tell him Judith had called in a favor with Judge Harding to try to get temporary custody of Floyd. Only in a small town could one woman get a judge to call a special hearing on the morning of Christmas Eve. Either there was more to the story of why Harper was in jail—hell, he didn't know *any* of the story—or if Harper were to be believed, Judith had embellished the story enough to get them in front of the judge.

Whatever the case might be, the hearing was set to convene that morning at nine, and Logan couldn't decide if he should go.

Should he try to help her out? Should he go and speak up for her?

But what the hell would he say? Did he even know Harper? He felt like he did. But how could he feel as if he knew her so well and not know one of the most important things in her life—that she was a mom?

The questions swirled through his mind as he walked outside. He'd been heading for the barn, but he found himself outside the bunkhouse door. The door was unlocked, so he let himself in and wandered around the small living space.

Grief squeezed his chest as he saw all the little touches of Harper around the rooms. She'd filled a mason jar with sprigs of evergreen and tied a red bow around the outside to create a centerpiece for the scarred wooden coffee table. An old picture of a mountain landscape had hung on the wall in the hallway, and she'd covered it in holiday wrapping paper so it looked like a present hanging on the wall.

Her bed in her room was neatly made, and her few shirts were folded in a tidy pile on the dresser. How could a woman who had so little have changed so much in his life? The scent of her hung in the room, and he had to get out of there. Backing out, he pulled the door shut behind him as if he could close off the memories of her as well.

The door to the second bedroom stood ajar, and he swallowed at the sudden burn of emotion that formed there as he stepped into the room. *When had she done all this?* he wondered as he gazed at the space-themed bedspread and the solar system mobile hanging from the ceiling. She'd hung a poster of a moon above the bed, and as he read the words printed on it, he knew what he had to do.

Regardless of what had transpired between them, Harper loved her kid—loved him to the moon and back, if the poster could be trusted. She'd done all of this, taken this crappy space that had previously been lived in by a drunken slob and turned it into a home. She had been trying. No wonder she'd been so excited to get an early paycheck. She must have used the money to decorate this room for Floyd.

And the kid would love it. He thought about Floyd's goofy smile and what a great kid he was to be around. That didn't happen by accident. That happened by being raised by a good and loving parent.

Logan checked his watch. He had time. But he needed to go now. He needed to at least show up. Even if he didn't say anything, maybe it would be enough that he was there.

His hurtful words from the night before replayed in his head. He'd told her that her apology wasn't enough, but he could see on her face that she thought he'd meant *she* wasn't enough.

And he knew that feeling. Had lived that scar of not feeling like he was enough—heck, he was still living it. He'd been feeling that emotion the last several days as he struggled with calling his dad to let him know he'd made an error that would cost the ranch dearly.

Maybe it was the fact he was distracted by thoughts of the mistake and rushing to get to the courthouse that he wasn't paying as much attention as he should, that he didn't notice Harper's door—the door he'd just closed—was now open until he walked into the living room.

He realized the shift in the air, smelled the faint scent of stale beer, and heard the soft footfalls behind him a second too late.

He turned just as the cast-iron skillet cold-cocked him in the side of the head.

He recognized the vindictive voice of his former ranch hand saying "Merry Christmas, asshole" as he sank to the floor and everything went black.

Harper smoothed her hair as she prepared to walk into the courtroom. Memories of her last court appearance played through her head. She'd had a court-appointed attorney who had skimmed over the notes of the case at the last minute and advised her to take the plea. It had all been over in less than ten minutes.

Was that what today would be like? Would she walk into this courtroom and walk out ten minutes later with nothing? At least she wouldn't be going back to jail. The cop, Mike Russo, had come in to talk to her the night before, and after hearing the whole story, he'd said he couldn't do much about Judith's claims, but he wouldn't be pursuing the assault charges against him he'd threatened. He'd even offered to help her find a bondsman to bail her out, but by that time it was after ten, and she had nowhere to go and no car to get her there if she did.

How pathetic her life had become that spending the night in jail—in a place she *swore* she'd never go back to—seemed preferable to being set free. Because for her, "free" was just another prison cell. She had no vehicle, no home, and thanks to her shopping spree to furnish Floyd's room, barely enough money to pay for a meal.

She probably could have called Bryn to come pick her up, but she didn't want to bother the woman who had already done so much for her. And she hated to think of herself as another one of the strays that the waitress took pity on.

Taking a deep breath, Harper steeled herself to enter the courtroom, knowing her side would be empty while Judith's side would be teeming with lifelong friends willing to go to bat for her sterling character. How could she compete against that? She'd just broken the heart of the only real friend she had in this town and chased him away.

She pushed through the door and spied four rows of people lined up behind her son's grandma. Judith was decked out in a black designer suit and sensible heels, and the same string of creamy pearls lay around her neck. With her perfectly coiffed and dyed dark hair, she looked like the impeccable image of a grandmother, which only made Harper more conscious of the day-old eye makeup smudging her face and the wrinkled jeans and shirt she'd slept in the night before.

She clutched her jacket and the scarf in her hands, the red color laughable now, since any inkling of that feeling of things going her way had vanished like a thief in the night. The only thing the scarf had done was provide a makeshift pillow for her head the night before.

As expected, her side of the courtroom was bare, and she fought to swallow the lump in her throat as she took a seat at the defendant's table. Had she really thought Logan would show up?

Of course he's not here, her conscience whispered. *Why would he be? You pushed him away. You lied to him. Why would he come to your rescue?*

Forget that. She didn't need him, or anyone, to come to her rescue. She might be in distress, but she wasn't a poor damsel, and she could dang sure rescue herself.

But what if she wasn't enough by herself? Logan's words came back to her from the night before, but she pushed them away. She had to be enough. For Floyd.

The bailiff announced the judge, and they went through the motions of standing and sitting as the Honorable Judge Arthur Harding settled himself on the bench and tapped his gavel.

The judge had a full head of silver hair but was probably still in his seventies. His eyes were sharp as he studied Harper. "Ms. Evans, I presume."

She nodded.

"I have to say I'm not too happy to be called in on Christmas Eve, but Mrs. Benning has assured me this is a matter of the utmost urgency, and I hate to see someone sitting in jail for Christmas."

He didn't seem like he'd hate it. His demeanor suggested

a bit of a Grinchy tone, but Harper still hoped he was fair, if a little on the grouchy side. She already knew he must have some kind of relationship with Judith. She'd said her husband played golf with the judge, so Harper wasn't holding out much hope he'd take her side against his golfing buddy's widow.

She wondered how much Judith had told him and how much he'd gotten from her file as he reminded her she'd just been released from jail for the embezzlement charges. As if she needed reminding.

"I don't appreciate you coming to his town and causing trouble. From what I understand, you are gainfully employed, but only in a temporary position, and your living arrangements are tenuous at best. Now, as this boy's mother, you do have rights, but it seems to me that Mrs. Benning has been doing a pretty good job with the boy, and he's settled and doing well in school. Even playing sports. Do you think it's right to take him away from all that? Do you think what you have to offer the boy is better than what Mrs. Benning has done?"

"Yes, I do. I'm his mother, and despite the events of the last few months, I'm a good mom. Yes, I made a mistake, and I know what I did was wrong. I was trying to save our house, and I trusted the wrong person. In my file you'll see my testimony that once I realized what was happening, I was going to go to the company and offer to make amends. I was just too late in my efforts, but I've paid for my mistakes."

She told the judge her side of what had happened with the embezzlement charges and shared a little of the screwed-up relationship with her own mother. "I know I messed up, but I don't ever want to be like my mom, and I'll never take a chance of losing my son again. He means everything to me. I'm not a bad person, Judge. I just did a bad thing.

"And I've changed. I know I spent last night sitting in a jail cell, again, the place I said I would never return to, but both times I've been to jail have been because I was trying to do what was right for my son. I know that Judith, Mrs. Benning, has been doing an amazing job taking care of Floyd, and I can't thank her enough. I appreciate everything she's done. We may not always get along, but I know she has to be a good person to have raised a man like Michael, Floyd's dad. And Michael was a great father. He loved our son, and we had a good life planned together, but then he was killed in an accident. Floyd is a great kid, but he's been through enough. He's already lost one parent. I don't want him to lose another."

She glanced over at Judith and was surprised to see her wiping the corner of her eye with a tissue. Had the kind words about her son gotten to her, or was this just part of the show for the judge?

"I hear what you're saying, Ms. Evans, but I'd like to hear it from someone else." The judge scanned the empty side of the courtroom. "Do you not have even one person, one friend or even an acquaintance, who can stand up for you?"

Harper hung her head. "No, sir. I don't. But I've only been in town a week or so. I haven't had a lot of time to make friends." She had though. She'd made one friend, a good one, but she'd wrecked that friendship and anything more it might have become when she'd hidden her past, and her son, from him.

She turned as the doors of the courtroom burst open, and Bryn and Zane rushed down the aisle.

"Wait, we're here, Arthur," Bryn said, sliding into the

bench behind Harper. "I mean, Judge Harding. We're here as character witnesses for Harper."

Zane sat beside her and solemnly nodded to the judge.

"And it's not just us. More are coming. We just found out about the proceedings, sir." Bryn winked and smiled at Harper.

More were coming? Who else knew her in this town? Besides those two? And Logan?

The doors swung open again, but it wasn't the tall cowboy who charged through them. It was Etta Perry, the woman Harper had helped at the grocery store, and she was followed by the young cashier who'd also been at the store that day. On their heels were Rachel and Josh, the mother and son who Harper had given her last five dollars to the first day she was in town.

Each one stood and told the judge how they'd met Harper, and even though they hadn't known her long, they knew what kind of person she was by the way she'd gone out of her way to help them.

The judge listened, and so did Judith. Harper could see her pinched expression soften as she heard their stories.

The judge looked to Judith after they had all had a chance to speak. "In light of these witnesses and what you've heard from Ms. Evans, are you sure you want to continue with these proceedings? It is Christmas, and I hate to see a family torn apart like this at the holidays. I can call for the boy to come in and talk to me, but I don't want to put him through any unnecessary trauma if I don't have to. What do you think, Mrs. Benning? Is there some way the two of you, his mother and his grandmother, can work together to come up with a solution?"

Maybe he wasn't so Grinchy after all.

Judith peered from Harper to the group of people rallying around her, then turned back to the judge. "I think so. I'd like Floyd to have both of us in his life. But there's still the matter of Harper's residence. How am I supposed to turn over my grandson to her if she doesn't even have a place to live? Where are they going to sleep? She doesn't even have a car." She pressed her hand to her chest, pink coloring her cheeks. "Not that I'm in any way suggesting they sleep in her car. I just meant that she has no way to even pick him up."

The judge studied Harper. "Is this true? Do you not have a place to live?"

No, she didn't have a place to live, not unless she wanted to take Floyd back to Kansas with her tonight. Which didn't seem likely, since, as Judith so helpfully pointed out, she also didn't have a mode of transportation. And now it didn't feel right to take him away from his grandma the night before Christmas. Not when Harper had just seen the first crack in the older woman's dragon-lady armor—the first inkling that gave her hope of them all having a relationship.

Before she could answer, a deep voice spoke from the back of the room. "She does have a place to live, Your Honor. She lives with me. Well, not *with* me. She has her own house, but it's on my ranch. She lives in the bunkhouse, which used to be a place for ranch hands to sleep, but now Harper has moved in and made it into a home. I've seen what she's done with it, and she's fixed up a bedroom real nice for Floyd."

She couldn't believe it. Logan was here. And sticking up for her. She hadn't even heard him come into the room. How long had he been there? And did he really mean it that she and Floyd could still use the bunkhouse?

"Is this true?" the judge asked again. "Do you live at the Rivers' ranch?"

She turned and looked at Logan—looked at all the people who had showed up to help her—and something inside her broke, some steely, hardened part of her that realized she couldn't do it all on her own. She had to trust other people, had to trust Logan. It was the only way she'd have a chance to get her son back.

And maybe it was okay to let other people in, to accept help. Even Logan. Especially Logan.

"Yes, it's true, Your Honor."

"Then it sounds like it's settled." He looked to Judith, who gave a small perceptible nod. "I'll leave the details up to you, but Ms. Evans does retain custody of her son, Floyd Michael Benning."

Harper pressed her hand to her mouth. She couldn't believe it. She started to sink into the chair, but instead was grabbed in a bear hug by Bryn, as she was surrounded by the people who had come to her defense.

"Thank you all so much. I can't tell you how much I appreciate the kind things you said about me."

"We meant them," Etta said. Romeo's small furry head popped out of the corner of her handbag and he gave a small yip, as if in agreement. "We all believe in you, dear."

"We heard you were in trouble, and we all wanted to help," Rachel said.

"But how did you hear? Who even knew I was here?"

Bryn nodded toward Logan who was still standing in the back of the room. "He called me and told me to rally the troops. He said you were in trouble and needed us."

Harper swallowed. He had called in the troops? For her?

After everything she'd done and all the things she'd said the night before? She excused herself from the group and made her way to where Logan leaned against the back wall of the courtroom.

As she got closer, she spied a purple knotted bruise on the side of his forehead. "Oh my gosh, what happened to you?"

He waved her concern away. His eyes were hard, with none of his normal teasing glints. "Nothing. A run-in with Ted and the flat end of a cast-iron skillet. I'm fine."

"Listen, Bryn told me what you did, how you called her. And I wanted to thank you."

"Don't. I didn't do it for you." His voice was hoarse and gruff, and his mouth was set in a tight line. "I did it for Floyd because that kid is too great to have to go through losing one of his parents again. He doesn't deserve to not have a chance to be with his mom."

She didn't know what to say, how to respond. But she didn't get a chance to.

"Don't let him down this time," Logan said, then turned and walked away.

CHAPTER 25

HARPER STARTED TO FOLLOW LOGAN, BUT STOPPED AS Judith cautiously approached her. "Are you ready to see Floyd?"

Yes. Yes. Yes. Her heart sang at the idea, but instead she looked down at her wrinkled appearance and shook her head. "I *am* ready, but I can't show up like this. I don't want him to see me this way. I slept in these clothes last night, and I'm pretty sure this stain on my shirt is from frosting, but I can't say for sure. I would really like to wash the stink of that jail cell out of my hair and change into fresh clothes." She looked around Judith's shoulder. "I can see if Bryn or Zane can give me a ride back to the ranch."

"There's no need. I can take you."

Harper jerked her head back. Who was this woman, and what had she done with Michael's mother? "Are you sure? I mean, thank you. I would really appreciate that."

The other woman gave a slight shrug and offered her a tentative smile. "I guess it's about time we got to know each other a little better. And after Logan's glowing report, I'd like to see this bunkhouse."

So they didn't turn into immediate besties, but Harper felt like they made a little progress as Judith drove her out to the ranch, and Harper showed her what she'd done in the bunkhouse.

The other woman seemed pleasantly surprised when they walked through the door. Harper had made some simple cinnamon-scented pine cones and left them in a bowl on the kitchen counter. Between the pine cones and the evergreen boughs she'd collected, they gave the living area a faint scent of Christmas. Judith complimented Harper's attempts at festive decor and acted genuinely delighted with the small bedroom she'd created for Floyd.

"He'll love this," Judith said, smoothing the star-covered pillow sham. "You've done a lovely job, Harper. Everything is so clean, and I can see you've gone out of your way to create little touches to make this place a home. I'm impressed."

Harper let out a breath. "Thank you. I've really tried."

"I can tell." Judith pulled a paperback from her purse. "Now I'll entertain myself while you get showered, then we can get back to Floyd. I'm sure he's anxious to see you."

Not half as anxious as she was to see him.

Thirty minutes later, Judith pulled into the driveway of her house. Harper had raced to take a shower, rub on some scented lotion, and dab on a smidgen of eye makeup. She'd taken less than four minutes to blow-dry her hair and throw on some fresh clothes.

She felt like a person again, and her heart clamored in her chest at the thought of how close she was to seeing Floyd. And not just seeing him this time, but actually spending time together.

On the way back from the ranch, Judith invited Harper to stay for lunch and suggested she take Floyd to the Christmas

Celebration this evening and then back to the bunkhouse for the night. They could be together for Christmas and make plans from there.

Judith turned off the car but reached to touch Harper's arm before she got out. "I want to make this work, Harper. I'm not ready to say goodbye to Floyd. He's become part of my life." She let out a soft breath. "In fact, he's given me back my life, and I don't want to lose him. I know you think I've been awful to you, and I probably have been, but Michael was my only child, and I was devastated when I lost him. I know it was an accident, but I didn't have anyone else to blame except you. I'm sorry for that. And for keeping Floyd from you. I didn't know you, and I was selfish. I wanted him to myself, and I was trying to do what was right for my son's son. He's the only part of Michael I have left, and I love him too."

Her words hit Harper square in the heart. She'd been so focused on her own grief at losing Michael that she probably hadn't tried to connect like she should have with his mother. Judith also had to have been devastated. "I'm sorry too. I should have reached out more after Michael died, made a better effort. I don't really know you either. But I'd like to change that."

"Me too."

It was a tentative treaty, but if they could work together, the end result would be good for all of them. Harper had been so close to her own grandmother that she wanted Floyd to have that as well. And it wasn't going to happen with her mom.

Her son deserved to have a family, which included both her and Michael's mother. If she were honest, Harper could also use a little family.

Judith opened the front door, and Harper spied Floyd at the kitchen table playing a board game with a cute elderly lady.

He looked up as the door opened, and his face lit with excitement as he scrambled out of his chair and ran to her. "Mom!"

Harper sank to her knees and pulled her son close, covering his head and cheeks with kisses. Her throat swelled so she couldn't say anything, could only hug her boy to her chest.

"Harper, this is Mrs. Ida May Phillips. She's my neighbor and was most likely Logan's Sunday school teacher at one point or another."

"I surely was." The white-haired woman pushed up from the table and came toward Harper. She had a hot-pink cast on her left hand but reached out to shake with her right. "I'm pleased to meet you. Floyd has told me so much about you."

"Thank you. I'm pleased to meet you too. And thanks so much for watching him this morning. I really appreciate it."

Ida May waved a hand away. "It was no trouble. Floyd's a good boy. You've done a good job raising him."

"Gosh, thank you. I appreciate that."

"Judith tells me you're currently without a car, and I happen to have one sitting in my garage that you're welcome to use."

"Oh no, I couldn't." Why in the world would this perfect stranger offer her the use of her vehicle?

"Sure you could. The car's just sitting there." She raised her casted arm. "I fell and can't drive for the next few weeks anyway. Someone might as well be using it. And it would please me to know I was helping you and Floyd."

Small towns were a funny thing. And the sense of community

Harper had seen in Creedence in the short time she'd been there was beyond belief. She'd spent so much time convincing herself she couldn't depend on anyone else that she didn't know how to handle this outpouring of support. First, the folks that showed up at court, then Judith softening, and now Logan's Sunday school teacher offering her a car to use. Maybe it wasn't so bad to let other people into their lives.

Harper let out her breath and let go of her pride. "Thank you. I would very much appreciate the loan of your car."

Ida May's face broke into a grin. "It's settled then. I'll get the keys from my purse."

"You'll stay for lunch, Ida May?" Judith asked. "I'm making spaghetti. It's Floyd's favorite."

"That sounds delicious. And I've never been one to turn down a good meal."

"You're staying too," Floyd said to Harper. "Right, Mom?"

"Yep, I'm staying. Then I'm taking you to the Christmas Celebration, and you're spending the night with me tonight. How does that sound?"

"Awesome." He threw his arms around her in another hug, but then his shoulders slumped and his excited expression fell. "Except I told Grandma I would go to the candlelight service with her tonight."

"Our church does a candlelight service every Christmas Eve," Judith explained.

"Well, why don't we all three go? Together?"

A smile curved Judith's lips, and she gave Harper a small nod. "I'd like that. And the Christmas Celebration is at our church, so I'll just meet you there and we can go into the sanctuary together."

"Sounds perfect," Harper said. "Now what can Floyd and I do to help with the spaghetti?"

Logan had been staring into the lights of the Christmas tree for the last twenty minutes. He didn't know why he'd turned them on in the first place. He sure didn't feel very Christmassy.

His thoughts were so jumbled over what to do about Harper that he hadn't given much thought to what he would do for the actual holiday. He couldn't get ahold of his dad, and Quinn was spending it with Rock's family this year. They were only going to be at the next ranch over, and his sister had invited him to join them, but right now all he wanted to do was crawl into a hole and lick his wounds. He didn't feel much like spreading Christmas cheer, more like having a Christmas beer.

A knock sounded at the door, and he looked up to see Bryn standing on the porch holding a covered dish. He waved her in.

"Hey there," she said, pushing through the door and crossing to the kitchen to set the dish on the counter. "We had an extra shepherd's pie at the diner, so I brought it over for you. I wasn't sure if you'd have anything to eat now that..."

"Now that Harper's gone? You can say it. It's obvious she isn't here." He'd followed her into the kitchen and held up the coffeepot. "Pot's fresh—well, mostly. I was gonna fix a cup. Want one?"

"Sure." She waited for him to pour them each a cup, then sat back down with him on the sofa. "How are you? Really?"

He shrugged. "Terrible. If you want to know the truth."

"I wasn't expecting you to lie to me."

"No, that's more Harper's scene."

Bryn took a sip of her coffee. "Did she actually lie to you about having a son or the jail thing?"

"No, according to her, she just omitted the facts."

Bryn chuckled. "That sounds about right."

"Why wouldn't she just tell me?"

"Why do you think?"

"I don't know."

"Have you asked her? Have you even talked to her? Called her?"

"No. She called me. Last night, I guess. She left me a message."

"What did it say?"

He shrugged. "I don't know. I can't bring myself to listen to it. I can't decide if I want to hear her voice."

"Do you want me to listen to it? Or we could listen to it together?"

"Yeah, I guess." He pulled his phone from his pocket and tapped the screen to play the message on speaker.

Harper's excited voice filled the room. "Logan, hi, I know you're still in practice, but I couldn't wait to tell you that I found the error you've been looking for with the cattle. And you're not really out twenty thousand dollars. I know I shouldn't have been in your office, but I followed the kitten in here and saw your calculations on your desk, and don't be mad, but I just took a quick peek to see if I could spot the issue. And I found it! It was in the price per pound. You switched two numbers around, and the beef price is really a dollar fifty-four per pound, not a dollar forty-five like you'd written. That nine-cent difference equals almost twenty thousand dollars. I'll show you when we get home, but I had to call and leave you this message. I'm so, so happy for you. Okay, can't wait to see you. We'll celebrate with the leftover frosting. Bye."

Bryn raised an eyebrow and offered him a teasing grin. "I'll have to ask her later about the frosting."

But he wasn't paying attention. His brain was processing Harper's message. Jumping up, he ran into the office, shuffled through the papers on his desk, and brought the market report back into Bryn. He held it out to her. "What does that say the price of beef is?"

Bryn scanned the page. "A dollar fifty-four per pound."

"Holy crap. She's right. Harper's right." He shook his head, still in awe of the news. "She found the mistake. She really did it." He sank down onto the sofa. "Why would she do that? Why would she help me?"

"Because she cares about you, you big lug." Bryn whacked him in the leg with the paper.

"Did she say that?"

"No. Not out loud. But it's obvious by the way she looks at you. And with the way you two acted the other day when we were making pies, it was no secret you all like each other."

"Of course I like her. She's funny, she's smart, she's beautiful. And we get along great."

"So, what's the problem?"

"The problem is we have no future. It doesn't matter how much I like her; she's not sticking around. When it comes to me, women never do."

"That's a little maudlin."

He lifted one shoulder, then let it drop. "It's true. That's what the women in my life do. Any woman I've ever really cared about has left. Come on, Bryn. We've been friends since we were kids. You know my mom ran off, and then the first girl I thought I loved left me too. And now my sister has even gone and left me."

"Oh geez. You can't blame Quinn for getting married. And please don't tell me you fell in love with Kimberly Cox!"

"Not really. I was just a kid, but the result was the same. So, I guess I've always figured it was easier to push someone away than give them a chance to leave. And I already know Harper's going to leave. She told me right from the beginning. There's never been any question. She has a house, a home, in Kansas. She told me she was planning to go back as soon as she settled some family stuff here. And I guess that family stuff was Floyd. Which now is settled. So there's no use even thinking about it. She's going to leave. End of story."

"Have you *asked* her to stay?"

Her question and the realization of the answer to it hit him like a punch to the stomach. "No. I've never asked anyone to stay."

"Then how do you know what she's going to say? Come on, Lo. You have to cut this woman a little bit of a break. The reason she came to town was to fight for her kid. I'm sure she didn't plan on falling for you. That has to be pretty scary for her too. I mean, I'm just spitballing here, but didn't Floyd's dad die? Harper's got to have some issues over being left behind herself and losing someone she loved. And the girl comes with a *lot* of baggage. Maybe the reason she didn't tell you everything was because *she* was afraid she'd lose you. Maybe she has some of the same issues you do, and maybe she thought as soon as you found out about all her stuff, *you'd* be the one to leave."

"Me? Why would I leave? I'm not like my mom. I don't walk away from the people I love."

Bryn inhaled a sharp breath. "Wow. That was a big statement."

He took a deep breath. "Yeah, I guess it was."

"Are you in love with Harper?"

He slowly nodded his head. "I think so. If the ache in my heart and the nauseous feeling in my gut are any indication, then I guess I am."

"That's kind of big deal," Bryn said. "Logan, you're a great guy. You're worthy of being loved, but of course people will leave if you push them away. Now you have to give someone a chance to prove they'll stay."

He scrubbed a hand through his hair, trying to decide what to do. This woman had already stomped on his heart. Could he give her another chance to totally obliterate it? Bryn was right. He hadn't given Harper a chance to stay. He'd shut her down and walked away. He hadn't even fought for her. Fought for them. Hell, he'd spent more time trying to round up his cattle than he'd spent trying to save what he had with her.

Bryn narrowed her eyes. "I can see the wheels spinning. But it doesn't help to sit around here and think about it. What are you going to *do* about it?"

He clapped his hands on his knees and pushed up from the sofa. "I guess I'm going to go find her. And ask her to stay."

His quest was easier said than done. Thirty minutes later, Logan was still trying to find her.

He'd known Harper wasn't with Bryn, and he'd already checked the bunkhouse, but she wasn't there either. His best guess was that she was at Judith's, but no one had answered when he'd rung her doorbell. He couldn't drive around town and look for Harper's car because she didn't have one.

The judge had said she could take Floyd. Maybe she'd already packed him up, and they were already on a bus back to Kansas.

He didn't know where else to look. All he could do was head back to the ranch. He stopped at the one stoplight in town and leaned his head on the steering wheel, praying for a Christmas miracle. Not that he believed in miracles.

The light turned green and he sighed, discouragement filling him as he drove down the street, the Christmas star twinkling on the top of the church a hard reminder that he'd be alone in the morning.

His brow furrowed as he noticed the church parking lot full of cars. What was going on there?

The Christmas Celebration. He'd made a date to go to it with Harper. His heart lifted as he turned into the parking lot.

Maybe he believed in miracles after all.

CHAPTER 26

HARPER HELD FLOYD'S HAND AS HE LED HER FROM ONE booth to the next until they'd visited every station of the Christmas carnival. They'd laughed as they'd raced plastic penguins, tossed rings over reindeers' antlers, decorated a gingerbread house, and played pin the nose on the snowman. They'd each made a holiday craft and eaten popcorn balls and drunk cups of hot chocolate chock-full of marshmallows.

When they'd first arrived, she'd searched every face to see if Logan had remembered their "date" to come to the carnival together, but after an hour, she'd given up. It didn't matter. What mattered was she was here with her son, and they were having a great time.

Ignoring the ache in her heart at losing the first man she'd had any real feelings for since Michael, she focused on Floyd and let the sound of his laughter, a sound she'd dearly missed, fill her heart instead.

"Are you two having fun?" Judith asked, walking up to them as they stood in line for the cakewalk. They'd done it once, but Floyd wanted to try again.

"Yeah, we're having the best time ever," Floyd told her. A grin covered his face, hot chocolate tinging the corners of his lips.

"I'm glad."

"We were just going to try the cakewalk again," Harper said. "Would you like to join us?"

"I'm always up for a game of chance. Especially when there's cake involved." She smiled and stepped in line with them just as the sound of a guitar strum filled the room. They were standing to the side of the small raised stage, and Judith nodded toward the band who were starting to warm up there. "This band is wonderful. They're here every year. They usually play a mix of Christmas songs and some contemporary stuff so folks can dance."

She might have said something else, but Harper couldn't hear her over the sound of her heartbeat pounding in her ears. She'd turned when she'd heard the guitar and had seen the tall cowboy standing on the other side of the stage.

Logan.

It was him, and he was walking toward her. He reached her side just as the band began to play a slow country song. "Can I have this dance?"

She nodded, her mouth dry, then looked back at Judith and Floyd. "Are you guys okay doing the cakewalk without me?"

Floyd shrugged. "Sure. We already did it once before."

Judith gave her a knowing smile. "I've got this covered."

Harper was still holding her son's hand, and she pressed it into Judith's, a gesture she hoped the other woman understood meant more than just taking her place in the cakewalk. They both loved Floyd, and having one of them in his life didn't mean that he couldn't have the other.

Love wasn't a small thing she was supposed to keep to herself and parcel out only to a select few people. Love was big, bigger than her, and even when she thought her heart couldn't hold it all, the last few days had shown her that it seemed to only grow bigger the more she offered it to others.

And she had the chance to offer it to Logan right now. She took his outstretched hand and let him lead her onto the dance floor and pull her into his arms. "I didn't think you were coming."

"We had a date, remember?"

"I remember."

"I wasn't sure you'd be here either," he said. "I wondered if you'd already taken off for Kansas. But I saw the star on the church, and I somehow knew you'd be here."

She leaned her head onto his shoulder. He felt so solid, so real. But none of this felt real. It felt like the last few days with him had been a dream. "I'm sorry," she said. "I'm sorry I didn't tell you. About Floyd."

"I don't get it. He's a great kid. And it wouldn't have mattered to me if you had a child. Why didn't you just tell me?"

"I wanted to tell you. I swear I did. And I tried several times, but I knew that if I told you I had a son, I would have to tell you why he wasn't with me. And then I'd have to tell you about being in jail. And I just couldn't bear to see the look in your eyes once you knew what kind of person I really was. For once, I'd met someone who didn't know any of the awful things I'd done, and I wanted to enjoy it, just for a little while.

"I knew once I got Floyd back you'd find out, and I was going to tell you last night after the hockey practice. I swear I was. I even considered having you come to Judith's with me. But then everything went crazy, and I never got a chance.

"You treated me like I was someone special, like I was worthy of being with a guy like you, not like I was the dirt under your shoe. But I knew all that would change when you found out I'd been to jail and lost my son. Especially after you told me about your feelings toward your own mom. How could I tell you that I'd lost my son after you'd shared your story with me?

"For so long now, I've felt like the only person I could count on was myself. Every time I trusted someone or let myself love them, they left me. After Michael died, then my grandmother, I felt like I had to stop believing in other people and just trust myself. Then I met you, and you made me want to believe again."

"You can believe in me." He reached up and cupped her cheek. "I understand how you feel. I was afraid to let myself care too much about you, because I knew you were going to leave, just like every other woman in my life. But I'm not like that. I won't hurt you. And I won't walk out on someone I love."

She inhaled a sharp breath of air. Everything else in the room dropped away, and all she could focus on was Logan's face, and the love shining in his blue eyes.

He tipped his forehead to meet hers. "Yes, you heard me right. I'm in love with you, Harper. For better or for worse. I've never had someone take my heart and wring it out and fill it up the way you have. I love the way you make me laugh and the way you're the first one to jump in and help when anyone needs you. I love your smile and your laugh and the soft sigh you make when I kiss your neck. I don't want you to leave before we've even had a chance to see where this thing leads. I want to get to know you as a mom and spend time with you and Floyd."

He leaned in and brushed her lips with a kiss.

Harper's heart—the one she was sure was broken beyond all repair—beat loud and strong in her chest. He'd just said he was in love with her. She knew that had taken guts. Now it was her turn to be brave. To let down her defenses and trust.

She took a deep breath and locked her gaze with his. "I love you too," she said, the words coming out in a rush.

His eyes widened, and a grin creased his face. "You do?"

She nodded.

"Harper, I've got to say this. I realized tonight that I've always felt as if I've been left behind, but I've never asked anyone to stay. And I'll still love you, whether you choose to go or stay. But I'm asking you now, will you stay? Here? With me?"

Before she could answer, the song ended and the other couples made their way off the dance floor, sweeping them along in their wake. Some of them looked at her with smiles or smirks, and she knew they'd heard at least some of what she and Logan had said to each other.

Floyd crashed into her legs, throwing his arms around her. "Mom, Mom. I won a cake. Look." He held up a small aluminum loaf pan, the sides bending and the top of the pan smeared with a thick layer of chocolate frosting. "Can we have some?"

She laughed. "Why not? It is Christmas Eve." She looked at Logan. "Would you like to join us for a piece of this lovely cake?"

His lips curved into a devilish grin. "Sure. I like cake. And I seem to recall you mentioning something about some frosting."

"I seem to recall that conversation too. I think that's a discussion we need to revisit." She laughed as she led them to the rows of tables and chairs set up on the side of the room. Judith found them forks, and they all sat around the table, laughing and talking as they ate the cake right out of the pan.

The lights dimmed, signaling the church service was about to begin.

"We're going to the candlelight service," Harper told Logan. "Would you like to join us?"

"I'd like that very much."

They filed into the sanctuary, and each took a candle before slipping into a pew. The service wasn't long, but Harper was aware of Logan's every movement as he sat next to her—his warm shoulder nestled against hers, the press of his thigh against hers, the sound of his rich voice as it joined hers in singing the old familiar Christmas songs.

As the last song ended, the choir filed into the aisles of the sanctuary, picking up and lighting a candle as they passed the altar. The room was hushed as they moved down the rows, lighting the candle of the person on the end who then lit the candles of the rest of their row.

Once all the candles were lit, the choir began to sing "Silent Night" as they traveled back up the aisles and into the choir loft. As they reached the chorus, everyone in the sanctuary lifted their candle, raising it to the heavens as they lifted their voices in song.

As the glow of the candles filled the room, Harper peered around and thought the sanctuary looked like a room full of twinkling stars. She closed her eyes, holding back the sting of tears that threatened to spill, as she made a wish upon all the glittering stars.

Opening her eyes, she peered up at Logan, her heart making its own wish upon a cowboy.

Logan looked down at her, smiled, and took her hand, the love shining in his eyes as brightly as the candle's flame.

The next morning, Harper held Floyd's hand as they made their way across the gravel to the farmhouse. They were having Christmas breakfast with Logan.

The night before had been one of the top ten best nights of her life, Harper thought as she walked up the porch steps.

They'd said goodbye to Judith at the church, after making plans to get together today, then Logan had followed her and Floyd home and walked them to the door of the bunkhouse. He'd said he knew how hard she'd worked on the place and wanted her to have the time alone to share it with Floyd. Then he'd given her a soft kiss good night—a kiss filled with promise and hope.

Floyd had loved the bunkhouse and all the decorations she'd made, and he'd gone crazy over the space-themed bedroom. They'd lain in his bed and talked for what felt like hours, and she'd been surprised when he'd finally fallen asleep.

The late night hadn't bothered him, though, because he'd been bouncing on her bed first thing this morning, asking her if she thought Santa had found him in this new place. She wasn't sure if he still believed, or if he wanted to still believe, but this wasn't the year she was going to tell him anything different.

The front door opened, and Harper grinned as she took in the best gift Santa could have ever given her. She wasn't sure which list she'd made of Santa's this year, but looking at the tall cowboy standing in front of her made her want to be both naughty *and* nice.

"Merry Christmas," Logan said, his face split in a beaming smile. He had on jeans and boots and wore a raglan T-shirt with red sleeves that had a picture of a cow wearing a Santa hat and read "Have a Moo-y Christmas."

"Nice shirt," Harper said, not sure if she should hug him or give him a Christmas kiss or just walk past him into the room.

"Thanks. Quinn found it in a clearance bin and gave it to me to be funny, and now I wear it every year just to annoy her." He saved her from having to decide what to do by pulling her into a hug. Then he stole her heart when he gave Floyd a hug too.

"Is Quinn going to be here today?" she asked as she followed him into the kitchen where he had a mess of pans and bowls covering the counters. "Geez, what are you trying to do in here?"

"Make breakfast," he said. "And Quinn and her crew may stop by. I couldn't sleep last night, so I invited a few other people as well. I figured we'd make it a Christmas potluck."

"A Christmas potluck?" The idea sounded kind of nice. "What are we making?" She liked using the word *we*. It felt a little foreign, but it was growing on her.

Logan shrugged. "I'm not sure. I figured I could smoke the ham that's in the fridge and maybe you could make a cobbler. What do you think, Floyd? What's your favorite dish for Christmas?"

"Macaroni and cheese."

"That's your favorite meal for every day," Harper said as she tickled his ribs. Hearing him giggle with laughter was the best gift she could get for Christmas.

"That's an excellent choice," Logan said, offering Floyd a high five. "Now who wants to help me make these pancakes?"

Floyd raised his hand, and Logan lifted him onto the counter while Harper attacked the mess of dishes. They spent the next hour in the kitchen, eating pancakes and preparing the dishes for the potluck. Harper was surprised at how easily Floyd and Logan got along and how much fun the three of them had together. She knew Logan was Floyd's hockey coach, but it still struck her how genuine he was with her son.

They had the cobbler baked, the ham in the smoker, the mac and cheese in the oven, and the kitchen back in order when the first car arrived. It was Judith, and Floyd ran out to greet her with a hug. He really loved his grandma, and Harper didn't want to ruin that relationship.

She didn't exactly hug Judith when she came in, but she touched her arm and helped take the piles of gifts she carried. Judith wore her trademark pearls, but today she had on jeans, short leather boots, and a bright red Christmas sweatshirt. She seemed younger somehow, and her face didn't have that severe, pinched look she usually got around Harper. She instructed Logan to bring in the slow cooker of stuffing she had on the floor of the car, then headed to the kitchen with an offer to help set the table.

Bryn and Zane showed up next with a turkey, a pie, and Rachel and Josh in tow. Etta's red convertible pulled in after that, and Harper burst out laughing as the older woman came through the front door wearing a headband of blinking Christmas lights in her silver hair.

Etta passed Logan a pan of sweet potatoes, handed

Romeo, decked out in a Christmas sweater, to Floyd, and gave Harper a hug. "I do love a good party. Got any eggnog? And by eggnog, I mean brandy."

Harper laughed. "I'll see what I can find."

It felt like a real family gathering as the house filled with laughter. They spread the dishes on the counter, and everyone filled their plates and settled around the table to eat. Their conversation jumped from hockey to football, from cattle to the latest television show to binge.

After Rachel shared a funny story about a customer at the diner, Harper asked her if she'd figured out what she wanted to do.

"I'm not sure," Rachel said. "It would be great to stay here, but I can't afford to live in Colorado. I'd love to find a small house to rent in a quiet town where I could start over."

Harper narrowed her eyes, the wheels in her head already turning. "How do you feel about Kansas?"

"I like Kansas. I have a sister who lives there."

"Why don't you rent my house? It's in a small town in eastern Kansas and available in a couple of weeks. There's a college student renting the basement for winter break, but she'll be moving back to the dorms soon. It's not big or fancy, but it has three bedrooms and a great kitchen." She quoted her a sum, knowing it was much less than what a rental cost in Colorado, but that it would cover the monthly mortgage payment plus give Harper a few hundred dollars extra.

"I love the idea," Rachel said. "Thank you."

Logan was seated next to her, and he leaned his head toward her ear. His breath tickled her neck as he lowered his voice to ask, "Does this mean you're staying?"

A grin tugged at the corners of her lips, but before she

could answer, the front door opened and a tall cowboy wearing a leather duster, boots, and a ten-gallon hat stepped through. His arms were laden with brightly colored packages, and with his thick, white mustache and red flannel shirt, he looked like a cross between Sam Elliott and a cowboy Santa.

"Merry Christmas, Son," he said, his voice deep and commanding as he looked at Logan. "Who the hell are all these people?"

"Hey, Dad." Logan's face broke into a grin as he got up to give the man a hearty handshake and a clap on the back. "You made it home. How's Uncle Mac?"

"Ornery as ever. He practically kicked me out the door. Told me I needed to be home for Christmas, so I drove all night to get here."

"Does Quinn know?"

"I called her when I hit town. I suspect she'll be over here shortly." He laid the presents on the sofa as most of the people at the table got up to greet him, and he almost smiled as Zane stepped toward him. "Good to see you, boy. You doing all right?"

Zane nodded and shook his hand.

"How's your dad?"

"Same."

"'Bout like I figured. Good to have you here." He nodded to Judith and Ms. Etta. "Ladies. Merry Christmas."

Bryn waved and introduced him to Rachel and Josh.

Harper wasn't sure what to do. Her hands were sweating, and Floyd stood a little behind her as if he was suddenly shy. Logan's dad *was* a little imposing, and he lived up to Logan's description of a rough, tough cowboy.

Ham turned to her, and his expression softened. "You must be Harper. And Floyd." He shook her son's hand and nodded in her direction. "I've heard a lot about you." He chuckled when she peered at Logan. "Mostly from Quinn. But she told me you're reported to make fried chicken that rivals my mother's."

"Oh, I'm sure that's not true." *Dang Quinn.* She'd rather Logan's sister would have said she cleaned the toilets well rather than insult this man's mother's home cooking.

"I look forward to testing the claim." His lips curved into a roguish grin, and he offered her a wink before turning to look around the room.

He winced as he took in the tree. "Wow. What happened to this poor thing? Who picked this tree?"

Harper pressed her lips together to keep from laughing as Logan offered her a wink similar to his dad's, then reluctantly told Ham, "Apparently I did."

"Then it's a good thing I'm home. I hope you've been taking better care of the animals. Although I'm not sure. That momma cat is sittin' on the porch, and she looks about half-starved."

Harper breath caught in her throat as she jerked her head toward Logan. "Did he say 'mama cat'?"

"It couldn't be," Logan said incredulously as they both rushed to the front door.

But it was. There on the front stoop sat the gray cat, her fur matted and her body thinner, but the notch in her ear unmistakable.

Harper leaned down and scooped the cat into her arms. "I can't believe it. How did she get here?"

"It looks like she walked."

"But didn't you say Gus lived twenty miles from here?"

Logan's eyes were wide as he stared in amazement at the cat in her arms. "At least. It must have taken her all this time to find her way back."

The cat struggled in Harper's arms as she heard the tiny meows of the three kittens who raced in from the kitchen. Harper set her on the floor and choked back tears as she watched the kittens tumble over their mother as she furiously licked their fur.

The group gathered around as Logan filled them in on how the cat had been gone for days. Harper made a saucer of shredded turkey and set it on the floor, and they all watched Nacho gobble it down, then go back to washing her kittens' heads.

Logan took Harper's hand and pulled her toward the Christmas tree. "I have something for you and figured now would be the time to give it you while everyone else is watching the cats." He took a small, flat box wrapped in silver from under the tree and pressed it into her hands.

Harper shook her head. "This is too much. You've already given me more than I could have ever imagined." She turned the box over in her hands, marveling at the pretty paper. "When did you even have time to shop?"

"I didn't. This belonged to my grandma. I thought of it last night and knew it would be perfect, so I dug through the boxes in the attic until I found it. I checked with Quinn and my dad, and they were both good with me giving it to you."

Her hands trembled as she unwrapped an antique jewelry case. She gasped as she released the gold hinge and opened the box, revealing a delicate silver chain with a pendant in the shape of a star. A small diamond in the center of the star caught the light from the Christmas tree, and Harper felt like she couldn't breathe.

"It's beautiful," she whispered.

"We talked about stars the other night and how they represented whatever it was you really wanted, like your deepest desire, and my deepest desire is standing right in front of me. I want to have a life with you, and Floyd. You said the Christmas star led the wise men to everything they would ever need. And I might not be the wisest man—in fact, I've done some pretty stupid things—but this thing with you, asking you to stay, believing we can really have something here, is the smartest thing I've ever done."

He lifted the necklace from the box, and she turned and raised her hair. The chain was cool on her heated skin, and she clutched the pendant in her hand as Logan fastened the clasp, then turned her back around to face him.

His voice was soft, earnest, as he cupped her cheek in his palm. "You said you see the star as a promise of something amazing ahead, so I'm giving you this star with the promise that we've got a lot of amazing things ahead. I'm in love with you, Harper. And I want a life with you. With you and your son. So, will you stay here? With me?"

She nodded, a smile pulling at her lips as she finally found her voice. "I love you too. I tried not to. I swear I did, but you won me over with your terrible singing, and your relationship with your marshmallow-eating girlfriend, and your awesome air-guitar moves. I've spent the last several years feeling like I couldn't depend on anyone but myself, like the only shoulder I had to lean on was my own. But I was wrong, because you've got some pretty broad shoulders, and you've proven that you'll be there for me. And for my son. I don't have to do everything on my own. I want to stay. I want to stay and build not just a life, but a family with you and Floyd. I want my son to have a relationship with Judith, and I want to introduce him to Star. I want to watch him play a hockey game with you as his coach. I want to fix mashed potatoes and your favorite gravy and sit at the table and eat meals with you. I want to wake up with you every morning and go to sleep next to you every night. Is that what you meant by 'stay'?"

"That sounds perfect. You're perfect."

She shook her head. "No. I'm not. I've done all sorts of terrible things. But I'm trying to make up for every one of them."

He pressed a finger to her lips. "I don't care about all that. I meant you're perfect for me."

She gazed into his eyes, searching for a trace of uncertainty, but all she saw was love. "And you're perfect for me. And so is this necklace. I love it."

She looked down at the pendant, then back up at him. "You said we've always used the stars to guide us. That if we're ever lost, or can't find our way, the stars will lead us home. And I look around this room—at your dad, at the sweet mama cat who traveled so far to be with her babies, at *my* baby as he stands there laughing with his grandma—and it feels like I'm witnessing a true Christmas miracle. Like we all somehow found our way home."

"I couldn't have said it better myself." Logan pulled her to him and pressed a tender kiss to her lips. "Merry Christmas, Peaches."

The End…

…and just the beginning…

ACKNOWLEDGMENTS

As always, my love and thanks goes out to my family! Todd, thanks for always believing in me and for being the real life role model of a romantic hero. You cherish me and make me laugh every day and the words it would take to truly thank you would fill a book on their own. I love you. *Always*.

Thank you to my sons, Tyler and Nick, for always supporting me and listening to a zillion plotting ideas. I love you both more than my heart could ever imagine.

I can't thank my editor, Deb Werksman, enough for believing in me and this book, for your amazing editing talents, and for always making me feel like a rock star. Thanks to Dawn Adams for this incredible cover that perfectly captures Logan Rivers and the setting of Rivers Gulch. I love it so much! I also love being part of the Sourcebooks Sisterhood, and I offer buckets of thanks to the whole Sourcebooks Casablanca team for all of your efforts and hard work in making this book happen.

Huge shout out thanks to my agent, Nicole Resciniti at The Seymour Agency, for your advice and your guidance. You are the best, and I'm so thankful you are part of my tribe.

A big thank you to my parents—all of them. I appreciate everything you do and am so thankful for your support of this crazy writing career. Thanks to my mom, Lee Cumba, for so many lunches where we talk writing and plots. And thanks to my dad, Bill Bryant, for spending hours giving me ranching and farming advice and plot ideas.

Ginormous thanks goes out to my plotting partner and dear friend, Kristin Miller. The time and energy you take to run through plot ideas with me is invaluable! Your friendship and writing support means the world to me—I couldn't do this writing thing without you!

Special acknowledgment goes out to the women who walk this writing journey with me every single day. The ones who make me laugh, who encourage and support, who offer great advice and sometimes just listen. Thank you, Michelle Major, Lana Williams, Anne Eliot, Ginger Scott, Cindy Skaggs, and Beth Rhodes. XO

Big thanks goes out to my street team, Jennie's Page Turners, and for all of my readers: the people who have been with me from the start, my loyal readers, my dedicated fans, the ones who have read my stories, who have laughed and cried with me, who have fallen in love with my heroes and have clamored for more! Whether you have been with me since the first book or just discovered me with this book, know that I write these stories for you, and I can't thank you enough for reading them. Sending love, laughter, and big Colorado hugs to you all!

ABOUT THE AUTHOR

Jennie Marts is the *USA Today* bestselling author of award-winning books filled with love, laughter, and always a happily-ever-after. Readers call her books "laugh out loud" funny and the "perfect mix of romance, humor, and steam." Fic Central claimed one of her books was "the most fun I've had reading in years."

She is living her own happily-ever-after in the mountains of Colorado with her husband, two dogs, and a parakeet who loves to tweet to the oldies. She's addicted to Diet Coke, adores Cheetos, and believes you can't have too many books, shoes, or friends.

Her books include the contemporary western romances of the Cowboys of Creedence and the Hearts of Montana series, the cozy mysteries of the Page Turners series, the hunky hockey-playing men in the Bannister Brothers books, and the small-town romantic comedies in the Cotton Creek romance series.

Jennie loves to hear from readers. Follow her on Facebook at Jennie Marts Books or Twitter at @JennieMarts. Visit her at jenniemarts.com, and sign up for her newsletter to keep up with the latest news and releases.

If you can't get enough of the cowboys of
Creedence, read on for a sneak peek at

A Cowboy State of Mind

Book 1 in Jennie Marts's new series,
Creedence Horse Rescue!

CHAPTER 1

THE STILL-NAMELESS DOG JUMPED INTO THE CAB AS Zane Taylor opened the door of his pickup. The late spring sun warmed his back, but the heat was light compared to the weight of the decision he bore on his shoulders. His former boss, Maggie, had been nagging him to come back to Montana, to his old job on the ranch. She'd texted him the day before to say she'd taken in a herd of wild stallions who needed to be broke. He'd texted back with a vague reply, but knew it was time to give her an answer. Time to get back on the road and out of Creedence. But the reason he was so fired up to leave was also the reason he wasn't quite ready to walk away.

He shrugged the soreness from his shoulders. He'd had a good morning with the horse—maybe Rebel, the black stallion he'd been trying to break for weeks, could feel the warmth in the air as well. Although it *was* Colorado, so they could still get a snowstorm or two before spring reluctantly slid into summer.

"Nice job today, Horse Whisperer," Logan Rivers, his current boss, and one of the few people he called a friend, hollered from the corral where he was putting another horse through the paces.

Zane waved a hand in his direction, ignoring the comment, as he turned the engine over and pulled the door shut. He wasn't fond of the nickname, even though Logan had been using it since they were in high school and Zane had started working summers at Logan's family's ranch, Rivers Gulch.

He could grudgingly admit he did have a gift with horses, especially the ones deemed dangerous or wild, somehow connecting with the animals better than he ever had with people. Maybe because he knew what it was like to be labeled and to endure abuse or trauma and something in his manner told the horses they could trust him—that he wouldn't hurt them. Or maybe because animals didn't care about or judge him for the two-inch ragged scar streaking down his face.

That damn scar. His fingers itched to cover the coarse skin that started at his eyebrow and ran a jagged course across his cheek and down toward his jaw. Instead, he brushed a hand over the dog's ear and focused on counting his breaths, an exercise he'd learned in the military.

The black-and-white border collie mix rested her head on Zane's leg, and he absently stroked her neck as he drove toward Creedence, the small town nestled in the mountains where no one was a stranger and everyone knew not just *your* business, but your cousin's as well.

He lowered the windows and turned on the radio, hoping to banish the dredged up memories now riding shotgun in the pickup. Instead, he contemplated the few errands he needed to run after grabbing a plate of biscuits and gravy at the diner. And maybe hoped to see a certain blonde waitress who had been taking up way too many of his thoughts the last few months.

He slowed, his brow furrowing, as he recognized that same waitress's car sitting empty on the side of the road. The car was an older nondescript blue sedan, but there was no mistaking the colorful bumper stickers stuck to the trunk. A bright blue one read, "What if the hokey pokey really is what it's all about," and the hot pink one above the back tail-light read, "It was me, I let the dogs out."

His heart rate hastened as his gaze went from the empty vehicle to a hundred yards up the road where a woman walked along the side of the highway, her ponytail bouncing with each step and a light-colored dog keeping pace at her heels. Which was pretty impressive, in and of itself, since the dog only had three legs.

But then, everything about Bryn Callahan was kind of bouncy, and she was just as impressive as her dog. The woman was always upbeat and positive. Even now, with her car sittin' busted on the side of the road, her steps still seemed to spring. The light glinted off her blonde hair— like the rays of the sun were drawn to her. Unlike him— who felt like the light was repelled and could only shy away from the dark places living within him.

He drove past the abandoned car and onto the dirt shoulder as he slowed to a stop beside her. "Need a ride?"

She turned, her expression wary, then her face broke into a grin, and it was like the sun shining through the clouds after a rainstorm.

"Hey Zane," she said, already reaching for the door handle. "I sure do. I was supposed to start my shift at the diner ten minutes ago." She lifted the dog onto the floor of the truck then blew her bangs from her damp forehead as she tossed in her backpack then settled on the bench seat and buckled herself in. "Good boy, Lucky," she cooed to the dog, who pressed himself into the space between her leg and the door.

Which only served to draw Zane's eyes to her legs. And the woman had great legs, already tan, and muscular and shapely from her work at the diner. Her white cross-trainers were scuffed with the red dirt from the road, and she had a smudge of dust across one ankle that Zane was tempted to reach down and brush away then let his fingers linger on her skin.

She wore a pink waitress dress, the kind that zips up the front with a white collar and a little breast pocket, and the fabric hugged her curvy figure in all the right spots. For just a moment Zane imagined pulling down that zipper—with his teeth.

Simmer down, man. He didn't usually let himself get carried away with those kind of fantasies. But he didn't usually have Bryn in his truck, filling his cab with the sound of her easy laughter and the scent of her skin—traces of honeysuckle and vanilla and the smell of fresh sheets off the line on a warm summer day.

"What happened to your car?" Zane asked, drawing his gaze back to the road as he eased the truck onto the highway.

"Who knows? This is the third time it's broke down since Christmas."

"Have you called someone about it?" *Like me.* Yeah, right. Why would she call *him*? Because they'd shared a few laughs when they'd spent some time together around the holidays? They'd only been hanging out together because they were helping Logan's girlfriend, Harper.

He'd thought there was a spark of flirtation, but with him, a spark often turned into a flame and people usually ended up burned around him. So he'd thrown himself into the work at the ranch and tried to forget about the perky waitress with the twinkling blue eyes and vibrant laugh. But like most things, other than horses, he'd failed.

"No. What good would it do to call someone when I don't have any money to pay them anyway? Last I checked, my bank account was holding steady at six dollars and eighty cents, and I don't know anyone who works for that cheap."

He shrugged. "I could take a look at it for you. And I wouldn't charge you more than a smile." Oh Lord, did that really just come out of his mouth? It hadn't sounded half as dopey in his head.

"That would be very neighborly of you," she said, ignoring his dorky comment and flashing him a brilliant grin. "And that's a price I can afford. But you don't have to. I know Logan's keeping you pretty busy at the Gulch."

Neighborly? He didn't want to seem neighborly. He'd been trying for flirty, but his efforts apparently fell flat. *Wait.* How did *she* know Logan had been keeping him busy at the ranch? Had she asked about him? "I've got time," he assured her. "I'll stop and take a look at it when I'm done in town. See if I can spot the problem, at least."

"That would be so great." She ruffled the neck of the black and white dog, who had shifted in the seat to inspect the newcomers. "You picked a name for your dog yet?"

"She's not my dog."

Bryn rolled her eyes and let out a small chuckle. "*You* might not think so, but *she* does. Once you fed her, she was yours. And she's been with you for months now. Every time I see your truck, she's ridin' shotgun. Why do you think she does that if she doesn't consider herself yours?"

He shrugged, his tone even and dry. "She must like my winning personality."

A laugh escaped Bryn's lips—a sound that filled the cab of the truck, and his heart, as if a door of a dark room had been cracked and let a shaft of light in. "I'm sure that's it," Bryn said, still chuckling.

A grin tugged at the corner of his lips. This woman made him smile, even when she was giving him a hard time.

"How's your dad doing?" she asked.

The smile fell from his lips. "Stubborn as ever."

His dad's heart attack had brought him back to town earlier that winter, and he'd planned to stay only long enough to get the old bastard back on his feet. But then Logan lost his hired hand and had offered Zane a job helping at the ranch and with the horses, and a couple of weeks had turned into a couple of months.

He'd found a sort of peace with his dad. As long as Birch took his meds and stayed off the sauce, Zane had agreed to remain in town and at the house. They mostly stayed out of each other's way, but occasionally found themselves watching a hockey game together, especially if the Colorado Summits were playing, and Rockford James, Creedence's hometown hero was on the ice.

But lately Zane had felt the familiar itch—the need to move on when he'd stayed in one place too long. An itch that was exacerbated by the blonde waitress who was taking up space in his mind and under his skin. An itch he had no business trying to scratch.

"He seems to be doing better lately," he told Bryn. "So I'll probably take off pretty soon. My old boss has been harping on me to come back to Montana. She took in a new herd of wild stallions and needs someone to break them."

"Oh," Bryn said, the word a soft breath on her lips. "I didn't realize you were thinking about leaving. When are you going to go?"

He murmured something noncommittal and lifted his shoulders in a dismissive shrug as he pulled into the parking lot of the diner and parked in the shade of giant elm tree. He got out but left the windows down for the dog. In this town, nobody locked their doors, and the dog hadn't jumped out of the truck yet, despite him giving her plenty of opportunities.

A dirty black pickup with out of state plates and a rusty horse trailer hooked to its bumper sat parked in front of the diner. The horse inside stamped and whinnied as Zane and Bryn approached the door. It butted its head against the side of the trailer, and peered out at them with a frightened brown eye that was crusted and leaky with infected goop.

"Whoa there, it's all right," Zane assured it, his voice steady and calm as they drew closer.

"Oh no, can you see its eye?" Bryn asked. "Poor thing."

"It's no wonder it's infected. This trailer is disgusting," he said, peering in at the mess of manure and sparse bits of hay. It looked like the horse had been trampling in its own waste for days.

"It doesn't look like they've cleaned this trailer out ever." Bryn pulled her head back to avoid the foul smell. "And that trailer has got to be baking hot." The horse's back was streaked with sweat and dust.

Bile rose in his throat, and Zane clamped his teeth together as his hands tightened into fists. He hated to see animals being abused. Especially when they didn't get the chance to turn old enough and strong enough to fight back. "I'd like to see the owner of this truck spend a day cooped up in there." Zane was tempted to loosen the latch as he walked by and let the horse free.

"I agree." Bryn lifted her hand toward the latch. "What if we just opened the back end of the trailer and the horse accidentally escaped?"

His lips curved in a wry grin. He liked the way this woman's brain worked. "I was thinking the same thing. But the horse is tied up in there, and even if we released the lead rope, where is it going to go?"

"I don't know. But I feel like we have to do something."

"Not our circus. Not our monkeys." Zane shook his head and stole a glance at the three-legged dog sitting devotedly at the waitress's feet. He put a hand on Bryn's back to guide her toward the diner entrance and softened his tone. "You can't save everybody, Bryn."

Her feet didn't move. She turned to stare at him, holding his gaze for just long enough to have sweat heating his back. "I'm still gonna try to save as many as I can."

Damn, but that woman had a habit of hitting him right in the heart. He gave a slight nod of his head, not trusting his voice to speak, as she tore her eyes from his and entered the restaurant.

"You're late," the fry-cook yelled from the kitchen. Gil had been frying eggs and slinging hash at the roadside diner for as long as Zane could remember. He'd learned to cook in the Navy, and as gruff as Gil sounded, Zane knew the old sailor had a soft spot for Bryn. *Who didn't?*

"I know," Bryn answered, the dog trotting at her heels as she raced into the back. Lucky must have taken his customary spot in the back office because Bryn emerged from the kitchen alone a few seconds later, hastily tying a white apron around her waist. She reached for the coffee pot as she apologized to Gil, the other waitress, and the sparse customers that filled the diner. "Sorry y'all. My stupid car broke down."

"Again?" Ida Mae Phillips, an elderly woman, and a regular, who had taught Sunday school down at the Methodist church for over thirty years, questioned from her customary table by the window. "You have got to do something about that dad-blamed vehicle."

"I know. I know." Bryn forced a smile at the two men sitting at the counter. The taller one wore a threadbare flannel shirt that was hard to tell if it was dirty or just faded. A chewed up toothpick clung to his chapped lips. The other, a shorter guy whose body was muscled, yet his rounded belly gave away a habit of either too much beer or too many chicken wings, had on a T-shirt so wrinkled, it looked like he'd slept in it. A green hat covered his unwashed hair, a greasy stain soiling the bill. "It looks like you're all set for coffee, so what can I get you fellas to eat?"

Zane slid onto a stool at the counter, leaving an empty spot between him and the two guys drinking coffee. He didn't recognize either one, but that didn't surprise him. He'd been gone for years, and the truck stop was next to the highway, so in addition to the regular locals, plenty of truckers and road trippers stopped in for the 'county's best chicken fried steak' the sign above the diner boasted about.

But these guys didn't fit any of those categories. They had a different air about them, with their grimy hair and dirty jeans and the oily way that one of them raked his eyes over Bryn's figure before giving her his breakfast order.

Zane was sure these were the guys driving the trailer, and just the sound of their voices nettled his nerves like rocks against a cheese grater.

But Bryn kept her cool as she passed their order to Gil. She poured Zane a cup of coffee as she took his order next then worked her way around the room, checking in with the few other customers, exchanging comments about her car and the nice weather while she cleared plates and filled water glasses.

Zane was content to sip his coffee and nonchalantly watch her work. Her movements were quick and efficient, like every action she took had a purpose. He noted, and appreciated, the way her curvy hips swayed as she maneuvered between tables and around chairs. She wasn't tall exactly, probably only five-seven or so, he knew this by how she fit against his over six foot frame the one time he'd danced with her, but she carried herself that way—her spine straight, her shoulders pulled back. Maybe it was from his time spent in the military, but he admired a woman with good posture.

He found he admired a lot of things about Bryn Callahan. She had a way about her that put people at ease, like they could tell she had a good heart. Just in the few minutes he'd been watching her, he'd seen her good-naturedly wipe up a child's spill and offer him a high five and a sticker, give Ida Mae a hug before she left the diner, and stand over old Doc Hunter's shoulder as they pondered a clue in his daily crossword puzzle. He liked the way she so easily doled out compliments and chatted with people, like they were old friends, instead of just customers. And some of them were. He and Bryn had both grown up in Creedence. They'd been a few years apart in school, and he hadn't paid much attention to her back then.

But she sure had his attention now. Watching her tuck

a loose strand of hair behind her ear and the sound of her laughter carrying through the diner had his gut doing the funny kind of flips he hadn't felt in a long time. Hadn't *let* himself feel.

And I have no business letting myself feel them now either, he thought as he picked up his fork and dug into the warm plate of biscuits and gravy Bryn set in front of him. He'd tried the 'feelings' route once before—tried the whole relationship thing but it had only ended in tragedy and pain. He'd been running from the memories of that relationship—the memories of Sarah—for years. Even now, the sound of an ambulance siren still caused his chest to tighten and his stomach to roil. And reminded him that love wasn't worth the pain, and he wasn't a bet any woman should take.

Bryn topped off the coffees of the two trailer guys as they ate then leaned her hip against the counter. Her manner suggested cool nonchalance, but Zane knew differently as he heard her casually ask, "Is that your horse out there?"

"Not ours," Flannel Shirt said, his tone boastful and derisive. "But she's in our trailer."

Bryn eyed them, the first hint of suspicion showing on her face. "Why do you have someone else's horse in your trailer? Who does she belong to?"

"No one. Not anymore."

Her brow furrowed in confusion. "I don't get it, but I noticed she didn't seem very happy."

"I'm sure she isn't," he answered, shrugging his shoulders. "But it doesn't matter. She's not gonna seem *anything* by this time tomorrow. That nag is on her way to "a farm in the country", if you know what I mean." He used his fingers to make air quotes.

Bryn's eyes widened as a gasp escaped her lips. "You mean you're taking her to…" She obviously couldn't say the words, and her skin took on a greenish pallor.

Green Hat nodded, and his lips curved into a sly grin. "Yep. We're what you might call a 'Waste Disposal' company."

The color drained from Bryn's face. "You can't be serious."

"As a horse's heart attack." He talked around the bite of hash browns in his mouth as he elbowed the other man in the rib and laughed at his own poor joke.

"But why?" she asked.

"Who knows? And who cares? Not our business to ask. We just collect the horse and the fee then it's our job to drop them off at the glue factory."

Just as "casually" as Bryn had been, Zane kept an eye on the conversation, and he swore he saw the light blink in Bryn's eyes as an idea occurred to her.

"Soooo, if you've already collected the fee for her, what happens if she never makes it to the…" She swallowed. "The final destination?"

Flannel Shirt shrugged again. "Nothing, I guess. Except they have one less horse to slaughter."

Bryn winced, but wasn't swayed by their obvious attempt to rile her. "So what if you just let her go? Or, what if I took her off your hands? I live on a farm so from what you said earlier, you'd still be fulfilling your obligation."

Green Hat's eyes went dark and predatory. "Where is this farm? Maybe we could stop by and visit before we leave town."

A low growl formed in Zane's throat, and his knuckles went white around his fork as he considered jabbing the utensil into the dirtbag's eye.

Flannel Shirt put a hand on his partner's arm as he eyed

Bryn, working the toothpick from one side of his mouth to the other. "I can see you really want this horse. So we might be able to arrange something. What did you have in mind?"

"Not the same thing he does," she answered, flashing Green Hat a disdainful look. She forced her lips back into a smile as she regarded Flannel Shirt. "How about I cover your breakfast *and* pack you a lunch for the road as well? I'll even throw in a couple of slices of pie."

He let out a scornful laugh. "How about you do all that *and* throw in a couple of hundred bucks?"

Bryn's shoulders sank. "I don't have a couple of hundred bucks." She pressed her lips together then inhaled a deep breath before offering, "But I'd give you my car in exchange for letting me have the horse."

"The one you just told this whole place is broken down on the side of the road? No thanks."

"Yeah, what are we gonna do with a broken down car?" Green Hat chimed in. As casual as she tried to act, they knew they had her. "Couple of guys like us, we work on a 'cash only' basis."

"I understand. I'm just a little low on cash right now." She glanced around the diner as if mentally counting up her morning tips. "And there's no way I can make that in tips today. But think about it, you giving me the horse only makes your job easier. That seems like a no-brainer for a couple of smart guys like you."

These two idiots were the 'no-brainers.' Zane held back a smirk as he reached for his wallet to pay his bill. He needed to get out of here before he did something foolish—like kicked these guys out on their greasy butts and let the horse go. Or worse.

Flannel Shirt tapped his finger on the counter, a thin line of grease visible under his nail. "No one's ever offered to buy our load before, but you have a point. If we don't have to drop off that horse, we can get home a day early. So maybe I'm feeling generous and willing to make a deal."

"I'm listening," Bryn said, crossing her arms protectively over her chest.

"You cover our breakfast and pack us a lunch, and we'll give you that horse for an even hundred."

"And don't forget the pie," Green Hat threw in.

Bryn chewed her lip, her gaze skimming over the diner patron's once more. Her eyes landed on Zane's, and he held them a moment, knowing already what she was going to say.

"Deal," she said. "Just give me a little time to drum up the cash. I'll make some calls while I put together your lunch."

Flannel Shirt's lips curved as his eyes went to the clock above her head. He knew he had a live one—he just had to reel in the line. "You've got twenty minutes. Or we're leaving. *With* the horse."

Zane rifled through the bills in his wallet. He'd just gotten paid. In fact, one of his errands that morning was stopping at the bank. Even as he fought it, knowing how stupid the idea was, he knew his deposit was going to end up being a little light.

He'd had the biscuits and gravy many times and knew his bill normally totaled a little over ten dollars, so he usually left fifteen. He sighed as he took two bills from his wallet and slid them under the edge of his plate.

"Thanks for breakfast, Bryn," he told her as he slid off the stool. "I'll check back in later to see if you need a ride home."